Exile Endgame

Preston Fleming

PF Publishing

Salt Lake City, Utah

PF Publishing
Salt Lake City, Utah

Publisher's Note: This eBook is a work of fiction. Names characters, places, and incidents are the product of the author's imagination or are used fictitiously. Locales and public names are sometimes used for atmospheric purposes. Any resemblance to actual events, locales, or persons, living or dead, is coincidental.

ISBN-13: 978-0-9994418-8-6

For more information, go to www.PrestonFleming.com

EDITORIAL REVIEWS

"[T]he book has all the bureaucratic complexity of a Cold War spy novel, with an intense focus on trade relationships, rival factions, and government policies. [F]ans of the series will enjoy the book's realpolitik take on dystopia. An intricate espionage thriller." — KIRKUS REVIEWS

"EXILE ENDGAME succeeds wildly as a political thriller set in a time when the U.S.—if not the entire world—is at a dangerous tipping point." —BESTTHRILLERS.COM

"A complex suspense novel that is sure to have readers on the edge of their seats. EXILE ENDGAME is perfect for those who love political thrillers and American dystopia fiction." —PACIFIC BOOK REVIEW

"EXILE ENDGAME is written in a compelling and gripping way, so the reader can tell right from the first page that this book is going to be hard to put down. [The] book is part of a series that is quite unlike anything else I've read." —SAN FRANCISCO BOOK REVIEW

"Fleming does a masterful job. [T]he complex story involves a huge cast of characters, [b]ut the individual exchanges will keep the reader quickly turning pages." —BOOKLIFE by PUBLISHERS WEEKLY

Contents

Chapter One: Washington

> "Every revolution evaporates and leaves behind only the slime of a new bureaucracy."
> –*Franz Kafka*

SATURDAY, 25 MARCH 2034

A fleet of leaden clouds swept in from the northwest, scudding low over the office towers of suburban Tyson's Corner, Virginia. The clouds, illuminated from below, sent stinging gusts of rain-drenched wind ahead. Thunder growled in the distance.

Victor Barbosa, chief of the Department of State Security's (DSS) Exile Division, parked his aging electric sedan in a reserved spot close to the mirror-faced office building where the Department leased expansion space. The walk from the nearly empty parking lot to the building's rear entrance was less than a hundred meters, but the wind soon turned Barbosa's umbrella inside out and nearly blew off his hat, bringing a curse to his lips as he lowered his head to trace a path across the puddled blacktop.

Once indoors, he submitted to a security scan and the uniformed guard waved him through to the elevators. The deputy director's office was on the seventh floor and Barbosa needed no help finding the way. When he arrived, the deputy director was seated behind his desk, speaking on a secure telephone, his massive black swivel chair facing a wall of windows where raindrops landed like handfuls of gravel.

Unlike the offices of many other high-ranking DSS officials, which displayed few personal objects that might open a window onto their owner's character, the deputy director's office was packed with memorabilia from his past postings as a mid-level CIA officer chasing Islamic terrorists across the Middle East. Tribal rugs covered the floor, framed Roberts and Bartlett engravings graced the walls, shelves were laden with Yemeni daggers, Egyptian statuettes, and Turkish coffee pots, while an intricate *mashrabiya*-style wooden screen lurked off to the side. Barbosa even spotted a half-dozen silver-framed family photos on the credenza behind the deputy director's desk. The children looked young, most likely from a second marriage, which was par for the course among lifers in the CIA and DSS.

DSS Deputy Director Gerrit DeWaart looked up and gave his visitor a perfunctory wave to sit down in one of the chairs facing the desk. DeWaart, a long-faced, high-shouldered blade of a man, slouched in the thickly upholstered chair, rotating it slowly to left and right as he spoke. Of all the men Barbosa had worked for in the CIA and the DSS, DeWaart was by no means the worst. Barbosa had been thrown in with him on many operations, though he preferred to keep his distance. For despite DeWaart's placid, almost austere manner, behind his well-trimmed goatee was the barren soul of a Beria, a Yezhov or a Yagoda. One false word, one errant slip under the wrong circumstances, and even Barbosa might be taken away and never heard from again.

DeWaart hung up the receiver on the red encrypted telephone and gazed at Barbosa across the massive walnut desk, his gray-green cat's eyes looking satiated and cold.

"So what brings you out here on a Saturday night," he began. "I've been stuck here all day. What's your excuse?"

"I just heard from my deputy that Warren Linder has been arrested in Boston. Apparently, someone at headquarters gave the order to grab him. You may recall that, earlier this week, we finally succeeded in luring Linder back into the country. The operation took nearly three years to develop and has put the department in a position to control nearly the entire the émigré opposition. But Linder's arrest puts that operation in jeopardy. If word gets out, our work could be set back for years."

"I see," the deputy director replied with an expression that gave away nothing. "So what do you want from me?"

Barbosa was not surprised to have the issue thrown back in his face and had a ready answer.

"I'd like to know who ordered Linder's arrest and why I wasn't informed. I'd also like the authority to release him back into the custody of the team running the operation. Which, by the way, you approved."

The deputy director listened with a poker face.

"You want to know who ordered his arrest?" he answered, pausing for effect. "I did. The General Secretary called me and demanded Linder's arrest after getting word that he was in country. If I'd let you block the arrest, you and I both would be a head shorter."

Barbosa remained silent for a moment, choosing his words carefully.

"Might there be some way of persuading the General Secretary to reconsider? If we could arrange to free Linder by morning, I'm confident our people could come up with a cover story for what happened and avoid irreparable damage to the broader operation. But the longer we keep Linder behind bars, the greater the risk that he and his supporters will realize that everything we've been feeding them is a fiction."

"I assume you're talking about the League operation?"

"Yes, and all its spinoffs, which by now are legion," Barbosa went on. "Listen, Linder met with the League's Political Council in Boston earlier today and gave them his blessing. Which means we've succeeded in co-opting nearly all the top émigré opposition leaders. And don't forget, the funds that the League brings in from the émigrés and their foreign state sponsors underwrites two-thirds of the Exile Division's hard currency budget. So once Linder goes back to the U.K. and endorses the League publicly, we will have gained effective control over the entire overseas anti-Unionist movement. But if Linder doesn't return, his people will smell a rat and the entire operation could unravel."

"You don't need to remind me what a success the League has been," DeWaart grumbled. "I backed it from the start. But the General Secretary seems to harbor a personal grudge against Linder. The chances of getting him released are nil. The best you can hope for is to delay his execution long enough for us to interrogate him and perhaps craft an alternative narrative around his disappearance."

"Damn." Barbosa gritted his teeth.

"So what will it be, Victor? Do you really want me to pick up the phone and give the General Secretary a call? You could be betting your career on it."

"If the League goes down in flames, my career won't be worth much, anyway. But this isn't just about me, Gerrit. I have officers and agents out in the field whose lives could be at risk if we don't find a way out of this. So, yes, I'll risk it. Go ahead and call the bastard. I'll take whatever I can get from him."

DeWaart raised an eyebrow, either impressed by Barbosa's courage or surprised by his recklessness, and picked up the red receiver to call. After being shunted from one White House functionary to another, he stiffened and motioned for Barbosa to be silent.

"Good evening, Mr. General Secretary. DeWaart here. You asked me to inform you when Warren Linder was in custody. I can report that he's safely behind bars in Boston. But I also have in my office the division chief who ran the operation that brought Linder in. Frankly speaking, sir, he's presented a solid case for releasing Linder back into the custody of our undercover officers and agents who arranged his visit. It's your call, of course, sir, but may I put Victor Barbosa on speakerphone to offer his reasoning?"

When Unionist Party General Secretary Paul Twitchell agreed, DeWaart pushed the speakerphone button and Barbosa, in a few sentences, summarized the League operation and its current plight.

"So what exactly are you proposing?" Twitchell interrupted.

"Linder has been in custody for only a few hours," Barbosa answered. "If we free him quickly, I believe we can salvage the overall operation by persuading him that the League used its influence to gain his release. If done well, such a move could enhance the League's credibility with Linder and his people. But time is of the essence, sir. We'll need to move quickly to keep the operation from falling apart."

"Need I remind you, Mr. Barbosa, that your prisoner has already been convicted of treason, insurrection, seditious conspiracy, murder, and a long list of other crimes? And that he's been sentenced to death not once, but twice? And, since his return to these shores, he's met with insurrectionists and called for riots, sabotage, theft of state property and the assassination of state officials—including me! Can you understand why I find your request unacceptable? And, while we're on the subject, could you tell me why I wasn't I informed of your plans to bring Linder here in the first place?"

It took all of Barbosa's resolve not to wither under this onslaught from the most powerful person in the ruling Unionist Party.

"The League is a sensitive compartmented counterintelligence activity that operates on a strict need-to-know basis, sir. Your National Security Advisor was briefed at every stage of the—."

"You mean to tell me, Mr. Barbosa," Twitchell interrupted again, his voice like an ice cold bath, "that you, a senior State Security officer, would allow an implacable enemy of the state like Warren Linder to enter the country and call for my assassination, and then let him waltz back out? What if someone had acted on his madness?"

Barbosa opened his mouth to speak, but DeWaart held up his hand to silence him.

"Mr. General Secretary," the deputy director intervened, "please accept our personal assurances that you were never at any risk from Linder's presence here. Every single League operative who came into contact with him was under DSS control. Setting Linder free to return to the U.K. would remove any further risk to your person. But more than that, it would demonstrate to the émigrés that the League has far-reaching influence inside the U.S. and that they should put their resources at the League's disposal. If so, for years to come the DSS would be in a position to control almost any plot that our overseas enemies might hatch against us."

Barbosa and DeWaart exchanged hopeful glances as they awaited the General Secretary's response. It came swiftly and was laced with menace.

"All right," he replied slowly. "I've let you state your case. Now here is my decision: request denied. You are to hold Linder and carry out his death sentence immediately. Am I understood?"

Barbosa winced at the news. But he couldn't let go easily, despite the risk of further aggravating the General Secretary.

"Certainly, sir. We will hold the prisoner per your order. However, with all due respect, I would be remiss if I didn't point out that vital national security interests are bound up with the League operation. While we can accept moving forward with Linder's execution, we urge you to consider a delay to let us interrogate the prisoner and prepare a suitable cover story for his disappearance. This will allow us to wind down the League in an orderly manner and mitigate the risks facing our officers and agents in the field."

The General Secretary let out an animal grunt.

"How long a delay?" he asked.

"Two or three weeks, I expect. Perhaps a bit longer."

"I'll give you a week. And I want Linder's interrogation reports delivered daily to my National Security Advisor. Am I understood?"

Barbosa looked across the desk at DeWaart, who murmured assent.

When the call ended, Barbosa pounded his fist on the desk, his face a mask of rage.

"What he wants is impossible," he snarled. "Linder's disappearance will destroy the League and undo all our hard work over these past three years. Just when we've finally gained control over the émigrés, their trust in the League will collapse like a house of cards. Our agents will be exposed and from then on, we'll be blind to the enemy's intrigues."

But to Barbosa's surprise, DeWaart merely shrugged.

"Orders are orders, Victor. The League has had a good run. You and your men deserve praise for it. But no intelligence operation lasts forever. Take satisfaction in what you've accomplished and start winding it down. Now. If you can break Linder within a week and protect the League at the same time, so much the better. But a week isn't very long when you're up against a hard-bitten S.O.B. like Linder."

A thin smile formed on the deputy director's lips.

"After all," he added, "Linder knows our tricks. He used to be one of us."

Preston Fleming

Chapter Two: Beirut

> "The dogs are barking. That means we are on our way."
> *–Don Quixote*

FRIDAY, 26 SEPTEMBER 2031 (TWO AND A HALF YEARS EARLIER)

Warren Linder rose from the desk in his study, where he had been answering emails since dawn, and stepped through half-open French doors onto the veranda of his sixth-story apartment. To the north, he enjoyed a panoramic view of Beirut's new container port, the city's rebuilt commercial district, and the sparkling blue Mediterranean beyond. Along the veranda's edge, potted gardenias, jasmine, and dwarf frangipani trees lent an intoxicating sweetness to the air.

Linder had gone to bed early the night before, after taking the dinner flight home from Geneva. The trip, made in part to raise money for the anti-Unionist Congress (AUC), an umbrella organization of prominent American émigrés, had been a disappointment. Leonard Fury, the organization's founder, no longer commanded its members' full support. Despite being a long-time Fury ally and personal friend, the time had come for Linder to distance himself. He'd left Geneva profoundly discouraged.

Seven years had passed since Linder's escape from a Unionist corrective labor camp near the Arctic Circle. Over that time, nothing he or the AUC had done had loosened the Unionist Party's grip on power. Today, most AUC members were a decade older than when they had fled America. While they still revered the Constitution and the Republic, most had lost hope in recovering either. Those most

9

active in the movement remained so chiefly out of a deep-rooted hatred toward the Unionist Party and a thirst for revenge.

Until now, Linder would not have called himself a revanchist. Over the past decade, he had struggled to forgive those who had conspired to send him to the camps. Of course, it helped that the person most responsible for betraying him, Neil Denniston, was dead, and the next one in line, Bob Bednarski, had gone missing in the Yukon. No, it wasn't what the Unionist machine had done to him that made Linder fight so hard, but rather that he had once been part of that machine. And now he aimed to atone for it.

Linder took a last look out to sea and re-entered the flat, heading directly for the kitchen, dimly lit by shafts of sunlight entering through high east-facing windows. He remembered how busy the kitchen had been when his sister, brother-in-law, and teenaged ward gathered there every afternoon for coffee or a snack. That was when Caroline would return in uniform from her Catholic girls' school, sometimes with friends. At that time, his life had seemed richer and more satisfying than he could ever have imagined before his arrest. Even during his best years in the DSS, when he would return to his rented flat from each overseas assignment, itching within days to go on the road again, Linder had often dreamed of putting down roots somewhere. And, to his surprise, he had achieved that dream, or at least had come as close as he was likely to get. But now the dream had turned to dust.

Linder's Beirut flat occupied a corner flat on the fourth floor of a red granite apartment block. It was a stately relic from French colonial days, located in the densely populated Achrafiyé section of predominantly Christian East Beirut, where ethnic cleansing had long ago tamped down the flames of sectarian strife. In some ways the flat was an odd choice, because both Linder's and his teenaged ward's period of captivity had begun in Beirut, at an apartment only a few blocks away, where Caroline's grandfather had settled briefly after backing the losing side in America's Civil War II (CWII).

At the time, Caroline and her parents had been visiting the Eaton family patriarch, Philip Eaton, while Linder had been working as an undercover DSS officer sent to entice the fugitive industrialist back to the United States, where he had been convicted of treason *in absentia*.

If a city like Beirut, synonymous with lawlessness and civil strife, seemed an odd choice for Eaton, and now Linder, to escape the long arm of America's police state, in many ways it was a sensible choice. For more than a century, Beirut had earned a reputation as a haven for political refugees. Since the end of its decades-long civil war, it had rolled out the welcome mat for wealthy exiles of all political stripes and did not tolerate meddling from foreign security services. Just as important, Lebanon had no extradition treaty with the United States and boasted some of the strictest bank secrecy laws in the world.

But this morning, Linder's apartment felt anything but secure and welcoming. He was alone in the flat because his sister April and her husband had chosen this particular week—the week when Linder was to drop off Caroline at the University of Lausanne—to desert the home that the four of them had shared for more than five years. On the eve of his return from Geneva, Linder had received a voicemail message from April announcing that she and her husband Jay had just boarded a flight to New York and did not know when they might be back. The message added that Linder would find a letter on the kitchen counter explaining their reasons for leaving.

On the flight back to Beirut, his mind had been in turmoil, blaming himself for whatever he might have done to drive April away, while seething with resentment that she had not shared her plans with him. There had been signs, of course, and perhaps he had chosen to ignore them rather than come to grips with his sister's unhappiness. For the past five years, April had devoted herself to becoming a second mother to the orphaned Caroline. The teenager's impending return to university in Switzerland seemed to have hit April especially hard.

By nature, April was a gentle soul who thrived on comfort, stability, familiarity, and the simple things in life. Though careful not to wax nostalgic in her brother's presence about her former life in Cleveland, she never felt at ease as an émigré. Of course, there was much she had hated about life under Unionist rule and about her job enforcing political orthodoxy as vice principal of an inner-city public high school. But that was the life she had chosen. She hadn't asked her wild-ass fugitive brother to show up on her doorstep and ask her to abandon everything to leave America with him. Linder knew that she loved him and felt obliged to him for many things, including the opportunity to meet her future husband, Jay. But Linder also knew that April resented that he often played top dog, as elder brothers tend to do, and seemed to take for granted that she would look after Caroline and manage the shared household simply because she was a woman.

Jay, too, bristled sometimes at living under his brother-in-law's roof. The two men had met when Jay's father hired Linder to work in the family's dietary supplement manufacturing plant in Coalville, Utah, near the former resort town of Park City. The job offer had been a lifesaver for Linder, since at the time he was an escaped political prisoner living under a false identity without any means of earning a living. For nearly a year, Linder and Jay had worked side by side at the factory before the two men, facing imminent arrest, took Caroline with them on a cross-country trek to Cleveland, Ohio. There Linder picked up his sister April, along with a fortune in rebel treasure looted from the city's downtown banks during the final days of CWII.

Now, six years later, Jay seemed a shadow of the high-spirited bachelor he had once been. He had become a stoop-shouldered mope whose sallow skin, sunken eyes and receding hairline made him appear a decade older than his forty years. Like April, Jay had never mastered French or Arabic and failed to thrive in his new environment, despite having landed a well-paying job as a bartender in a Phoenicia Street speakeasy frequented by affluent English-speakers.

Even before Jay received the fateful letter from his father, claiming that the DSS had released him from custody and urging Jay to come help him rebuild the family business, Linder had sensed Jay's and April's discontent. The couple never let an opportunity pass to cite press articles about how life was returning to normal in America, and how Party General Secretary Twitchell was fostering the revival of small business with his New Economic Plan (NEP). They also marveled at how a new class of upstart "NEP men" had sprouted up almost overnight, launching pop-up shops, restaurants, and factories with astounding speed and building them into brands, chains, and fledgling commercial empires. Even chronically underfunded local governments were experiencing a renewal of sorts, reinvesting at last in decayed urban school systems like the one in Cleveland where April had worked.

"Could things really be so bad over there, now that the fighting is over and the regime has relaxed its grip?" April asked Linder one day at breakfast, not so rhetorically. "Jay's dad just qualified for the Congressional amnesty of former insurrectionists. He says Jay could qualify, too, if he went back."

April looked up from her coffee with expectant eyes, which Linder declined to meet.

"Jay's been in the camps, just like me," Linder answered in a sour tone. "He ought to know better than to believe anything coming from the Unionists."

"But the letter was from Jay's dad, not from the government."

"Really? How can you be sure that Larry wrote it and not some DSS minion?"

"Because it was in Larry's handwriting," April replied. "The letter said that Utah has a new DSS Regional Director. And that the regional office assured Larry that his son had no reason to fear re-arrest if he came back. Larry also mentioned that there's an opening for vice principal at Coalville's high school and that a friend of his on the school board could put me up for it."

April's voice was suffused with hope, and Linder hesitated to throw a wet blanket over her.

"So have you applied for the position?" he asked in as neutral a tone as he could muster.

"No, but I did take a look at the job description online. And it looks like I'd be more than qualified."

"April," Linder replied, shaking his head and peering into his coffee cup. "Can't you and Jay see you're being played? The DSS never lets bygones be bygones. Not ever. Even if the letter were genuine and Jay somehow qualified for amnesty, do you really think that the DSS would leave you and Jay in peace after having fled the country to live in exile with a convicted traitor like me? They'd find new charges to throw at you the moment you stepped off the plane."

"Jay doesn't think so. He says the letter rings true. He's also inclined to believe what Larry says about the new DSS Regional Director. And he can't bear the thought of refusing to help his father bring the family business back to life at a time when prospects look so good."

"But I thought you and Jay wanted to make a fresh start here. Sure, Lebanon isn't America, but we're settled now. And it's a pretty good life, if you ask me. Why can't you just accept what we have and be happy?"

"Happy?" she shot back, her face clouding over. "What would ever make you think that? We're ten thousand miles from home, living among total strangers. We don't speak the language. And we have to hire bodyguards and look over our shoulders wherever we go for fear of Unionist assassins or kidnappers."

Linder felt a bitter taste in his mouth.

"It is what it is. The important thing is that we're together and we're relatively free to live our lives as we want."

"I'd hardly call it being together when Caroline is going off to study in Switzerland and you're away two weeks out of every month crusading against the Evil Empire. You talk of settling down, but you never socialize here, and you won't let any woman your age get close to you. I hardly know you any more, Warren. The way you've become, I pity any woman who'd marry you. It would be a living hell."

"Maybe so," Linder replied, swallowing the hurt. "But that's my problem. As for you and Jay, don't think for a minute that boarding a plane for New York will make your life any easier. Look, I spent eight years in the Exile Division. In my professional opinion, that letter from Larry Becker reeks of provocation. We used to fabricate letters like that all the time to lure enemy exiles back to their doom. Don't fall for it, April."

But his sister remained unconvinced.

"Your work with those people has made you paranoid, Warren. You see nothing but danger everywhere and distrust everyone. Jay and I refuse to live like that any more. It's our lives at stake here, not yours, and we're inclined to take our chances going back to help Jay's father."

"But that's suicide! Please don't do anything more till I've had time to do some investigating. I'll want to take a very close look at that letter, for starters..."

"I'm sorry, Warren," April concluded with her head held high. "You can talk to Jay about it if you like. But I doubt anything you say will change his mind."

Linder read his sister's note one more time before stuffing it back into its envelope and returning it to the kitchen counter. By now the note's contents were seared in his memory. If April were right and the DSS didn't plan to arrest her and Jay on arrival, whether in New York or Salt Lake City, then he would likely hear from her by evening. If she didn't call or send a message soon, he would have to assume the worst. Meanwhile, he would do all he could to keep his mind occupied and shake off the gloom.

Linder dropped his empty coffee mug in the sink and pulled out his mobile phone.

"Okay, Valery," he began, addressing his Russian bodyguard. "Get ready. We're going to the gym as soon as I get dressed. We can pick up groceries on the way back."

Linder preferred Russian security guards. First, they were highly skilled. And he got along well with them, even though some had the personality of an ice cube. Second, having worked often in Beirut during his former career, he knew that native Lebanese bodyguards often harbored religious, tribal, and other loyalties that presented unknown risks. And third, while Israeli contractors were top-notch, they were also high-priced. And many Israeli firms maintained uncomfortably close ties to the U.S. national security establishment, even after the Unionist takeover. So he relied on Russian contractors, hired through a Cypriot-registered firm, who worked in pairs on month-long rotation.

Linder's current daytime bodyguard, Valery Chupin, didn't look the part at all. Short and pot-bellied, with a gregarious personality, he had a knack for putting people at ease and spoke English with an educated British accent. Few would have guessed that Chupin had been a *Spetsnaz*[1] major with combat experience in Syria, Armenia, Moldova, and the Donbas. Also to his credit, Chupin always brimmed with energy, was deceptively light on his feet, and possessed seemingly inexhaustible powers of endurance.

While en route to the gym in his thinly armored Audi Q9, Linder engaged Chupin in light-hearted banter. After a minute or two, the Russian turned serious.

---

[1] Soviet or Russian Special Operations Forces.

"The company asked me to remind you that my rotation ends in two weeks. After that, I return to Russia on home leave. They are selecting my replacement now."

"Good for you, Valery," Linder replied with a smile. "You've earned a proper rest. How long will you be away?"

"Two months. A week in Moscow for business, and the rest in Novosibirsk to see my girlfriend. We're thinking of marriage."

"Really? What for?" Linder asked, regretting at once the bitter note he detected in his own voice. It was a foolish thing to say to a man like Chupin. Like many Russian officers, Chupin was a traditionalist who could be expected to place a high value on family life.

"What for?" Chupin repeated. For a moment the Russian seemed taken aback, but then he brushed aside his client's cynicism with a soft laugh.

"Forgive me, Valery," Linder added. "I didn't mean it badly. Congratulations to you both."

A few minutes later, the Audi approached Linder's favorite gym, one of three that he used in irregular rotation to avoid displaying a consistent daily routine. The gym, located near Place Sassine in East Beirut, occupied the floor above a trendy men's clothing boutique. As usual, Chupin dropped off Linder near the entrance, then found a parking spot on the crowded street and took a seat at a sidewalk café nearby. There he ordered sweet Arabic coffee and joked in English and pidgin French with the old men playing backgammon and with a table of young Kalashnikov-toting Christian militiamen. It was Chupin's strategy to befriend militia and private security guards wherever he went, both to avoid friction and to have more firepower on his side should trouble arise.

One of the off-duty gunmen, a lanky teenager dressed in a cheap track suit, had met Chupin weeks before and never wasted an opportunity to pump the veteran for tips on the warrior's craft. Chupin had nearly finished his second coffee with the youth when his cell phone vibrated and Linder asked him to bring the car around.

Chupin did as promised and stood beside the SUV while keeping an eye peeled for his client. At the same time, his attentive young friend watched cars drive by with his assault rifle stretched across his lap.

As Linder emerged from the gym, an idling motorcycle engine roared to life fifty meters up the street. At Chupin's outdoor café, the noise caught the ear of his teenaged friend, who noticed a pair of helmeted riders approaching from uphill. Because motorcycle-borne assassinations were frequent in Lebanon, the teenaged gunman went on alert, flipped down the safety on his assault rifle and jacked a cartridge into the chamber.

The Russian's attention was still focused on his client when Linder emerged onto the sidewalk. Just then the motorcycle's rear passenger pulled a short-barreled machine pistol from his jacket and fired, hitting Chupin in the torso with a three-round burst and dropping him hard. But before the shooter could shift his aim to fire at Linder, the youth with the Kalashnikov sprayed the motorcycle with automatic fire, sending the riders flying sideways and the motorcycle into a screeching metallic skid. When the bike came to rest, the shooter lay lifeless while the driver struggled to regain his feet. As he rose, he drew a bulky black pistol from his belt. In the blink of an eye, the Lebanese felled him with a single shot to the chest and jumped off the curb toward his inert victims.

For what seemed an eternity, Linder remained frozen by the gym door, only a few strides away from where Valery Chupin lay bleeding. Seconds later, the other militiamen sitting at the café sprang into action, administered first aid to Chupin and packed him quickly into the rear seat of Linder's idling Audi. Two of the fighters rode with Linder and directed him to the nearest hospital, only a few minutes away. The moment they arrived at the emergency room entrance, a team of first responders raced out to meet them. They lifted Chupin onto a gurney and sped off on foot into the hospital. Linder and one of the fighters followed them all the way to the operating room. There the chief surgeon examined the Russian and promptly declared him dead on arrival.

Preston Fleming

Chapter Three: Bristol

> "Three may keep a secret, if two of them are dead."
> —*Benjamin Franklin*

FRIDAY, 26 SEPTEMBER 2031

T he Great Western Railway train pulled into Bristol's Temple Meads Station shortly after four on a cloudy and windswept September afternoon. Owen Quist rose to fetch his roller bag from the overhead rack but paused first to examine his reflection in the window. Quist was a fireplug of a man, not long past middle age, with the face of one who has lived too well. He took care to straighten his tie, smooth his Van Dyke beard, and adjust the collar of his newly purchased tweed sport coat, which despite skilled tailoring did not flatter his tubby form.

After waiting for the other passengers to leave the carriage, Quist stepped briskly onto the platform. From there he made directly for the taxi stand, where he gave his driver a handwritten address in the nearby suburb of Filton, a hub of Britain's aerospace industry and home to units of Airbus, BAE Systems, and Rolls-Royce. Ten minutes later, Quist paid the cabbie and watched him drive off before he walked around the corner and rang the doorbell at a handsome two-story semi-detached house faced with red brick.

The man who opened the door was a trim-figured fellow of military bearing, also in his early fifties, but appearing years younger. Harold Acker sported the same buzz-cut hairdo that he had worn during his quarter century as a U.S. Air Force bomber pilot. He was dressed modestly in gray woolen slacks and a striped cardigan over a black turtleneck. He greeted the traveler with a firm handshake and a genial smile.

"My, don't we look prosperous?" the former pilot remarked after looking Quist up and down. "Going socialist doesn't seem to have hurt you one bit, Owen. But tell me, how on earth did you ever wangle an exit visa from the Workers' Paradise?"

Quist blushed as he stepped indoors and allowed Acker to take his roller bag.

"Oh, I'm traveling on company business," Quist answered. "They sent me here to expand U.S. LPG[2] exports to Bristol's new Avonmouth sea terminal."

"But isn't foreign travel still tightly restricted, even for government officials? Or is the State Oil Company turning a blind eye to former seditionists these days?"

Quist let out an uneasy laugh.

"Fortunately, my brief indiscretion with the militias seems to have eluded the background checkers. I'm a Party member now and all that mess is behind me. Still, I'd appreciate it if you kept quiet about our time fighting together in Colorado. Not just for my sake, but for Denise's."

"Ah, my lovely wife. How is Denise doing these days?"

Quist went silent for a moment and gave Acker a searching look.

"If it's okay for me to ask, when was the last time you and Denise spoke?" Quist asked his host.

"Four or five years ago. It was just after she'd landed a big new government job. Since then, it's been crickets until she wrote about your coming to see me."

---

[2] Liquified Petroleum Gas, which consists primarily of propane. LPG differs from LNG (Liquified Natural Gas) in that the latter consists mainly of methane and is generally cheaper but requires expensive cryogenic storage.

Quist relaxed imperceptibly, seeing that Acker had not taken offense at his question.

"Well, Denise's career has really taken off since then," he told his host. "She's a big wheel at Treasury now."

"How generous of the government not to begrudge her having a notorious political exile for a husband," Acker commented with a smile that his eyes didn't share.

"Of course, she had no choice but to denounce you, Harold. But, fortunately, Denise's legal work has nothing to do with sensitive criminal or intelligence cases. Only financial disputes. And, apart from marrying you, she's always toed the line with her politics."

Acker's jaw clenched and a momentary shade darkened his face. Then, as if nothing had happened, he stowed his guest's overnight bag in a corner and led him into a well-appointed kitchen.

"Well, if we're going to jump right into the matter of Denise, then perhaps we'd both better have a drink. How about a wee dram of malt whisky to get us started?"

"If you insist," Quist replied with an eagerness that sprang in part from the near impossibility of finding good Scotch whisky in the States ever since import controls went into effect.

Acker poured a generous shot of the straw-colored liquid into a cut-crystal tumbler for his guest and poured another for himself.

"Not that we'll need this on Denise's account," the ex-pilot noted, raising his glass in salute. "To be perfectly honest, she and I were already on the outs even before I joined the insurgency. But, as Catholics, we weren't in a hurry to divorce. And once I left the country, there never seemed much reason to follow through."

"So you haven't been inclined to remarry?"

"Nah, British women can be very appealing, but they're an odd breed. Frankly speaking, I haven't found one yet that I could see eye to eye with. Not that I've stopped kicking the tires," Acker concluded with a half-smile.

"As well you might. I expect you'd appear a fine catch for some enterprising woman. Aeronautical engineers must be paid pretty well. Are you still toiling away at Airbus?"

"No, I jumped ship for Rolls-Royce this spring. They're working on some new engine prototypes and wanted someone with experience flying long-range bombers."

"So then you have no objection to Denise filing for divorce?" Quist inquired, abruptly changing tack. He felt a chill in the air while awaiting a response.

"I might, if she were marrying some asshole *apparatchik*," Acker answered in a mock-serious tone. "But since she's picked you, Owen, I'm pleased she'll have someone reliable to look after her."

Acker took a deep gulp of whisky while continuing to fix Quist with a steady gaze.

"Though Denise has always been quite capable of looking after herself," he added before raising his glass again. "Anyway, Owen, here's a toast to your happiness together. And I really mean that."

Quist tended to be suspicious of people who prefaced their remarks with "to be frank" or "honestly," or concluded them with "I really mean that." But he took his old friend at his word and raised his glass in unison.

"You can't imagine what a relief it is to me that you don't object to our getting married," Quist replied, feeling unexpectedly buoyant. "It's been a long time since you left for England, and I couldn't be sure how you'd take the news."

"Well, as I recall, it was me who first stole Denise away from you. So it's only fair for me to give her back."

Acker poured more whisky into each glass, this time evading eye contact with his guest. "Listen, Owen, are you hungry?" he added after they drank again. "I'm not much of a cook. Why don't we hop over to my local pub, grab some bangers and mash, and catch up on old times?"

After downing what little remained in their whisky glasses, the two men walked three blocks to an unassuming stucco-fronted building whose antique signage read "The Horsehead." Once indoors, they waded through the crowd to a small table at the back.

"Would you care to sample some of our local ale?" Acker offered.

"Sure, I'll have whatever you're having."

The barmaid brought them two pints of copper-hued real ale drawn from a wooden barrel with an antique hand pump.

"To Denise, the love of our lives!" Acker pledged as he raised his glass.

Not long after, having downed half his pint, Quist loosened up sufficiently to address more serious questions.

"I've often wondered," he began, "have you stayed in contact with any of the guys who fought with us in Colorado? I imagine that the ones who escaped capture have scattered to the four winds, but I can't help thinking of them now and then."

Acker had nearly finished his pint by now and his eyes seemed to glow with alcohol-fueled well-being.

"Oh, I hear from a few of them occasionally. But you're right—when we saw the writing on the wall, most guys took off in all directions. Those of us who keep in touch do it mostly through the FAP."

"The what?"

"Free American Patriots. Ben Payne's group," Acker noted. "They're the ones who put up the money to exfiltrate a lot of us out of Mexico after the fighting. It's a good outfit, though the leadership isn't what it used to be. They're mostly washed-up Republican politicos and purged Pentagon brass who spend their time organizing fundraisers and conferences to take back America from the Unionists."

"Good luck with doing that from across the pond," Quist answered on a bitter note. "Payne and his elitist cronies had their chance in CWII. But they let the Unionists roll right over them. Now they're wealthy émigrés, while ordinary folks back home are left to pay the price. Why should any of us trust the likes of them again?"

"Fair enough. But if it's too late for the émigrés to unseat the regime, what are the prospects for an internal opposition?"

Quist looked around as if to check whether anyone might be listening.

"I think I might need another pint before I tackle that one," he replied, picking up a menu. "And something to eat."

Acker waved over the buxom young barmaid, who took their orders for another round of ale, along with a mixed grill for Quist and a steak and kidney pie for himself.

"As you were saying," Acker went on after fresh pints were served, "just how restless have the natives been growing lately back home?"

"Having lost CWII and suffered through the Blue Terror, most Americans are too terrified to utter a word against the regime. Everybody knows someone who's been sent to the camps. And no one wants to lose his ration card or housing permit by sticking his neck out. Though many came close last summer."

"Why? What happened then?"

"It's more about what didn't happen," Quist replied. "The economy was at a standstill, and we had severe food shortages, power outages and fuel rationing, all at once. Fistfights were breaking out in supermarket aisles. Had it not been for the NEP, we might have seen food riots and possibly worse."

"Excuse me, but what's the NEP?"

Quist shot his friend an incredulous look.

"Surely you've heard about the New Economic Plan? It's all that the state-controlled media has been talking about for the past year."

Acker shrugged and took another sip of ale.

"You have to remember, Harold," Quist explained, "all through the Twenties the Unionist system of state capitalism and central economic planning was circling the drain. We had major labor strikes, farmers burning their crops, and hunger strikes by small business owners demanding an end to high taxes and regulatory stranglehold. What's more, the police and the military were showing clear signs of unrest. The Unionist Party had won CWII, but it was losing the peace—badly. The Gang of Three feared outright revolt and Zuckerman wanted to bring back the Blue Terror to crush it. But Twitchell nixed that. Instead, Ted Terzian dreamed up the NEP and Gang of Three went along with it."

"Did it work?"

"To an extent. There was a short-term economic boost from shifting resources away from failing state-controlled enterprises toward small businesses and family farms. Lifting wage and price controls also helped. But the government couldn't afford to rescind currency controls without risking capital flight, so they kept a tight lid on imports. As for exports and inbound foreign investment, those had already collapsed years before when the President-for-Life repudiated the country's foreign debt. Which is why Twitchell surprised everyone by inviting back American émigrés to become investors, in hopes of attracting a gold rush of entrepreneurial capital and know-how."

"That's a pretty harsh assessment, coming from a senior Party member like you, Owen. Are you sure you're okay sharing it with a political heretic like me?"

Quist snorted. The truth was that he had long thirsted for an opportunity to speak openly about the Party's disastrous economic policies. At home, he had taken on a quiet and deferential demeanor to divert attention from his past political sins. But here in England, outside the Party's reach, with a sympathetic audience and ample rations of whisky and ale under his belt, Owen Quist was ready to let it rip.

"You don't intend to repeat any of this to the DSS, do you?" he asked Acker with an ironic frown.

"Not bloody likely," Acker guffawed. "But tell me this. If U.S. exports are blocked, what are you doing in Bristol peddling American propane?"

"Energy exports are the exception to the rule. They're our trump card, the key to reopening trade and foreign investment. And, for the moment, the Brits are quite happy to buy our LPG at the sizeable cash discounts we're offering."

"So you're relying on the U.K. to bail out your failing economy?"

"Not me. I'm just a lowly propane salesman," Quist parried. "My job is to boost monthly shipments to you blokes. Beyond that, I think your Tory government knows better than to prop up the Unionist Party by reopening trade on a broader scale. Frankly, I suspect that Whitehall is still hoping to smother the infant American regime in its cradle."

"Do any of your friends in Washington see things the same way, or are you the only misfit among your crowd?"

"Oh, I'm far from being alone in my thinking," Quist insisted, his face flushed now as he downed the dregs of his second pint. "But those of us who see things my way never speak out in public. Even privately, we meet only in twos and threes. Still, I've been hearing that secret cells have formed in Washington to discuss alternatives to Unionism. I've put out feelers to learn more."

"Wow, I'd love to know what you find," Acker replied, showing unexpected enthusiasm. "Would you mind if I passed along what you've said to the guys at FAP? The more information we have about what's going on over there, the more effective we can be in fighting the Party from over here. I wouldn't use your real name, of course."

Quist drew a sharp breath and bit his lip, realizing he had stepped onto sensitive territory. But, having come so far, he didn't want to risk offending his friend. Heaven forbid that Acker might withdraw his consent to Denise's divorce. And by now, Quist's head was muzzy with alcohol.

"The FAP are good lads," Acker assured him as he waved on the barmaid who was wending through the crowd with their meals. "You have nothing to fear from their sort."

"I suppose it's okay to share my material with them, as long as they don't know it's coming from me," Quist replied, while sensing a frosty chill creep across his skin.

An hour later, the two men left the pub to polish off Acker's bottle of whisky at his place. By then, Quist had lost any recollection of what he had told his friend, or how easily it might be traced back to him if the material fell into the wrong hands.

Two nights later, while Quist typed up his sales contact reports after dining alone in his Bristol hotel room, Harold Acker was busy at home drafting a report of his own. It was addressed to Benjamin Payne, the Berlin-based leader of the Free American Patriots, and contained a detailed account of what Quist had told Acker about American economic policy, oil and gas production, LPG and LNG exports, dissident cells within the U.S. government, and other topics that an authoritarian regime might consider sensitive.

While Acker's report was professionally done, owing to his military experience and basic intelligence training, the description of Acker's source, when combined with the report's content, made it a cinch for any competent counterintelligence outfit to identify the source as a senior State Oil Company official who had visited Bristol recently. That was unfortunate for Owen Quist, given that the DSS already had an informant in place inside Benjamin Payne's Berlin office, who promptly forwarded a copy of Acker's report to his Washington-based DSS handlers.

Nor did Acker inform Quist that, as the holder of a British security clearance, he was obliged to disclose all contacts with foreign nationals to the chief of security at his employer, Rolls-Royce, whose office routinely relayed such disclosures to MI5, the British domestic security service.

As it happened, both Americans went to sleep that night with a warm feeling about their reunion two nights before. They had shared their memories, gained new empathy for one another, and cleared the path for Quist and Denise to marry. What could be the harm in that?

Chapter Four: Heathrow

> "The strong do what they will and the weak suffer what they must."
>
> *—Thucydides*

TUESDAY, 30 SEPTEMBER 2031

L inder's flight to Heathrow arrived early and the lines at passport control were shorter than expected. Since he was entering on a British Refugee Travel Document, he queued up in the line for British passport holders. When his turn came, he stepped forward and presented his papers.

For what seemed like an eternity, the young immigration enforcement officer stared at the travel document while also consulting a computer screen below Linder's field of vision. Then, without looking up, the officer entered a series of keystrokes, punctuated by brief pauses, in apparent communication with some higher authority. At last, the officer rose from his chair and, without handing the travel document back, invited Linder to accompany him to a side office. There a pair of uniformed police led Linder to a bank of hard seats.

"What seems to be the problem, officer?" Linder asked, his anxiety rising. This was not supposed to happen. He had given his flight information to his MI5 contact, Allen Hackett, who promised to be on hand to expedite his arrival.

"I'm sorry, sir, but you are denied entry into the United Kingdom."

"But I've been granted political asylum here and have a valid residence permit. I gave you the document that proves it."

Linder took a deep breath and did his best to keep his cool. Before boarding his flight, Hackett had assured him that there was zero chance of being turned away. So much for Hackett's assurances. They always sounded good, but sometimes didn't hold water.

"Our records show that Interpol has issued a Red Notice against you," the immigration officer explained. "They say you're a fugitive from justice in the United States. So I'm afraid we're going to have to turn you back. Please empty your pockets and place all the contents on the table. That includes your mobile phone."

Linder did as he was told but would not be silenced.

"Excuse me, officer, but a Red Notice is not an arrest warrant. And, even if it were, official U.K. policy bars the arrest or deportation of American nationals accused of political crimes in the United States. Nor has any British court issued an extradition order against me. So why are you denying me entry?"

"I understand your position, sir," the immigration officer pointed out. "But refusing entry is not the same as an arrest or deportation. If you wish to contest your removal, you'll have to do it from a British embassy located abroad."

Linder stiffened and answered through clenched teeth.

"May I speak to the ranking MI5 officer on duty here? All this was supposed to have been worked out in advance."

By now Linder suspected Hackett himself might be the cause of the problem. He had first met Hackett nearly a decade earlier when assigned as a DSS officer to the U.S. Embassy in London. The two men had worked together on a counterterrorism case involving an American citizen and became occasional drinking buddies. At the time, Linder didn't particularly like or trust Hackett, who came across as a quintessential English snob.

Three years later, when Linder returned to London as an escapee from an American corrective labor camp, the two men met again. This time, Hackett was the MI5 officer assigned to interview him for his political asylum application. But by then, if the two had ever considered each other friends, there was no longer any pretense of it. While the asylum application was approved, was it possible that Hackett still distrusted Linder and had arranged behind the scenes to block his re-entry into Britain?

The young immigration officer exchanged distrustful looks with the two uniformed police before answering Linder's request to summon the MI5 duty officer.

"Wait here, I'll see what can be done."

An hour later, the immigration officer returned with a bald fellow of slight stature whose face reminded Linder of a baby bird.

"How can we help you," the presumed MI5 man began without offering his name or rank.

Linder summarized the situation for him and asked the man to call Allen Hackett to sort things out.

"You mean, just now?" The MI5 man's eyes moved from Linder to the three immigration employees and back again.

"Yes, why not?" Linder demanded.

A smirk spread across the MI5 man's face.

"I have another idea. Why don't you write down the name and phone number of this person you want me to call?" He removed a small bound notebook from his suit jacket and handed it over. "I'll get back to you when I'm able to reach him."

Again, Linder did as he was told. Ten minutes later, the MI5 man returned with a scowl on his face.

"I notice that you have legal residence status in Britain but have been residing outside the country," he noted, giving Linder a wary look. "May I ask what prompted your return?"

"Of course. You see, when the Unionist regime filed an extradition request against me with the British government, I decided to move to Lebanon, which lacks an extradition treaty with the United States. I planned to return as soon as my case here was resolved. But years have passed and the case hasn't even been docketed with a court. When a couple of killers tried to gun me down last week in Beirut, I decided to come back to London and take my chances with the British legal system rather than with Lebanese gunmen. And to that end, MI5 offered me certain assurances."

Linder felt a sudden chill. If those assurances turned out to be empty, and the British put him on the next plane back to Beirut, another team of hit men might be waiting there to kill him. Could he persuade the authorities to send him somewhere other than Lebanon? Perhaps to Cyprus, where he could pick up a fresh Russian bodyguard?

"Interpol claims that you are a suspect in a series of bombings in the United States," the MI5 man went on. "And that you've provided funds to Leonard Fury's insurgent network. Is there any truth to that?"

Linder collected his thoughts in time to stifle a bitter laugh.

"Leonard is a friend of mine. I confess to giving him money from time to time, but never for anything illegal. If you'll check my record as a refugee, my political activities have been completely nonviolent."

At that moment, the MI5 man's mobile phone vibrated audibly. He fished it out of his pocket to read an incoming text message. Then, without changing his deadpan expression, he gestured for the immigration officers to return Linder's travel document and belongings.

"Yes, I see now that Officer Hackett will vouch for you and has confirmed your asylum status. I have only one more question for you, Mr. Linder. Do I have your earnest commitment to refrain from political violence while on British soil and to report any such activity you may come across?" the MI5 man continued.

"But of course."

"Then you're free to enter, Mr. Linder. Good day to you."

Chapter Five: London

> "The discontentment is there; now it's up to us to go in and rub raw the sores of discontentment and galvanize them for radical social change."
> –*Saul Alinsky*

TUESDAY, 7 OCTOBER 2031

T he call came from the hotel's front desk.

"Mrs. Bowles is here. Shall I send her up?"

Linder was staying at the five-star Milestone Hotel, located opposite Kensington Palace. In fact, his junior suite had an excellent view across the gardens to the royal residence. He had stayed there many times before and had gone out of his way to befriend the staff as a first line of defense against hostile action.

"Please do," Linder replied.

A brief silence followed, after which the desk clerk spoke again.

"Mrs. Bowles would prefer to meet you in the lobby, sir, if you don't mind. She says you have a busy schedule this afternoon and will need to make an early start."

"All right, then. I'll be down in a moment."

Fiona Bowles, who had been his private secretary for several months before he moved from London to Beirut, had also been his occasional lover during that time. She was married now, to a prosperous American banker, and he imagined that she didn't want to appear indiscreet by meeting him in his suite. So be it, he thought. She had come today as a favor to help him find a rental flat in the area. That morning they were to meet an estate agent and view half a dozen flats.

In the lobby, Linder and Bowles exchanged pecks on the cheek before moving to an adjacent lounge to sit. The room was empty, so they took places on a settee that looked out onto Kensington Gardens. Bowles had been in her early thirties when the two had first met, a willowy, dark-haired beauty who had just lost her job as executive assistant at a major advertising agency. Now, though her hair was streaked with gray, she had kept her youthful figure, good looks, and supremely confident manner. Today, Bowles wore an expensive-looking double-breasted trench coat over a knee-length knit dress, both of which looked like upgrades to her wardrobe from six years before.

"I'm sad to hear that Beirut didn't work out for you, Warren," Bowles opened.

"Actually, Beirut was quite agreeable while Caroline was in school and my sister was living with us," Linder replied. "But now that April has returned to the States with her husband and Caroline is at university in Switzerland, I'm on my own. London seems a better fit."

"Certainly less hazardous," Bowles added with raised eyebrow. "I'm so pleased you're looking for a flat in this part of the city. What with the proximity to Parliament, Buckingham Palace and the like, security here is very tight indeed. It's not a place where rogues and villains can lurk about unnoticed."

Linder smiled. He sensed a repressed sexual energy between them, though Bowles seemed intent on keeping her distance. As her hands fidgeted in her lap, Linder couldn't help notice her massive diamond engagement ring.

"Congratulations on your marriage, by the way," Linder remarked, changing the subject. "Tell me about your husband. Have I met him?"

"I doubt it," she replied. "Thomas came here from New York in 2020, before the Unionist coup, and has had very little contact with American political exiles. In fact, I would call him a political agnostic."

"So what's it like for you as a Brit being married to an American? Is it true what they say about our two peoples being separated by a common language?"

"Oh, I had my concerns about it early on, but we've been together four years now and I think we get along quite well. My family positively adores him. And he gets on swimmingly with my British friends."

Bowles's enthusiasm for her marriage seemed genuine, though it seemed odd she hadn't mentioned her husband's last name. So why had she agreed to help her old lover look for a flat? Was it purely out of kindness, perhaps tinged with curiosity? And if her husband was so well off, why had Bowles also agreed to work several days a week to help set up Linder's office? Not for the money, apparently. Without further thought, Linder brushed off such concerns as unfair.

"Well, I'm very happy for you both," Linder replied with an open smile. "I'd love to meet Thomas sometime."

"Let's do that. Meanwhile, perhaps you should consider finding a British wife to look after you. I could send one or two candidates your way, if you like."

Linder laughed uneasily.

"I'm not sure you'd be doing them any favors, given my situation," he replied.

And it wasn't just the latest assassination attempt he was thinking about, or the fact that the DSS would never stop pursuing him so long as the Unionist regime held power. Rather, it was his sister's biting remark that she pitied any woman who became his wife. Was it true?

"Well, you let me be the judge of that," Bowles replied. And as she looked up at the antique wall clock, a concerned look came over her face. "Oh, my, we really must get started if we're to be on time for our first showing."

Linder was inspecting a tastefully furnished three-bedroom flat in Chelsea, not far from Sloane Square, when his mobile phone rang. The flat was the best prospect he had seen all day, with both a tube station and a Sainsbury's grocery located a short walk away, and in a neighborhood that exuded quiet safety. Though, ironically, it was less than a mile from his old DSS office in the now-shuttered U.S. Embassy at Nine Elms. He did his best to banish the thought from his mind.

"Hi, sweetheart," Linder answered after accepting the call.

"Greetings from the Alps," Caroline replied. "Sorry about the delay in calling you back. I've been working on a research paper. So what are you doing in London? Are the Lebanese at war again?"

"No, things are quiet in Beirut," Linder lied, neglecting to mention the attempt on his life. "It's just that things got lonely there without you and April and Jay. So I thought I'd get away for a while and do my work from here. I have plenty of meetings lined up on the Continent this fall and it's easier to manage the travel from London. In fact, I'm looking at a rental flat right now. I think you'd like it."

"That's brilliant!" Caroline declared. "Now I can visit you there! As it happens, Aunt Wendy Eaton has invited me to her house in Oxfordshire next weekend, so I'm free for dinner Friday night. Could I come see you on the way?"

"Ah, sadly, I'll be in Berlin next weekend."

"Oh, rats. I was really hoping we could check out some cool London clubs together. Besides, I don't know quite what to make of Aunt Wendy's invitation. I mean, the last time we lived in London, she acted as if she didn't want to know us. As if you and I were somehow responsible for Mom and Dad's death."

Caroline fell silent and Linder imagined her eyes welling with tears.

"Anyway," she went on, "she seemed nice enough on the phone this time, so I decided to give her a second chance. But they'd better not say anything unkind about you, or I swear I'll walk right out the door."

Linder smiled, idly wondering if Caroline's threat represented genuine loyalty or just youthful contrariness.

"Never mind what they say about me, sweetheart," he replied. "Just do your best to stay on good terms with them. The Eatons are your blood relatives. Life is long. You may need each other one day."

Though Linder was sincere in urging Caroline to get along with her aunt, he had no illusions about why the Eatons had invited Caroline to visit them. Most likely, their purpose in taking her under their wing was to wean her away from Linder, whom they blamed for the DSS's extra-judicial rendition of Caroline, her parents, and her grandfather back to the Unionist State a decade earlier, an operation in which Linder had played a key role. No doubt they also believed reports that the cached rebel booty that Linder had spirited away from the U.S. rightfully belonged to Caroline's grandfather, and thus to the Eaton clan at large. Though this was untrue, Linder doubted that the surviving Eatons could ever be persuaded otherwise. The important thing for him was that Caroline reconnect with her extended family and gain the social standing and support network that only they could offer her. And if it meant that Caroline might fall under their influence and drift away from him, he could accept that risk. After all, who knew how long he'd be around to act as a surrogate parent?

Linder was so lost in his own thoughts he didn't hear what Caroline said next.

"Excuse me, what were you saying?" he asked.

"I was asking about Aunt April and Uncle Jay. Have you heard from them? Did they make it back to Utah okay?"

Now Linder realized why he had tuned out the question.

"No word from them yet," he told her, without sharing what he feared had happened to them. "I'm assuming no news is good news. But, just in case, I've asked my sources over there to check on them."

"Well, let me know the moment you hear anything more, okay? I had a bad feeling about their going back. Before they left, I told April that I couldn't understand how she and Jay could trust the Unionists to leave them in peace. But she didn't want to hear it. And the next day they were gone."

"I know how you feel, sweetie," Linder replied, sharing the girl's sadness. "But sometimes a person's native soil can exert an irresistible attraction. And April and Jay never felt quite at home living overseas."

"You wouldn't ever go back, would you?" Caroline answered in a voice that trembled. "Warren, promise me you won't! I can't bear the thought of you back in one of those camps."

Linder affected an easy laugh.

"Believe me, dear, I have no intention of ever letting the DSS get their filthy paws on me again."

"Will you promise?"

He hesitated before answering. And at that moment Bowles entered the room. But she stood back when she saw that Linder was on the phone.

"Frankly, I'd rather not promise," he told Caroline. "Over the years, I've learned that making a promise is often a bigger mistake than breaking it."

Rather than object, Caroline let out a laugh.

"Funny. Mom used to say something like that. Her version of it was that promising not to do something made it all the more likely that you'd go out later and do it."

"I miss your mom."

"So do I," the teenager replied softly.

Bowles waited to speak until Linder had put away his cell phone,

"Your ward?" she asked quietly.

"Yes."

"Will she be coming to live with you?"

"No, she's at university in Switzerland," Linder answered. "But I think she'll like this place when she sees it. Tell the owner I'll take it."

The quarterly meeting of the Anglo-American Freedom Committee (AAFC) met for lunch at its usual venue, the Hotel Café Royal, on Regent Street near Piccadilly Circus. The eighty or more attendees were seated at a dozen round tables in an upstairs dining room, with a raised dais at the front. Linder arrived a few minutes late, missing the sherry pour but seating himself in time for the salad course.

Linder's media relations consultant, Dwight Calder, cast a relieved look at the late arrival, since he had been the one to book Linder as the event's major speaker. Calder had been one of the organization's founding members, launching it within a year after the Unionist coup in America. Over the next few years, as wealthy American refugees flocked in from across the Atlantic, he had helped build the committee into London's most influential association of anti-Unionist émigrés.

Within days after Linder's initial arrival in London following his escape from a Yukon labor camp, Calder persuaded him to write a memoir, entitled My Book of Revelations, a modern-day Gulag Archipelago describing the American corrective labor camp system, his experiences there, and his harrowing trek to freedom. Linder and Calder wrote the book together and published it in record time. And, on the strength of its rapid rise on the international best-seller lists, Linder spent the next two years on the celebrity speakers' circuit, connecting with anti-Unionist militants everywhere he went.

But Linder had attended only a few meetings of the London-based committee since decamping for Beirut five years earlier and found the modest size of today's crowd disappointing. In the AAFC's early years, meetings had been monthly and often packed the hotel's spacious ballroom. For many members, the meetings offered a networking venue to help them find their feet in a strange city. For others, the committee was an outlet for their hostility toward the Unionist Party. For Linder, it had been both. But his primary use for the group was to recruit donors and activists for his own organization, the Anglo-American Information Bureau (AAIB), whose mission was to broadcast anti-Unionist propaganda throughout North America via radio, the internet, and clandestine photocopying.

Once Linder's entrée was served, he wolfed it down quickly, as he had little time to eat before being called upon to speak. He had scarcely finished his roast beef when the meeting's chairman tapped his fork loudly against his water glass to command attention.

"We are indeed fortunate to have Warren Linder back as a speaker after a long absence. I daresay we can expect to see much more of him now that he has relocated to London. Today, Warren will address us about a recent shift in his strategy against the Unionist regime and what it means for the émigré opposition movement. Please welcome Warren with a hearty round of applause."

Linder rose to the podium and looked upon his well-fed audience. Most were members of America's moneyed elite who had fled their native land after the Unionist coup d'état. To their surprise, upon seizing power, the Party had immediately turned the full force of state power against those who considered themselves above it; and offered them a choice between exile and the camps. These moneymen—and some prominent women among them—had escaped the new Unionist State of America with their offshore cash but left behind their businesses, their professions, their clubs, their gated enclaves, and their connectedness to the communities and institutions that defined who they were. Linder had come to know many people like this during his years as a scholarship student at Exeter, Kenyon, and Columbia Law. They were the handsome, talented, sophisticated, well-traveled youths from Greenwich and Rye, Brookline and Cambridge, Wilmington and Philadelphia's Main Line, who by adulthood had little time for anyone outside their intersecting circles of privilege.

Many of the AAFC's exiled members had never intended to start life afresh in London. Rather, they had hoped to reproduce their old lives there on a temporary basis until the Unionist regime collapsed of its own weight. But now, a decade later, that collapse had not occurred. And while the younger generation had taken new jobs, opened new businesses, married locals and sought permanent residence in the U.K., their elders refused to turn the page on America. Instead, some aimed to make up for lost time by doing business with the same scoundrels who had cast them out. And the longer they waited to return, the more strongly they justified their collaboration with the Unionists.

Linder made a conscious effort to banish resentment from his mind as he smiled and nodded to the notables who surrounded him on the dais.

"The last time I spoke here," he began, "I had just returned from my European book tour. While on the road, I met many American patriots who were waging the struggle to defeat Unionism from exile. I respected these men and women and vowed to support them as best I could."

Linder saw the faces of his audience fall as he drew a deep breath and fixed them with a stern gaze. And at that moment he wondered how many among them had given up the fight and came to these meetings merely to socialize.

"Tonight, five years later," he went on, "we live in a different world. The armed insurgency has failed, and what remains of it is now widely viewed, both within and outside North America, as wanton terrorism. So let me be clear: If I thought that more violence would bring us victory over the Unionists, I wouldn't hesitate to pursue it. But I don't believe that any more. To defeat Unionism, I believe we need to change our tactics and draw on the lessons of Gandhi, Mandela, and Martin Luther King. They succeeded against tyranny with non-violence. They strengthened the people's will through facts and argument. Call it propaganda, if you will.

"But how can we who live outside America reach a mass audience inside when all mass media are state-controlled, the internet is censored, and those who speak freely among friends risk secret denunciation and arrest? Means exist to penetrate the Unionist firewall, but they are vulnerable to DSS countermeasures. At the moment we're using encrypted emails, Virtual Private Networks, the Dark Web, shortwave radio, and other means to spread the word about Unionism's failures. At the same time, we use mockery and satirical memes to portray Party leaders as weak and feckless. Not only do these tactics undermine the Party's public approval, but our own people also get a huge kick out of applying them."

Here Linder paused to offer a conspiratorial smile, drawing polite laughter and applause from his audience. He closed his remarks with a brief description of the newly created Anglo-American Information Bureau, which he funded out of his own pocket with the goal of creating dissident cells around the country that one day might coalesce into an organized resistance. Afterward he took questions from a modestly enthusiastic audience.

At every opportunity he used the words "peaceful" and "non-violent" to make absolutely clear that he renounced violent insurrection. He did this knowing that the audience included not only fellow anti-Unionists, but also a sprinkling of MI5 officers, left-leaning journalists, and DSS informants whom he hoped to persuade that he was no terrorist and could safely be left alone to peddle his propaganda.

Linder stepped off the dais to circulate among the attendees who remained behind. Dwight Calder stood at his elbow and steered him toward the most influential AAFC members and donors. Calder, a tall, burly man with a full black beard and unruly head of graying hair, made a comfortable living as the owner of an advertising and media relations agency. Born on Manhattan's Upper West Side, he had fled America with his parents fifteen years earlier, not long before the Unionists seized power. Now past forty, he still behaved like someone who thought himself young.

Having demonstrated his value to Linder as a media strategist during the latter's tenure as a popular author and speaker, Calder had gone on to assist Linder in his efforts to influence the British public and its government against the Unionist regime. Stopping short of directly lobbying legislators, the two men had assembled a team of influential bloggers, op-ed writers and talking heads who could be relied upon to generate a drumbeat of invective in the U.K. media against the Unionists. Now, with the launch of AAIB's new propaganda campaign, Calder stood to greatly expand monthly billings from his wealthy client.

But as Linder shook hands with one admirer after another, he was dismayed at how little zeal they seemed to show for supporting his informational campaign or indeed doing anything of substance against the Unionist Party. When the AAFC was young, the vast majority of its members were diehard anti-Unionists who had fought in CWII, suffered under the Blue Terror, or otherwise paid a steep price for having stood against the Party. Now it seemed that many in the audience were there purely for mercenary reasons and would leap at the chance to do business with the enemy the moment trade relations were reopened.

Just as Linder and Calder bellied up to the cash bar, one of these sunshine patriots, a fellow of about Linder's age dressed in an elegant three-piece banker's suit, intercepted him and held out a well-manicured hand.

"Welcome back to London, Warren," the man said in a crisp mid-Atlantic accent. "You and I met when you spoke here on your book tour. I'm Tyler Voss, from Barclay's Bank."

Linder shook the man's hand, which was soft and weak.

"I'm pleased to hear you've disentangled yourself from Leonard Fury with your reputation intact," he went on. "Your new project seems much more in keeping with the times. And I applaud you for launching it with your own funds."

Linder could see that the remarks were merely a windup and braced himself for the pitch.

"But why keep poking the beast with a stick? The Unionist Party is here to stay. Why not come to terms with them? It could be quite lucrative for a man like yourself, I can assure you."

"If you think I would ever do business with the Unionists, you don't know me," Linder replied, cold as a stone. "Renouncing violence against tyrants doesn't mean throwing in with them."

"But neither does doing business with them at arm's length. Anyway, Warren, if you ever change your mind, please give me a call."

And, with that, Voss handed Linder his business card.

Linder took it and slipped it into his breast pocket without giving it a glance. But the encounter with Voss left him feeling soiled. Was this what the émigré movement had come to? Had the spirit of resistance faded so much? Linder surveyed the other men waiting at the bar and wondered whether they were all sleek collaborators like Voss. He turned to Calder with a curdled expression.

"I've had enough of these people. Let's grab a drink somewhere else."

"I know just the place," Calder replied.

A few blocks away from Regent Street, Calder led his client down a flight of stone stairs to a watering hole marked only by a red neon sign reading "Lounge" in cursive lettering. Inside was a 1950s-style American cocktail lounge complete with walnut veneer paneling, red leather seating, and a marble-topped bar that ran the length of the watering hole. At its far end was a low stage where a musician wearing jeans, cowboy boots and a fringed buckskin jacket sat tuning his guitar.

Although the place was bustling, the waitress recognized Calder at once and escorted the two men to a booth at the rear.

"What can I get you gentlemen to drink?"

Linder detected a Southern accent in her voice, possibly from Kentucky or Tennessee, and guessed that the woman was in her late thirties. She wore black jeans, a hipster plaid flannel shirt and an easygoing smile.

"An Old Fashioned for me," Linder replied, "with hundred-proof rye and extra bitters, please."

"The same for me," Calder echoed, drawing an appraising look from his friend.

"When I was in pharma sales, right out of business school," Linder volunteered with a wry smile, "we were trained to drink whatever the client was drinking. But, really, Dwight, aren't you and I beyond that? Go ahead, have your single malt if that's what you really want."

"No, really," Calder protested. "Rye is the perfect spirit for a place like this. Of course, they'll probably pour us some thin Canadian stuff. Can't easily get full-bodied American rye these days."

"Is that so? I had no trouble finding it in Beirut."

"That's because Lebanon has a thriving black market," Calder explained. "Here, we still have a trade embargo against the Unionists, though it's riddled with exceptions. For example, if it weren't for American natural gas imports, we'd all be shivering in our overcoats."

At that moment, the waitress interrupted to bring them some kettle-style potato chips and spicy peanuts before flitting off to the next table.

"So tell me more about this trade embargo, Dwight. Are the Tories still holding firm on it? I've heard that Labor is breathing down their necks, eager to reopen trade with Washington."

47

"Labor is pushing hard for it, to be sure," Calder answered as he reached for the chips. "The argument is that France and Germany are getting ready to drop their own trade restrictions and will steal a march on Britain if we don't open soon. With the European Union in shambles, trade competition has become a total free-for-all on the Continent."

"Hence Whitehall's willingness to discuss a new trade pact with the Unionists?"

"That's the gist of it. The new U.S. trade rep, Kreutzer, has already set up shop in Mayfair at the Four Seasons. Preliminary talks are due to start any day."

"Kreutzer, did you say? That wouldn't be Irwin Kreutzer, would it?"

Calder nodded. "Why, do you know him?"

"He was deputy commercial attaché when I was posted to the U.S. Embassy here," Linder replied. "Kreutzer used to help us run the DSS's foreign currency operations. For a while, he also worked with me to size up émigré bankers who might be sympathetic to the Unionist cause. We used to go out together to wine and dine them on the government dime. Even then, Irwin was a man of expensive tastes. It might be interesting to try and get back in touch with him."

"Are you implying he might be corruptible?"

Linder smiled as if at some private joke.

"Well, the Kreutzer I knew was insanely ambitious and always up to his eyeballs in intrigues."

At that moment, Linder noticed the waitress approaching with their drinks and fell silent. When she left them, Calder was the first to speak.

"Whether Kreutzer is worth pursuing or not, one thing seems clear. The Unionists are dead-set on re-opening trade with both Europe and the U.K. to bail out their economy. At the moment, the Tories are holding the line against it, but maybe not for much longer. So if you really want to stick it to the Unionists, I don't think you could find a more effective way than to torpedo their trade initiative."

"Hmm. You may have a point there," Linder mused, raising his glass to his partner's health. "Do you have a plan in mind?"

"I wouldn't say it's my plan, exactly. You see, I work with a consortium of companies in the energy sector, and some of my clients have come to me for help. They point out that the collapse of U.S. oil and gas production has made it essential for the Unionists to attract foreign energy investment. But my clients, having seen their U.S. properties nationalized by the Unionists, take a dim view of the U.K. restoring trade and investment with the new regime. Their idea is to veto any Anglo-American trade agreement unless they receive compensation for what they've lost."

A predatory smile spread across Linder's face as he put down his cocktail.

"I like their veto idea. It could open opportunities for us. Do you suppose your clients and I might be able to team up?"

"These are very private people who prefer to work behind the scenes," Calder cautioned, affecting a sober mien. "But they might welcome a public figure like you taking a position consistent with theirs. And if you threw in some money for a joint media effort, they might see synergies."

"How much money are we talking about?"

"Oh, low six figures to get the thing off the ground. Plus a monthly retainer."

"Send me a proposal. I can have the funds wired to you."

"From the same Swiss shell company?"

"No, I'll use a different one for this. I'll let you know."

The cost of the campaign was steep, but Linder had invested well with the assets recovered from the rebel looting of the downtown Cleveland banks and could afford it. After all, this was exactly what his money was for.

The moment Linder finished speaking, the Western-attired musician launched into his first song, a wistful ballad about the loss of the cowboy way of life. Linder listened closely as he downed the last of his cocktail. He had heard the same song years ago in the Yukon and it provoked a feeling of deep sorrow to think of the men who had perished in the camps while he managed to get out.

"Let's go," he said abruptly.

"Okay," Calder replied with a puzzled look. "I'll find the waitress and collect the bill."

"Don't bother. I've got it covered."

Linder pulled out his wallet and left a large bill on the table worth more than double the price of their drinks. Then he stepped away to drop an identical bill in the open guitar case of the musician. On his return, he noticed Calder's raised eyebrow.

"I may spend most of my time with moneymen," Linder said barely audible above the music and chatter, "but it's guys like this I'm fighting for."

Chapter Six: Kreutzer

> "The louder he spoke of his honor, the faster we counted our spoons."
> *–Ralph Waldo Emerson*

MONDAY, 13 OCTOBER 2031

Over the next few days, Linder ruminated over how best to approach the new U.S. trade representative and what to say if they met. Years earlier, Linder and Kreutzer had developed a degree of mutual trust through their work together at the London embassy. But how was he to reach the trade representative now under the prying eyes of both the DSS and MI5? As it happened, the opening he needed came from an unexpected source.

Fiona Bowles, having lately resumed her earlier work as Linder's private secretary, presented him one morning with a handwritten note on U.S. Trade Representative stationery, delivered by messenger. The note was unsigned but said that an official in the trade delegation would like to meet with him privately. To avoid unwanted scrutiny, it recommended that Linder provide the official's messenger the next day with a secure email or text address where detained contact instructions could be sent.

Linder did as instructed. And the following day, Bowles reported that her note containing Linder's secure email address had been picked up. That evening, a message appeared in Linder's encrypted email inbox telling him to appear at six P.M. the next evening at a celebrated Michelin-starred restaurant on Kensington Park Road, where he should tell the maître that he was to join "Mr. Gottfried's birthday party." He would then be taken to a private dining room. The instructions were vintage Kreutzer.

The next evening, Linder hailed a taxi to the appointed address, paid the fare in cash, and recited the magic words about Mr. Gottfried's birthday party at the restaurant's reception desk. With an inscrutable smile, the hostess consulted the computer at her standing desk and escorted Linder through an unmarked door to a private dining room where a round table was set for eight.

"May we bring you a cocktail, sir, while you await your party?"

"A glass of Lillet on the rocks would be nice."

"Of course. Someone will bring it to you shortly."

Linder waited five minutes for the aperitif and another fifteen for his mystery contact. Then the door opened and Irwin Kreutzer stepped in. It had been a decade since they had met, and the years had not been particularly kind to the trade representative. Despite the crisp bespoke suit and spruce Burberry raincoat, Kreutzer had a drawn and bloodless look, with some hard miles showing on his face.

That the man was under stress did not surprise Linder. By his estimate, Kreutzer was at bottom an ambitious, pragmatic, and moderately corrupt technocrat who, far from being a devout Unionist, seemed more of an ideological poseur. Early on, it seemed, Kreutzer had taken a career risk in championing Gang of Three member Ted Terzian's call for a resumption of foreign trade under the Party's New Economic Plan. And while the bet had paid off handsomely in landing Kreutzer his current post, it had also raised the stakes.

For not only was Kreutzer tasked with persuading the U.K. government to reopen trade, but his bosses would also expect him to

[3] Abbreviated name for the Progressive International, an organization controlled by the Unionist Party of America that advocated world Unionism and the overthrow, by armed force, if necessary, of capitalism and populist nationalism around the globe.

exploit that reopening to resume DSS subversion in Britain. The problem was that the two assignments were incompatible, so that any misstep by the DSS or the Progintern[3] threatened to lay waste to his career. Thus, Linder expected that Kreutzer might be casting about for a way to feather his nest against the day when he might want to defect rather than return to Washington under a cloud.

Yet, if the trade representative aimed to squirrel away hefty sums during his London tenure, he would need accomplices. And since bribery, kickbacks, self-dealing and the like were forbidden to state officials, he couldn't turn for help to anyone loyal to the Unionist regime.

What he needed was someone with no qualms about cheating or stealing from the regime and the skill to pull it off. Now, who in London, Linder thought, fit that description better than he?

The Unionist trade official removed his coat and draped it across a chair before urging Linder to take a seat at the table. He did the same.

"I'm sorry I can't stay long. But the moment I learned you were back in London, I knew I had to see you." He gave Linder the once-over before offering him an approving smile. "You've done remarkably well for yourself, Warren, considering all you've been through. I must say, I thought your arrest was most unfair."

"An odd claim, coming from a senior Party member like you, Irwin."

"Come, now, Warren. Yes, you suffered for a while, but look at your remarkable career since you escaped! Who would have guessed that we'd be meeting again under such agreeable circumstances?"

"I've been following your, career, too," Linder replied. "And I imagine you've also faced your share of risks, having been a protégé of Ted Terzian, who is one step away from being purged. You must have done some fancy footwork to land where you are. But then, you were never a revolutionary like Terzian. More of a survivalist, I'd say."

"If, by that, you mean I like to take a long view of things, that would be correct. And with both of us having endured what we have, perhaps we've come to think alike to a degree. Who knows, perhaps the time has come to cooperate again."

Linder feigned surprise.

"Surely you must know by now that I would never collaborate with the Unionist regime. So what's your angle?"

"What if I were to make a proposal that would benefit the two of us, as well as your oppositionist friends, all at the expense of the ruling party? Would you be interested in hearing more?"

"Sure, why not? I suppose you could report me to the DSS, but then they already know who I am."

Kreutzer leaned in toward Linder, his elbows on the table.

"Do you remember General Secretary Twitchell's speech, delivered just after he launched the NEP, announcing the unilateral withdrawal of U.S. forces from our overseas bases? The so-called 'Speech Heard Round the World'?"

"How could I not?" Linder replied in an acid tone. "In one fell swoop, he declared victory in the global war on terror, renounced the role of world policeman, and promised a huge peace dividend from America's exit on the world stage."

"Did you ever wonder what was going to happen with all those overseas bases after we abandoned them?"

"Of course I did. In my past life, I'd been to many of them, both in the U.K. and in Europe. These days they're empty and falling to pieces."

"That's about to change," Kreutzer declared. "U.S. trade representatives in the various host countries have been tasked with selling those properties. There's a tremendous amount of money to be made if things are handled right. Something in it for everyone."

Kreutzer cast a meaningful glance at his guest.

"So how might that apply to me?" Linder replied with narrowed eyes.

"Would your clients be interested in picking up any of the U.K. properties—at a substantial discount?"

Linder laughed. "How much of a discount? How would your scheme work?"

"It's quite simple. You and I would fix the bidding. Once an award was made, most of the payment price would go into the U.S. Treasury. But a certain part would go elsewhere. A little for you, a little for me. Everybody walks away happy."

"You're taking quite a risk in telling me this, Irwin."

The boldness of the scheme took Linder by surprise. It must have shown in his face, because now it was Kreutzer's turn to laugh.

"Not really," he explained. "Everybody knows you're a sworn enemy of the Unionist Party. If you went to the press and claimed the property sales were rigged, I'd deny it, and everyone would chalk it up to sour grapes. But you'd be blowing the opportunity of a lifetime if you did."

"And you'd trust me not to rat on you later? You wouldn't be able to deny it once I had my hands on the receipts."

"I think I know you well enough to believe you wouldn't take that step, Warren. It would be a case of mutually assured destruction. Neither of us would escape unscathed."

Kreutzer inched up his sleeve to consult his wafer-thin gold watch.

"Damn. I'm already late for dinner down the hall and I'm the guest of honor. Listen, why don't you sleep on it and get back to me via encrypted email. If you decide to come in, you can do anything you want with your share of the money. Use it for your propaganda crusade, for all I care. By the time the DSS figures out what we did, I'll be outside their grasp."

Chapter Seven: Quist

> "Those who can make you believe absurdities can make you commit atrocities."
> —*Voltaire*

TUESDAY, 14 OCTOBER 2031

Owen Quist arrived at Washington's Dulles Airport in the early afternoon. He stood in the immigration queue set aside for U.S. citizens and used the passport control kiosk to scan his passport and answer the routine questions presented. But shortly after completing his interview with a uniformed immigration inspector, two scowling plainclothes federal agents intercepted him.

"Passport, please," one of them demanded.

This was not good. Quist felt an immediate jolt of adrenaline, as if a snarling grizzly had just crossed his path. He handed over the passport and the agent opened it to the photograph page. After a quick look, the man closed the document but didn't return it.

"Mr. Quist, please come with us."

Quist suppressed an urge to bolt. This had to be a mistake. He hadn't done anything wrong.

The agent beckoned toward a nearby door, which his partner held open. Quist followed them a short distance down a narrow corridor before reaching a walk-through metal detector. The uniformed policeman who manned the detector held out a plastic bin for Quist to deposit his wallet, cell phone, belt, keys, and other metallic objects. Then he handed the bin to one of the two plainclothes agents, who carried it into a nearby interview room.

"You can leave your roller bag here. We won't be long," the second agent said. Once inside the interview room, he closed the door behind them.

"Please identify yourself and state the reasons for your travel," the agent ordered.

"My name is Owen Quist." Quist felt a twinge of shame that his voice quavered as he spoke. He took a deep breath and did his best to pull himself together before continuing. "I was traveling with a delegation from the State Oil Company to sell American petroleum products in Europe. Now, may I ask you a question? What agency are you with and why have you singled me out for questioning?"

"We're with State Security and we need some more information about your trip, Mr. Quist. Please, wait here while I invite my colleague to join us. It'll just be a moment." The tone was polite but distant.

The agent gestured toward a pair of straight-backed aluminum chairs on opposite sides of a metal table. Then he left the room while his partner remained standing at the door. But it wasn't just a moment. No one appeared for ten minutes, then fifteen. Quist tried to empty his mind to avoid panic, but he couldn't stop his thoughts from racing out of control. After twenty minutes, the agent returned alone.

"My colleague can't come right now. I'm afraid we'll have to go to him. Follow me, please."

But this time Quist stood his ground.

"Wait a second, officer. I was traveling on official government business. You can see that from my red official passport. Please return it to me now and let me go on my way."

"You'll get it back after we finish our business together."

"This has gone far enough," Quist protested, his anger rising. "And while you're at it, why don't you hand me my cell phone so that I can call my supervisor at the oil company. I'm sure he'll be able to address whatever concerns you might have about my travels."

"All in due time, sir. But the sooner we go see my colleague, the sooner we can get this resolved. Bear with us a moment longer."

Without another word, the federal agent opened the door and gestured for Quist to follow him to the end of the corridor. It happened so fast that Quist was at a loss to do anything else. So he went along while the second agent trailed behind, pulling Quist's roller bag. At the corridor's end they turned left, soon reaching another door, which opened onto an alley. There a black SUV stood waiting with its engine idling and its trunk and passenger doors flung open.

"Climb in. We're not going far," the first agent directed, while the second loaded the roller bag into the trunk. Quist hesitated before recognizing that he'd been duped. The time to resist had passed.

As they drove away, Quist's anxiety level rose the further they traveled from the arrival hall. At last the SUV rolled through a barricaded gate into a fenced compound and halted outside a nondescript three-story building that looked more like a warehouse than any government office Quist had seen.

Once inside, they proceeded to a security desk manned by a solitary uniformed guard, who stowed Quist's roller bag in a corner and buzzed the three visitors into an antiseptic corridor. Along each wall was a row of metal doors, each featuring a small glass window at head height, a horizontal feed slot just above the knee, and two odd-looking round keyholes. The lead agent opened the nearest door and gestured for Quist to enter.

For the first time, Quist noticed the scowl leave the agent's face. And when he spoke, Quist detected a note of sympathy. Was it because there was no longer any possibility of escape?

"Go ahead and rest until my colleague is ready for you," the agent told Quist. "There's a sink and toilet inside for you to freshen up. Someone will fetch you when it's time."

As Quist entered the cell, its heavy metal door clanked shut behind him. Only then did he realize what a fool he'd been to follow these men blindly into a DSS interrogation facility. What could he possibly have done to deserve this? Panic seized him as he racked his brain to recall any act on his European trip that might be considered illegal or even improper. He certainly hadn't taken bribes or engaged in any illicit dealings. Nor had he taken drugs, gone whoring with his customers, or gotten wasted in any seedy dive where he might have rubbed elbows with shady characters.

At last Quist's thoughts settled on his weekend in Bristol with Harold Acker. To be sure, he had consumed far too much alcohol and spoken loosely with his old friend. But how could the DSS possibly know what the two had discussed, unless they'd learned it from Acker? But Acker despised the DSS even more than he did and had nothing to gain from informing against him. On the contrary, the two men had gotten along perfectly all weekend. Acker had even acquiesced to his wife's filing for divorce so Quist could marry her. So what motive could the engineer possibly have for ratting on him to the DSS?

All at once a fresh wave of dread swept over Quist. Acker had said he belonged to an anti-Unionist exile group and asked if he might share Quist's comments with his politically active friends. How foolish he had been to agree! What if one of Acker's friends were a DSS informant?

When a pair of black-uniformed prison guards finally came for Quist, the two bound him in handcuffs and leg irons before leading him down the hall to an interrogation room furnished with a wooden table, four chairs, and a one-way mirror that filled an entire wall. Once inside, the guards clipped his leg shackles to a steel ground anchor and sat behind him, just beyond his field of view.

Less than a minute later, a black man entered the room wearing a gray cotton jumpsuit and carrying a hardbound laboratory notebook and a slender manila file folder. The man was of middle height, with a rotund build, pudgy hands and face, and a *café au lait* complexion. His was a deceptively benign appearance. Yet Quist, having heard dreadful tales about what occurred inside DSS interrogation prisons, expected the worst. He felt the grip of fear seize him while cold sweat trickled down his spine.

The man in the jumpsuit took a seat opposite Quist, opened the file folder, and began to read it silently. For a moment, the prisoner felt not relief, but anger, with confusion not far behind.

"Who are you? And why have you brought me here? I haven't done anything wrong!"

The interrogator ignored him, flipped the page, and read to the bottom before closing the file.

"My name is Darrell Otis," the man declared. "And you're here because you've been charged with disclosure of classified information, membership in a subversive organization, and seditious conspiracy to overthrow the U.S. government. All are serious felonies, punishable by long sentences at hard labor."

Quist's eyes opened wide with horror.

"What? But none of that is true!" he objected.

"If that's so, then why did you tell your co-conspirator, Harold Acker, that the U.S. economy was 'circling the drain' and that America was experiencing food shortages, power outages, labor strikes and violent unrest among the military and the police? We also have conclusive evidence that you passed classified information about U.S. energy production to an enemy of the state, knowing that he would deliver it to a foreign subversive organization. And we have evidence that you are in clandestine contact with secret insurgent cells operating in or near the nation's capital."

Quist gasped. While he remembered bad-mouthing the condition of the U.S. economy to Acker, at the time he certainly hadn't thought of it as rising to the level of treason. And the information he had shared about U.S. oil and gas production was hardly of the kind whose disclosure could cause the country serious damage. As for his throwaway comment about secret dissident cells in Washington, it was mere puffery. He had never belonged to such a cell. It was all intended to make himself look important in Acker's eyes.

But before Quist could deny the charges, the interrogator began reading aloud from a letter addressed to one Benjamin Payne, chairman of the Free American Patriots, located in Berlin. The text quoted Quist's boasting in embarrassing detail, and now he remembered just how far out on a limb he had climbed that night. After reeling off three or four paragraphs to Quist, Otis laid the letter down and fixed the prisoner with a stare that left no doubt who was in control.

"Listen, I had no idea Harold was going to put me on the spot like that," Quist complained.

"Do you mean to say your friend was lying?"

"Well, not exactly."

"In that case, we're going to have to take whatever time is required to sift through your statements and weigh the charges against you," Otis replied. "I hope you weren't in any hurry to get back to your job at StatOil."

"As a matter of fact, I…"

"That is, assuming your job still exists, once your superiors learn that you abused your foreign travel privilege to meet secretly with our nation's enemies."

"But that's not at all what happened!" Quist exclaimed. "The only reason I visited Harold was to get his consent for his wife to divorce him so that she and I could get married. You can confirm that with Mrs. Acker. She's a senior lawyer at the Department of…"

"Treasury," the interrogator cut in. "We've already spoken to her. She's in custody, too, charged with aiding and abetting your conspiracy with the FAP. And she's not very happy about it. Quite a scrapper, that woman."

Quist could only imagine Denise Acker's fury at the accusation. Her entire legal career reduced to ashes merely because the man she had married refused to give up his grudge toward the Unionist Party and her new fiancé was a naïve fool. Even if they got out of this mess somehow, he was sure Denise would never forgive him for dragging her into it.

"If you've spoken to Denise, then you must know she couldn't possibly be guilty of a political crime. She's a loyal Party member and has been from the start."

"You'd be surprised, Mr. Quist, how Party members with otherwise immaculate credentials can get themselves entangled in rebel conspiracies. You see, traitors and counter-revolutionaries are like ants. Where you find one, there's generally a whole nest of them. And if you don't root them out all at once, the infestation will spread like wildfire."

"But Denise and I are not traitors!" Quist argued. "Surely you must see that! How can I prove it to you?"

Otis offered his prisoner a condescending smile as he picked up the file to leave.

"I'm afraid you'll just have to let the investigation run its course, Mr. Quist."

Upon exiting the interrogation center, the officer who called himself Darrell Otis returned to his parked car, drove out the compound's security gate and headed east on the Dulles Access Road. Less than a half hour later, at an office park near the Tyson's Corner Mall, he parked beside the mirror-faced DSS Annex. It was already late in the afternoon when he arrived to find a stream of workers on their way out to the parking lot under the slanting rays of an orange-tinged sun.

Otis wasted no time after clearing security and made a beeline for the elevators. On the sixth floor, he went to his boss's office, knocked twice, and walked in.

"Just came from seeing Quist," he said, taking a seat without being invited.

Victor Barbosa, chief of the DSS's Exile Division, was a big, square-shouldered man with a somber gaze who carried his head stubbornly bent, as if nothing in the world was to his liking. He generally uttered as few words as possible and, when he spoke, was inclined toward irony. Yet, in an organization where trust was rare and friendships paper-thin, Barbosa had a reputation for fairness and not letting his men down. Otis, whose real name was James Jenkins, revered his boss. And though, at thirty-five, Jenkins was only five years younger than Barbosa, he modeled himself after the older man.

"So what do you make of Quist?" Barbosa asked, putting down the file he was reading.

"Complete lightweight," Jenkins replied. "He inflated his dissident credentials to his friend Acker, who further inflated them to Payne and the FAP. What amazes me is how eager the boys in Berlin were to stay in contact with Quist, considering how little of substance he gave them."

"So where do we go from here?"

"I've hauled in Acker's estranged wife to compare her story with Quist's. So far, they match. She denies any anti-government activity by either of them. What's more, she describes Quist as very bright, but with a Walter Mitty complex, someone who always felt intimidated by her estranged husband. She claims Quist would have gone along with anything Acker wanted if it would get him to agree to a divorce. Sure, he may have told Acker too much about U.S. oil and gas production, but that's hardly a hanging offense."

"I tend to agree," Barbosa replied. "The charges against Quist don't amount to much. But what about Payne and the FAP? Benjamin Payne happens to be a former Vice President of the United States. He's a big cheese in émigré circles. How might we leverage this Quist fellow and his friend Acker to get closer to Payne?"

"Are you proposing that we send Quist back to Europe and run him against the FAP?"

"Possibly," Barbosa mused. "Do you think Quist could handle it?"

Jenkins winced and fidgeted in his seat.

"I don't know, boss. Give me a few days to see if he has the right stuff. I'll also need to read up some more on the FAP to see whether they're even worth the effort."

"You do that, Jim. And hold onto that Acker woman. We may need her to persuade Quist to play ball."

Two days later, Jenkins returned to Barbosa's office.

"I've done some digging into the Free American Patriots and I think you might be onto something," he told his boss. "It turns out that Benjamin Payne has hired some top-notch fundraisers and now the FAP is rolling in cash. The trouble is, they have no discernible intelligence assets inside the U.S. So being in contact with Quist promises them access to dissident circles in D.C. Now, you and I know those dissident cells are a total fantasy. But what if Quist went back to the FAP with proof that they were real?"

Barbosa let out a short, hard laugh.

"Do you think he might be able to wheedle some cash out of them?"

"We've done it before," Jenkins replied with a crooked smile. "Handled right, we could feed the enemy disinformation, while he bankrolls our foreign operations."

"I like it. But does Quist have what it takes to pull it off? I remember you calling him a lightweight."

"It remains to be seen. He'd need a lot of coaching."

"We'd also need a detailed target assessment on Payne and the FAP," Barbosa added, stroking his chin. "Can our people in Berlin come up with one?"

"I expect so. But I have another idea, chief. What if one of our officers paid a follow-up visit to Acker in Bristol, posing as a member of Quist's dissident network? We could use the visit not only to assess

Acker and his U.K. émigré friends, but also to set up a meeting for Quist at FAP headquarters in Berlin. By then we'd know better whether Quist is the right man to work with. If not, we could try someone else."

"Do you think Acker would fall for it? Your report said he's had intelligence training."

"Long ago and it was only an introductory course," Jenkins noted. "Remember, Acker's a bomber jockey, not an intel professional. No, I think an experienced undercover officer could get Acker to open up if Quist set up his visit in advance."

"Do you have someone in mind?"

Jenkins had intended to nominate himself for the job. But that was before he noticed the wolfish expression on his boss's face. For he knew that Barbosa was one of those men who, from time to time, felt the urge to put his lucky star to the test. And having spent so much time in the field before becoming a division chief, there were few men more qualified for the assignment than Victor Barbosa.

"Nobody in mind just yet," the interrogator replied with the hint of a smile. "The assignment is yours if you want it."

"In that case," Barbosa replied, returning the smile, "I'd like you to draw up a plan."

A week later, Quist let Acker know by email that a member of his dissident circle would be coming to Bristol. Not long after, Victor Barbosa, posing as Carl Yoder, a member of that circle, arrived in Bristol and hailed a cab to The Horsehead pub in Filton. Stepping out onto the curb, he felt a surge of exhilaration to be overseas again and back in the undercover game.

It was dinnertime on a Wednesday evening and the pub was not crowded. Barbosa spotted Acker at once, a fit-looking man of fifty with short gray hair, dressed in charcoal slacks and the same striped cardigan that Quist had described during his interrogation. The two men exchanged polite greetings and ordered ale at the bar before retreating to a quiet table along the far wall.

"I've never been out this way," Barbosa commented, putting on his most winsome smile. "It's quite a charming train ride. What do they call this area?"

"South Gloucestershire," Acker replied. "The town dates back to the twelfth century. And before that, the Roman legions camped out here."

"Fascinating. What's it like being an American expat in a place like this? Do the locals accept you?"

"By and large," Acker replied with an amiable smile. "The Brits can be terribly insular at times, but with Filton being an aerospace hub, this area is more cosmopolitan than most. And, with my being a former colonial, they tolerate me."

"So do you find yourself missing the old country very much? I mean, working abroad is one thing, but not ever being able to go home must be quite another."

For a fleeting moment, Acker's smile faded and his head seemed to droop. Barbosa sensed that he had hit a nerve. Was it loneliness?

"Well, I do hope to return one day, once the Unionists are gone," Acker answered, "but I don't expect that will happen any time soon. So I've resolved to make a new life here."

"I admire your attitude, Harold," Barbosa replied, launching into a well-practiced monologue. "Unfortunately for me. I missed my chance to get out of Dodge after the coup. So I'm stuck in D.C. and have to put on an act every day just to survive. I live for the day when the Unionist State cracks up. That's why I joined Owen's group. And it's why I also like keeping in touch with anti-Unionists outside the country. Each of us has strengths that the other lacks. Together, I believe we can do to the Unionist Party what Soviet dissidents and the international human rights movement did to Soviet Communism."

"Well, as Owen may have told you, Carl, I'm active with a group of Yanks here who belong to the Free American Patriots," Acker explained, suddenly lowering his voice. "Do you know them?"

"Only what I've heard from Owen. I understand that the FAP gathers information about events inside the U.S. and broadcasts it to the world. Does the FAP also help support internal opposition groups?"

"Yes, that's also part of our mission," Acker nodded. "But, to be frank, we haven't had much success with that of late, largely because it's so difficult to find reliable people on the inside."

Barbosa smiled inwardly. The fish was rising to the bait.

"Well, I'm not due back in Bristol till Friday," Barbosa noted. "Why don't we spend some time figuring out how we can work together for the cause?"

"Wow, that would be fantastic," Acker replied, his eyes aglow. "By the way, Owen mentioned that you don't work together at StatOil. Would you mind telling me what you do for a living?"

"I'm at the Department of Energy. Before that, at the Pentagon."

Acker raised an eyebrow.

"And they let you roam free here in Britain without any keepers?"

Barbosa laughed.

"My keepers wanted some time off over the weekend. So we agreed to cover for each other. You wouldn't believe the amount of mutual back-scratching that goes on in a socialist system."

"Well, I'm eager to find out. Listen, Carl, do you have a place to stay tonight?"

"Not yet. I was hoping you could suggest an inexpensive hotel."

"Why not stay with me? I'll show you around in the morning, and in the afternoon, I can gather the blokes to join us for a few hours of discussion. Would that work for you?"

"Perfectly," Barbosa replied with a winning smile. "That means I can hop an evening train tomorrow and be back in Bristol by midnight."

The fish was on the line.

The next day, DSS division chief Barbosa, posing as Carl Yoder, sat down with a half dozen stalwarts of the Bristol chapter of the Free American Patriots and answered their questions about the political situation in Washington, adhering to a well-crafted script that he had rehearsed repeatedly before leaving home. Barbosa's answers were larded with sensational intelligence nuggets crafted to impress the émigrés, but without exposing sensitive state information. By the end of the debriefing, Barbosa did not doubt that the émigrés viewed him as a genuine patriot fighting Unionism quietly from inside the system.

Barbosa's success emboldened him to ask whether the FAP might be willing to provide funds to help expand his and Quist's dissident network. If so, on his next trip across the pond, he would like to visit the FAP leadership in Berlin. Acker considered it a splendid idea and agreed to convey the proposal to his FAP superiors. In the meantime, as a goodwill gesture, he took up a collection from those in the room and handed the cash to Barbosa in an unmarked envelope.

Suppressing an inward smirk at the group's naiveté, Barbosa bid them farewell. Then, once safely inside his taxi, he ripped the envelope open and considered how much of the money to keep for himself. Yes, the money belonged technically to the State, but who exactly was the State if not a hard-working officer like himself?

Chapter Eight: Geneva

"When injustice becomes law, resistance becomes duty."
–Thomas Jefferson

WEDNESDAY, 12 NOVEMBER 2031

"**M**r. Hackett is here. Shall I send him up?" Ficna Bowles announced from the kitchen of Linder's London flat.

"Yes, please. I'm expecting him."

But Linder wasn't looking forward to the visit. For while Alen Hackett was his designated contact at MI5, and Linder needed his protection from the Unionists in more ways than one, the Brit seldom called unless he wanted something. And he rarely offered anything in return.

Once the two men had settled in Linder's study and Bowles had brought them their mid-morning coffee, Hackett got down to business. He placed his cup and saucer on the low table before him and peered at his host over gold-rimmed bifocals. Hackett was a divinely tall man with a high forehead and receding hairline, whose courtly bearing implied an elite upbringing.

"Have you ever heard of an American resistance group called the American Constitution League?" the MI5 man asked.

"Doesn't ring a bell," Linder replied. "Care to share more?"

"We've had two visits this fall from Americans claiming ties to resistance cells in the Washington area. Both are federal officials engaged in promoting petroleum exports and both visited the same American émigré residing in Filton. The émigré belongs to an anti-

Unionist organization called the Free American Patriots. Do you know them?"

"Quite well, actually," Linder answered. "The FAP are a well-intentioned bunch, though ineffectual. If they had any assets working inside the U.S., it would be news to me. But Filton's an aerospace hub. Do you suppose your visitors might be trying to steal British military technology?"

"Possibly, though I doubt it. You see, one of the local FAP blokes reported the meetings to us immediately," Hackett explained. "He said the visitors were looking for help from the FAP to organize a dissident network inside the U.S. They offered intelligence about the Unionists in exchange for cash support and technical assistance."

"Sounds dodgy to me. When I was in the Exile Division, we used to mount that sort of provocation all the time. We'd offer émigré opposition groups doctored intelligence about U.S. events to infiltrate them. Which group did the visitors claim they represented?"

"The American Constitution League. We have no prior record of them."

"That doesn't mean much either way," Linder offered, finishing his coffee and hoping the meeting was near an end. "Most likely, they're a stalking horse for the DSS aimed at penetrating the émigré opposition."

"In that case, I'd ask that you not share the organization's name with any of your émigré friends. If we get more visits from the League, I rather not have to deal with false confirmations."

"My lips are sealed."

"While we're on the subject of provocations," Hackett went on, "our analysts are detecting a new influence campaign in the foreign press aimed at painting a rosy picture of the American economy under their New Economic Plan. Apparently the goal is to lure wealthy émigrés back to the U.S. to invest in new businesses. To that end, they have been dangling lucrative concessions to bait the hook. What do your sources have to say about that?"

Linder's jaw clenched and he stiffened involuntarily, thinking of his sister's return to Utah to work in her husband's family business.

"Your analysts are right. The DSS is using every trick in the book to ensnare the homesick and the naïve into returning. Even people who ought to know better, like my sister. April and her husband flew to New York just a couple days before the attempt to kill me in Beirut. I haven't heard a word from them since."

"I'm sorry to hear that," Hackett said, his face showing surprise.

"Returnees have become a profit center for the Unionists," Linder went on. "Like the Nazis looting property from dispossessed Jews. But some people just can't help themselves. The will to believe is their fatal weakness."

Hackett nodded but seemed uninterested in hearing more. After downing what remained of his coffee, he changed the subject.

"One more question before I go," he added. It was the old 'Colombo' tactic used by seasoned detectives everywhere, and Linder sensed that this question would probably be the one that had prompted Hackett's visit. "Have you been following the news about a new Anglo-American trade agreement? The new U.S. trade representative, Mr. Kreutzer, seems to be cutting a wide swath among the City's banking crowd."

"Is that so," Linder answered with a deadpan expression, hoping to stonewall further questioning about Kreutzer.

"I thought you might be following Mr. Kreutzer rather closely, since the two of you served together at the U.S. Embassy some years ago. Did you know him well?"

"Not really. Our paths rarely crossed," Linder lied.

"Well, Kreutzer brings a formidable reputation as negotiator, along with close ties to the Unionist Party leadership," the MI5 officer noted. "People who know about these things are laying strong odds that he'll bring home a British trade deal."

"That's certainly what Labor would like to see," Linder countered, "but I'm betting against it so long as the Tories stay in power."

"Of course, Warren, political exiles like you would be dead set against any such deal. But I would warn you to tread lightly if you intend to interfere with any agreement on trade. The issue of restoring commercial relations with the United States is highly political, and His Majesty's Government frowns upon interference from non-citizens in our domestic affairs."

"In that case," Linder responded with a thin-lipped smile, "you'd be wise to remember that Unionist diplomatic representation brings with it a heavy dose of DSS subversion. If a deal gets signed and the U.S. Embassy opens up here again, I suggest you impose some very strong prohibitions against political agitation so you'll be able to kick the bastards out the moment they step out of line."

Once Hackett was gone, Linder went back to work at his desk. But soon he found that he couldn't concentrate. The mere mention of the DSS's success in luring émigrés home to their doom was enough to trigger a fresh bout of depression over his sister's disappearance. Unable to dispel these dark thoughts, he decided to go out for an early lunch. But even after returning from his favorite local pie shop, his mind was still too deep in turmoil to focus on correspondence. So he went out for a short run in Hyde Park to clear his head.

At age forty-six, Linder had reached a crisis of sorts. Until the failed rendition operation in Beirut that had led to his arrest and captivity, he had been on a winning streak. From the day of his decision to join the CIA, through his voluntary transfer to the DSS on the eve of Civil War II, and until that fateful afternoon on Philip Eaton's Beirut veranda when the DSS turned against him, all his ventures had met with success. Since that day, most had ended in failure, except for his escape from a Yukon labor camp and his collection of millions in rebel loot on his way to freedom.

For example, his brief post-escape career as an author and lecturer had been a flash in the pan. Similarly, his efforts to form an effective émigré opposition movement had begun well, but had run into stiff headwinds, with a steady decline in paid membership, fundraising, and overall fervor. The only project since his escape in which he took genuine pride was having brought his sister, her husband, and his ward Caroline to Beirut for five years of relatively stable and happy domestic life. But now April and Jay were gone, likely in DSS custody or perhaps dead, and Caroline was away at university and slowly falling into the orbit of her Eaton relatives.

So what now? Looking ahead, Linder saw little but obstacles and threats. Even worse, he began to feel he was weakening. Clearly, his middle-aged body had logged more than its share of wear and tear over the years. And having endured interrogations, beatings, malnutrition, hard labor, and frostbite in the camps and during his winter escape from the Arctic, today he suffered from heart arrhythmia, hypertension, arthritis, insomnia, and occasional shortness of breath. When he looked in the mirror, he saw dark circles under his eyes, furrows in his forehead and cheeks, and an infiltration of gray in his hair and beard. In recent days, he had begun wondering how much longer he might have to live.

Nonetheless, on this particular morning, the most compelling problem on Linder's mind was money. Among the messages he had received the evening before was one from his legal counsel in Basel, who reported that the Swiss authorities had frozen several of his accounts there in response to legal filings from the U.S. Department of Justice. According to his attorney, the DOJ had traced to Basel certain assets that Linder had spirited away from Philip Eaton's rebel cache in Ohio and later converted to cash. The DOJ now claimed that this cash represented the proceeds of illegal money laundering. While the asset freeze hadn't reached all of Linder's Swiss accounts, or any of the ones domiciled in London or Beirut, now nearly half of Linder's liquid assets were out of reach until he could defend himself in the

Swiss courts. Success was unlikely, his legal team warned, since the U.S. government lawyers possessed some compelling evidence. And where they lacked specific proof, the Unionists would not hesitate to perjure themselves or fabricate whatever documentary evidence they might require.

For the moment, Linder had enough funds in his London accounts to meet his near-term living expenses and his obligations to vendors and employees. But until the legal challenges were overcome, and perhaps for some time after, he would need to scale back the ambitious information warfare campaign that he'd planned for the coming year. No court date had been set yet, but he expected to spend a week or more in Basel once the date was known.

Linder's spirits sank when he thought of the Unionist regime's latest line of attack. Having failed to gun him down in Beirut or prevent him from entering the U.K., they now focused on ruining him financially. Of course, the Unionists had tried to destroy him before and failed. So he would have to revise his defensive strategy once again. Each time they hit him, it was essential to hit back twice as hard. And while Linder no longer espoused physical violence, he remained open to every manner of fraud, deceit, spying, hacking, and other underhanded tactic. Since his arrest, he had learned the bitter lesson that the ends sometimes did justify the means. Not every end, nor all the means, but when fighting tyranny, nearly anything was fair game.

Later that week, Linder was scheduled to depart on a fundraising tour of European capitals where American émigrés had settled and formed anti-Unionist political organizations. In Geneva, Paris, Amsterdam, Berlin, Warsaw, and Prague, he would pitch his information warfare strategy to émigré activists and to their allies in the local security and intelligence services.

His first stop would be Geneva, where he was scheduled to speak at the newly created International Anti-Authoritarian Entente (IAAE), a loose coalition of non-government organizations (NGOs) that opposed autocracies around the world. His message there would be to promote non-violent resistance to authoritarian tyranny based on the methods of Gandhi, Mandela, and Martin Luther King.

The prestige of the IAAE's current membership was reflected in its choice of hotels for the conference. The Beau-Rivage was one of Geneva's landmark hotels, with an unrivaled location opposite the Jet D'eau on the shores of Lake Geneva. The ballroom, where the plenary sessions were scheduled to take place, enjoyed a breathtaking view of the lake through French doors that bathed the room in dazzling sunlight.

The first full day of the IAAE meeting was uneventful, with most of each plenary session consumed in sterile debate over goals, ways and means. The speakers agreed that armed counter-revolution had failed in the U.S.A. and that future opposition to the Unionist State would likely require a long-term campaign of passive resistance inside the country, combined with information warfare waged from outside.

What Linder hoped for by the end of the conference was an official endorsement of his Anglo-American Information Bureau as one of the most effective émigré groups working against the Unionist regime. But, as the conference entered its third and final day, Linder realized that no such endorsement would be forthcoming.

Linder was scheduled to address the IAAE's plenary session on the morning of the conference's last day. But rather than deliver his planned speech, a stem-winder that focused on his experiences in the corrective labor camps, he shortened the autobiographical material in favor of a plea to shift from armed insurgency toward information warfare.

While the audience listened with rapt attention to the first portion of his speech, their absorption faded the more he talked. To them, Linder had always personified vigorous action, not the steady drip of persuasion that he proposed now. After the speech, as he circulated among the remaining attendees in the ballroom, he was unable to spot the legion of wealthy donors whom he had hoped would help fund his AAIB. It was nearly time for the next speaker to begin when a tall, stoop-shouldered fellow with a head of silver hair confronted Linder with a face wreathed in smiles.

"You mentioned Kamas in your speech," the man began, seizing Linder's hand and pumping it long and hard. "I was an inmate at Kamas when the tanks rolled in. Thank you for keeping our story alive."

Linder's eyes widened.

"I heard that they sent all the Kamas survivors to the Yukon," he replied. "I nearly died up there myself. How on earth did you manage to get out alive?"

"It was a miracle," the stranger replied, "Actually, I never made it as far as the Yukon. They released me on a technicality and allowed me to emigrate after my in-laws paid what amounted to a hefty bribe. My wife and daughters flew with me to the U.K. and later to Poland, where we've lived for the past six years, keeping out of the public eye to stay safe. You see, I, too, wrote a book about my experience in the camps. I also did a speaking tour, but had to cut it short because of the threats on my life."

"Oh, I know who you are!" Linder exclaimed. "You're Paul Wagner. I bought your book the day after I arrived in London. You know, if the Kamas inmates hadn't revolted when they did, I probably wouldn't be alive today. The revolt forced me to leave Utah early and head for the border. The fact that I made it out is another miracle."

"Well, I'm grateful that at least one good thing came out of our revolt," Wagner said with a hangdog look. "You're doing the Lord's work in spreading the truth about Unionism."

"Thanks, Paul. But tell me more about you and your family."

"Well, my wife and I were fortunate in having preserved some capital to start a business that qualified us for Polish residency. But life in Warsaw can be hard on Americans. Many arrive as stateless refugees, unemployed, not knowing the language, and can't make ends meet on the government dole. To get through it," Wagner continued, "you have to prop up your sense of self-worth. Fortunately, the American colony in Warsaw sticks together and offers us a certain status. Among the Poles, we're nobody; but when we mix with other Americans, we're somebody."

"How about your wife and kids, Paul?" Linder asked. "Have they adjusted to Poland? My family went through some rough spots in Beirut, though we lived fairly comfortably."

"Well, like many Americans who fled, I wanted my daughters to keep their American identity, because we all thought we'd be going back soon. So we sent both girls to an American school, where they learned about American history, culture, and the American way of life. As a result, they've grown up thinking of the old America as a sort of paradise lost. Everything they remember about the old country is idealized, and all its negatives forgotten. They want to go back someday, but I expect they'd find the new America unrecognizable."

"And your wife? How is she holding up?"

"She hated Warsaw from day one. To her, Unionist America is, after all, still America. I feel bad about all she's gone through, but we had no other choice but to leave."

Linder took a long look at the frail figure before him and imagined what Paul Wagner might have been like before his arrest. Even a few months in the camps could do irreversible damage to a man.

"You mentioned that you received threats after you wrote your book," Linder went on. "Did they continue when you moved to Warsaw?"

"No, the Polish security service is very good at keeping foreign agents at bay. Our small circle of anti-Unionists in Warsaw has been left largely alone. Our counterparts in Berlin haven't fared as well. The FAP is a much larger organization and gets much more attention from the DSS. Especially now that they've linked up with a new internal opposition group led by government insiders. Are you familiar with an organization called the American Constitution League?"

The hairs went up on Linder's neck. Several days before, Allen Hackett had described an organization by the same name and told him not to mention it to anyone.

"I've heard of it," Linder replied, without giving more away.

"Rumor has it that they're looking to get help from émigré groups like ours." Wagner noted.

"What kind of help?"

"Funding, mainly. But I've also heard they're looking for experienced operatives to go into the U.S. to train their members." Wagner ended his sentence with a questioning look.

"Sounds fishy to me," Linder said.

"I thought so, too. Several people I know have gone back recently to take jobs or start businesses under the New Economic Policy. None has been heard of since."

Linder bit his lip.

"The same thing happened to my sister and her husband. They received a letter from her father-in-law urging them to come back to Utah and help rebuild the family business. Even though the letter was in the old man's handwriting and appeared authentic, I warned them not to trust it. But what good is a warning when someone is desperate to believe?"

"That's how I see things, too. But my wife…" Suddenly Wagner's voice dropped and his eyes filled with tears. He reached into the breast pocket of his well-worn suit and pulled out a check already written out. "Here, take this for your campaign. It's not much, but I feel I owe it to the guys I left behind at Kamas."

Chapter Nine: Cao

> "The boldest moves are the safest."
> *—Vice-Admiral Horatio Nelson*

SATURDAY, 15 NOVEMBER 2031

After Geneva, Linder's next stop was Paris, where two of his closest allies in the anti-Unionist movement lived. One of them was Colonel Barton Cao, a former U S. Army officer of Vietnamese extraction who had risen to battalion commander in Iraq and Afghanistan and later served as brigade commander in the ill-fated Manchurian War. Interned in Alaska with other American officers after the evacuation to prevent them from bearing witness to the betrayal of U.S. forces in that war, Cao led his fellow officers in a daring escape to Canada, and from there traveled to France.

Linder arrived at his Paris hotel on a Saturday evening, indulged himself by sleeping late, and arrived at his friend's townhouse in time for Sunday dinner. In the ornate upstairs parlor, he was greeted by Cao and his Vietnamese-French wife, his niece, the niece's husband, and Jacques "Jack" Poirier, a former U.S. naval officer who had fought on the rebel side in Texas during CWII and until recently led Cao's intelligence organization in Canada. Linder had met Poirier twice before and considered him a capable fellow, shrewd but no eagle.

Linder found Cao's niece, Maria Silva, far more interesting. She was in her late twenties, of medium height and lithe of figure, with jet-black hair and an olive complexion that she owed to her Brazilian father and Vietnamese mother. She also seemed to burst with energy. In contrast, her husband, Gordon Mook, though a nice enough fellow and certainly good-looking, came across as insipid and lacking drive. To Linder, the couple seemed a rather odd match, with Maria being the brains of the outfit and likely the one who wore the trousers.

When Cao mentioned that his niece had begun her undercover work against the Unionist regime years before, Maria acknowledged the remark with a stiff smile.

"Is that how you and your husband met?" Linder ventured.

Maria shook her head.

"No, we met here in Paris, three years ago, not long after I arrived from Mexico City, one step ahead of a Unionist hit team. Gordon had come much earlier."

Linder's eyebrows rose at her mention of the assassination squad.

"So you were active in the resistance even before you came to France?"

"Yes," she replied without volunteering more.

"Maria is far too modest," Cao broke in to fill the void. "She got started in the movement organizing protests against the Manchurian War as a sophomore at UC-Riverside. After the Unionist takeover, she went underground, running a series of resistance cells until the DSS finally closed in on her. It's a miracle she made it out alive."

"I'm lucky that I had someplace safe to go when it happened," she noted. "Others didn't."

For a moment Maria's face clouded over. Only later did Linder learn that her first husband died in a Utah corrective labor camp after being captured.

"Of course, safety is relative," Poirier added. "Maria has been a key member of our organization from the moment she joined us and has never shied away from risk."

"Let us drink then, to risk and reward," Cao interjected, removing a bottle of champagne from an ice bucket on a nearby table.

When they finished the bottle, the party adjourned to the dining room for dinner, which consisted of delicious homemade *coq au vin*, served with a luscious red Bordeaux. During the meal, discussion revolved around personal anecdotes, with no business matters being raised, out of concern over possible electronic eavesdropping. The same was true when brandy was served after the meal. Only when Cao invited Linder to his study, a windowless interior room built to meet most of the specifications of a SCIF,[4] did Linder address the purpose of his visit.

"What did your agent learn about April when he traveled to Utah? Did he talk to any of her father-in-law's friends or neighbors?" Linder pressed. "Has anyone laid eyes on April or Jay since they flew back to the U.S.?"

At Linder's urging, Cao had sent one of his Colorado-based stay-behind agents to Utah to locate the nutritional supplement facility that April's father-in-law had planned to reopen with his son's help. Cao's agent had found the building shuttered, with no trace of April, her husband, or her father-in-law.

"Not a one. The only person in Coalville willing to talk was the old woman you said ran a boarding house."

"Mrs. Unger?"

"That's the one," Cao nodded. "She also checked with the local police chief. He was pretty sure that the father-in-law died in the camps a few years ago."

"Which means that his letter to Jay must have been a forgery."

"I'm afraid so, Warren," Cao added, laying a sympathetic hand on his friend's shoulder. "As for your sister, I'll tell my people to keep looking. But you know even better than I that trying to find anyone in the camps is like searching for a needle in a haystack."

"Understood. But thanks, anyway."

---

[4] Sensitive Compartmented Information Facility, a room or building used by U.S. government offices to discuss classified information. Its primary purpose is to prevent the hostile interception of data or information, whether physically or electronically.

While Cao's news came as no surprise to Linder, it still hit hard. He stared into his brandy snifter for a long moment before raising his head to speak again.

"I just returned from the IAAE conference in Geneva," Linder began. "If the people at that event represent the front line against Unionist tyranny, then the tyrants have victory in the bag. Most of the people there were wealthy globalists kept afloat by old money and obsolete ideas. Now their nostalgia for the good old days seems to have overcome their fears of another Blue Terror. I'd say they've set their sights on getting on good terms with the Unionists so they can make some easy money again."

"I'm not surprised," Cao answered before taking a sip of cognac.

Of all his fellow resistance leaders, Linder considered Cao the most practical and insightful, and the one whose advice was generally most valuable. After having been betrayed by America's political leaders during the Manchurian War, locked up in an Alaskan labor camp, and hunted down after escaping, Cao had dedicated his life to bringing down the Unionist regime.

"Unfortunately, you and I appear to be outnumbered these days," Linder went on. "The movement has become packed with weak, gutless, self-deluding sellouts who are one step away from peddling their souls to the DSS in the hope of becoming players again."

"When you talk of sellouts, Warren, are you thinking of anyone particular? If so, we might have the same person in mind."

"If your person happens to be located here in Paris, then we probably are," Linder answered with a long face. What saddened him was that the person he had in mind was arguably the most prominent leader in the émigré movement.

"I told Leonard I was coming to Paris this week and requested a meeting," Linder went on. "He declined, claiming he'd be out of town. Would you happen to know if that's true?"

"Leonard told me he was going to the south of France," Cao answered.

"I could send someone to his flat to confirm, if you like."

"No, I'll take him at his word, for now. But I'm worried about Leonard. He's running out of money and losing supporters fast, which is driving him toward increasingly desperate schemes. One wrong move and he could make serious trouble for all of us."

The last time Linder had seen Leonard Fury had been on his fundraising tour during the week before he fled Beirut. At the time, Linder had been in Geneva to support the Anti-Unionist Congress, of which Fury was founder and general secretary. But he and Fury parted ways over the latter's reliance on violent tactics, and Linder resolved to keep his distance thereafter.

Fury, a sometime lawyer who had been among the most celebrated militia leaders during CWII, had continued launching cross-border raids into the Unionist State long after the war's end. Then, after his retreat from Mexico to Europe, he kept up the pretense of waging armed struggle, though with negligible results. Now, like Cao, Fury called Paris home and lived under French intelligence protection.

"I share your concern about Leonard," Cao confided. "I've never seen him under so much stress. He drinks far too much. And I thoroughly distrust the people in his entourage. In my opinion, they are a nest of vipers who feed his absurd overconfidence and indulge his worst vices. What's more, his current favorite, Mrs. Geiger, is the worst of a bad lot."

"In what way?"

"As his personal assistant, and as his lover, she controls not only Leonard's schedule and the information reaching him, but also his mental well-being. Lately, my sources tell me that Geiger has been feeding him reports that the American public is growing impatient with Unionist tyranny and that dissident cells are popping up all across the nation. She's telling him that he ought to lead them."

"Where is she getting this information? And could there be any basis for it?"

Cao's face registered disbelief.

"A spontaneous uprising all over the country? Hardly," he scoffed. "And, if there were one, how could it happen without the DSS swooping in?"

"Either way, who could be putting out such reports? Leonard's own sources in-country?"

"Leonard has no sources left," Cao snorted. "I suspect Geiger is getting them from Berlin. The FAP claims to be in touch with a new group of well-placed dissidents in Washington. One of them plans to visit Berlin soon and Leonard is thinking of meeting him there."

"The group wouldn't happen to call itself the American Constitution League, would it?" Linder asked, a faint smile forming on his lips.

"How did you know?" Cao asked with narrowed eyes.

"Two members of the League visited the U.K. earlier this fall to meet with local members of the FAP. MI5 says they're on top of it, but they question whether the group is real."

"I'd be skeptical, too. Do you mind if I pass along your info to Leonard the next time I get him alone?"

"Be my guest," Linder offered, breaking his promise to Hackett not to share it. "When is he due back from the south?"

"I have no idea," Cao shrugged. "He's been incommunicado lately. My suspicion is that Leonard is planning something to disrupt the international trade conference in Cannes next spring."

"Trade conference? Why would Leonard be interested in that?"

"Because the conference is aimed at reopening trade between the G7 nations and the Unionist State. The conference will kick off just before the G7 Summit in Genoa and continue until a new multilateral trade arrangement is worked out with the Unionists. Except that Leonard is dead-set on preventing it."

"And how do you suppose he intends to do it?" Linder jeered. "You and I both know that Leonard isn't half the man he used to be, and his resources are dwindling fast."

"Yes, but don't underestimate his determination. Leonard is a genius at playing the spoiler, and he doesn't give a rat's ass how much collateral damage he causes."

In that moment Linder's thoughts turned to the Anglo-American trade talks in London. Cao's news about Fury's plans planted the seed of an idea.

Chapter Ten: Berlin

> "Nearly all men can stand adversity, but if you want to test a man's character, give him power."
> —*Abraham Lincoln*

TUESDAY, 16 DECEMBER 2031

Two weeks after Victor Barbosa's return from Bristol, he called his deputy, James Jenkins, into his office in the mirror-faced DSS Annex at Tyson's Corner. Jenkins, dressed in gray corduroys and forest green sweater over a white button-down shirt, took a seat on the opposite side of Barbosa's desk and returned his boss's smile with a quizzical look.

"I hope you're not planning a vacation any time soon," Barbosa began.

"I might be," Jenkins answered. "Why do you ask?"

"I just spoke to the deputy director. He's approved our new deception operation against the émigré movement in Europe."

"You mean against Payne's organization in Berlin?" Jenkins asked.

"For starters. But we're authorized to extend the operation to as many opposition groups as we can. The concept is for a network of notional anti-Unionist dissidents inside the U.S. that seeks cooperation with like-minded émigrés. Of course, the top people in the network would be DSS undercover officers or contractors. But the front men will have to be outsiders. They can't be veteran operators like you or I because the deception could go on for years. There'd be too high a risk of someone identifying us. What we need as front men are people with credible anti-Unionist bona fides who have never been associated with the DSS. How about your man Quist? Do you think he's up to it?"

Jenkins let out a long breath.

"I don't know, chief. He seems to fit the profile well enough, as a former rebel and all. But to succeed as a provocateur, you need to be a world-class liar and have nerves of steel."

"So you don't think he's bent enough?" Barbosa challenged, holding up a manila file. "Look, I've read Quist's file. The guy is an out-and-out con artist!"

Jenkins made a sour face.

"It's not that he's too straight, boss. My concern is that he may lack the nerve. On the other hand, I expect that he could be had rather cheaply right now."

"Well, then, let's put him to the test."

Shortly after lunch, James Jenkins arrived at the DSS's satellite interrogation facility at Dulles International Airport and brought out Owen Quist for questioning.

After initial formalities, Jenkins, posing as Darrell Otis, got to the point of his visit.

"I'm not going to sugar coat it for you, Quist. You're in deep shit. If we were to remand you to the National Security Court, you could be facing ten years at hard labor in the camps."

"But that's a death sentence!"

Quist had been in custody for more than two months and had lately begun to doubt whether he would ever see freedom again. Otis's comment made him wonder if the imagined scenes of Arctic labor camps in his nightmares might be prophetic.

"But it doesn't have to be the end," Otis replied. "For a moment, think of that dissident circle of yours that you told Acker about."

"How many times do I have to tell you that I don't have a dissident circle!" Quist interrupted. "I made it all up to get on Harold's good side so I could marry Denise!"

"Yeah, yeah, yeah," Otis said with a dismissive wave. "I get that. But I didn't come here to make you rat on your friends. Think of it this way: What if that dissident circle of yours were real? What if they were seeking outside help from the exile movement? And what if they sent you back to Bristol to procure that help from Acker and his buddies? What kind of reception do you think you'd get there?"

"I don't understand why you're asking me this," Quist replied, his head swimming from the unexpected line of questioning.

"Okay," Otis answered slowly. "What if you and I were to invent a secret dissident organization located in D.C. along the lines of the one you described to Acker? Only larger and more ambitious. With members in law enforcement, the armed forces, the Unionist Party, and every key locus of power in Washington. Imagine that our organization aimed to overthrow the U.S. government but needed outside aid to do it. Do you think Acker's bosses in Berlin would lend a hand?"

"Of course they would," Quist answered on a note of exasperation. "That's what those guys live for. But how could such a dissident organization possibly exist in D.C. without being rolled up by the security organs?"

"It couldn't. You and I know that," Otis answered. "But the émigrés don't, because they've been away for too long. Nor do they even want to know how impossible it would be to evade notice. For more than a decade, the émigrés have been hoping and praying that the Unionist experiment would collapse of its own weight. Now, what if we gave them reason to believe that a crackup was right around the corner?"

"I suppose some would swallow that. It would depend largely on the quality of the evidence and the credibility of the person telling the story."

"What if the DSS created the evidence and you were the one to present it?"

Quist drew a sharp breath and Otis regarded him with an expectant look.

"Me? Pitch it to the FAP? But how?"

"It's quite simple," Otis responded, leaning back casually in his chair. "We want the FAP leadership to believe not only that your notional dissident circle exists, but that it can offer them valuable insights into U.S. affairs and help them achieve their anti-Unionist goals. We also want the FAP to think they could play a key role in the new government that would take over once the Unionist system fails."

"I still don't get it," Quist answered, throwing up his hands. "How do you people benefit if I persuade the FAP that my fictitious dissidents are ready to work with them? Wouldn't I also have to deliver the goods at some point?"

Otis let out a short sharp laugh.

"What we want from the FAP is for them to share with you their plans, intentions, methods, and whatever resources they have inside the U.S. Later, we'll exploit this collaboration to gain control over the FAP and, eventually, over the entire émigré opposition. We'll do that by feeding the émigrés disinformation, co-opting their leaders, infiltrating their membership, and siphoning off their cash to support operations that we will secretly control. In time, they won't make a move without our knowing it. And, operating inside the U.S., the organization will act like a giant bug light, attracting, capturing, and zapping genuine dissidents before they can bite us."

"Okay, okay, I can see why you'd want the FAP to fall for your ruse," Quist conceded. "But what if they don't take the bait? I wouldn't want to be the one sent to persuade them if they were able to see through the con. I expect the FAP deals rather harshly with spies."

"Would you rather take your chances in the Yukon?"

"No. But if I failed to convince them and lived to tell the tale, why wouldn't I just run off and never see you again?"

"Because we'd find you. And because we'd send Denise to the camps in your place. But let's not dwell on the negatives, Owen. Look on the positive side. If you succeed, we'll let your fiancée out and the two of you will be free to marry. You'll also get to keep your job at StatOil so you can continue to travel abroad on business. With bonus pay from us. And, while you've overseas, you'll be dining at fancy restaurants on our nickel and staying at posh hotels where you'll hobnob with wealthy émigrés and their foreign intelligence agency sponsors. By the way, I understand from your file that you were once active in amateur theatrics. If you still enjoy that sort of thing, working with us could offer you the role of a lifetime."

This stunning reversal of fortunes threw Quist completely off-balance. He didn't know what to say. So he said the first thing that came to mind.

"Would I have to kill anybody?"

Otis roared with laughter.

"Not at all!" he asserted, before adding with a sly grin, "Don't worry. We have plenty of other people to do that sort of thing."

"Then why not use one of them for this job? I'm an engineer, not a spy."

Otis shook his head and gave Quist a disapproving look.

"Come now, Quist. You may not agree with everything the Party does," he scolded, thrusting a finger under the prisoner's nose, "but you and Denise appear to value the benefits of Party membership. So I'd say that leaves you under an obligation to defend the Party against all enemies, foreign and domestic. And right now you are in a unique position to do just that."

Quist remained unpersuaded, wringing his hands and squirming in his seat.

"But Harold is my friend," he protested. "It wouldn't be right for me to trick him into helping the DSS."

"Let's make something perfectly clear, Quist. You owe nothing to Harold Acker or his friends in the FAP. These are people who betrayed their country."

"But what if my work led to them getting renditioned or killed? I'm not sure I could live with that."

"No, no, no. You're looking at this all wrong," Otis contended, shaking his head. "This is not cloak and dagger stuff. Think of your role as that of a salesman. You sell propane for StatOil, right? Well, you'd be selling other things for us. Things like information, influence, and hope for a brighter future. That's what the émigrés want. So let's give it to them—good and hard."

Having been offered a clear idea of what the DSS expected from him, Quist's thoughts began to settle. Yet he remained troubled by the images conjured in his mind.

"But all the risk would be on me," he fretted. "If the FAP found out I was working for the DSS, they could kill me. Or torture me. Or both."

"Not likely," Otis argued. "Their goons might rough you up a bit, but then they'd turn you over to the local authorities, who would hold you for a few days or weeks and deport you back home."

"And then what? Would I get to go back to my job at StatOil? Would you still let Denise go free? You know very well that I did nothing wrong when I was in England. You have no right to exploit me like this!"

Suddenly Otis's expression turned icy and his eyes stone hard.

"Do you know what the conviction rate is in the National Security Court? About ninety-nine percent. Would you rather take your chances with the court or with me? Pick one or the other. This is not a negotiation."

One month later, Owen Quist's taxi stopped at the entrance of Berlin's Hotel Adlon Kempinski shortly before sunset as reddish-orange clouds lit up the midwinter sky. Quist stepped onto the cobblestoned pavement and looked out to find the floodlit Brandenburg Gate an imposing presence less than a block away.

As he looked up at the luxury hotel's massive stone edifice, his nerves grew taut. For while he had won an introduction to the FAP's Berlin-based leaders by convincing their British followers that he represented an important Washington dissident network, Quist's critical test lay ahead. Judging from the lavish accommodations the FAP had arranged for him, the men he would be meeting tonight would be sophisticated and well-informed, not ones easily duped by specious claims and empty promises. But he had no choice but to move forward. For, having embarked upon a sequence of lies, going back was impossible.

Quist let the bellhop take his bags and followed him into the hotel's limestone-walled lobby with its iconic elephant fountain and glass-domed ceiling. At the registration desk, he checked in quickly and was handed a message with the name of the private dining room where he was expected to appear for cocktails and dinner at seven. Before stepping into the elevator, he checked his watch. He had just over an hour to shower, dress, and psych himself up for the ordeal.

At seven sharp, Quist appeared at the door of the private dining room, where a pair of dark-suited security men frisked him for weapons and took his cell phone for safekeeping before letting him enter. Inside, he found an elegantly laid table for six and five distinguished-looking men engaged in spirited conversation beside a moveable bar.

The person at the center of attention was the oldest of the five, a portly fellow of about seventy years, dressed in an impeccably tailored gray houndstooth suit. Quist recognized him at once by his lush mane of white hair: Benjamin Payne, former two-term governor from a

Midwestern state and one-term Vice President of the United States—the last of his breed before the Unionists seized power.

Payne suspended his conversation when Quist came through the door and offered him a broad smile. The other men, all but one dark-suited and past middle age, gazed upon the visitor with expressions of bland curiosity. The older men were FAP officers whom Quist identified on sight from his DSS briefings. The fifth man, the youngest and fittest of the group, likely in his early forties, wore a brown tweed sports jacket and gray flannel trousers. From his lean, chiseled face and close-cropped salt-and-pepper hair, Quist guessed he had a military or intelligence background.

Once introductions were made and small talk exchanged, the headwaiter offered Quist a drink. He chose dry *fino* sherry to keep a clear head.

"You come to us highly recommended," Payne opened as Quist took his first sip of sherry. "Our British colleagues were excited to hear that a vigorous underground opposition has stepped up to challenge the Unionist State. Tell me, Mr. Quist, how has your organization been able to grow so rapidly under the baleful eye of State Security?"

"It's because we already operated in another form, even before the Events," Quist replied. "In those days, we called ourselves the Constitutional Officers League and our members came from law enforcement, the military services, and first responders. We pledged to fulfill our oath to defend the Constitution against all enemies, foreign and domestic. Little did we know then that our pledge would mark us for persecution under the Unionists. Many of our members were imprisoned, and others fled after the Unionists took over. But some stayed behind to form underground cells in every major law enforcement department and on military bases across the country. Now we're recruiting civilian members so we'll have more patriots standing by to take down the Unionist Party when the time comes."

"So what do you call your organization now?" one of the men asked, a tall and cerebral-looking fellow of about sixty years with the chilly politeness of a diplomat on assignment.

"We're the American Constitution League now, or just the League."

"You must be aware, Mr. Quist," Payne noted, "that our group and others like it have done absolutely everything in our power to foster an internal opposition movement since the Unionist takeover. We've spent millions, and sacrificed hundreds of lives, in that effort. Yet we have little to show for it. Somehow your group appears to have succeeded where ours failed. So, given these results, what can we offer you that you aren't able to manage on your own?"

"And why has it taken so long for you to make yourselves known?" Payne's cerebral-looking colleague added after a pause.

Quist took a moment to scan each of the others' faces, all of which seemed to display sincere interest in his answer rather than suspicion. So far, so good.

"Our primary reason for waiting was to make sure that we could reach out securely," he replied. "But also, the time came when we realized we needed greater resources if we were to grow more quickly."

"What sort of resources?" Payne asked.

"Well, funds, obviously. Our members have been donating their time and covering expenses out-of-pocket. But to professionalize our movement, we need to start paying stipends to full-time organizers and to cover their travel and incidentals. We also need technical assistance, particularly with secure communications. We lack state-of-the-art encryption, reliable access to the Dark Web, and other means of communicating securely with each other and with members of the public."

Benjamin Payne cast a glance at another of his colleagues, a wiry, fussy little man with a nervous tic that caused his right eye to twitch.

The latter met Payne's gaze with a tight-lipped smile that his eyes did not share.

"Ira, do you suppose that our technical staff might be persuaded to help Mr. Quist?" Payne inquired.

"I don't see why not," the little man responded without relaxing his forced smile.

"Then I suggest the two of you get together later to explore details. In the meantime, I'd like to hear from Mr. Quist over dinner about what he and his people have done to weaken the Unionist regime. Does anyone else have an appetite?"

The others nodded and murmured assent.

During dinner, which included local perch filets in a mustard sauce, accompanied by a dry Mosel Riesling, Quist delivered a meticulously rehearsed speech outlining the League's origins and recent achievements. He fielded each question as it arose, and his responses seemed effective at reducing the level of skepticism among the group. By the time dessert arrived, which consisted of house-made vanilla ice cream with *sabayon* sauce, Quist was hopeful that he had passed muster with the FAP leadership and might at least live to see another day. His confidence faltered, however, when the resistance leaders began to press him for details on the sort of sensitive and exploitable intelligence that the League could deliver on the Unionist regime's strategic plans, capabilities, and weaknesses.

Quist dodged the most difficult questions and put off responding to several others as best he could, until one of the five men, the one in his forties with the military bearing, spoke up after a long silence. He had introduced himself as Jack Poirier and seemed to be the only one of the five who didn't represent the FAP. Instead, he came from the ultra-hardline Anti-Unionist Congress and was a last-minute replacement for the Congress's founder, Leonard Fury.

"You mentioned that you used to work for the Department of Transportation," Poirier began. "Is that so?

Quist felt his chest muscles relax ever so slightly at the question, which was an easy one and would help establish his credentials.

"That's right," he replied. "Before the Events, I was an oil and gas pipeline engineer for the Pipeline and Hazardous Materials Safety Administration. After the Unionists gained power, PHMSA suffered an acute shortage of qualified professionals and was folded into the State Oil Company."

"May I ask what position you held with PHMSA before you joined StatOil?"

"I was Deputy Director of Pipeline Safety. They promoted me to director when the office merged into StatOil."

"Then you must be familiar with the DOT's critical infrastructure plan. According to our sources, there's a classified section of the plan that covers LNG terminal safety. Might you be able to get us a copy?"

Quist caught his breath and felt his body stiffen once again. The obvious reason for wanting information on terminal safety was to plot sabotage, something at which Poirier's organization, the AUC, was highly experienced.

"Uh, that section is classified," Quist answered slowly. "And, since I'm no longer in PHMSA, I don't have access to it."

"But surely you must remember a good deal of what's in the plan. Would you be willing to let one of our experts debrief you on it?"

"I suppose so," Quist answered while struggling to think of a way to avoid it. "But it's been quite a long time since I last reviewed the document. I'd hate to give you outdated information. It might be better if I took another look at it before trying to describe it. I still have contacts in PHMSA. I expect they might let me see it again."

"When you get access, is there any way you could make a copy of the key sections dealing with security at the LNG terminals?"

Quist was certain that his DSS handlers would never let him hand over anything that émigré insurgents or foreign intelligence services might use to sabotage American critical infrastructure. If he promised to deliver it but failed to do so without having an ironclad excuse, the failure could raise suspicion. On the other hand, an outright refusal would be inconsistent with the League's professed eagerness to help the FAP bring down the Unionist regime. So how could he show a present willingness to supply the information while excusing a failure to do so later?

But before Quist could answer, he received help from an unexpected source. Ira Levin, the fussy little man who specialized in communications, offered a temporary reprieve.

"Before we ask Mr. Quist to risk stealing classified documents for us, I think we should work out a secure communications plan. And that may take time. Might it be better to delay the critical infrastructure document until we're ready to handle it?"

To Quist's surprise, Poirier's expression softened and he offered Levin a deferential nod. After all, Poirier didn't belong to the FAP and perhaps was reluctant to overstep his bounds as an outsider.

The remainder of the dinner event went more smoothly. Though Payne would not commit to a specific sum in financial aid, he proposed a range that was substantially higher than what the DSS had expected. Likewise, Quist's later one-on-one with Ira Levin came off exceedingly well. The two men set up several communication channels, including an encrypted email account by which Quist was to report weekly about the League's activities. When the time came to leave the dining room, Quist felt as if he had carried off his dramatic performance as well as anyone had a right to expect.

Chapter Eleven: Cannes

> "The great strength of the totalitarian state is that it forces those who fear it to imitate it."
> —*Adolf Hitler*

WEDNESDAY, 14 APRIL 2032

Linder rose from bed and pushed aside the blackout curtains in his room at the Hôtel Martinez in Cannes. When he last stayed here, he had booked a prestige suite with sea view, but that was before the Swiss froze nearly half his assets. Now he had to settle for an ordinary room without sea view. Not only was he on a budget, but this was also the week when delegates from the G7 nations plus the United States were gathering down the street for their multilateral trade conference, driving luxury hotel rates sky-high. For a minute, he looked out the picture window onto the shimmering blue of the Mediterranean, thinking of the challenges ahead. Then he retreated to the shower to get ready for his first meeting of the day.

The meeting was to be with Nelson Furness, at the Carlton, located two blocks down the Boulevard de la Croisette, which was the official venue for the Cannes trade conference. Furness, a former pro-Brexit Member of Parliament and one-time Tory Prime Minister, was one of Britain's most prominent opponents of an Anglo-American trade deal, or indeed any deal granting formal recognition to the Unionist State.

Linder arrived early at the Carlton to clear the multi-layered security measures for the conference. To his relief, his journalist credentials were accepted without objection. On reaching the lobby, he made his way to the Carlton's fifth floor, where Furness had booked his suite. The politician, now nearing his seventieth year,

101

looked crisp as a new banknote in his raw linen suit, knitted cravat and olive-hued suede loafers. He escorted his guest to a pair of fan-backed Art Deco chairs located just inside the French doors that lay open to the suite's sun-drenched private terrace.

"Coffee?" Furness offered before pouring each of them a cup from a thermal carafe.

"Thanks," Linder replied. "It's going to be a long day. Did you catch the Prime Minister's press conference last night?"

"I did. Pretty standard stuff. 'Peaceful coexistence' and all that. 'Better to do business with a rival than exchange missiles.' Just what you'd expect before the conference gets down to brass tacks."

"Yes, but I could have done without the PM's comment that the Twitchell regime is here to stay," Linder added. "Do you think Bledsoe is going soft on Unionism?"

Furness offered an indulgent smile. Dwight Calder had introduced the two men while he and Linder were readying *My Book of Revelations* for publication. At the time, Furness was one of very few leading Tory politicians willing to condemn human rights abuses in Unionist America. On a whim, Calder had sent Furness an advance review copy of Linder's book in hopes of picking up a favorable review. Far better than a review, Furness had volunteered to write the foreword, and ever since had taken Linder under his wing and become his confidential advisor on U.K. politics.

"Not exactly soft," Furness answered. "The PM giveth and the PM taketh away. I think you'll see some very stiff preconditions this week from our Tory negotiators."

"I'm afraid my clients won't find that terribly reassuring," Linder grumbled. "They don't want any trade deal, not even one on Bledsoe's terms. Most of them are dispossessed owners of U.S.-based properties who fear that the politicians will negotiate away their claims. Their position is this: no trade deal until the Unionists compensate them for all the property they've taken."

"That may have been a tenable position a few months ago, Warren, but your clients need to realize that, to get back on its feet, the global economy must have access to American markets, energy and raw materials," Furness explained. "At present, the U.K. and Europe are in a mad scramble to fill the U.S. trade vacuum. No country wants to be the first to formally recognize the Unionist regime, but now that Mexico signed a peace treaty with Washington, and a new North American Trade Agreement followed soon after, it's only a matter of time before one of the G7 nations offers diplomatic recognition in exchange for concessions on trade. Your clients would be well advised to accept whatever compensation they are offered."

"My clients and I understand the changed circumstances," Linder conceded, returning his coffee cup to its saucer and fixing Furness with a firm gaze. "But we also recognize that many of the PM's supporters are chiefly interested in opening a lucrative business with their collaborators across the pond. We won't stand idly by while the Gang of Three reaps an economic bonanza that could shore up their power for years."

Furness sat back in his soft-backed chair and gave Linder a hard stare.

"So how do you intend to stop them?"

"The Tories have many constituencies," Linder replied. "Prime Minister Bledsoe should be careful not to alienate any of them. We've been busy forming alliances with his anti-Unionist Tory supporters to raise his political cost of conceding to Washington."

"Do you really think that will suffice?" Furness asked with raised eyebrows. "The globalist free traders in the City of London wield far more influence in Whitehall than your clients ever will. And we both know that DSS agents will attempt to bribe, blackmail and bend conference delegates to their will by all possible means. In my opinion, it's a foregone conclusion that trade with the U.S. will reopen very soon. The only question is on what terms."

"You may be right about the forces arrayed against us, Nelson. And, as you know, I oppose violence. But some anti-Unionist groups are not so scrupulous. If my faction fails to disrupt a G7 consensus on trade with America, more extreme factions may step in. For example, Leonard Fury and his Anti-Unionist Congress have made it clear that they intend to disrupt the Cannes conference any way they can. And the French security services cannot be relied upon to stand in their way, knowing that Germany and the U.K. will likely eclipse France in the race for trade with the U.S."

"Why have I not heard of this Fury fellow before?" the former PM groused. "And what are Britain's security services doing to stop him?"

Linder shrugged while a stealthy smile crept across his face.

"MI5 and MI6 know Leonard well, but neither is eager to see an expanded Unionist trade office in London, let alone a reopened American Embassy, with all its potential for subversion. So it seems they've thrown up their hands and maintain that stopping Fury is a matter for the French, since his organization is Paris-based and the conference is taking place on French soil."

"Well, I shall certainly do my best to see that stricter measures are taken," Furness replied in strong tones. "If not by the French, then by our own security apparatus. We cannot let the most extreme elements determine the outcome of this conference."

"Certainly not," Linder agreed. "Fanatics like Leonard will always be circling around. They'll never be satisfied and there's no point trying to appease them. But they do have their uses."

"Is that so?" the older man challenged, rising from his chair with a curdled look on his face. "And what might those uses be?"

"They make me appear reasonable."

Linder spent the rest of the morning and most of the afternoon buttonholing conference delegates and their aides in areas of the hotel open to journalists and non-government organizations. That day he drank more coffee than he had consumed on any other day of his life. But at half past four he left the Carlton and hired a taxi to take him to the nearby resort town of Antibes-sur-Mer, located some twenty minutes to the east.

Upon arrival, he set out on foot for the old city to find the bar where he had arranged to meet the U.S. trade representative to Britain, Irwin Kreutzer, for a quiet drink away from other conference participants. As with the invitation to their earlier clandestine meeting in London, Kreutzer's note had come by messenger. It gave precise directions to the Absinthe Bar, located between the Antibes covered market and the Cathédrale Notre-Dame.

Linder found the bar without difficulty just before the appointed meeting time at five o'clock. On arrival, he descended the winding stone stairs into a cave-like room with vaulted limestone ceilings. The walls were festooned with vintage French advertising posters and an enormous variety of silly hats, some of which were currently in use by the clientele, who had turned raucous. Linder spotted Kreutzer at a far table, dressed in a navy blue summer suit with a Mexican sombrero perched atop his head. Arrayed on the table before him were a bottle of spirits, two glasses, and an odd contraption that resembled a small antique water fountain.

Linder took a seat opposite the trade representative, who immediately handed him a beat-up brown derby.

"Go ahead, put it on," Kreutzer urged with a mischievous smile. "I already tried it on for size. It should be large enough for you."

"Ingenious choice of meeting place," Linder answered as he glanced around the room. "Not the kind of bar where we're likely to see fellow conference types. And the hats make it devilishly hard to recognize anyone even if you know exactly who you're looking for."

"Quite so. Listen, Warren, I've taken the liberty of ordering our drinks. Have you had absinthe before?"

"Once or twice, but never with an apparatus like this," Linder answered, pointing to the fountain-like contraption.

"Good. Our bottle is one of the best. What we don't drink I'll take back with me to the hotel."

Linder picked up the bottle and examined its ornate Art Nouveau label. It looked expensive.

"It's the original Vieux Pontarlier, from Pernod," his host pointed out. "I'm eager to try it. Shall we?"

It seemed to Linder as if Kreutzer were seizing every possible opportunity to live high on the hog so long as an ocean separated him from the Unionist Workers' Paradise.

"Let's do it," Linder answered. "I never refuse a drink when someone else is buying."

Kreutzer poured a shot of the pale green liquid into each stemmed glass, placed a perforated absinthe spoon across its mouth, dropped a sugar cube into the bowl of the spoon, and positioned each glass under one of the two tiny spigots of the fountain. Then he opened the dual spigots and poured a thin stream of water over each sugar cube until they dissolved slowly into the liquor below.

"That looks just about right," the trade official said when turning off the spigots. "This stuff is 130 proof and isn't meant to be drunk neat."

He nudged a glass across the table to Linder and raised his own.

"*Santé*!" Kreutzer toasted to his guest before taking the first sip.

"*A la tienne*!" Linder replied.

The taste was not the strong licorice flavor he had expected, but more nuanced, with notes of anise and fennel. He liked it more than he'd expected. But he had a lingering concern about the bottle's wormwood content, based upon absinthe's sinister reputation for inducing hallucinations and eventual madness.

"Very nice," Linder commented. "But will it make us go insane?"

"Not if we stop at three," Kreutzer answered before letting out a guffaw.

Linder was surprised at Kreutzer's buoyant demeanor, for the canny trade rep had to be aware of Linder's active lobbying against reopening Anglo-American trade. After their autumn meeting in London, where Kreutzer had proposed a scheme for the two men to profit from rigging the bids on U.S. surplus property sales in the U.K., neither had contacted the other. As for Linder, he found the bidding scheme attractive but didn't need the money badly enough to risk compromising himself by becoming Kreutzer's business partner. But why had Kreutzer called for another meeting? Was it to push the bid rigging scheme again? Or had Linder finally become enough of a thorn in Kreutzer's side that he wanted Linder to throttle back his lobbying against the U.K. trade agreement? The answer came quickly.

"My people tell me that you've been quite busy turning out propaganda against resuming trade with Washington. While that's what I would expect of you, Warren, what interests me more is that you've been advising your clients to require restitution for expropriated properties or, alternatively, fair compensation, as their bottom-line demand. Am I correct in that?"

"More or less," Linder answered while wondering what lay behind the question. "Of course, I oppose any trade agreement so long as the Unionists remain in power. But I realize that a deal with the U.K. may be reached, anyway. If so, I would insist that restitution be one of its core principles. After all, my clients expect me to put their interests first."

At this, the corners of his host's mouth lifted in an unexpected smile.

"In that case, Warren, what if I told you that my government is willing to negotiate a fair settlement of all outstanding property claims raised against us by foreign-based parties, to include protections for any future investments. Might that help to mitigate your opposition to a trade agreement with the U.K.?"

Linder's jaw dropped and for a moment he was at a loss to respond.

"It might," he answered at last. "But why on earth should I believe you?"

"Because you and I have worked together in the past and know each other well. Have I ever lied to you or led you astray?"

"No, but you're playing a very high stakes game now and I expect you'll stop at nothing to win. In such situations, my motto is 'trust but verify.'"

"In that case, perhaps we could reach a compromise," Kreutzer proposed, taking a moment to recharge his glass with absinthe. "A moment ago I gave you a valuable piece of inside information about the U.S. negotiating position. You are free to use it as you wish for your clients' benefit. Tell them, if you like, that the Unionist government is so eager for a trade agreement with Britain that it will offer generous property settlements to all foreign claimants who drop their opposition to an overall agreement on trade. Using this information, there's nothing to stop you or your clients from pre-emptively snapping up discounted shares of nationalized mining firms, oil drillers, power utilities and the like, and then reaping a tidy profit after compensation occurs. Whether or not you trade personally on this information, surely your clients ought to be most grateful for it."

"And by buying off your opponents like this, you reckon to wrap up your agreement and win a fat promotion on your return to D.C.?"

"Ah, but there you are wrong, Warren. I have no intention of going back to work in D.C. My goal is to stay in London until diplomatic relations are re-established, and then continue as American Ambassador to the Court of St. James until my retirement."

"Optimistic, are we?"

"Oh, yes," Kreutzer agreed, recharging Linder's glass and putting spoon and sugar cube in place before dispensing water to melt the cube. "And I hope you haven't forgotten my earlier proposal about helping to divest surplus U.S. real estate in Britain. Have you given it any thought since we talked?"

"Ah, I see. Another neatly wrapped bribe to get me to go along with the trade deal," Linder replied, leaving the freshly prepared absinthe glass untouched. "I'm afraid you're wasting your time, Irwin. I'd much rather see your trade agreement go down in flames than line my pockets, even if it is at the Party's expense."

"But what if you could do both?" Kreutzer held Linder's gaze, seemingly undeterred by the latter's rejection. "All I ask is that you keep an open mind until after the Cannes conference. Whether a trade deal with the U.K. happens now or not, you can still benefit your clients by helping them acquire valuable properties at highly discounted prices. While helping yourself, as well."

The last time Kreutzer had made him such an offer, Linder hadn't risen to the bait. But that was before almost half his assets were frozen in the Swiss courts. In principle, Linder had no objection to his clients speculating in the shares of nationalized American companies. Nor did he mind them making a profit from buying and selling surplus U.S. military facilities in the U.K., even if a portion of the purchase price wound up in the secret offshore bank accounts of Kreutzer and his Unionist cronies. Even if Linder did no more than to make introductions and guide interested clients through those acquisitions, he could make his clients very happy, at little risk to himself. What if he did as Kreutzer suggested, took his cut in the deals, and used the money to fight the Unionist regime? Now that, he thought, might be interesting.

"Okay, Irwin. I'll think about your proposition," Linder answered, feigning disinterest.

"I always knew you were a reasonable man, Warren," Kreutzer replied with a grin. "Once we're back in London, I'll be in touch. Meanwhile, let's have another absinthe and see if it really can drive us crazy."

On the morning of the third and final day of the Cannes Trade Conference, Linder was shuttling from one meeting to another at the Carlton, urging his clients to hold fast to their demands for full compensation from the Unionists, when he received a cell phone call from Dwight Calder in London.

"Have you heard about the assassination plot at Sanremo?"

Linder swallowed hard. Sanremo was a popular tourist town located between Cannes and Genoa, where the G7 Summit was scheduled to open in two days. The target site's location relative to the two international conferences could not be a coincidence.

"No. Tell me."

"It just popped up in my news feed," Calder went on. "According to Reuters, the Italian police have arrested a team of heavily armed American émigrés just across the French-Italian border in Sanremo. They're being charged with conspiracy to attack members of the U.S. delegation as they were about to leave Cannes. Your friend, Leonard Fury, was detained separately and released without charge on condition that he return to France immediately."

"Oh, my God," Linder replied, feeling his heart sink. "Every time I think Leonard has hit bottom, he surprises me."

He thought at once of the disrepute that Fury's fiasco would bring to the anti-Unionist movement and how badly it would demoralize the movement's rank and file. Fundraising would suffer, as well.

"Do you have more details?" Linder asked.

"A few," Calder replied. "Apparently, the team intended to ambush Kreutzer and his motorcade at a congested spot in Sanremo while they relocated from Cannes to Genoa for the G7 Summit. One of the shooters told police that killing Kreutzer was intended to convey the message that the Unionists would have no peace till they restored constitutional rule. And they wanted to deter Washington from sending any more high-profile delegations to international meetings."

"Damn," Linder groaned, looking around in vain for something he could punch with his fist. "Now I know why Leonard's been avoiding me. He knew I would have tried to stop him."

"So how much of an impact do you think the news will have at Cannes?" Calder asked.

"Doubtless it will generate sympathy for the Unionists and shift the tide in favor of reopening trade. Opponents like us will be forced back on our heels. But it's anyone's guess what the official delegates will do. I expect that most of them came to Cannes with their decisions already made for them. "

"Well, good luck, old boy. I leave the situation in your capable hands," Calder signed off, clearly happy to be many miles away.

For the remainder of the day, Linder watched while journalists cornered prominent opponents of U.S. trade and pressed them to denounce Leonard Fury and the AUC for the alleged assassination plot. All but a few knuckled under and only those who did so were allowed to speak on air. But, despite feeling anger that Fury had let the anti-Unionist side down, Linder would not be provoked into commenting either way about Fury or the alleged plot. Instead, he ordered his bank to stop Fury's monthly cash transfer and resolved to cut off further contact. If there were to be a reconciliation somewhere down the road, Fury would have to take the first step.

To Linder's relief, the final day of the Cannes conference came and went without a joint communiqué laying out commonly agreed-upon terms for reopening trade with the United States. Instead, each country's delegation either flew home or moved on to Genoa for the G7 Summit. In the days that followed, commentators attributed the lack of consensus to the obstinate demands of America's foreign creditors and those insisting upon compensation for confiscated properties. Meanwhile, Linder's clients moved quietly to buy up the discounted shares of nationalized American companies, particularly those in the mining and energy sectors, in hopes of reaping outsized profits if and when the Unionists compensated those companies for their nationalized assets.

As if to confirm that the fix was in for an eventual Anglo-American trade deal that would make speculators rich and the Unionist Party strong, Tory PM Humphrey Bledsoe announced a week after the Cannes adjournment that Irwin Kreutzer's trade team in the U.K. had been upgraded to a permanent trade mission and that bilateral trade talks were being fast-tracked. Those of Linder's clients who had risked buying up the discounted shares were ecstatic. But rank and file members of the émigré opposition movement, having rejoiced prematurely at the failure of the Cannes conference, were downcast that a resumption of U.S. trade with Britain now seemed closer than ever.

Chapter Twelve: Fury

> "Men are more easily governed through their vices than through their virtues."
> *–Napoleon Bonaparte*

WEDNESDAY, 19 MAY 2032

A month after his travel to Cannes, Linder took the train from London to Paris at Barton Cao's request. Cao expressed concern that, ever since Leonard Fury's failed Sanremo operation, their wayward friend had sunk into a deep depression and seemed unable to snap out of it. Worse still, he saw a risk that Fury might become so desperate as to lash out with actions even more damaging to the émigré movement than those at Sanremo. So, despite his resolution to remain distant, Linder agreed to pay Fury a visit.

Arriving in the late afternoon, Linder made his way to the taxi stand, limping due to a painful plantar wart on his foot, and caught a ride to the Hotel Raphael. The five-star hostelry, which stood a few blocks south of the Arc de Triomphe and only a twenty-minute walk from Fury's flat, was Linder's first choice whenever he visited Paris. Built in 1925 and known for its Art Deco style, the hotel was also notorious for having housed senior officers of the SS, Gestapo, and Wehrmacht during the Nazi Occupation

After settling into his room, a pall of gloom soon fell over Linder. It was the eight-month anniversary of his sister's return to Utah and he hadn't heard a word from her or Jay since. He missed April terribly and could not help imagining her sufferings if sent to a corrective labor camp. At the same time, he sensed that his teenage ward,

113

Caroline Kendall, was also slipping away from him under the influence of her Eaton relatives in Oxford.

To dispel the gloom, Linder resolved to take a glass of champagne at the hotel's rooftop bar, known for its stunning views across the rooftops of the City of Light. Upon emerging from the elevator, he filled his lungs with the scents of flowering jasmine, lilacs and wisteria and felt his entire body release pent-up tensions. Only after finishing his first glass of *brut* and ordering another did his thoughts return to Leonard Fury.

According to Cao, Fury's affairs were in total disarray. Since Sanremo, his supporters had deserted him in droves and his detractors had written him off as a spent force. In Cao's view, however, Fury had lost more than support—he had lost his judgment, and perhaps even his fabled nerve. Linder knew from hard experience that weak people make dangerous partners and that, sooner or later, they tend to fail anyone who depends on them. Uneasy at the prospect of confronting Fury the next day, and bothered by his painful foot, Linder finished his second glass of champagne without even tasting it.

The next morning Linder walked out of the Hotel Raphael and headed south along Avenue Kleber through the wealthy 16th Arrondissement, allowing extra time for his ailing foot, and for random stops to help him detect anyone who might be following. At ten sharp he entered Fury's building and rode the wrought iron Art Nouveau elevator to the fourth floor.

To Linder's surprise, no one was posted on the landing. On his last visit, a sinister-looking Israeli bodyguard had stood guard outside Fury's door. Today, no security man was in sight, most likely because Fury could no longer afford it.

In the years immediately following Linder's escape from the Unionist State, Fury had been the leading figure in the émigré opposition and its last great hope. Accordingly, Fury was the very first émigré opposition leader Linder supported after retrieving the cached treasure that Philip Eaton's militia had looted from Cleveland's downtown banks. Over the next few years, Linder had grown to admire Fury's tactical skill, resourcefulness, and dogged will, and the two men became fast friends. More recently, however, after reckoning the human cost of Fury's increasingly fruitless armed insurrection, Linder reluctantly stopped bankrolling his cross-border raids and paramilitary cells. Going forward, Linder gave Fury only a modest allowance solely for his personal maintenance.

Thus, as the rebel leader's financial resources dwindled from year to year, he was forced to cut back on his far-flung agent network and vacate his expensive office located among the embassies and wealthy NGOs of the 8th Arrondissement. Now his offices inhabited the back portion of his sprawling residential flat in the Rue de la Tour. All the while, Fury's financial position continued to weaken because of his profligate lifestyle, lavish travel budget, and bloated personal staff. Doubtless, Fury would expect Linder to go on bankrolling him till the bitter end. Yet without full access to his Swiss accounts, Linder could no longer bear the cost. Persuading his old ally to accept that fact would not be an agreeable task.

Before the door to Fury's flat opened, Linder could hear the clacking of a woman's heels on the parquet floor inside. Moments later he came face-to-face with Doris Geiger, Fury's personal assistant and, according to Barton Cao, current lover. The woman appeared to be in her late thirties, with a petite plump figure, pale complexion, and dark bobbed hair. But her most characteristic feature was the scowl she showed to everyone but Fury and her long-suffering husband, as if her favorite emotion were disgust.

The Geigers, who had worked for Fury in one capacity or another ever since he arrived in Paris, had in recent years made themselves indispensable to their employer, thereby gaining near-complete control over his schedule and the people who were allowed access to him. Beyond offering her body to Fury, Madame Geiger was also reputed to supply him with drugs to cope with recurring symptoms of post-traumatic stress left over from CWII. According to Cao, Fury had gone from an occasional user to a full-blown addict under her care. But then, Cao admitted to detesting the woman, whom he referred to as "that stinking cow" behind her back.

As Linder had taken to heart Cao's advice never to criticize Madame Geiger in Fury's presence, the woman treated him with wary politeness. On this occasion, she admitted Linder and led him in silence to the sitting room, where he found Fury slouched in an easy chair with a tablet computer in his lap. Now in his late forties, Fury was a small, dark, balding, sloe-eyed man whom most people would never have picked out as someone who had murdered hundreds during a decade-long rampage of bombings, ambushes, and assassinations.

Yet somehow this ordinary-looking man possessed a monumental ego and had come to see himself from a young age as a Nietzschean superman who transcended conventional moral limits. Without a doubt, Fury possessed a rare organizational talent, with a quick wit, boundless energy, and a gift for inspiring followers. But, at the same time, he could be unfathomably credulous, irresponsible, conspiracy-prone and, on occasion, childishly romantic. In Linder's experience, such personalities often achieved impressive results, but just as often made puzzling errors at critical moments and placed blind faith in the wrong people.

Fury raised his head at the sound of approaching footsteps, appearing momentarily distracted. He rose slowly, put aside the tablet computer and extended a hand in greeting. Madame Geiger hovered for a moment but left the room when Linder pointedly looked her way.

"It was kind of you to come," Fury began without looking his guest in the eye. "It can't have been easy for you, considering the fallout from Sanremo."

"I might not have come at all if Barton hadn't been so concerned about your state of mind," Linder replied. "What's done is done, so I won't beat you over the head with it, but your bungled attack undid a year of work for us in the U.K. A week after Sanremo, Prime Minister Bledsoe upgraded the Unionist trade delegation to a permanent mission, paving the road toward a formal trade agreement. You hurt us badly, Leonard."

"Yes, but only because the operation failed," Fury shot back. "We took a risk and it didn't pay off. But we had no choice, Warren! Don't you see? Idle talk is getting us nowhere. Half-measures never work against the Unionists. We had to go after their delegation to Cannes to put them back on their heels."

"Surely you don't mean to say that assassination was your only option," Linder replied. "There's always an alternative to killing." While Linder had grown accustomed over the years to Fury's doubling down on bad bets, the latter's answer was disappointing. Was the man completely incapable of learning from his mistakes?

Fury scoffed. "Have you forgotten so quickly why we resorted to assassinations and bombings after losing the civil war?" He was clearly unwilling to cede the high ground. "Political murder has two basic goals. The first is to remove dangerous persons from the enemy camp. But it's just as necessary to charge our own movement with electricity, to jolt it out of apathy, and to destroy the enemy's myth of invulnerability. Without terror, the movement loses vitality."

Linder shook his head and twisted his lips into a frown.

"Maybe that was true early on, when we were fighting for our lives against the Blue Terror. But now that the Party has consolidated its grip on power, our attacks represent little more than pinpricks. Even worse, violence does our enemies the favor of making martyrs of them. Frankly, I'd rather hold them up to ridicule. Better to point out their incompetence and make people feel the consequences of the regime's failures."

"Is that so?" Fury asked, feigning surprise. "And just how does one go about doing that?"

"Through propaganda and protests. We collect information about Unionist corruption and incompetence and help local dissidents get the word out through social media, graffiti, posters and the like. We offer rewards for the best memes, videos, and political jokes—whatever puts Party leaders in a bad light."

"That's all?" Fury sneered. "Nothing kinetic? Have you really gone that soft, Warren?"

For a moment, Linder wasn't certain if the question was meant to be serious. He decided it wasn't and answered in like manner.

"Not completely. I avoid physical violence to the extent that I can. But I remain open to fraud, deceit, blackmail, and other dirty tricks. Does that reassure you?"

Fury's expression eased and a faint smile played on his lips.

"Well, good for you. Warren. I'm glad you've found a niche for yourself. But I'm afraid propaganda is too weak a brew for me."

"That's your prerogative, of course," Linder answered. "But you mustn't think you can go back to your old ways after Sanremo. Your financial backers have abandoned you and your grass-roots followers are doing the same. Nor is Italy the only country where you're declared *persona non grata*. I have it on good authority that MI5 has put your name on a watch list to keep you out of the U.K."

"I'll miss London," Fury replied with a sigh, but his eyes showed no regret.

"Listen to me, Leonard. You've got to get it through your head that the kinds of operations that made your career aren't an option any more. If you intend to play any role in the opposition movement from now on, you've got to do it from the sidelines. Your Anti-Unionist Congress might still be viable, but only if you resign the chairmanship and allow someone else to replace you."

"Well, now that you mention it, that's something I've been considering."

"How soon?"

"At the next annual meeting, in the spring."

"Not soon enough," Linder snapped. "Resign now. And scale back your public statements and appearances to allow time to rehabilitate your image. Otherwise, there may not be a Congress by next spring."

Fury's face went pale, and for the first time Linder thought his message might be getting through.

"You think it's that bad?"

Linder nodded. "And it's not just me," he pressed. "Barton is of the same mind. As I said before, he's very concerned about the stress you've put yourself under. Cut back now. Get some rest. Let others carry the torch, at least for a while."

Fury rose to his feet and gazed around the room, as if searching for a successor right then and there.

"But there are so few I can trust! There's you, of course, and Barton, but…"

"Yes, and neither of us will ever give up the fight. But these are desperate times for us, too. Barton gets some support from French intelligence, but his private contributors are offering him less and less. I'm seeing the same with my own backers. And, though I haven't had an occasion to tell you, I've suffered a major financial setback recently."

This seemed to shake Fury out of his reverie, for he turned to face Linder with a look of disbelief.

"Financial, did you say?"

"Yes. The Swiss authorities froze the greater portion of my assets there after the Unionists claimed that the funds derived from money laundering. I'm appealing the seizure through the courts but I'm not sanguine about the outcome. So I've had no choice but to cut back on all my activities, including support to others."

Here Linder fixed Fury with a pointed stare.

"Permanently?" Fury demanded.

"I'm afraid so. If I were in your shoes, I'd look for new funding sources."

"Easier said than done," Fury grumbled, looking away. "Do you have any candidates in mind?"

While Linder was wary after Sanremo of the damage that a well-funded Fury might still cause, he didn't want to let the man down entirely. It seemed fair to at least offer him a fundraising lead or two.

"Well, there's Nascimento," he told Fury. "He just won the presidential election in Brazil and has vowed never to do business with the Unionist regime. Have you tried him?"

"No, but I will."

"And how about Payne and the FAP?" Linder suggested. "He's rolling in dough and seems widely respected among the moneyed crowd. If he made even a token contribution, his endorsement might open doors for you."

"Payne?" Fury answered with a look of disdain. "Odd that you should mention him. The man is an utter buffoon, of course. All money, no sense. But lately he seems to have stumbled across an interesting opportunity. Some of his people have made contact with the representative of a new resistance group operating inside the U.S. Payne invited me to Berlin to meet the fellow, but I wasn't free. So I sent one of my top men to check him out."

Was Fury talking about The American Constitution League? Up to now Linder had dismissed the group as a likely DSS provocation. But if the League had sent an emissary to Berlin to meet with Payne and the FAP leadership, might there be more to it?

Without waiting for his guest to comment, Fury shouted down the hall.

"Doris, is Jack in his office? If so, could you send him here, please?"

A few moments later, Jack Poirier entered the parlor wearing a brown tweed sport coat and khaki trousers. Linder had met Poirier on two or three occasions and, though Fury considered him one of his top cross-border agents and Cao still used him from time to time, Linder thought of him as one of those irritating freebooters who always volunteered for hazardous missions to collect a hefty bonus, yet always managed to skate through unscathed. Coincidence? He wondered. Otherwise, Poirier was an engaging sort, clever and alert, with a mordant sense of humor.

"Tell us about your trip to Berlin to meet that fellow from the League," Fury addressed Poirier, omitting introductions. "What was his name again?"

"Owen Quist," Poirier replied while acknowledging Linder with a nod.

"Have a seat, then, and tell us what you learned."

The veteran cross-border agent plopped down on a stuffed chair between the other two men and summarized his dinner meeting in Berlin with Quist, Paine, Ira Levin, and others from the FAP. He began with his initial suspicions that the League seemed too good to be true, which deepened when Quist balked at disclosing the Transportation Department's critical infrastructure plan.

"In the end, Quist said that, if I wanted to learn whether the League was for real, the best way was to travel to the States with him and let him show me around. At first, I was suspicious because, the last couple times I'd been over there, security had been extremely tight. I just didn't see how the two of us could get in and out safely, let alone travel all across New England and maybe even New York City."

Poirier appeared composed as he related the story, his attention glued upon Fury. But upon meeting Linder's gaze, he shifted uncomfortably in his seat and looked away.

"Anyway," he went on, "after going over their plan, I decided to take the chance of going with Quist to the Vermont border, with an option to cross over if all looked well. I knew it was risky but, in the end, I couldn't pass it up. What clinched it for me was a phone call I made to my brother in Boston, who vouched for a couple of League members he knew there."

"So how did the trip go?" Linder asked, trying to conceal his disbelief that Poirier could have made such a foray into the Unionist State without being caught.

"Incredibly well," the agent replied with a smile that did not reach his eyes. "Wherever we went, League people seemed to have the police in their pocket. We never had so much as a tense moment."

Linder narrowed his gaze.

"Not once?" he asked.

"Nope, it was smooth sailing all the way."

Poirier quickly broke eye contact and went on to describe places he saw and his impressions of how conditions had changed since the end of the Great Blue Terror and the launch of the NEP. For while security conditions had eased in America and the standard of living had improved, it seemed that this very easing had fostered a restless spirit among the people. And it was that spirit which had fueled the League's rapid growth.

It was a tidy story that made the League look very attractive indeed, but Linder wasn't ready to buy it. Not yet, at least.

"So what's next in your plans, Jack? Are you going back in?"

"I'm planning another trip with the League now. I'll be bringing along someone else from Leonard's team, and possibly one of Barton Cao's people. His niece, Maria, is very keen to come. Things are moving fast, I'm telling you."

"Maybe too fast," Linder replied. "Your comment that the League seems to have the police in their pocket makes me nervous. It's inconceivable to me that a group could pop up and grow like Topsy over there without coming to the DSS's attention. They'd be penetrated immediately. And why haven't we come across any protests or demonstrations organized by the League? It sounds like the dog that didn't bark."

"Maybe demonstrations aren't their thing..."

"Possibly," Linder went on. "But what about Quist's refusal to turn over the critical infrastructure plan? Or any other exploitable vulnerabilities on the Unionist side? Doesn't that bother you, Jack? And has the League claimed credit for any acts of sabotage? Or assassinations? Or defections? I think somebody needs to press them hard on these questions before we put any of our people in their hands."

But before Poirier could answer, Fury cut in.

"We will press them. Believe me, we will," the insurgent leader assured him. "But for the present, Jack's work with the League has presented some intriguing prospects for us. Not least of them is expanded collaboration with the FAP. You see, Payne has agreed to finance Jack's next trip. And wasn't it you, Warren, who proposed that we seek funding from the FAP?"

The response was typical of Fury. When he wanted something, he would invent any pretext to pursue it, even if it contradicted positions he'd taken before.

"So if the League invited you to cross the border along with Jack, would you run off and go?" Linder pressed.

"To be perfectly frank, I've been giving it serious consideration," Fury replied, drawing himself up to his full height. "Quist reports that the League intends to appoint someone with national stature as its new head. Someone who can put forward a comprehensive plan for governing the country when Unionism falls apart. They've asked Jack whether I'd consider taking the job."

Linder bridled at the words. Cao had been right to worry about Fury's state of mind. The man's colossal ego was finally cracking under the weight of his latest setbacks. Now he had become so desperate to stay relevant that he was grasping at straws. And Poirier, witting or otherwise, was feeding his boss's false hopes of returning to power.

Fury seemed to notice the ominous hardness in Linder's eyes and confronted him.

"Oh? You think I shouldn't accept?"

"Not necessarily," Linder evaded. "I'd need to know more before I could say that for sure. Let me do some research."

"And how long do you suppose your research might take?"

"I don't know. A week or two. A month, perhaps."

"In that case, would you consider restoring my regular stipend for another month? It would help me bridge the gap until the FAP's first payment arrives."

Linder had fully expected that Fury would hit him up for money during his visit. After all, he had cut off Fury's stipend without notice. One more transfer wasn't entirely unreasonable. He would provide it. But he resolved it would be the last.

Chapter Thirteen: Annabel

> "The essence of dramatic tragedy is not unhappiness. It resides in the solemnity of the remorseless working of things."
> *—Alfred North Whitehead*

THURSDAY, 20 MAY 2032

Linder had planned to see Barton Cao, if only briefly, before leaving for southern France to meet with prospective contributors. But, as Cao's return to Paris had been delayed by a day or two, and the plantar wart on his right foot was making it increasingly painful to walk, he decided to remain in Paris for a few days and have the wart removed. He asked the hotel's concierge for a dermatologist referral and was offered an appointment the next morning at an exclusive private clinic in the nearby 9th Arrondissement, a short walk from the Paris Opéra metro station.

Upon entering the spotless white reception room, whose walls were decorated with oversized canvases of abstract art, he checked in and then turned around to find a seat. Sitting in one of a half-dozen neo-futuristic womb chairs was an attractive woman, about a decade younger than he, dressed in a gray tweed suit that looked like it might be from Chanel or Lagerfeld. When Linder's gaze fell upon her, the woman was busy sending a text on her cell phone. When she raised her eyes, Linder found himself gazing into a face that conveyed intelligence and strength, with steady blue eyes that seemed kind, but at the same time sad, as if the woman had known love and lost it, not once, but perhaps many times.

"*Bonjour, madame,*" he greeted her before sitting.

"*Bonjour,*" she replied with a sheepish smile. "Excuse me, but do you speak English?"

"Much better than my French, thank you. Are you British?"

"Very much so. And you? Let me guess: American?"

"Formerly. I'm stateless now, living in London as a refugee, thanks to your great country."

"Well, you seem to have landed on your feet," she replied, looking him up and down with a bold smile, as if assessing the cost of his Savile Row suit. "May I ask what brings you to Paris?"

"Meetings with sponsors, mainly," he evaded, while pulling out a business card that showed him as Chairman and Founder of the Anglo-American Information Bureau. "I run a non-profit that puts out information critical of the Unionist regime back home. By the way, I'm Warren."

"And I'm Annabel," she replied with a smile, removing from her purse a card that listed a Mayfair address.

"Is Paris a second home for you, Annabel?"

"No, but I come as often as I can. Sad to say, I'll be leaving in a few days."

Before Linder could reply, the receptionist appeared from behind her desk to escort him through a glass door into the clinic.

"I'm so sorry we can't go on talking," he said as he rose from his seat to follow the receptionist. "I expect to be back in London by the end of the month. Would it be all right if I gave you a call?"

"I'd be delighted," Annabel replied, offering him her hand and a broad smile.

Upon returning to his hotel from the clinic, Linder searched the internet for Annabel's name. He found it under both Annabel Bishop and Annabel Haddon, the former being her maiden name, which she had used during her career in the London musical theater, and the latter being her married name.

Years earlier, when Linder had worked in London for the DSS, he had taken an avid interest in the West End theater scene and had dated several actresses at the time. So it seemed possible that he and Annabel might have shared some mutual acquaintances back then. But while Linder was away felling timber and mining tungsten in the Yukon camps, Annabel had married the prominent British film director and producer, Richard Holmes Haddon, and retired from the stage not long after. Her husband, nearly three decades her senior, died of a stroke five years into the marriage, leaving Annabel moderately wealthy by London standards. She did not remarry.

To Linder's delight, the opportunity to meet Annabel Bishop Haddon again came sooner than expected. The next day, while returning in late afternoon from a short stroll around the Arc de Triomphe to test his convalescing foot, he spotted her at the Hotel Raphael's concierge desk. Was it coincidence or fate? Either way, here was an opening he didn't intend to miss. So he stepped up behind her and waited until she finished her business.

"What a lovely surprise," he said as she turned to leave. "Is this your hotel, too?"

"Why, yes," she replied with a bright smile.

"Have you had tea?" He looked at his watch. "It's just past four o'clock," he added. "Would you care to join me?"

Her smile widened.

"I'd be delighted. I must admit that I was hoping we might see each other before leaving Paris. The clinic whisked you away so quickly..."

"To be frank, I felt quite the same way," Linder answered, gesturing toward a free table near the lobby bar. "But, considering the nature of the clinic, how do you know I wasn't there to treat some dreadful disease?"

"It never occurred to me," she replied with an amused look. "Why, do you have one?"

"No, just a wart on my foot, since removed. But, if you don't mind my asking, why were you there?"

"I had a terrible rash on my arm."

"Well, I figured it was something harmless or you probably wouldn't have offered me your card so quickly."

Now Annabel's look was one of perplexity.

"And why do you say that?"

"Didn't you know?" Linder replied with a wry smile. "That dermatologist is also the premier V.D. practitioner in town."

At that, Annabel threw back her head in laughter, and Linder sensed he was off to a good start. Summoning the waiter, he ordered a selection of finger sandwiches and a pot of Darjeeling tea and embarked upon a long conversation that led into Annabel's early career as a dancer and Linder's as an intelligence officer. As it happened, not only was Linder a devotee of the musical theater, but Annabel had long nursed a fascination with spies and foreign intrigue. They swapped tales for an hour or more, by which time the dinner hour loomed large. So Linder took a chance and invited Annabel to dine with him. She declined but accepted for the following evening.

The next morning, Linder woke up with misgivings. Though he had found Annabel alluring, and genuinely wanted to see her again, now he harbored second thoughts. Was it solely due to his secretiveness, born of his career in the CIA and DSS, and of his experience as a fugitive? Certainly, having worked under cover for so long, he had missed out on more than one opportunity to form a lasting romantic relationship. The women with whom he had paired off from time to time in casual flings had come and gone, leaving scarcely a trace behind. None had loved him; of that he was fairly sure.

His rediscovery in Utah of Philip Kendall's daughter, Patricia Kendall, and their brief but tragic relationship, had been the exception.

After losing Patricia, his teenage sweetheart, he doubted he would ever find someone to take her place. As a result, he had kept his distance from most women of marriageable age since his escape. Was it too late to try again? Had his sister been right to pity any woman unwise enough to become involved with him?

Fortunately, by evening, his nerve recovered. He took Annabel to a Michelin two-star restaurant in the 8th Arrondissement. There the degustation menu dragged out the meal for hours and the wine pairings loosened their tongues, encouraging each to tell his or her life story, from childhood to the present day. Annabel's began with early dancing lessons, which led to casting as a young dancer in a West End musical, and advanced from there to more and better roles. Owing to her natural flamboyance and high energy, she attracted the attention of numerous moneyed suitors who spoiled her, though she fended them off until past the age of thirty, when she met Richard Haddon, then nearing sixty. He soon became her guiding star, as loving husband, career coach and surrogate father, until his sudden death after only five years of marriage. They had no children.

Linder told a carefully redacted version of his own life story, omitting the worst of his misdeeds working for the Exile Division, his suffering in the camps, the DSS's attempts on his life, and his fears about the fate of his sister and brother-in-law. He dwelt mainly on his recent work against the Unionist regime and his hopes for a better future. By the end of the evening, Linder felt more comfortable with Annabel than with any other woman in his adult life, possibly including Patricia, whose role in his story he left out, as well.

Linder extended his stay in Paris for a week on the excuse that the minor surgery on his foot required more time to heal. Though Barton Cao returned to Paris during that week, Linder never found time to see him. Instead, he and Annabel roamed Paris together each day, visiting museums, attending the theater, shopping, and dining out. It didn't take long before they discovered they had similar tastes in music, drama, art, food, and other things. For despite his straitened financial circumstances, Linder spared no expense while courting Annabel. One night he even found somewhere to take her dancing, where his skill as a ballroom dancer surprised her and won him her professional respect. And before long they ended up in bed. Having distanced himself from women for so long, Linder felt as if he were dry grass being swept up in flames. He told her that she had caught his heart off guard but that he was grateful for it.

As for Annabel, having already married a man three decades her senior, she seemed to have no qualms about starting an affair with a man only ten years older. On one occasion, she joked about her "Pygmalion syndrome," possibly due to her father having deserted the family when she was a child. She added that Linder was one of several unlikely soul mates to whom she had felt drawn during her adult life. She said he made her feel whole again after her husband's death.

Similarly, Linder told Annabel that she had given him a new source of hope and a reason to savor life, despite the setbacks he had suffered over the past year. He found her to be fun-loving, outspoken, and quick to pull him out of his occasional funk. Also, like him, Annabel was a *parvenu*, a schemer, a go-getter who had learned to live by her wits and get by on her looks and talent. Yet, having acquired independent wealth upon becoming a widow, Annabel had managed her finances prudently. Thus, her practicality further put Linder at ease.

Linder felt drawn to Annabel as tides are drawn to the moon. Even so, he remained conflicted about starting a lasting relationship with her. His mission to bring down the Unionist Party had always demanded his full concentration and freedom from serious entanglements. Also, he hadn't yet shared with Annabel some of the darker aspects of his past, particularly his decade-long fight with the DSS. If he and Annabel were to become a pair, she might become a target, as well. And if the Exile Division killed or abducted him, she would be widowed once more. She was strong, of course, and would go on with her life, as she had when Richard Haddon died. But was it fair to bring her into a life as turbulent as his?

Linder completed his fundraising circuit through southern France and northern Italy and returned to London on a Friday. That night, at dinner, he told Annabel about Patricia Eaton Kendall, and how her daughter, Caroline Kendall, had come to be his ward. On Sunday afternoon, they met again at his flat and Linder answered the questions raised by Annabel's reading of his memoir, a copy of which she had found online. Afterward, he confessed that he was falling in love with her and hoped she was willing to go on seeing him.

"I would understand if you chose not to," he added. "Please believe me, Annabel, I really don't go around looking for trouble," he told her over coffee. "Since my escape, I've chosen a non-violent path. While I believe fully in my mission, I don't see why I should have to die for it. But it's impossible to know how far the Unionists might go to silence me. A life spent with me wouldn't be free of risk."

"I'm willing to face it, if you are," she replied, taking his hand.

"Then so be it," he said, giving her hand a squeeze. "If troubles come our way, I'll protect you as best I can. With my life, if need be."

A month later, they announced their engagement to a small circle of family and friends, with a wedding date set for September. They married in a quiet civil ceremony at the Westminster Register's Office, with Caroline Kendall and Annabel's older sister as bridesmaids. Dwight Calder and Barton Cao served as groomsmen, with Linder's assistant, Fiona Bowles, and Allen Hackett of MI5, as witnesses. Linder wished that his sister April could have been there, if only to see that he was marriageable material, after all. He had sent

April and Jay a wedding invitation in Coalville, in the care of his and Jay's former landlady, Mrs. Unger, but received no response.

At the ceremony, the bride wore a sleeveless chiffon gown and carried a bouquet of orchids and lilies of the valley. When the time came to toss the bouquet, Annabel aimed at Caroline, who ducked. Also attending the wedding reception at the Savoy Hotel were many of Annabel's friends from the theater, as well as Linder's closest backers in the émigré community. A few of the latter had known Caroline's parents when they had lived in London and invited her to visit. One notable friend of Linder who did not attend, however, was Leonard Fury, to whom a U.K. visa had been denied.

In Linder's remarks to his guests, he joked that, having become notorious for the treasure he brought from America, the freezing of his Swiss assets now made him appear like a fortune hunter for marrying a wealthy widow. And having given up his Chelsea digs for Annabel's fancy Mayfair flat tended to confirm it. Annabel responded promptly by taking Linder's hand and declaring that their marriage had made her feel like the luckiest woman in the world.

Chapter Fourteen: Basel

> "For the thing which I greatly feared is come upon me."
> —*Job 3:25*

WEDNESDAY, 15 SEPTEMBER 2032

L inder and Annabel had originally planned to depart immediately after their wedding for a honeymoon on the French Riviera at Théoule-sur-Mer, but when the Swiss cantonal court handling Linder's asset freeze set a trial date in Basel for September 20, they were forced to make new arrangements. They left London by train on the Wednesday after their wedding, with a plan to visit Caroline Kendall in Lausanne after the verdict, followed by a weeklong honeymoon hiking the mountain trails at Zermatt.

For Linder, it was a time of great stress, knowing that the Unionists would play every trick in the book to win their case and might try even more extreme measures if they thought they might lose. He kept on the lookout around the clock for suspected DSS agents. After arriving in Basel, he and Annabel rarely left their hotel, except for meetings at their lawyers' offices. Even then, they traveled with an armed guard hired from a local Swiss VIP protection agency. They also remained circumspect when indoors, though security at the five-star Hotel Les Trois Rois was extremely tight.

To prepare for the trial, Linder spent three days with his litigation team reviewing facts and arguments, anticipating tactics of the opposing side, and rehearsing his testimony. His senior attorney explained that the U.S. government's seizure request rested upon its claim that Linder's Basel-based bank accounts had been funded with property stolen from safe deposit boxes in Cleveland's downtown banks, which property Linder later retrieved from a cache buried south of the city. The government would also likely support its case with a claim that the property had been removed from U.S. territory in violation of capital controls and tax laws then in effect.

Linder's chief counsel then explained that his chief argument in Linder's defense would be that the assets in his Basel accounts had not been stolen at all, but instead had been the rightful property of Philip Eaton, and that Linder had acquired them through a legal chain of custody. Thus, he argued, the accusation of money laundering was baseless. In addition, the U.S. Treasury's capital controls and exit taxes were irrelevant to Linder's case, as they were unenforceable under Swiss law.

"Okay, I'm feeling a bit better," Linder replied before letting out a slow breath. "But, when all is said and done, how do you think the court will come down?"

"One never knows in a case like this," the attorney replied. "But to be perfectly honest, I would put your odds of success at less than even. Substantially less."

Linder pleaded with Annabel not to attend the trial, lest she be exposed to the libelous tales that the U.S. government attorneys were likely to tell about him. But she insisted on being in the courtroom to show support for her husband and promised that nothing the U.S. side could say would diminish her faith in him. In the end, Linder relented and Annabel attended all three days of the trial.

On the first day, the chief counsel for the Justice Department recited at length the crimes of which Linder had been convicted in U.S. courts, including treason, seditious conspiracy, espionage, sabotage, terrorism, prison escape, and not to be overlooked, violations of currency controls and tax laws. Certified documents were placed in evidence to verify each conviction. Government witnesses also testified to the lurid details of his alleged crimes, some of them true, some not. Cross-examination failed to efface the picture drawn of Linder as a complete and utter scoundrel.

On the trial's second day, Linder was compelled to testify under oath or lose by default. He could not claim protection against self-incrimination because he was not in criminal jeopardy in Switzerland, his case being civil rather than criminal in nature. Under cross-examination, the U.S. Justice Department litigators pummeled Linder with artful questions that substantially weakened his position.

"Mr. Linder, were you present when the valuables that you removed from that Ohio barn first arrived there?" the U.S. chief counsel asked him. "Yes or no, please."

"I was not."

"Do you have any documentary proof that the valuables you removed were the rightful property of Mr. Philip Eaton?"

"I do not."

Here the government counsel paused for effect.

"The United States has submitted extensive evidence to the court about the source of the assets you deposited in your Basel bank accounts," the government counsel went on. "Our evidence traces those assets directly to property looted by rebel militias from the downtown Cleveland banks. Do you intend to submit evidence that contradicts this?"

"With all due respect to the court," Linder replied with a sour expression. "I believe the United States evidence to be fabricated and therefore inadmissible."

"So you claim, Mr. Linder. But I repeat my question. Will you submit evidence to refute the U.S. government's assertions about where you obtained your funds?"

"Not at this time."

Linder glanced briefly at the table where his legal team sat. None of them would meet his gaze.

"Let the court record the defendant's answer as a 'no,'" the Justice Department attorney declared. "Now, let us assume, if only for the sake of argument, that the valuables in question were the legitimate property of Philip Eaton. You've claimed that Mr. Eaton entrusted the valuables to Charles Yost for the benefit of Eaton's daughter and granddaughter, and that Yost entrusted them to you for the same purpose. You then converted them to cash and deposited the cash into Basel-based trust accounts with Caroline Kendall as ultimate beneficiary. Do you have any documentary evidence to substantiate this chain of custody?"

"Only the trust documents and the bank's receipts for my deposits," Linder answered.

"Are you aware that both Philip Eaton and Charles Yost were leaders of the rebel militia that looted the Cleveland banks to which your valuables have been traced? Again, yes or no?"

"The documents that the government is using to claim that the valuables were stolen are forgeries and thus inadmissible as evidence."

"On what basis do you make that assertion?"

"I refer you to my affidavit," Linder replied.

"So, it's the naked word of a convicted criminal against a stack of official government documents," the government's counsel commented, looking up at the three-judge panel with eyebrows raised. "I think the matter speaks for itself. But back to my original question. Do you deny that Philip Eaton and Charles Yost were leading members of the Cuyahoga River Militia, which the U.S. government has conclusively linked to the downtown bank lootings?"

"I can neither confirm nor deny that."

Now Linder turned his head to catch a glimpse of the judge, whose face wore a dark expression. Meanwhile, Annabel sat stiffly and bit her lip, a pained look in her eyes.

"Let the record read that the defendant does not deny Eaton's and Yost's membership in the Cuyahoga River Militia," the opposing counsel went on. "Now, one final question, Mr. Linder. Did you obtain prior approval from the U.S. Treasury Department to remove the valuables in question from U.S. territory? And did you pay all U.S. taxes due on the transfer?"

"I was fleeing for my life, for God's sake. Of course I didn't ask the permission of an illegitimate totalitarian regime," Linder added, showing his irritation.

The government lawyer cast a mocking glance toward his fellow co-counsels before turning back to Linder.

"Then did you act later to pay the relevant exit taxes on the properties you removed?" he asked the defendant.

"The question is absurd."

"Did you pay or not? Yes or no."

"Of course not."

"Let the defendant's answer be recorded as a 'no.' I have no further questions."

It took all of Linder's self-control not to lose his temper. But he bit his tongue, as a rant would have destroyed any remaining credibility he might have.

On the trial's third day, the court delivered its decision at mid-morning. It found that, though Linder committed no crime under Swiss law, the funds held in his Swiss trust accounts were subject to seizure as the product of money laundering. It ruled that the funds be turned over to the U.S. government for the purpose of restoring them to their rightful owners.

"Sure, of course they'll track down the owners of those safe deposit boxes," Linder muttered to his Swiss defense counsel. "If anyone believes that one, I've got a bridge in Brooklyn to sell him."

Without giving so much of a glance toward his adversaries, Linder took Annabel's hand and left the courtroom with her at his side. They went to their hotel immediately, where their luggage was packed and waiting. By late afternoon, the couple was aboard a train bound for

Lausanne, having dismissed their bodyguards. Now that the case was lost, there seemed little need for armed protection.

But while Linder had put the city of Basel behind him, he was far from reconciled to the loss of his Basel-based funds. For not only had income from the Swiss trusts offered a significant source of funding for his information warfare projects, but now Caroline Kendall would no longer receive the trust principal on her twenty-first birthday, as Linder had planned when he set up the trusts. He had always known that he would lose access to trust income when Caroline became twenty-one, but to lose it early meant that he would have to accelerate his search for new sources of funds or else curtail many of the AAIB's projects. But where could he find so much cash so quickly? And how could he afford to make up Caroline's loss of principal from his remaining assets without shutting down projects?

These questions weighed heavily on his mind as he rode the fast-moving Swiss train past fields of brown stubble and bales of hay waiting to be put aside for the winter. Every ten minutes or so, he left his seat to walk up and down the center aisle of the first-class carriage. Annabel commented that she had never seen him so distraught.

"Come now, Warren, you're far from ruined. You still have other funds," she chided when he returned from one such ramble.

"Yes, but not enough for what I want to do. A man must have sufficient money not to have to think of it. Now I'll be thinking about money quite a lot."

Though Linder had not grown up wealthy by any stretch, in recent years he had become quite accustomed to wielding the assets recovered from the Ohio rebel cache. And while he had put aside many of them for Caroline's benefit, and spent a smaller amount fighting the Unionist regime, he resented the prospect of having to make do with less. For a moment, he felt a shudder as his thoughts turned to Leonard Fury's increasingly desperate finances. Was he headed down the same path as Fury?

"Well, if it makes you feel any better, we can live off my income until you get back on your feet," Annabel offered with a reassuring smile.

"No, I won't allow it," Linder objected, stiffening in his seat beside her. "I insist on meeting my financial obligations, whether they're for daily living or my political activities. And I refuse to give the Unionists a moment's rest while I rebuild my capital."

"Really? But why?" Annabel probed. "I understand how important your work is to you, Warren, but you mustn't let it eat at you from inside. Why not take a breather from this crusade of yours until you secure new funding? For the past decade, you and your émigré friends have exhausted yourselves trying to defeat the Unionist Party. And what do you have to show for it? Can't you let it rest, at least for a while?"

Linder turned to her with a pained expression.

"You make the movement sound like some sort of personal vendetta, Annabel. Listen, this isn't about revenge. It's about justice. And not just for the people whose lives the Unionists have destroyed, like my sister and the men I knew in the labor camps. It's for people we can still help. People like Caroline."

"Well, while we're on the subject of Caroline, it seems to me that it's time to ease up on her, too," Annabel replied firmly. "I know you're concerned about her gravitating toward her relatives in Oxfordshire, but Caroline is an adult now. And the Eatons are her flesh and blood. You've fulfilled your obligations to her and to her late mother. Let Caroline get to know her aunts and uncles and let them help her in ways that you cannot. If you keep Caroline away from her family, who can she turn to when you're gone?"

"Let go?" Linder snapped, his eyes suddenly blazing. "Listen, I let Patricia go. I let April go. I let five good men go on our escape from the Yukon. Why am I always the one who must let go of people close to me?"

He gave her a piercing gaze that seemed to unsettle her. Annabel responded by taking his hand and holding it tight.

"You won't ever have to let go of me," she assured him. "I'm sticking to you, like glue."

Chapter Fifteen: Lausanne

> "Freedom is the only worthy goal in life. It is won by disregarding things that are beyond our control."
> *–Epictetus*

WEDNESDAY, 22 SEPTEMBER 2032

Warren and Annabel arrived in Lausanne just before sunset and checked into a junior suite at the Lausanne Palace. Though the hotel was in the city center, the couple enjoyed a panoramic view from their balcony across the pale blue surface of Lake Geneva toward jagged peaks with pink clouds perched above.

A short while later, Caroline called from the lobby to let them know she had arrived. The three met at the hotel's Parisian-style brasserie, where Linder had made dinner reservations. The maître led them to a leather-upholstered booth at the back, with Linder following last. Observing Caroline from behind, he found that she reminded him more than ever of her mother, dressed as she was in pressed jeans and a white embroidered blouse, her mahogany hair tied behind her head in a ponytail with a blue satin ribbon. For a moment, an image flashed in his mind of Patricia Kendall as she had first appeared to him in Coalville, Utah.

Over dinner, Caroline talked at length about her studies, her Swiss roommate, and the boys she had met since beginning her second year at the university. She particularly enjoyed her studio art lessons at a local atelier, as well as racing small sailboats on Lake Geneva and meandering through the Old Town on market days. She also looked forward to the upcoming ski season at nearby Gstaad, Morgins and

141

Villars. Annabel used the occasion to draw Caroline out on a variety of topics, deepening the budding friendship they had developed during Annabel and Linder's wedding.

"I'm sorry to break the news, Caroline," Linder said, pausing to take a sip of water. "But my court loss in Basel may require some belt tightening from both of us. There's enough income from your remaining trusts to keep you at university, but not for all the extras you're used to. I'm afraid your monthly allowance will go down by about thirty percent starting next month."

Linder expected an outcry but received none. Though Caroline could be sullen and irritable at times, she could also be delightfully levelheaded. Fortunately, this was one of those moments.

The dinner ended on a positive note, with Caroline planning a trip to London for the Thanksgiving holiday, along with an extra night in Oxford to visit her Eaton relatives. After some coaching from Annabel, Linder encouraged Caroline to become better acquainted with the Eaton clan since they were, after all, her flesh and blood.

Once they saw Caroline off, Linder and Annabel retired early for the night. Though Linder felt dog-tired from the stress of the trial, his mind remained restless and he couldn't sleep. In Basel, a doctor had prescribed sleeping pills, but he was loath to take them. After an hour of lying awake, he rose from bed and went to the window. The street below was quiet, with only a few well-dressed couples passing by, doubtless after a late dinner out. But then something caught his eye. It was a man in a dark loden overcoat wearing a Tyrolean-style hat pulled low over his brow. He stood in the shadows of a shopping alcove directly across the street. Why was he there? In that moment the man raised his eyes and looked up toward Linder's window. A chill went up Linder's spine and he called out to Annabel, waking her from a deep sleep.

"Annabel, come quick, to the window!"

She did as she was told and followed Linder's gaze as he pointed across the street toward the alcove.

"Do you see him?"

She hesitated before answering.

"No, darling, I'm sorry, but I don't see anyone at all."

"You're right," he answered, taking a long breath. "I turned away for an instant and he vanished. But he was there. I saw him. A big man in a dark overcoat."

"He was probably just stopping to check his watch or catch his breath. Don't let it bother you, darling. Besides, we'll be leaving for Zermatt right after lunch."

But Linder couldn't get the man's image out of his mind.

"Perhaps I shouldn't have dismissed the bodyguards so quickly," he added.

The next morning, Annabel rose early and phoned Caroline to invite her for breakfast at the Lausanne Palace. She explained that Linder planned to spend the morning on his computer and that she would love to pass some time alone with Caroline. As Linder had planned to work until lunch, he accepted the arrangement and ordered a room service breakfast for himself.

Though Annabel's main reason for inviting Caroline to breakfast was to learn more about Linder and his increasingly frequent dark moods, she began by encouraging the young woman to talk about herself.

"Do you miss Beirut?" Annabel began.

"I loved Lebanon," Caroline replied with a wistful smile. "And I miss my friends. But I miss Aunt April and Uncle Jay even more. Has Warren heard anything from them since they left for Utah last year?"

"I'm afraid not. But he is doing everything he can to investigate. Perhaps by the time you visit us over Thanksgiving, he might have something. And, by the way, don't worry about leaving us a night or two early to visit your relatives in Oxford. We understand how important they are to you."

At this, Caroline's face took on a pensive look.

"I think one night at Oxford ought to be enough," she replied. "It's hard to be comfortable around my aunt and uncle sometimes. I mean, the last time I saw them, I felt as if they were trying to drive a wedge between Warren and me. One time, my aunt referred to him as a terrorist, and implied that he was living off stolen money. And she wouldn't let go of wanting me to go study at Oxford. She even offered to use her influence to help me get admitted."

"I'm sure they just want what's best for you, Caroline. Oxford is a fabulous place to study, and very difficult to get into."

"Maybe so," Caroline answered with narrowed eyes, "but I would never want to do anything disloyal to Warren. He was so kind to my mother and me at a terrible time in our lives. He found us a safe place to live and did so many other things for us. Not to mention taking me away from Utah when Mom died. He saved my life."

"Warren told me that the year after you and he escaped from America was extremely difficult for him. What was he like back then? How did you and he manage to start over after all you'd been through?"

"I just remember that Warren seemed very unhappy, even though he had brought all that money with him from Ohio. We lived in a very nice rented Georgian townhouse in Earls Court. But then somebody took a shot at Warren on his way home from buying groceries. That's when we moved to Beirut. Things were much better for us there. Maybe it was the sunny climate, but Warren seemed a lot happier."

"How about when he moved back to London last year?" Annabel pressed. "Wasn't he worried that someone might come gunning for him again?"

"I wouldn't say worried, exactly. More like frustrated. And determined to get back at the Unionists, no matter what."

"And how would you compare his state of mind then to what you saw last night?"

"Quite similar, actually. He was on cloud nine all summer after meeting you. But his court loss in Basel seems to have shaken him. I've rarely seen him so out of sorts."

"Nor have I. That's why I wanted to see you alone," Annabel confessed. "I just hope that a week of peace and quiet in the mountains will help settle his mind. And if you think of anything else that might help me to understand Warren better, I hope you'll share it. I want to do everything I can to help him."

"Well, there is one thing," Caroline suggested. "But it's kind of odd. I hope you won't think me weird for saying it."

"You're speaking to someone who spent years on stage pretending to be someone she wasn't. Who am I to call anyone weird?"

"All right, then," Caroline replied, bracing herself to share a secret. "I don't talk about it much, but sometimes I get dreams of the future. Dreams more real than life. And often they come true. My mother hated hearing about them; it really creeped her out. But the very first time I saw Warren, I dreamt that he was going to change things for us. And he did."

"Have you dreamt anything like that about him recently?"

"Not exactly. But last night at dinner, I got a powerful sense that Warren is moving toward some great crisis in his life, something that's been hanging over him for a long time. And even if he comes out on top, I sense that he'll pay a terrible price."

Annabel felt a chill pass through her on hearing those words, not least because something about them rang true.

After breakfast, Annabel brought Caroline up to the hotel suite and chatted with her while she and Linder packed their bags for Zermatt. Afterward, Caroline accompanied them to the railway station and saw them off. Linder waved at her through the window with mixed feelings as the train left the station. Caroline was an adult now and her path was diverging from his. Where would life take each of them next?

The train proceeded eastward along the northern shore of Lake Geneva past the photogenic towns of Vevey and Montreux, and onward through deep wooded valleys to Visp. There they transferred to the scenic mountain railway that climbed steep slopes to the mountain resort of Zermatt, located at the foot of the world-famous Matterhorn peak.

The couple checked into their hotel, ate an early dinner in its formal dining room and went to bed not long after to get an early start the next day. In the morning, they rose before dawn, rode the gondola up to the Schwarzsee Loop trail, and hiked among glacial lakes and streams to the base of the Matterhorn. After a hearty lunch at a mountain hut, they returned to town, where they enjoyed some leisurely window-shopping along the Bahnhofstrasse before taking a well-earned afternoon nap.

They followed a similar schedule the next day, riding the Sunegga funicular and Blauherd gondola up to the Five Lakes Trail. Though they started early, they were far from being the first hikers on the trail. Linder kept a close eye on the others, stopping from time to time to rest and to make sure no one was following. But it didn't appear that anyone was, so by the time they returned to town, Linder was feeling more relaxed than he'd been in weeks.

That night, however, just before dressing for bed, Linder had an odd sensation that something wasn't right. On impulse, he went to the window, which overlooked the town's main shopping street, and peered down onto the dimly lit cobbles below. At first he saw no one. Then, scanning the deep shadows of store entrances and alcoves, he spotted a gray figure in a dark overcoat, whose bearded face was concealed by an upturned collar and an Alpine-style hat pulled low over his forehead. The bulky figure raised its eyes and took a step forward into the half-light. A moment later, it extended one arm toward Linder's window and waved slowly as if beckoning him to come out.

Seeing her husband standing motionless at the window, Annabel went to his side and followed his line of sight down to street level. She saw the figure at once and put her arms around Linder's shoulders in fright.

Linder turned away from the window, leaving Annabel alone as he went to the door, grabbed his down-filled jacket from a hook, and left the room without a word. He was unarmed and, for a moment, he regretted having dismissed his bodyguards. But he was determined to learn who had followed him from Lausanne. If someone had meant to kill or kidnap him, they could have done so at any point along the way without calling attention to themselves by standing outside his window. No, there had to be more to it, and he was prepared to take a risk to find out.

The man was still standing there when Linder reached him.

At first, Linder didn't recognize him. For he resembled neither the bull-necked DSS Base Chief he had known in Cleveland and Beirut, nor the beaten-down stool pigeon he had encountered in the Deputy Camp Commandant's office in the Yukon. But this version of Bob Bednarski appeared to have recovered at least some of his physical bulk, along with much of his arrogant manner, that he had lost when Linder saw him in the camps. What's more, Linder recognized instantly the ex-DSS man's badly frostbitten left ear, not fully concealed beneath his narrow-brimmed hat.

"It's been a long time," Bednarski began in a wary monotone as he offered Linder a fleshy hand with a band of scar tissue across the knuckles. The former base chief spoke with a thick Cleveland twang that reflected his blue-collar origins before he joined the army and, later, the CIA and the DSS, rising to a civilian rank equivalent to that of full colonel.

"Not long enough," Linder replied.

"Now, now, Linder. You ought to be happy to see me. Until a few days ago, I was on the team sent to Basel to fake your suicide. But I didn't have the stomach for it. I jumped ship, which forced the others to abort the mission. Lucky for you."

Linder looked at him as if he had sprouted two heads. Bednarski had never lacked the stomach for foul play.

"You don't say."

"But I do," Bednarski insisted. "You see, Exile Division made a big mistake in using me to go after you. They thought I hated you. But I don't. The one I hated was Denniston. I laughed out loud when I heard you'd blown his sorry ass to hell in Ohio. So I've come to offer you a deal, Linder. Let's call it even between us. I'll tell you all I know about the DSS's plans to kill you if you help me disappear."

"Good luck with that. Disappearing from the DSS radar screen is no easy thing. I'll do what I can if your information is good, but after that it's up to you. What do you need to get started?"

"A new identity and some cash. I aim to go somewhere outside their reach."

"Of course you do. But what can you tell me that would make it worth my while to help you try?"

Bednarski launched into a detailed account of the DSS plan to enter Linder's Basel hotel room while he was sleeping and make it look as if Linder and Annabel had died in a classic murder-suicide.

"So what will they try next, now that their Plan A has fallen through?" Linder asked.

"After failing to nail you this time, they'll probably wait a bit, hoping you'll lower your guard. Or they may go after you in a place where they can think they can capture you alive."

"But why go to all that trouble? It's been nearly eight years since I escaped."

Bednarski shook his head.

"Doesn't matter how long it's been. DeWaart and Barbosa see you as the most dangerous exile on the planet."

"More so than Fury?"

Bednarski nodded slowly.

"They think Fury is finished, a goner. They see your propaganda machine as the greater long-term threat."

"Good to know," Linder replied, swallowing hard. "What else can you tell me that's worth giving you a pile of cash?"

"They've got a mole close to you. A woman."

Linder caught his breath.

"What's her name?"

"I don't know, but she has an American husband and has worked for you before. That's all I've got, but it shouldn't be hard to figure out."

There was only one possibility: Fiona Bowles. Linder cursed himself. How had he failed to spot the signs?

"Okay, how much do you need?" Linder growled.

"A hundred grand should do it. Along with a fresh passport. One that will work anywhere outside the U.S."

"Where are you thinking of going? Not that I care. It's just that some places require better documentation than others."

"Somewhere in the Balkans, I think. How soon can you deliver?"

"I can't do much from Zermatt. But if you can get to Paris, I've got a partner who can fix you up with a passport and forty or fifty thousand Swiss francs. That's all I can spare right now after losing my court case in Basel."

"Make it fifty."

Linder opened his wallet and emptied it of cash, about two thousand Swiss francs. He would have to repay Barton Cao out of capital for the fifty thousand, and it would hurt. But it had to be done.

"Take this. It ought to be enough to get you to Paris. And here's your contact."

He wrote Cao's name and address on the back of a dinner receipt, along with the phrase, "Fortune favors the bold."

"Go to his office and tell him this phrase. He'll be expecting you. I'll wire him the money tomorrow."

"That works for me," Bednarski replied with a grim smile. "Now, since you've been straight with me, I'll be totally straight with you. A couple of DSS torpedoes are on their way up here to find you. For all I know, they may have arrived already. So you and your wife need to get out of Dodge fast. Pack your bags and leave them in your room. You can send for them later. Pretend that the two of you are going out for a nightcap. Then ditch any tails you see and lie low until midnight. That's when you take the last train down to Visp. There's no road, so if you hole up there and take the first train to Geneva, there's no way the goons can catch up."

"What about you? Won't they be after you, too?"

Bednarski laughed and his teeth sparkled in the moonlight.

"No, you're the only one they'll be looking for. Besides, by the time you pack up and leave your hotel, I'll be long gone."

And without another word, Bednarski took off down an unlit alley and was gone indeed.

Chapter Sixteen: Amsterdam

> "There are no absolute rules of conduct, either in peace or war. Everything depends on circumstances."
> *–Leon Trotsky*

FRIDAY, 1 OCTOBER 2032

Owen Quist drove his aging hybrid sedan past the sprawling Tysons Corner mall complex and turned off Chain Bridge Road into an upscale section of suburban Vienna, Virginia. It was a place where the townhouses were so similar to one another that he might easily have lost his way if he hadn't been to this particular DSS safehouse nearly every week for the past six months. Quist clicked open the ground-level garage door with his remote, parked in the unlit double garage, and quickly shut the door behind him. Darrell Otis's Jeep Cherokee was already parked inside.

He climbed the stairs to the first floor and found the DSS case officer waiting for him in the living room.

"Go ahead and grab some coffee if you want," Otis told him. "I put a fresh pod in the machine. Our meeting today may run a bit long."

Quist winced at the comment, sensing that his workload from the DSS was about to grow even heavier. Ever since his return from Berlin, he had been contacted by a growing number of genuine dissidents seeking information about the American Constitution League, steered to him by DSS provocateurs in the D.C. area. After each contact, he met Otis to receive instructions about how to handle it. In most cases, his instructions were to turn them over to other DSS operatives, who initiated them into phony ACL cells to draw in other unsuspecting dissidents. Lately, the pace of such turnovers had

151

accelerated to the point where Quist was seeing Otis twice a week and the demands on his time were encroaching upon his home life.

Until very recently, Quist's domestic life had been highly agreeable. He and Denise Acker had married a month after his return from Berlin and were enjoying the material and social benefits of his DSS-backed promotion to a higher post at the State Oil Company. But in recent weeks he was out most evenings doing DSS work. And though Denise knew that this was an essential element of the deal he had struck with the DSS, she was growing impatient. Even worse, he knew that he was due for another overseas trip, and that the next trip might be considerably more challenging than the one to Berlin.

Once Quist retrieved his coffee and took a seat opposite Otis, what he had feared came about.

"It's time for another junket, Quist. We'll need you to take a month's leave from StatOil. Don't worry, your bosses won't object. They've already given us the green light. In fact, you can expect a tidy raise when you come back, assuming you do good work for us over there."

"And where, exactly, is 'over there' this time?"

"You'll be going to Amsterdam, Brussels, and Paris for some very important meetings. The trip will require you to up your game quite a bit. That's why we've scheduled you for two weeks of prep time before you go."

Quist felt a cold chill up and down his spine. Stepping up his game doubtless meant peddling larger and more complex lies to anti-Unionist émigrés like Benjamin Payne. But Payne and his lot weren't fools. By now they would have had time to investigate the claims Quist had made in Berlin and to lay some nasty traps for him. What if they exposed him as a fraud? Would the DSS come to his rescue? Not bloody likely.

"Look, Darrell," Quist explained. "You know as well as I do that all my free time is taken up these days skulking around with these dissident types you keep sending me. Denise is not happy; she wants her husband back. It's even begun to affect my work at StatOil. A month on the road right now would be a disaster for me. I know I'm passing up a terrific opportunity, but isn't there someone else you could send?"

"I'm sorry, Owen, but we're not changing horses midstream," Otis declared. "You're the League's leading mouthpiece now. You speak directly for the shadow foreign minister."

"Come on. How could I be that important after only two trips? Couldn't you groom someone else to take over for me? You must have people who'd jump at the chance."

Otis's expression hardened and his tone turned sharp.

"Don't forget how we started, Quist. You were in deep shit. We gave you a chance and turned you into Cinderella. But we can make the clock strike midnight any time we want. Do you want to lose your job, your Party membership, your marriage, and spend your last days felling trees in the Yukon?"

Quist blanched.

"Well, do you?" Otis demanded.

"No," Quist replied in a tone barely audible.

"Good. Then let me give you the big picture on what's coming. You see, when this whole thing began, the Department had no idea that the League would develop so quickly from your weekend with Howard Acker into the far-flung operation that it's become. Since your meeting with Payne in Berlin, we've sent a number of other undercover agents to the U.K. and Europe to meet with émigré opposition groups and persuade them to support the League. Now we're ready for you to take it to the next level."

"Oh? And exactly how am I supposed to do that?" Quist asked, casting a bitter look at his handler.

"By convincing émigré leaders that the League is winning over more and more Unionist Party members and state officials. And that soon it will be ready to form a true shadow government. Which is why the émigrés and their state sponsors need to refrain from bombings.

assassinations and aggressive propaganda against the U.S. until the League is ready to make its move."

All at once Quist's interest was piqued. This didn't sound quite as challenging as he had thought. In fact, he imagined that it might just be doable.

"And what evidence will I be able to show of the League's growing strength?"

"Don't worry. We'll come up with the evidence. Your job will be to persuade the émigrés to give the League cash and technical support. In return, you'll be able to provide them a wealth of intelligence about the Party's plans and intentions. We'll even give you classified government documents and let you invite émigré operatives on fact-finding trips to the U.S. that include meetings with secret members of the League. And in special cases, we might be able to arrange the release of their people from detention. You're going to be very popular among the émigrés, Mr. Quist."

But the list of goodies left Quist puzzled.

"Promises are one thing," he noted with a skeptical expression. "But you can't be serious about the DSS handing over sensitive intelligence and releasing prisoners. Why would the DSS do that? Where's the catch?"

"Every document we hand over will be doctored to deliver only the information we want the émigrés to have. No more, no less," Otis replied with a twisted smile. "The secret League members will be our own men, role-playing as dissidents. The émigrés' visits to America will be stage-managed from start to finish, like the Potemkin villages that Western journalists visited in 1920s Russia. And if we release a prisoner, it will be only temporarily and under controlled conditions. But we'll paint such a rosy picture of the League that the émigrés will be eager to hop into bed with us."

"And who will I be meeting on this particular trip?" Quist inquired with growing interest.

"Ah, so you're warming up to the idea, are you?" Otis replied. "Well, you'll learn who the targets are once we're ready. Meanwhile, training starts first thing tomorrow morning."

Quist landed in Amsterdam on a bright sunny morning two weeks later. A driver sent by the Free American Patriots met him at the airport. He drove Quist to his hotel, located on the Herengracht, a block away from the famous Golden Bend, the canal stretch where the richest Amsterdammers lived during the city's seventeenth-century Golden Age. Quist looked forward to strolling along the city's concentric web of canals later in the day, once he'd taken a nap. But his plans changed minutes later when Benjamin Payne caught up with him in the hotel lobby.

"We've had a marvelous stroke of luck," the former U.S. Vice President and FAP leader gushed after the men exchanged greetings. "We have an interview in an hour with Gordon Butts. His house is less than a ten-minute walk away, on the Keizersgracht. I realize you just flew in and may be a bit jet-lagged, but President Butts is keen to meet you. And a morning meeting is ideal for him because, at age eighty-six, his attention tends to flag by lunchtime. Could you check into your room, freshen up, and meet me back here in, say, forty-five minutes? I can prep you on the way over."

Word of the meeting hit Quist as a complete surprise. Butts, whose two terms as U.S. President had ended eight years before Payne's terms as Vice President began, fled to the Netherlands soon after the Unionist takeover but steered clear of émigré politics from then on. Instead, he focused on shoring up his personal balance sheet, which had suffered major losses when the Unionist regime expropriated his U.S.-based ranchland, sports teams, and oil and gas interests. Fortunately for Butts and his family, he had shifted the bulk of his liquid assets offshore before the Unionists seized power. Among his current investments was a leading Dutch soccer team, purchased to indulge his lifelong passion for professional sports.

"The President has heard about your work," Payne explained as they crossed the bridge to the Keizersgracht. "He's a great admirer of what the League is doing and takes heart that it might spell the beginning of the end for Unionism."

"Do you suppose he'd consider a contribution?" Quist probed.

"If he does, it will likely be a small one. But even a lukewarm endorsement from him will open more doors in émigré circles than you can imagine. And with foreign governments, as well."

"Wonderful. What message do you think will appeal to him most?"

"If I were you, I'd focus on your grass-roots support," Payne suggested. "Gordon is a politician at heart, and he knows that retail politics is where everything starts. But one caveat: Deliver your most salient points in the first thirty seconds. That's your window. If you miss it, his eyes will glaze over and you'll risk losing him."

Five minutes later Payne and Quist climbed the stone stairs to the entrance of Butts's double-wide canal house, built by a member of the East India Company in the seventeenth century and held in the family for generations until the American ex-President purchased it. Payne used the ornate brass knocker to rap on the door and waited until a dark-suited security man opened it. The latter led the two visitors from the entrance hall into a reception room whose walls were covered by photos of a smiling President Butts posing with world leaders, sports stars, country-western singers, and other notables. A moment later, the door opened to a *bel-étage* sitting room where Butts sat facing tall windows that overlooked the canal. He was a slender man of medium height, fit-looking for a man approaching ninety, and dressed modestly in an olive tweed jacket over gray flannel trousers. His face wore an expression of polite interest—friendly but noncommittal.

Introductions were brief. After a few minutes of small talk, the former President's personal assistant suggested that Quist begin his presentation.

"Mr. President," Quist began, "as you may be aware, one of the most important developments in America since the Unionist Party seized power has been the New Economic Plan, which the Party unveiled two years ago at its Tenth Party Congress. What the NEP did was shift national resources away from state enterprise toward small business, family farms and foreign trade."

Quist paused for a moment and Butts nodded for him to continue.

"Without question," Quist went on, "the NEP represents an admission of political weakness. That's because a shift away from state enterprise weakens state power. But, at the same time, the NEP is essential to the Party's survival. The reason is that any major rollback of the plan will almost certainly create food and energy shortages that could lead to serious political unrest."

The former president frowned at the mention of political unrest, suggesting that he still followed Quist's argument.

"We in the League favor the NEP because we believe that, over time, it will pave the way toward a market economy and a more open political system. The Unionist leadership fears this, of course. They worry that the émigré opposition will lobby foreign governments to demand political concessions in return for restoring foreign trade and investment under the NEP. Which is why the Party has kept its citizens in the dark about any ongoing trade negotiations. And it's why we believe Europe should continue to pursue trade talks with the Unionists. The key is to use the free world's leverage on trade to demand a relaxation of authoritarian controls."

Quist stopped his speech there, realizing that he had gone longer than thirty seconds and that the former President's eyelids had begun to droop. But, to Quist's relief, the old man's eyes opened wide again and he seemed to rally.

"Ben has told me about your organization and the success you've had in winning over émigré opinion," Butts commented after a moment's pause. "But what about your grass-roots support inside

America? What kind of people are you attracting, and where is your support strongest?"

Quist was well prepared for the question, having rehearsed the answer with Otis many times.

"I'm glad you asked that, Mr. President. We're attracting people all across America: the same kind of people who created the Tea Party, and the populist-nationalist movement after that, and who later joined the militias to fight the Unionists in CWII. Americans love freedom, and they won't put up with tyranny forever. As for where we're strongest, I'd say it's moving into the big cities now, where people have greater access to information and the means to gather with one another. But the spirit of liberty is strong all across the land, Mr. President, and people are reaching out to us from every state."

Quist's answer must have hit home because he could see his host's tired eyes welling with tears. The former President looked away for a moment before speaking again.

"Mr. Quist, you've brought hope to an old man. I realize I may not live long enough to see a free America again, but I'd do just about anything to let my sons and grandchildren go home and live in the land of their forefathers. So how can I help you?"

As agreed during their walk to the meeting, it was Payne who fielded the question.

"Gordon, you've already done a great deal to support the Free American Patriots, and the Patriots are putting our full weight behind Mr. Quist and his League. If you could give the same kind of public endorsement to the League that you gave us, it would help enormously to draw the émigré movement together and win the backing of those European intelligence services that remain active against the Unionist target. Is that something you might be comfortable doing?"

"Damn right I would!" the old man replied with a sparkle in his watery blue eyes. "Hash out the wording with my people and I'll sign it by day's end. Along with a check to help keep you going. Hell, at my age, what good is having a pile of money if I can't spend it on causes I believe in?"

"I can't thank you enough, Mr. President," Quist replied, reaching out to take the old man's gnarled hand.

"Don't mention it," Butts said. "Now, how about a photograph together, or would it be too dangerous for someone in your situation to be seen with someone like me?"

Quist was taken aback for a moment, but then thought of how much fun it would be to show his DSS handler hard proof of his meeting with the ex-president.

"I'd be delighted, Mr. President," Quist beamed. "All I ask is that you keep your copy somewhere safe and not give it to the press. It might be hard for me to explain at home."

Butts motioned to the security man, who pulled out a cell phone and took photos of the ex-president with his two guests, and then with Quist alone. Payne gave the security man an encrypted email address, to which the photos were sent immediately.

"One more thing, are you a soccer fan?" the President asked as Quist and Payne rose to leave.

"I certainly am," Quist answered with a smile.

"Then take one of these." The old man reached into a low drawer, removed a fresh jersey with the colors of his Dutch pro soccer team, and tossed it to Quist with an expression of boyish delight.

Quist and Payne left the canal house on cloud nine. Despite his jet lag, Quist felt as invigorated as if he'd just taken an icy shower and downed a double shot of chilled vodka. After lunch, instead of taking a nap, he walked the streets of Amsterdam with Payne, taking in the sights and discussing how best to exploit the League's presidential endorsement.

The next morning, Payne made a call to the chief of Dutch General Intelligence and Security in The Hague. The two men were given an appointment for late afternoon per prior arrangement and made the trip by car.

Delivering a short speech he had prepared and rehearsed with Otis for the occasion, Quist described the League as a widely dispersed dissident network whose members included low- and mid-level officials across multiple U.S. military branches, intelligence agencies and urban law enforcement departments. None of what he claimed was true, of course, but he and Otis had spent days composing a narrative outlining how the League might have achieved such success, including profiles of typical League members. Yet, despite the shakiness of Quist's narrative, the Dutch intelligence chief seemed receptive.

Quist had challenged Otis on the story's defects weeks earlier in Virginia, doubting that European intelligence officials would accept that a League-like organization could sprout up in full view of the DSS. Yet, as Otis had argued then, what evidence could an outsider present to refute Quist's claims?

Nearly a decade had passed since the Unionist takeover. During that time, America had been isolated from the rest of the world, much as the Soviet Union, Red China, Albania, and North Korea had been during the height of the Cold War. By now, European intelligence services would have few, if any, well-placed spies in America, and the small number of diplomats and journalists who were allowed to enter the country were kept on a short leash and shown only what the Unionist authorities wanted them to see. Foreign-based intelligence analysts who covered America would have little to go on but rumors and official propaganda. If fed a consistent narrative of Unionist decline and dissident resurgence, backed by a flood of fabricated documents, why wouldn't the European intelligence analysts accept what their superiors wanted to believe?

"The League asks for your support, but we don't expect something for nothing," Quist told the Dutch intelligence chief as the interview neared its end. "We are prepared to share with you a steady stream of intelligence about the Unionist State. Let our information speak for itself. If you find it useful, then we ask that you provide us with technical and financial support so that we can expand our activities. What we have in mind is a mutually beneficial alliance that can grow in scope over time."

"We would be happy to review as much or as little intelligence as you choose to provide to us. We will respond promptly with our evaluation," the Dutch official replied with cool detachment. "How would you prefer to communicate?"

"Encrypted electronic messages would be best at this time. I can work out the details with your technical staff before leaving the building, if you wish."

The Dutch intelligence chief agreed, and the messages started flowing within a week. To build credibility at this sensitive stage in the relationship, the League provided impeccable information on topics that could not fail to pique the interest of Dutch analysts. Follow-up reports were of a similar high quality. Before long, the Dutch service would come to value the League's reporting on America above that from all other sources.

Quist's visit to Belgian State Security followed a similar pattern. The Belgians accepted Quist's offer of free intelligence without hesitation, though they could provide little in return. But that was no problem for Quist or his DSS masters, as their goal was to make the Dutch, the Belgians, and other European intelligence services dependent on the League and thus elbow out alternative sources of intelligence on the Unionist State. After all, who could know America better than an organization with so many well-connected sources on the ground? And one endorsed by both a former U.S. President and a Vice President?

Quist's visit to Paris the following week took quite a different turn. There, the French foreign intelligence service, the Directorate-General for External Security (DGSE), lacked a pre-existing relationship with Payne's FAP. It maintained ties instead with Barton Cao's Inner Line organization and with Leonard Fury's Anti-Unionist Congress, though relations with the latter had cooled after Fury's botched attack on the U.S. trade delegation at Sanremo.

Quist's introduction to the DGSE came through Fury's right-hand man, Jack Poirier, whom Quist had met in Berlin some months before. The chief of the DGSE's American section met Quist in the company of both Cao and Poirier, for Fury was unable to attend. The DGSE official listened to Quist's presentation on the League with polite interest, leaving questions to his subordinates, who seemed to have conferred earlier with their Belgian counterparts, for they tested Quist on several of the same points.

"How did your organization develop such broad access to classified intelligence information?" one French analyst asked. "And how are you able to evade DSS interdiction?" Quist was quite prepared for such questions and many others. By the time his grilling was over, the DGSE had agreed to set up a secure channel to receive intelligence from the League, though it offered nothing in return.

But that was all right with Quist, for his primary objective in Paris was entirely different than the one he had in The Hague and Brussels. It was to wean the DGSE away from Cao and Fury and to prepare the groundwork for Leonard Fury to return to America under the League's auspices. This he did by pointing out that Poirier had already traveled to the Unionist State and that the League would be pleased to receive further visitors from Fury's AUC, Cao's Inner Line, or even from the DGSE itself.

At this, the French intelligence officials cast quizzical glances at one other but made no reply. It was Cao who broke the silence.

"Congratulations to Jack for daring to travel to America with the League. As for me, I have too much respect for the DSS to follow his lead. Lately, the Unionists have lured far too many patriots back to America, never to be heard from again. Not that I would accuse Mr. Quist of being complicit with the DSS, of course, but at this point, for me to join him on a visit seems, let us say, premature."

Quist brushed off the remark with a smile and a shrug. Poirier shifted uncomfortably in his seat.

"Of course, colonel, due diligence would be advisable before taking up our offer," Quist conceded to Cao. "I'm sure Mr. Poirier did his own investigation before travelling with us. But today, opportunities for exiled patriots who join the League grow by the day. Leaders like Mr. Poirier and Mr. Fury who have a proven record of fighting the Unionists are exceedingly valuable to us. When regime falls, enormous opportunities will be open to them."

Quist did not intend the statement so much for the DGSE or even for Poirier or Cao, but rather for Poirier's egotistical boss, Leonard Fury, whose hunger for relevance had reached pathological levels since his failure at Cannes. But was Fury ready to take the bait?

Chapter Seventeen: Roll Up

> "When you are in the light, everything follows you. When you enter into the dark, even your own shadow doesn't follow you."
> *–Adolph Hitler*

SUNDAY, 3 OCTOBER 2032

L inder and Annabel took Bednarski's advice and holed up in a quiet bar in Zermatt until the time came to catch the midnight train down the mountain to Visp. To their immense relief, they were able to reach London via Geneva and Paris without spotting even one surveillant along the way.

With his Swiss-based assets severely reduced and the unplanned payment to Bednarski further stressing his funds, Linder was obliged to cut back temporarily on his anti-Unionist propaganda activities and to redouble his consulting efforts. Now that Anglo-American trade negotiations were heating up once again, he focused on advising holders of repudiated U.S. debt, former owners of nationalized U.S. properties, and others opposed to reopening Anglo-American trade.

By now, the U.S. trade office in London had commenced its program of divesting surplus U.S. properties in the U.K. by sealed-bid auction. The properties on offer, chiefly U.S. Air Force bases in south central England, were highly attractive to developers. Ideological opponents of the Unionist Party, however, strongly opposed the auctions. Prospective buyers received thousands of angry messages from American émigrés threatening boycotts and lawsuits if they submitted bids. As a result, most prospective purchasers hired political consultants from the émigré community to help manage the risk of participating in the auctions.

165

This created an opening for Linder to manipulate the bidding by organizing a secret bidders' cartel. Its aim was to minimize total sales proceeds to the U.S. government while, at the same time, to help Linder's clients pick up desirable properties at rock-bottom prices. Under the cartel agreement, a target bid was agreed upon for each property to be sold. Then the target bid for each parcel was assigned to a specific cartel member, with the other members committing to submit lower bids. To prevent outsiders from outbidding cartel members, Linder secretly obtained a list of all qualified bidders from Kreutzer and had the latter disqualify on made-up grounds any bidder unlikely to go along. This Kreutzer did in return for Linder's agreement to kick back half of his sale commissions. Though Linder didn't like the idea of doing business with the enemy, he saw little personal risk in this scheme. And he certainly needed the money. Since the net effect of the cartel would be to weaken the Unionist regime, he decided that the ends justified the means.

When the winning bids were announced for the divestitures, the U.K. press reported that the proceeds were far lower than expected, which helped dampen blowback from the anti-Unionist opposition. And the various cartel bidders, having secured their favored properties on the cheap, offered plausible reasons for their low bids. Linder's total commissions on sale, though far less than what he had lost in Basel, represented a nice down payment toward rebuilding his capital.

Linder continued to raise cash by making fundraising appeals at émigré events around the U.K. and Europe. On top of that, he sold his prized collection of Abraham Lincoln memorabilia to a rival collector. He even suggested one evening, after reviewing his downsized personal budget, that he and Annabel move out of her sumptuous Mayfair flat in favor of a more modest one, as he could no longer afford to contribute half the rent as before. Annabel vetoed the idea, offering instead to cover the entire rent until such time as Linder's finances recovered.

After his encounter with Bednarski in Zermatt, one expense on which Linder could no longer afford to skimp was security. For not only had the DSS plotted to abduct him from Basel but, according to Bednarski, they had also inserted an informant in his midst. And all signs pointed to Fiona Bowles.

Immediately upon his return from Switzerland, Linder devised a new security plan that included engaging a local security consultant, hiring a night watchman to stand guard outside the Mayfair flat, and setting a trap to catch Bowles. Even so, Annabel confided to Linder that she still felt watched by unseen eyes and sensed that their comings and goings were being marked. Unable to substantiate her fears, she had concealed them from her husband. Then, late one night, after being unable to sleep, she slipped out of bed and went to the window. There, in the shadows of the street below, she saw a dark figure in a trench coat and slouch hat gazing up at her. She couldn't breathe. But a moment later, the figure was gone.

It was at one of Linder's fundraising events in London during December that he once again ran across Paul Wagner, the former Kamas inmate who had been released shortly before the tanks rolled through the camp. The last time he had seen Wagner was at the IAAE conference in Geneva, nearly a year before.

"How is life in Warsaw these days?" Linder asked with an amiable smile, recalling that Wagner and his family had been living in Poland. "Is the Autumn Festival still going on there?"

"I'm afraid I can't answer that," Wagner replied with a tired look. "We left Warsaw a week ago and are making our way back to Pennsylvania."

Linder could tell from the man's expression that he wasn't entirely happy about the move.

"I'm very sad to hear that," he ventured, doing his best not to show alarm. "May I ask what prompted you to return?"

"Our business in Warsaw was failing and we didn't want to hang on until we ran out of cash. Lately, friends and relatives back home have been telling us that the NEP offers fantastic opportunities. Plenty of pent-up demand, rock-bottom operating costs, and generous tax abatements for investors. After selling the house and the business in Warsaw, we expect to have just enough capital to make another go of it back home."

"I don't get it," Linder declared, eyeing the man as if he'd just landed from Mars. "After all that you and your family have suffered under the Unionists, why would you ever consider going back?"

"I hear conditions are a lot better now," Wagner replied with a shrug. "The Blue Terror is over, camps like Kamas are closed, and the DSS is losing its grip on the population. It's only a matter of time before things return to some semblance of normal. Juliet and I want to get in on the ground floor and make up for lost time."

Linder thought of his missing sister and doubted that the fate of political dissidents could have improved to the point where it was safe for Wagner and his family to return. But he held his tongue. If Wagner didn't know this, he probably didn't want to.

"Well, I can't deny that the NEP is making a favorable impact on the economy," Linder told him. "But the word I'm getting is that things could easily go south again. How well do you trust your sources? Is it possible the DSS could be manipulating them to trick you into going back?"

Wagner looked away and his face took on a sheepish expression.

"With the DSS, anything is possible, I suppose," he answered with a face wrapped in gloom. "But Juliet misses her family, and the girls miss their friends. Life was very hard for us in Poland, Warren. I just can't say no to them."

"I understand, Paul. It's a tough decision and one that only your family can make. But don't forget how attractive a target you are to the regime. You wrote a best-selling book about the Kamas revolt. So you're living proof that the atrocities at the corrective labor camps were real. I'm sure the DSS would love to get their hands on you to make you recant your story or discredit you in some way."

"Of course. But that's all in the past. What's important now is giving my wife and daughters a better future."

"Funny," Linder commented. "That's what my sister said before she and her husband left Beirut and flew back to Utah last year."

"And how have things turned out for them?"

"I don't know. I haven't heard from them since they left. Nor has anyone else."

At this, Wagner gave a mournful nod, as if he knew that he was taking a grave risk in returning, but still hoped that he and his family would be safe. Linder didn't have the heart to press his case further, and the two men parted with a silent handshake.

That evening, after returning to the Mayfair flat, Linder poured himself a stiff brandy in the drawing room and perched uncomfortably on an arm of the sofa, his head bent low.

"Promise me one thing," he said to Annabel as she put down her cup of tea. "Promise that you'll never go to America. Whatever happens, however great the temptation, however sincere the people who ask you, and whatever assurances they might give. Even if I should write from America and ask you to join me there, you must never go."

Linder took his wife's hands in his and held her gaze until she made the pledge.

"I promise," she said. "But why?"

"Because there are a mere handful of people left on this earth against whom the Unionist criminals would give their eyeteeth to exact revenge. So long as these people draw breath, Twitchell and his minions must sleep with one eye open. Fury is one. Barton Cao is another. And I am one, as well. The DSS has tried to kill each one of us and failed. But what they want most is to capture us alive. And they will tell any lie, commit any fraud, pay any price, to achieve it."

❖   ❖   ❖

A few days after Linder's encounter with Paul Wagner, he received a visit from Barton Cao, who was in London on business. They met at Linder's flat.

"Have you heard anything new from Bednarski since he left Paris?" Cao inquired not far into their conversation.

Linder shook his head. "Not a word. Have you?"

"No, not that I expected to. I sent him off to Moscow with a fresh South African passport, a five-figure Zurich bank account, and ten thousand Swiss francs in cash. I figured he wouldn't have trouble finding a place to hole up in Russia or in one of the ex-Soviet *stans*. And none of those places would make it easy for the DSS to find him."

For a time, some years earlier, Linder had also considered relocating to Russia or Kazakhstan, but had rejected the idea. For one thing, having served in both the CIA and the DSS, he didn't relish having the FSB hound him to work for them. Nor did he care for Russia's frigid climate, its difficult language, or the fact that many American émigrés took such a dim view of Russia that they would never trust him again if he set up shop there. But Russia was such a vast country that perhaps Bednarski would find a place there to settle down and call home.

"Anyway, thanks for taking care of Bednarski for me," Linder replied to Cao while pouring his visitor a cup of coffee.

"No problem. He was quite appreciative. But he wanted me to remind you that you shouldn't feel safe just because you dodged the bullet in Switzerland. The fact that the DSS has failed so far won't stop them from targeting you again. I do hope you're taking precautions."

"No more or less than usual. This isn't a new situation for me."

"Bednarski seemed remarkably well-informed about your living arrangements," Cao persisted. "He also said the DSS has an informant close to you. Did he tell you that, too?" Cao asked with narrowed eyes.

"Yes. And I intend to deal with the situation soon."

Linder's tone made it clear that he didn't want to discuss it.

"Well, good luck," Cao replied. "If you need any help…"

"I'll let you know. But, while we're on the subject, do you ever wonder whether the DSS might have turned Poirier around while he was over there?"

"Jack? Switch sides?" Cao gasped.

"I don't think we should rule it out," Linder replied. "Have you seen much of Poirier lately?"

"Not since he and I visited the DGSE last Friday with Quist."

"Poirier seems to be awfully close to Quist and the League," Linder noted. "Something doesn't add up. Or is he just a fool who's allowed the League's grandiose ambitions to turn his head and make him feel self-important?"

"Can't be sure of either," Cao replied with a shrug. "What bothers me more is how hard he's been working on my niece to travel to Canada with him. Maria is a clever girl, but sometimes she's too gung-ho for her own good. I've told her it's not safe, but she keeps pushing me to let her go."

Linder gave Cao a searching look.

"Have you been paying attention to how many people from our side have gone back to the U.S during the past year? There's my sister, of course, and her husband. But over the summer there have been plenty more. To my knowledge, none of them has resurfaced. Have you heard from anyone who's gone home and made it back out again?"

"Not a one," Cao replied with a solemn look.

"Earlier this week," Linder went on, "I ran into Paul Wagner, the Kamas revolt survivor. He said he was taking his family home to Pittsburgh after some heavy lobbying from family and friends on the other side. Do you suppose the DSS is behind the campaign to reel him in?"

"Possibly," Cao ventured. "The League's been inviting everyone and his brother on field trips to the U.S. Let's see how many of those come back."

"I hope you can keep Maria from making the pilgrimage," Linder told his friend. "If it's true that the DSS is the puppet master behind the League, then your niece is exactly the sort of person that they'd want to recruit."

Despite Linder's offhand answer to Cao's inquiry about the traitor in his household, the topic had been very much on his mind since returning from Switzerland. But dealing with someone who was feeding secrets to the enemy required time and extreme caution. His first step after arriving in London, even before hiring a security consultant and a night watchman, was to observe closely whether his movements were being watched. After a few days, he noticed that nobody seemed to follow him when he made routine trips to and from his office to fetch coffee, to take lunch alone, or visit the doctor or dentist. But on days when he visited consulting clients, joined someone for a meal, or met clandestine informants, there was always a highly skilled surveillance team on his tail.

Linder's next move was to order a technical sweep of both his residence and his office for eavesdropping devices. This was done late at night on a weekend so that his office staff and domestic help were off duty. Electronic devices were found at both locations but were left in place. The next morning, Linder took his wife out for a stroll in a nearby park and gave her the news. As Annabel was not yet fully accustomed to being the target of hostile surveillance, she voiced outrage over the intrusion.

"You mean to say that strangers have been listening to our intimate conversations at our private residence?" she railed. "Please don't tell me that devices were found in our bedroom."

"No, nothing found there," Linder deadpanned. "Just the living room, dining room, and my study. Until we resolve this, Annabel, we'll have to assume that each of those rooms, as well as all our telephones and electronic devices, are being monitored."

They stopped a few moments later at a café to order coffee. Once seated, Linder handed his wife a prepaid burner phone.

"Use this for any phone conversations you don't want to share with the Unionists. I've also opened a new encrypted email account for you. Until further notice, we'll be holding any confidential discussions either outside the flat or in the laundry room. It's clean there."

"I should hope so," Annabel replied, acknowledging the pun without a smile.

Later that day, Linder directed his security consultant to monitor Fiona Bowles's movements and her communications on a 24/7 basis. Three days later, the consultant's surveillance team photographed Bowles meeting a U.S. Trade Mission staff member at a bar close to her flat. The male staffer fit the profile of a DSS officer like a glove. And after tracing the man's name with Barton Cao and another anti-Unionist émigré group, the staffer was found to be an ex-Philadelphia cop and former FBI agent, thus likely an undercover DSS officer. At that point, Linder had to assume that Bowles had been spying on him ever since he re-hired her when he'd returned from Beirut.

That evening, he took Annabel out for dinner at a noise-filled Italian restaurant and delivered his findings about Bowles.

"Are you shocked?" he asked her afterward.

"Of course I am. Nobody wants to believe that a trusted employee is disloyal. But I must confess, I've long had an odd feeling about Mrs. Bowles and her husband."

"What sort of odd feeling?"

"Oh, just the way she looks at you sometimes. May I ask: Were the two of you once an item?"

Linder blushed and then nodded.

"Yes, when I first lived in London, before Fiona married her current husband. If you must know, April and Caroline didn't care much for Fiona, either. Our relationship ended shortly after an attempt was made on my life here. That's when I relocated the family to Beirut."

"Do you suppose Fiona had something to do with that, too?"

"I didn't at the time, but now that you mention it…"

The blood drained from Linder's face when he realized how heedless he had been.

"So what are we going to do with her? Dismiss her? Turn her in to the authorities? Or perhaps slit her throat and dump the body in the Thames?"

For a moment Linder wasn't entirely sure Annabel was joking.

"We'll play along, at least for a while," he answered, picking up his glass of wine. "First, we'll feed her false information. After that, we can go ahead and finish her off… I mean, report her to MI5."

Annabel drew a sharp breath that turned quickly into an awkward laugh.

For the next two months, Linder did his best to behave as usual around Fiona Bowles. He went about his daily business, assigning Bowles the same tasks as before, such as setting up appointments and arranging travel, without restricting her access in any way. At the same time, however, he inserted misleading information into many of the communications to which Bowles enjoyed access, so that her DSS handlers would be misinformed as to key elements of his plans.

At the end of the two months, Linder tipped off Allen Hackett that Bowles would be meeting her DSS handler at their usual time and place. MI5 arranged for the London Metropolitan Police to arrest the pair. Under interrogation, Bowles confessed to having worked for the Unionists. She told her interrogator that, soon after meeting Linder to help him find a London apartment, DSS agents threatened to arrest her émigré husband's elderly parents in the U.S. and send them to a labor camp if she didn't cooperate. After conferring with her husband, she complied.

The British authorities released Bowles without criminal charges twenty-four hours after her arrest. Two days later, she and her husband disappeared. Their Notting Hill flat was sold a few weeks later, fully furnished, on the authority of their solicitor. Linder could find no trace of the couple after that. He suspected that they were back in the U.S., but whether they had gone voluntarily or under duress was anyone's guess.

Linder received a visit from Allen Hackett not long after Bowles's disappearance to thank Linder for identifying members of the U.S. Trade Mission suspected of working in secret for the DSS and the Progintern.

"Unfortunately, our political class is hopelessly naïve about Unionist subversion in this country," Hackett complained. "Out of one side of their mouth, the Unionists tell us they want to normalize relations. But from the other side, they instruct their covert allies on how to subvert British democracy."

"So what will happen to the undercover DSS officers we busted?" Linder asked.

"Whitehall will likely declare them *persona non grata* and issue a stiff *demarche* to the U.S. Trade Representative's office. Kreutzer will send the villains home, to be replaced by others whose illegal activities we will then be at pains to detect."

"Does either MI5 or Scotland Yard have any evidence that Kreutzer himself has committed any crimes in Britain?"

"Not that I am aware," Hackett replied. "Though they may be keeping it under wraps, since the Prime Minister seems intent on pushing his draft trade agreement through Parliament, come hell or high water."

"But what if Bledsoe's back benchers were to learn that Progintern agents were carrying out subversion through the trade office?"

Hackett offered Linder a faint smile.

"I think you're beginning to see our dilemma," the MI5 man replied with a raised eyebrow.

Linder certainly did. He filed away the idea and quickly changed the subject.

"Have you heard from that fellow Quist lately?" he asked Hackett next. "You recall, the one who came to Bristol a year ago claiming to represent dissident cells in Washington? I'm told he's been making the rounds on the Continent, soliciting help from various European intelligence services. Has he called on your blokes yet?"

Hackett's response was a derisive snort.

"I think Quist may be avoiding us," he said. "Perhaps he's intimidated by MI5's reputation. But our analysts think the League is a serious organization and bears watching. Why, have you run into Quist during your travels?"

"No," Linder answered. "Do you think I should?"

"I don't see why not. There's no substitute for meeting face to face to take the measure of a man. What do you have to lose?"

"Oh, nothing important, I suppose. I'd just like to know more about Quist first."

"Well, do let me know your impression if and when you meet him," Hackett remarked in conclusion. "It would be lovely if the

League were genuine, of course. But if anyone can expose it as a fraud, it's you."

Chapter Eighteen: Acapulco

"The dirtiest work often requires the most trustworthy people."
–Reinhard Gehlen (Cold War era West German Intelligence Chief)

MONDAY, 14 MARCH 2033

When Linder had last visited Leonard Fury in Paris, he'd advised his friend to resign as chairman of the Anti-Unionist Congress if he wanted the organization he had founded to survive. After Fury's failed ambush of the U.S. trade delegation at Sanremo, the rebel leader's reputation had hit rock bottom. And yet Fury rejected the advice, which led Linder to expect the organization would die a quiet death.

Accordingly, the invitation Linder received nearly a year later to a meeting of the Congress's central committee in Mexico City came as a surprise. It was to be a small gathering, no larger than would fit into the elegant private apartment of Fury's leading expatriate supporter in Mexico. But the Congress still appeared to be a viable organization. And its three-day agenda was an ambitious one, focusing on the future of the anti-Unionist movement in the Western Hemisphere, particularly Mexico, Canada, the Caribbean, and several Central and South American nations. The subtext of the gathering would almost certainly be Fury's attempt to reassert his leadership over the émigré opposition movement. Though Linder doubted Fury would succeed in that goal, he decided to attend the event.

He and Annabel flew to Mexico several days in advance to overcome jet lag and to enjoy the tropical sun at Acapulco before the Congress opened. They chose Acapulco over other Mexican resort towns because it was one of the closest to Mexico City and attracted

179

mostly Mexican vacationers, unlike Puerto Vallarta, which was overrun with Americans. Once the choice of Acapulco was settled, Annabel took delight in selecting a rental villa located in a gated community overlooking Puerto Marques Bay and boasting its own private pool.

The only drag on their brief vacation was that Linder had scheduled some business meetings nearby during their first few mornings in Mexico.

"Have a morning swim and enjoy the sun while I'm at work," he had told her on the night of their arrival, without revealing the nature of the business he had planned.

The next morning, a young associate of his local contractor picked Linder up at his villa and drove him to the garden condominium that the contractor had rented nearby. That person was Frank Werner, an American expat who had spent three years in the corrective labor camp system, survived the revolt at Kamas, and been sent to the Yukon to die of cold and overwork. Fortunately for Werner, and unlike most other Kamas survivors, he lived long enough to benefit from a Congressional amnesty.

Thus Werner eked out a living in Boston for the next several years. He found work as a bartender, bootlegger, and small-time arms trafficker, until he led the team that assassinated Fred Rocco, the Kamas camp's former commandant. By a stroke of good luck, after fleeing Boston he found passage to Havana, and from there to Mexico City, where the Free American Patriots landed him a job tending bar at an upmarket hotel. Soon after, he put his skills to work helping the FAP with intelligence operations. Among other services, Werner assembled a team of master forgers to create false identity documents for the FAP's border-crossers.

Before long, being both ambitious and resourceful, Werner found a more lucrative occupation for his team of forgers. At the time, a brisk trade was emerging in Canada and Mexico for stolen or leaked U.S. government and Unionist Party documents. Since quality intelligence on the U.S. regime was scarce, entrepreneurs like Werner filled the gap with authentic-looking documents containing plausible but fabricated information. Media organizations and foreign embassies paid handsomely for these documents, for lack of anything better. And, over time, even the DSS waded into the lucrative market, peddling genuine documents as well as impossible-to-detect forgeries that spread useful disinformation and brought in much-needed hard currency.

On Linder's first morning in Acapulco, Werner greeted him in his rented condo's private garden, which was alive with jasmine, honeysuckle, poinsettia, and orchids.

"You've come to the right place, Mr. Linder," he began, reaching out to shake hands. "My team has the most complete assortment of Unionist documents this side of Washington. Using our templates, we can create any electronic or paper record you might imagine, all at a reasonable price."

"What I have in mind is very specific," Linder replied. "If you can do it, you'll be paid well. But absolute secrecy is essential. Can you guarantee it?"

Werner offered his visitor a knowing smile.

"Positively. Come inside and we'll talk details," he said as he led Linder to the dining room, on whose massive hacienda-style table he had laid out a wide array of file folders.

Apart from Werner's gray hair, it was difficult to judge the man's age. For he had both the tanned complexion of someone who had spent much of his life outdoors and the lean physique of a man who was no stranger to physical exertion. Linder guessed that Werner was north of sixty, but appeared exceptionally healthy for one who had survived hard labor at Kamas and in the Yukon.

"So what kind of project do you have in mind, Mr. Linder?" Werner asked once the two men were seated at the table.

At first it was difficult to hear Werner speak because a pair of cheap boombox radios filled the room with competing blasts of mariachi music to defeat possible eavesdropping. Linder moved his chair closer to his host and leaned in.

"How much experience do you have with overseas Progintern documents?" he asked Werner.

"Ah, you're going top shelf. Excellent."

"How do you mean?"

"You see, Unionist Party communications take place at three security levels. The first consists of public messages to the masses. The next involves confidential intra-governmental and intra-Party messages. And the highest security level applies to secret messages exchanged with covert DSS and Progintern representatives posted abroad. So which geography are you focused on?"

"Great Britain."

"Okay," Werner nodded. "We have several recent examples of messages to Progintern U.K. that we can draw on."

"Fine, then. This is what I'm looking for…"

For the next three days, Linder spent each morning with Werner at the garden condominium shaping details of the fake Progintern document he wanted. They finished each day at noon, after which Linder joined Annabel for lunch, a siesta, and an hour or two of relaxation by the pool.

On their last day together, Werner brought out a bottle of aged mescal and two glasses. Between sips of the smoky liquor, Linder asked whether the forger planned to attend the Anti-Unionist Congress later that week in Mexico City.

"Not invited," Werner replied. "The meeting is intended for Fury's moneymen. And I wouldn't give the guy a dime even if I had one to spare."

"Oh? Why is that?" Linder asked, feigning indifference.

"Let's face it, Warren. Fury is washed up over here. The Canadians have locked him out, now that they've signed a peace treaty with the Unionists. And in Mexico, the same is about to happen. You see, during CWII, the Mexican government looked the other way while gringos waged guerrilla war across the border with help from the cartels. In those days, Fury's people smuggled arms and fighters into the U.S. while the cartels brought refugees out at a tidy profit. Then the Unionists completed the border wall and cut off traffic both ways. Which meant that the rebel payoffs to Mexican politicians also dried up. So, with the money cut off, it's just a matter of time before the Mexican government throws out the rebels and makes peace with Uncle Sam."

"So what would peace with the Unionists mean for you personally?"

"Well, I can probably stay here a while longer if I keep my nose clean," Werner mused before taking a sip of mezcal. "But making a living in the documents business will likely get a lot harder. I may just head back to Cuba They still have a lively cross-border trade over there."

"You won't have any trouble finishing my project before you go, will you?"

"Oh, no, you needn't worry about that. I'll have it finished in a couple of days," Werner replied. "But if I were you. I'd be extra careful at Fury's soirée this weekend. Never underestimate his capacity for screw-ups. His botched job at Cannes is just the latest example. I'd hate to see something bad happen to you before you paid me."

Werner offered a smile that was so dissolute and yet so oddly charming that it gave Linder chills.

On the day scheduled for Linder and Annabel to depart for Mexico City, Werner called early to ask if Linder could come back to the condo to settle a final detail. Linder agreed and Werner's young associate arrived a half hour later to pick him up.

About twenty minutes after her husband left, Annabel's housekeeper announced that a visitor was at the door demanding to see her on urgent business. The housekeeper's face was sallow and she seemed unusually nervous. Though the situation was odd, Annabel went to the door.

"*Señor*a Linder?" the visitor asked with a troubled expression. He was a good-looking Hispanic of about forty, dressed in a beige summer suit, and spoke in English with a Mexican accent.

"Yes? How can I help you?"

"There has been an accident on the highway and your husband has been injured," the man said on a note of urgency. "An ambulance is taking him to the hospital, but he asked me to come find you since I was the first to stop and help him. Can you come with me? My driver spoke with the paramedics and knows the way to the hospital."

Having learned to look for the DSS's hidden hand behind unusual events, Annabel was not prepared to accept the stranger's claims at face value. She began at once to pepper him with questions.

"What kind of accident?" she demanded. "Tell me exactly what happened."

"Your husband's car was hit at an intersection just in front of me," the man explained. "My driver scarcely avoided a collision himself. I cannot say how serious *Señor* Linder's injuries might be, but he was still conscious before he left for the hospital and urged me to find you at once."

The stranger was polite and well spoken, and his car parked outside was a sleek new Mercedes. Given the possibility of serious injury to her husband, Annabel put aside her misgivings and called for the housekeeper to bring her purse. As she followed the man outside, he introduced himself as Diego Machado, a local builder, before opening the car's rear door for her and circling around to take a seat beside her.

But first, Annabel took her mobile phone from her purse and called her husband's number. It went immediately to voicemail, as it always did whenever Linder was in a meeting. But why would it do that if he were still en route…?

"Please, *Señora* Linder, we must hurry if we are to catch up."

For a moment Annabel hesitated, but as Machado's tone was solicitous rather than assertive, she entered the Mercedes.

Once the car had left the gated compound, she spoke again.

"Which hospital is it?" she asked.

"The Farallón. It's quite close. We'll be there in a few minutes."

In the next moment Annabel detected a slightly sweet chemical odor. At the same time, the car lurched to the right and the stranger was thrown against her. She felt a sharp prick in her thigh and the thought flashed through her mind that she was being drugged. So she reached for the door handle. But the door was locked.

"Stop the car!" she screamed before the stranger held a thick cloth over her mouth and nose. Then the medicinal odor became overpowering, the soft leather seat seemed to slip out from under her, and everything turned black.

Out of the darkness, a beam of light flickered ahead before coming closer. Annabel felt nauseous and imagined that she was in a deep abyss whose walls revolved slowly around her. Then the light grew steadily brighter until it hurt her eyes. She found herself sitting in a folding chair, bent over with elbows on her knees.

"Ah, that's better," said a voice nearby. As her vision cleared, she could see a bespectacled older man looking at her with concern. Behind him stood a wall of shelves lined with bottles of every shape and size.

"Drink this," the old man added in heavily accented English as he held a glass of water to her lips. "You are all right. Don't be alarmed."

Annabel opened her eyes wide and realized that she was in a storefront pharmacy and that the old man wore the starched white coat of a pharmacist. His young female assistant watched from behind the counter. A half-dozen curious customers gathered just beyond arm's reach.

"What happened? Where am I?" she asked the pharmacist.

"You went faint in your car but you'll be fine," he replied.

She stiffened when she remembered the needle stick in her thigh and the cloth held over her face, realizing that she must have been drugged.

The pharmacist offered a sympathetic smile and laid his hand on hers.

"Don't worry," he repeated. "You'll be fine now. Your husband has gone to fetch a doctor."

"Husband?" Annabel bristled, struggling to collect her thoughts. "What husband?"

"The young man who brought you in, of course," the old man replied with a confused look.

"That was not my husband!"

Annabel reached for her purse and fished out her mobile phone. She dialed Linder's number again. This time the call went through.

"Annabel, what happened? Are you okay?" he demanded. "I just got back to the villa and heard about your accident."

"*My* accident?" she demanded. "What are you talking about?"

"The maid called and said a car hit you while you were out for a walk."

"But I never went for a walk!"

"Then why did the man who hit you come to the house to find me?" Linder stammered. "He offered to drive me to the hospital. Listen, he's right here. I'll put him on."

A moment later, Linder spoke again, more quietly than before.

"He's gone. And so is the maid. What on earth is going on, Annabel? And where are you calling from?"

"I'm at a pharmacy on the airport road. A man came to the villa claiming that it was *you* who were injured in an accident. You didn't answer your cell phone so, like a fool, I let him take me to the hospital. But before I realized what was happening, I felt a needle in my leg and woke up here."

When Linder spoke next, his voice conveyed relief.

"Now I see. Taking you away from the villa was a diversion to lure me out on a wild goose chase so they could kidnap me. All they needed to do was keep you on ice long enough to get me to go with them."

Annabel glanced at her watch.

"But I've been gone nearly a half hour," she replied. "So why didn't their plan work?"

"I think because you woke up too soon. What's more, you had the presence of mind to ring me again just now. If you had called even a minute later, I would have gone off with the man who said he was taking me to you. And we might never have seen each other again."

Linder and Annabel finished packing their bags an hour later and called their hired driver to request an early departure for Mexico City. While shaken by her abduction, Annabel recovered quickly and seemed more indignant than intimidated. While it was unlikely that the kidnappers would come back the same day for another attempt, Linder wanted to leave nothing to chance. Once on the highway, he phoned Leonard Fury to alert him that additional security might be needed for his AUC event. He also warned Frank Werner to be on the alert in case the DSS men came after him, too. Werner insisted that he was at no risk, which only tended to make Linder more suspicious of him and his young assistant. Could he rely on Werner to produce the

Progintern document he ordered, or might his plan for the forged document be foiled before it started?

Linder and Annabel arrived at their hotel in Mexico City's fashionable Polanco district just before dinner. After the morning's events in Acapulco, neither was inclined to leave the building for dinner. So they ate a light meal at the hotel's gourmet Mexican restaurant and retired early after knocking back some tequila from the minibar. Recalling Werner's cautionary words about Leonard Fury's rocky relations with the Mexican government and his propensity for screw-ups, Linder did not have a good feeling about the coming days.

The opening session of the Anti-Unionist Congress Central Committee started early at the apartment of Fury's leading Mexico-based supporter, located in a gleaming residential tower not far from Linder's hotel. Linder arrived a half hour beforehand to sip coffee with the other delegates, most of whom were American expatriates residing in Mexico, Canada, the Caribbean, or any one of several right-leaning nations in Central and South America. Everyone Linder spoke with over coffee feared the long-term impact of an authoritarian U.S. that sought hegemony over the entire Western Hemisphere. Several attendees asked Linder how much support Latin America could expect from the free nations of Europe, the Russian Federation, India, Japan, and Southeast Asia against growing Progintern subversion.

"Not much," was Linder's response. He reminded them that many of those free nations were at that very moment working to expand relations with the Unionist State.

To Linder's relief, the balance of the day went rather well, with an upbeat introductory speech from Chairman Fury, updates from the AUC's various standing committees, and presentations about the current state of the Unionist regime and Progintern subversion abroad.

The second day started almost as well, but hit turbulence after lunch, when Mexico's state news agency released a story that Fury had bribed Mexican officials to allow the AUC to keep its office in

Mexico City in the face of demarches from the Unionist regime. Even worse, a second article alleged that one of the criminal border cartels had paid off Mexican police and border officials to allow it to smuggle Fury-backed saboteurs into Texas. At a time when the Mexican president was seeking normalized relations with the Unionists, the revelations embarrassed his administration to the point where news commentators expected him to expel Fury and his devotees at any moment.

That moment came the following morning, when Fury received an order to vacate his offices and leave the country within twenty-four hours. When Linder arrived at the residential tower where the Congress had been meeting, he found a sign in the lobby stating that the group's final day of sessions was canceled. As if that weren't enough, a team of uniformed Mexican policemen blocked non-residents from using the building's elevators and stairways. Linder returned to his hotel room straightaway, where he found Annabel taking breakfast.

"As soon as you finish eating, we'll need to pack our bags," he announced. "The Congress is over."

An anxious look spread over Annabel's face as she dropped her fork.

"What's going on? Is there a problem?"

"Yes, a big one. The Mexican government has put its foot down. We'll need to leave the country right away to avoid being detained."

"Detained?" she exclaimed. "Whatever for?" Her face grew pale.

"The Unionists have accused the Mexican government of harboring émigré terrorists. They're demanding that everyone associated with the AUC be held for questioning and possible extradition to the U.S. under the new Mexican-American peace treaty."

"Oh, my heavens," Annabel gasped. "The Mexicans wouldn't really do that, would they?"

"I don't intend to stay long enough to find out. Let's catch a flight out while we can."

Chapter Nineteen: Two Men

> "Absolute power does not corrupt absolutely. Absolute power attracts the corruptible."
> —*Frank Herbert*

WEDNESDAY, 13 JULY 2033

Linder and Annabel succeeded in catching a midday flight from Mexico City to Panama before an order for their arrest could be carried out. After a stopover in Cuba to recover from the turmoil of the past few days, they arrived safely in London and spent a quiet couple of months close to home.

On a sunny mid-June morning, however, they awoke to news that the British Labor Party, having won an upset election victory over the Tories earlier that week, had agreed to form a new government with the Liberal Democrats.

"What exactly does that mean?" Annabel asked her husband over coffee as he carried a stack of morning newspapers to the breakfast table.

"It means that Humphrey Bledsoe is out as Prime Minister and Robert McKay is in."

"Not that horrid McKay who proposed the wealth tax?" she protested.

"The wealth tax isn't half of it," Linder replied with a scowl. "McKay has also pledged that one of his first acts on taking power would be to expand official relations with the Unionists in Washington. Last month, Labor's policy forum released a draft treaty giving the Unionists official recognition in return for a promise to guarantee America's pre-revolutionary overseas debt."

191

"So why is that important?"

"Because it means the new government intends to let the Unionists reopen their London Embassy. And once that happens, London will be crawling with DSS agents. MI5 and Scotland Yard can't possibly keep up with them. And I will be at the top of their target list."

A troubled look came over Annabel's face.

"Then you'll just have to stop them, won't you?"

Later that day, Linder and Dwight Calder met to craft their battle plan to thwart Labor's pro-Unionist initiatives. The good news was that they now enjoyed an influx of new consulting clients and their business was thriving. The bad news was that the reopening of bilateral relations with the U.K. would make a similar diplomatic opening with Western Europe more likely, giving the Unionist regime just the kind of boost it needed to secure its grip on power.

Meanwhile, Linder received a series of increasingly desperate appeals from Leonard Fury for more money and a face-to-face meeting. Since Fury was barred from entering Britain, a meeting meant that Linder would have to take time away from his duties to visit Paris. Still troubled over Fury's recent fiascos at Sanremo and Mexico City, Linder responded to each successive appeal with a terse message claiming that he was unable to travel due to the press of business. Finally, in July, Fury pleaded that Linder come see him "on a matter of grave importance."

"If he wants to talk, why doesn't he just pick up the damned phone? He's got secure commo," Linder groused to Dwight Calder after receiving Fury's latest appeal. "I really can't justify traveling to Paris right now."

"I understand," Calder answered in a conciliatory tone. "But Leonard is still your friend. And you are probably one of very few people on earth he can turn to for advice. You'd feel terrible if he did something stupid to further harm himself and the movement. I'm sure the operation here could spare you for a few days if you really wanted to go."

"Let me think about it," Linder replied. "I'll let you know."

"I truly pity Leonard's situation," Linder began in a call later that day to Barton Cac, Fury's other close friend in the émigré movement. "But damn it, he's brought it down on his own head. He was so desperate to keep his operation going in Mexico that he failed to see how badly the Unionists wanted to shut it down. He completely closed his eyes to how reckless it was to gather the AUC's leadership there. So now Leonard is *persona non grata* in Canada, Mexico and in half of Latin America. The only country that will still have him is France. And even the French don't seem too happy about it."

"All that may be true, Warren," Cao replied, "but Leonard remains a symbol of the resistance to many in our movement. It would reflect well on you to lend him a hand in his hour of need. Besides, Leonard's keepers continue to keep me at arm's length, so I haven't been able to get through to him. I think you should pay him a visit. If nothing else, it would be smart to keep an eye on that flock of buzzards circling around him."

The next morning, Linder relented. He wrote to Fury that he and Annabel would arrive in Paris on Friday to see him.

From the moment that Linder and Annabel left their Mayfair apartment, Linder felt certain they were being watched. At St. Pancras Station, the face of every stranger in the premier class lounge seemed charged with menace. Annabel, too, seemed very much on edge, paying close attention the comings and goings of the other passengers.

Once aboard the train, Linder rose every half hour to pace up and down the aisle of the business class carriage and enter the adjacent cars to look about.

On arrival in Paris, Linder noticed a small middle-aged man with a neatly trimmed beard dressed in a beige suit and straw hat. Linder watched as the little man joined a huddle of four or five men waiting on the platform. But Linder lost sight of him until Annabel stepped off the carriage and he began lowering their roller bags to her. Then, no sooner did Linder's foot hit the pavement than the little man rushed up to greet him.

"Mr. Linder, Mr. Linder, what a pleasant surprise to see you here in Paris!" he exclaimed in a Northern English accent, seizing Linder's hand and pumping it vigorously. "You probably don't remember me, but we've spoken several times at meetings of the AAFC. I'm Sam Nadler. I help sometimes with the committee's accounting work."

"Well, thank you for your service to the cause, Mr. Nadler," Linder replied with a distracted smile. "What brings you to Paris?"

"Oh, one of my London clients has offices here and I've come to perform an audit. And you? Have you come on behalf of the committee? I hear that Paris is flooded with Unionist agents since the French allowed the U.S. Embassy to reopen."

Linder felt the smile fade from his face at the man's gratuitous mention of Unionist agents. At the same time, Nadler cast a sidelong glance toward the cluster of men he had left. All were staring back at Nadler, but shifted their gaze away the moment they noticed Linder watching them. The tallest of the men, who wore a raincoat and a slouch hat, immediately began moving back down the platform toward the station.

Meanwhile, Nadler tied Linder down with rapid-fire questions and offers to help by showing him around Paris and keeping troublemakers at bay. Yet whenever Linder asked him a question about himself, such as the name of his Paris client or of his hotel, Nadler evaded. Not until Annabel pleaded fatigue and demanded to contact their driver did Linder break free at last from the pesky little man.

Only after they were safely in their hired car en route to the Hotel Raphael did Annabel mention the tall man on the platform who so closely resembled the figure in a raincoat and slouch hat she had seen months ago outside their London flat.

"I never saw that person," he replied, placing a hand on her arm to reassure her. "But if you believe the man on the platform might be the same as the one outside our hotel in Switzerland, that can't be true. The man we saw in Zermatt is long gone. He was intent on starting a new life in the Balkans under a new identity and I helped him get there."

"But how can you be sure he hasn't come back?"

"Anything is possible, I suppose," Linder answered. "But I know Bednarski. After betraying his DSS mission in Basel and gaining the means to disappear, he would be crazy to show his face in Paris. You can bank on that."

But, for whatever reason, Annabel did not look reassured.

As if to underscore her fears, later that evening Annabel and Linder had another encounter with the pesky accountant. They had just exited the elevator in the Hotel Raphael's lobby to go to dinner when they ran into Sam Nadler once again. Yet neither had told the man where they were staying.

As before, Nadler brimmed with false *bonhomie* and insisted again on offering his services during their stay in Paris. Then he peppered Linder with questions about the state of the anti-Unionist movement in France and asked whether Linder planned to visit that other renowned émigré leader, Leonard Fury, while in the City of Light. Linder's answers were curt to the point of rudeness, but Nadler was undeterred.

Only when Linder firmly refused to let him take a selfie photo with the couple did the accountant finally take his leave.

When at last the couple was alone in the hotel's dining room, Annabel asked whether Linder thought Nadler was a DSS agent.

"Perhaps not," he replied after a moment's thought. "I recall having seen him at AAFC meetings in London, so he does have a legitimate connection to the anti-Unionist movement. All the same, I'll keep an eye out for him and will ask Cao to check whether Nadler has popped up in Paris before."

"And what about the man outside our hotel in Zermatt? Could you check on him again as well?"

"Certainly, dear, if it would make you feel better."

The next morning, Linder and Annabel ate an early breakfast and made the short walk from their hotel to Leonard Fury's apartment. Just before ten o'clock, Fury's assistant, Doris Geiger, met them at the door. It was clear from her startled expression that Geiger had not been expecting their visit and was none too pleased to see them. When she failed to open the door wide enough to let them in, Linder took the bull by the horns.

"Leonard asked me to see him on urgent business," he announced. "Would you be so good as to let us in?"

"I'm afraid Leonard is not here," she replied, cold as the moon. "He was summoned to Milan. I'm sure he will be available to see you on his return."

"And when would that be?"

"I expect him back by evening. Barring unforeseen events, that is."

Linder detected a haughtiness in Geiger's demeanor that rubbed him very much the wrong way.

"All right, then," he replied, maintaining his composure. "I wouldn't want to impose on Leonard so soon after his trip. Unless he calls me first, I'll plan on returning tomorrow morning at around this time. Will you tell him that?"

"Of course."

"One more thing, while we're here," Annabel said to Geiger as she and Linder turned to leave. "Would you happen to know a man named Samuel Nadler, an American accountant visiting from London?"

"I do," Geiger replied, unfazed. "He visited us not long ago with Jack Poirier, whom I believe your husband knows well. I'm sure either Leonard or Jack would be happy to tell you more about Mr. Nadler when you see them."

"Thank you, Doris," Linder answered with a half smile. "Till tomorrow, then."

Not until they were on the street did either of them speak.

"That woman gives me the creeps," Annabel said at last. "How can your friend stand to have her skulking about?"

"I really don't know," Linder answered. "Barton Cao has warned him many times not to trust her. I probably shouldn't say this, Annabel, but people like Doris Geiger stay alive only because it's against the law to kill them."

On the following morning, Linder arrived at Leonard Fury's door alone, as Annabel declined to go with him. This time, Mrs. Geiger led Linder to the sitting room, where he expected to find Fury alone. Instead, he found Geiger's husband and two strangers seated there.

"You have met my husband, I believe," she said to Linder with a perfunctory nod toward the fellow, a chubby little man who dressed as if he'd been tossed through a thrift shop window.

"Yes, good morning." Linder replied, remembering little about Mr. Geiger from their earlier meeting except that he had seemed entirely in thrall to his wife

"And these are our visitors from Canada," she added. "Andy, Wade, please meet Warren."

Both men offered monosyllabic responses without meeting Linder's gaze.

As Linder was accustomed to bumping into all manner of informants and undercover agents when around Fury, he was not surprised that Geiger failed to mention the visitors' last names. In fact, he doubted that even their first names were genuine.

Linder recalled having seen the younger man once before, at the AUC gathering in Mexico City. Andy had assisted then with seating, serving refreshments and other mundane tasks. A studious-looking bearded fellow in his mid-twenties, he had seemed earnest and energetic in Mexico. Now, however, Andy appeared pale and fearful, with despairing eyes and a forehead beaded with perspiration.

Wade was a couple of decades older than Andy, likely in his mid-forties, a big, square-shouldered man who carried his head tucked into his shoulders like a boxer. His eyes were cruel and piercing and he kept them fixed on Andy, like a cat aiming to strike terror into a mouse.

"Andy and Wade arrived earlier this week from New York," Geiger added. "They brought a message from Jack Poirier, who's away visiting the League."

But before Linder could follow up with a question about New York, Leonard Fury shuffled into the room. The change in his friend's appearance unnerved Linder. It was as if Fury had become a shadow of his former self. No longer the charismatic leader, here was a stout little man with a high brow, small eyes, and undershot chin, whose head was bent low as if in contrition.

"How was Italy?" Linder asked, hoping that Fury had returned with good news.

"A complete waste," the rebel leader responded in a monotone.

"Oh?"

"President Nascimento called me last weekend, offering to resume our discussions." Fury said as he plopped down heavily in an overstuffed armchair. "He urged that we meet again in person before he returned to Brasilia. But the meeting went nowhere. We'll get no financial aid, just a handful of Brazilian passports for our covert operators. And perhaps some in-kind assistance from their Paris embassy. A total bust, if you ask me."

He spoke in a sepulchral tone. Doris Geiger jumped in at once, as if to distract him from his foul mood.

"Well, it is what it is," she said dismissively. "Tomorrow is another day. And this morning Andy and Wade have brought you a message from Jack in New York. Wouldn't you like to see it?"

Fury gave her a sidelong glance before responding.

"Of course," he said, holding out his hand. Andy unfolded a sheet of notepaper and handed it over. Fury read Poirier's message out loud.

"'Today I met with members of the League's Political Council. They told me that the League has a pressing need for seasoned leadership at the top and wants you to return to America to lead the organization. Through their agents in the Justice Department, they have worked out an arrangement to get you into the country on terms that will let you participate in political life there. The conditions are that you surrender yourself to the League's people at Justice, confess to past acts of insurrection, and nominally acknowledge the Party's present authority. In return, you will receive a suspended sentence for past offenses and the restoration of all civil rights, along with the League's protection from retaliation by the DSS. I grant that the plan may seem risky, but the League is offering you a clear path to ride with them into power when the time comes. If, after considering their terms, you find them acceptable, the bearers of this message will arrange for your safe conduct to Washington. I apologize for not being able to deliver this message in person, owing to a recent injury that prevents me from traveling.'"

To Linder, the offer seemed ludicrous. How could the League possibly make such a proposal unless they were in cahoots with the Unionist Party leadership and not just the League's agents in the DOJ? And what was Poirier's injury that kept him from coming to Paris in person? It seemed an obvious trap. After Sanremo and Mexico City, however, Fury was likely at the end of his rope. The League was dangling the opportunity for him to be a major political player on the American scene, and perhaps even have a shot at real power if the League were to replace the Unionist Party. It was a long shot, to be sure. But Fury was nothing if not a gambler.

Thus, it didn't surprise Linder that the rebel leader's voice swelled and his eyes brightened with each sentence that he read aloud to the group.

"I know Poirier's handwriting. This message must be from him," Fury declared with an exultant expression before handing the paper to Linder.

Linder did his best to conceal his alarm, both at the message's content and at Fury's triumphant response. He remembered all too well the rebel leader's comment a year before, when Poirier had reported that the League sought a leader of national stature to take it to the next level. At that time, Fury had confided that he would seriously consider heading the League. Upon hearing this, Cao had warned Linder that Fury appeared so desperate to remain at the helm of the anti-Unionist movement that he was capable of doing most anything to remain relevant. Now, it appeared that Cao's prediction had come true.

"Everything Jack says in his letter is spot on," Wade affirmed, speaking directly to Fury as the latter handed the note to Linder to examine. "Right now the League stands on the verge of taking on the Unionists, but we've been holding back for lack of a proper leader. What we need is someone who can take command and get things done. Someone whose orders won't be questioned. Everyone in our current leadership circle recognizes we need someone like you to lead us, Leonard. We stand ready to strike. All we lack is a steady hand. Yours."

In a matter of minutes, Leonard Fury had become transformed. The stout little man who wore his head bent low became once again the charismatic leader. He rose from his seat and strutted around the room, as if contemplating the League's offer. Letting loose a flurry of pointed observations and rhetorical questions, he struck a bold pose before the mantelpiece. Next, he displayed his noble profile from one side and then the other and thrust his hand between shirt buttons in the Napoleonic style. Every pose seemed carefully studied to impress his tiny audience. Yet he scarcely looked at them. Nor did he need to, for when he frowned, a cloud settled on the group. And when he smiled, answering smiles appeared on every face. Except for Linder's.

That Fury could be so easily inflated and deflated by transitory events aroused Linder's contempt. While Fury had once seemed a latter-day Napoleon, now he appeared little more than a ham actor. The scorn showing on Linder's face must have been easy to read, because the moment Fury stopped speaking, all eyes turned to the apparent skeptic.

"Your thoughts?" Fury inquired icily after a moment of strained silence.

"I think the note is bogus," Linder announced, handing it back to Fury. "Either that, or Poirier has gone over to the other side. Really, how is it possible that the League, having popped up out of nowhere less than two years ago, could be ready to face off with the Unionist Party? To do that would also require taking down the DSS. The same DSS that controls every major institution in America. Don't you wonder how the League manages to operate without the Department's knowledge?

"Think of the churches," he went on. "All of them: Catholic, Protestant, Jewish, Muslim, New Age, whatever. They all fall under the government's Council for Church Affairs. The DSS also controls the universities, the media, the banks, the corporations, and the labor unions. It does that by putting trusted Party members in positions of control. How could the League possibly remain outside the Party's grasp, when the DSS controls every other institution in America?"

"So you dismiss everything we've come to know about the League as a hoax?" Fury confronted him. "And you consider any émigré who cooperates with the League, including the FAP and the AUC, an arrant fool?"

"I can't tell you exactly how much of the League's story is true," Linder replied, meeting Fury's hostile gaze. "But I strongly question their claims. In my opinion, for you to go to America relying on their capabilities would be madness. My advice: Don't go."

Suddenly, Fury waxed thoughtful, sinking his chin into his palm while casting a worried look at the Geigers and the two visitors from Canada. This seemed to raise an alarm with Doris Geiger, who licked dry lips before venturing to speak.

"I disagree completely with Warren about the League's capabilities," she asserted. "Those abilities are by now fully established through the comings and goings of men like Andy, Wade, and Jack. I myself wouldn't hesitate to cross the border with any of them. But if you harbor any doubts, Leonard, why not delay your departure a while until you can resolve them?"

Geiger shot a half-apologetic smile toward Andy and Wade before looking once more to her boss.

"To be perfectly frank," Fury answered, "I do have a few questions about how the League operates. But I trust Jack implicitly. And I look forward to hearing his answers in due time. But, at the moment, the main thing going through my mind is the difference I could make to the League if even half of what Poirier says is true. If I lived to a thousand, I might not see such a chance again."

Linder felt a strong urge to seize Fury by the scruff of the neck and trot him out into the hall to talk sense into him. He wanted to warn his friend in no uncertain terms not to trust Poirier, the Geigers, the pair from Canada, or anyone else associated with the League. But to denounce Madame Geiger would be dangerous, as she had a keen sense of who her enemies were. And she wouldn't shrink from attacking them in any way she could. Linder wasn't quite ready for that. Not yet.

A few moments later, Fury took Geiger aside, while her husband did the same with Wade. Linder seized the moment to sit beside Andy and pump him for information.

"So, what sort of accident did Poirier have that kept him from traveling?" he asked the younger man.

"I don't know," Andy replied, looking at the floor. "I heard he fell off a bicycle."

The answer seemed ridiculous. Linder pressed harder.

"Are you sure Poirier hasn't been arrested?"

Andy bit his lip but made no reply.

"Do you know of any other League members who've been arrested lately?"

The younger man shook his head.

"Okay, tell me who from the Party delivered the DOJ's clemency offer to Poirier?"

But the more Linder peppered Andy with questions, the more deeply the latter seemed to withdraw. No matter how Linder phrased his question, Andy shook his head, pressed dry lips together, and remained mute.

Only when Fury rejoined the general conversation did Andy appear to relax.

But by then, Fury no longer seemed interested in discussing Poirier's letter. Nor did he have anything more to say until he rose to escort Linder to the door. Just before letting his friend out, Fury asked Linder to resume the monthly payments that he had halted after losing the Basel court case. By now, disgusted with Fury's weakness and self-delusion, Linder refused.

"No. If you want to turn yourself in, let someone else cover your airfare."

"Then let's say our goodbyes," Fury answered with a glance cold and heavy.

"I prefer a simple goodnight," Linder answered with equal coolness. "I have a superstition against goodbyes."

❖　　　❖　　　❖

Linder left Fury's apartment feeling profoundly discouraged. His old friend, once a genuine force of nature, seemed burnt out. How could he have relied upon so flawed a character as Fury for so long without seeing it? Yet who else could have taken Fury's place in the movement? No one. And then a thought hit Linder that made him shudder. What if he, too, might end up like Fury someday, played out, a pale vestige of who and what he had once been?

That night, while he and Annabel were at dinner, someone gave the couple's hotel suite a systematic search. The tripwires that Linder had left on their laptops, dresser drawers, luggage and among their papers had all been disturbed. While most items remained in place and none of their possessions appeared to be missing, the fact that someone had gained access to their rooms in a five-star Paris hotel worried Linder. Was it the DSS, or Fury's team, or possibly the League? When Linder took Annabel out onto the balcony to tell her what he had detected, she blanched.

"Must they really dog us so, wherever we go?" she complained.

Linder had no answer.

The next morning, while eating a room-service breakfast, he received a phone call from an unidentified number. Despite a fleeting apprehension, he put it through. The call was from Doris Geiger.

"I'm calling to let you know that our flat is being watched this morning. I would advise against coming. It may be dangerous for you."

"Thanks. I'll take it under consideration," Linder replied.

He went there anyway.

Geiger answered the door. There was no mistaking the cold malice in her eyes as she opened it just wide enough to speak.

"Mr. Fury says he's not in the office today," she sneered, her stiff posture as unwelcoming as her voice.

"Fine. Please tell him I'm here, anyway."

"He's sleeping."

"Then wake him up."

"No. Come back tomorrow. Or, better yet, don't come at all."

Then she shut the door in his face.

Linder considered making a scene but decided against it. Instead, he wondered why he had even bothered to come.

Upon returning to the Hotel Raphael, Linder sent Barton Cao a secure message asking what he knew about Andy and Wade. He even offered to pay Cao's people to tail the pair to and from Leonard Fury's apartment. Cao replied that no payment was necessary, as he had already sent a team to follow the two men back to their fleabag hotel in the 12th Arrondissement, near the Gare de Lyon. They discovered that Doris Geiger had visited Andy and Wade every evening since their arrival. But Cao could learn nothing more about the two men, except that they were Americans traveling on Canadian refugee documents. For good measure, Linder also asked Cao about the gadfly Samuel Nadler. According to Cao's database, Nadler was a low-level émigré activist based in London who traveled often to Paris. But he was unable to confirm any connection between him and the DSS.

On reflection, Linder stood by his assessment that Jack Poirier's letter was a provocation intended to lure Leonard Fury back to the U.S. for capture by the DSS. But how could he confirm if the League itself was under DSS control? There had to be a way.

Chapter Twenty: Kuroda

> "Our doubts are traitors, and make us lose the good we oft might win, by fearing to attempt."
> *—William Shakespeare*

WEDNESDAY, 20 JULY 2033

Linder had one source in Paris who might be able to reveal the hidden link between the League and the DSS, if one existed. She was a former U.S. Department of State employee who years ago had provided under-the-table passports to American dissidents fleeing the country. Landing in London shortly after Linder's escape from the Unionist State, Grace Kuroda had arrived penniless and fearful of DSS retribution. After seeing Linder interviewed on GB News to promote his book, she reached out to him for help.

In recognition of her assistance to fellow U.S. émigrés, Linder gave Kuroda five thousand pounds and sent her on to Barton Cao, who offered to help her find work in the French capital. Not long after, Kuroda was hired to work in the consular office of the Canadian Embassy's U.S. interest section in Paris, on the strength of her fluency in French and her experience at the State Department. Apparently, the consular officials in Paris either didn't know or didn't care about her past help to dissidents, perhaps because she applied for a low-paying clerical position that offered no access to classified information.

But by virtue of her presence in the consular section, Kuroda was able to monitor the comings and goings of American citizens who visited that office and identify those who appeared likely to be DSS operatives. Later, when the full U.S. Embassy reopened in Paris, she kept her job in the consular section and moved quickly to recruit a pair of sub-agents who gave her access to the chancery's visitor log as well as video coverage of the building's entrances. In view of Kuroda's favorable new situation, Linder asked Cao if she could identify Andy, Wade and Nadler from surveillance footage and report whether any of them had appeared at the U.S. Embassy. Since Cao was about to depart on a weeklong trip, he instructed Kuroda to deliver the results directly to Linder at the Hotel Raphael.

This lapse in tradecraft nearly led to disaster, for as Kuroda passed through the hotel's lobby, she spotted none other than Samuel Nadler pretending to read a newspaper while keeping a close eye on the elevators. She flinched on seeing him, and he also noticed her. By the time she reached Linder's door, she was a nervous wreck. Linder opened the door and saw the panic on her face. Neither spoke a word as he motioned for her to enter.

To Linder's eye, Kuroda was a well-dressed, well-tended Japanese-American woman of fifty-some years. While her petite figure now tended toward a dumpling shape, Linder imagined she had been quite attractive in her day. But what Linder admired most about Kuroda was her courage in helping dissidents in Washington and then resuming her clandestine work in Paris, all at substantial risk to her safety. No one would have blamed her if she had taken a tame job in a bank or insurance company or taught classes in Japanese flower arranging, without daring to deliver secret intelligence reports to Barton Cao.

"I saw Samuel Nadler in the lobby," Kuroda began, still out of breath when the door closed behind her. "And he saw me, too. I don't think he recognized me, but all he has to do is check with his people at the embassy and I'm finished. It's impossible to go back there now, Warren. What can I do?"

"First, have a seat," Linder told her, leading her into the suite's sitting room. Once they were seated opposite each other on a pair of chintz-covered chairs, he spoke again.

"You spoke of 'his people' at the embassy. Do you have any reason to think Nadler is working with the DSS?"

"Positively. I saw one of the DSS guys meet him in the chancery lobby and take him upstairs."

"Okay. That's enough in my book," Linder replied. "Which means we have to assume that Nadler will report your coming to my hotel."

"And what if he's still downstairs when I leave?"

"We'll have to slip past him somehow. The question is whether he's still in the lobby or has come up here to stake us out. My bet is that he's still downstairs. Either way, we'll need to move fast. So come with me. We're going to try on some disguises."

They retreated to the bedroom, where Linder opened the closet.

"Find one of my wife's outfits that fits you. Preferably one as different as possible from what you're wearing now. Then join me in the bathroom for your makeover. Don't worry about complaints from my wife. She's out shopping and won't be back for hours."

Kuroda found a beige knit dress that hung low on her, though its hemline likely fell above Annabel's knee. She also selected Annabel's mid-length Burberry trench coat that was also a couple inches too long for her. She carried both garments into the bathroom for Linder to approve. He nodded upon seeing them and held out a blonde wig for her to try.

"Really?" Kuroda objected. "A Japanese blonde?"

"Doesn't matter. We're aiming for distraction. Pick out some makeup that agrees with the wig and try to give yourself an entirely different look. Then put on the dress and let's go. I'll be waiting in the bedroom."

When Kuroda emerged from the bathroom, she was totally transformed. Meanwhile, Linder had donned a black Nehru-style tunic and a chauffeur's cap that he kept in his suitcase for occasions when he might need to evade surveillance.

"I'll walk with you to the elevator posing as your chauffeur. That's the moment of greatest risk. Once we're in the lift, things will get better."

And so they went. The corridor remained empty while they waited with taut nerves by the elevator bank. Once the lift door closed behind them, Linder pushed the third-floor button and revealed the rest of his plan.

"When we step out, we're going to switch to the service elevator and take it to the basement. Then we'll walk to the freight exit, where we'll ditch our coats and hail a cab to the Châtelet metro station. From there we can catch the express line to Place D'Italie, which is only a few blocks from Barton's office."

Kuroda seemed fine with it until they caught the cab to Châtelet. Halfway there she began breathing rapidly and sweating, as if struck by a panic attack.

"It's no use," she moaned. "Once the DSS realizes I've been working with you and Barton, they won't rest until they hunt me down."

"Nonsense. We'll get you to a safe place where you can start an entirely new life. You've done it before, Grace. You can do it again."

But Kuroda was not easily consoled. Her face darkened, her hands trembled, and her eyes stared blankly ahead. By the time they reached Cao's office, she was nearly in a stupor and could barely put one foot ahead of the other.

Linder and Annabel remained in Paris for another week until Cao returned from abroad. When Linder finally met Cao at his office, one of the first things he did was to praise Cao's niece, Maria Silva, for her resourcefulness in finding Kuroda a place to hide until Nadler and the two men from Canada left town.

"Thank God Maria was here when we arrived," Linder declared. "She was amazing. She cut Grace's hair, dressed her as a man, and hid her in a part of the Quartier Asiatique where nearly everybody spoke Chinese or Vietnamese. If the DSS were looking for Grace there, they would have had a devil of a time. Then, after five days of tense waiting, Maria put her on a flight to Sydney, where Grace has friends and can start a new life."

"My niece is a master of improvisation," Cao announced with pride.

"Is Maria here today? If she is, I'd like to thank her in person."

"Regrettably, she's not. Maria and her husband are taking a brief vacation in the south of France before traveling to Canada."

"Canada? Could that be related to...?"

"Yes, she's going to spend some time with the League. Jack Poirier set it up."

Linder winced.

"I remember you telling her last year that going there wasn't safe. Did you change your mind?"

"Not really," Cao answered with a sour look. "But Maria is a headstrong young woman. And old enough to make her own choices. I've warned her not to cross the border into the U.S., but who knows what she and Gordon will do once they're in Canada?"

"Well, at least they'll have Poirier to look after them," Linder pointed out, not without irony. "If even a third of what he says about the League is true, they should stand a decent chance of getting out safely."

"With Poirier, thirty percent accuracy wouldn't be far off," Cao sniffed. "Sometimes I wonder if the League isn't paying him. But enough about my problems. I understand you've got plenty of your own in London, now that the Labor Party has ousted the Tories."

"You have no idea," Linder grumbled, rolling his eyes. "When the Prime Minister called a snap election, nobody dreamed that Labor and the Liberal Democrats could raise enough votes to dislodge the

Conservatives. Now, McKay's Anglo-American Trade Agreement is sailing toward approval in Parliament. And, once it does, other countries will follow suit. The economic boost will bail out America's economy and keep the Unionists in power for another decade."

"So is there any way to stop it?" Cao asked, shifting uneasily in his seat.

Linder shrugged.

"Hard to say," he said. "I've been working on a plan for months. But it's risky, and I have absolutely no idea if it will work."

Chapter Twenty-One: The Zuckerman Letter

> "A hair divides what is false and true."
> –*Omar Khayyam*

MONDAY, 22 AUGUST 2033

Late on an August afternoon, when London's air hung heavy with heat, Linder and Dwight Calder appeared at the Westminster office of former Tory Prime Minister Nelson Furness, one of Britain's foremost opponents of normalizing relations with Unionist America. It was after office hours, when his partners and clients were least likely to notice the arrival of the two Americans, who were not in good odor with the Tory establishment for having fought former PM Bledsoe's attempts at reopening Anglo-American trade.

Now it was Labor's turn to sell the benefits of trading with the Unionists. And by all accounts, Prime Minister McKay's trade agreement seemed heavily favored to win its vote in Parliament. The coalition of anti-Unionist American émigrés, like-minded Britons, and dispossessed holders of repudiated U.S. debt had done its best to derail the trade pact, but that effort had not been enough.

Once the two visitors were seated opposite their host and coffee was served, Linder kicked off the discussion by asking Furness what else he thought might be done to thwart McKay's trade initiative.

"The two sides are so deeply dug into their trenches by now that I'm hard pressed to think of a move that could break the stalemate," the veteran politician replied. "Labor has staked its political future on the promise to boost British exports and open new financial markets in America for British bankers. The Tories, in contrast, oppose government loan guarantees in principle and insist on full repayment of capital and interest to British holders of American debt. Neither side can afford to disappoint its constituency by backing down. Only some major event outside the scope of the present stalemate has a chance of changing facts on the ground."

"I agree," Calder added. "I fear that our lobbying efforts have reached a point of diminishing returns. And the press seems evenly divided on the trade issue. Warren, can you think of any another way to break the impasse?"

This was Linder's opening. He certainly did have a way in mind, but he would need to be circumspect in proposing it if he were to have any chance of winning Furness over.

"It occurred to me on the way over here," Linder went on, "that perhaps we should take a closer look at the text of McKay's trade agreement. The enforcement provisions are usually where one finds the points of maximum leverage. Deal breakers, in other words."

Linder opened his briefcase, removed three copies of the draft trade agreement, and handed one each to Calder and Furness. Then he summarized each of the document's key provisions, identifying potential breaches and permissible remedies, until Furness interrupted him.

"Wait a moment. I recall that the original Tory trade proposal contained language prohibiting subversive activity by either party against the other. At the time, McKay and the Laborites accepted that language in the Tory bill. Can you find similar language anywhere in the new draft?"

A few moments later, Linder found it.

"Here it is, on page fourteen. Section 8(a)(iv)(B) declares subversion to be a material breach of the agreement. And the succeeding subparagraph allows either side to suspend trade with the other, unilaterally revoke trade credits, and declare loans to be in default, following substantial allegations of subversion. And it revokes the entire agreement if the breach is not timely corrected."

"So, if proof of subversion is sufficient to revoke the agreement, then why not submit such proof to prevent the agreement from going into effect?" Calder proposed.

"Fair question. But do we have any proof?" Furness challenged.

"Not yet. But I think I know where to look for it," Linder replied. "Clearly, the Progintern is up to no good in Britain, and the same can be said of the DSS. It's a matter of gathering evidence and bringing it forward. But tell me this: If we were to submit compelling proof of Unionist subversion, could we rely on our allies in Parliament to beat the drum for it?"

Furness took a sip of coffee and sat back in his chair before answering.

"That depends on the British public. If our evidence were to outrage the voters sufficiently, our Tory backbenchers might summon the courage to speak out. But don't tell anyone I said that. If you find your evidence, tout it any way you can."

Which was exactly what Linder had hoped to hear.

A few days later, while Linder and Calder were out canvassing their contacts in the Metropolitan Police, MI5, and various émigré groups for evidence of Unionist subversion against Britain, they had a major stroke of luck. Following a summer of anarchist-inspired demonstrations and rioting, the chief editor of a notorious anarchist website published an "Open Letter to the Police Forces" calling on British police and military personnel not to use force against the rioters but instead to join them in bringing down Britain's ruling class. When the Labor-run Crown Prosecution Service declined to bring charges against the anarchist editor, the Conservative Party put forward a censure motion and, to everyone's surprise, the resulting vote of no confidence passed. As a result, a new general election was called for late October.

During the campaign that followed, a leading issue advanced by Tory leader Bledsoe was Labor PM McKay's alleged sympathy toward the Unionist regime. Summer rioting in London, Birmingham, and Manchester had already left British voters in a surly mood and sensitive to claims that British anarchists were collaborating with a foreign power. This, in turn, sapped public support for the Anglo-American trade agreement. But the race between Tories and Labor remained close through mid-October. Both parties remained nervous about the other pulling what the Americans might have called an October surprise.

Accordingly, it seemed odd that, all through September and early October, Linder kept his distance from Calder and their team of lobbyists and publicists who were working against the trade agreement. Whenever Calder expressed concern about the latest poll numbers, Linder assured him that he was working on a special project that promised to advance their cause. The fruit of his labors finally became evident on the Sunday morning immediately before the Thursday election.

Linder was sitting down to breakfast when Annabel brought in the Sunday newspapers. He shuffled through them quickly until he found *The Mail on Sunday*. There, on page one and above the fold, he found the article he was looking for. The headline was "American Regime Plots British Insurrection." The article described how MI5 had intercepted a letter of instruction from Jeffrey Zuckerman, chairman of the Progressive International of the Unionist Party, better known as the Progintern. The letter was addressed to Allen McKinney, chief British delegate to the Progintern. It called on British progressives and their anarchist allies to prepare for armed insurrection in working-class areas of Britain. It also called for steps to subvert the allegiance of British police and military personnel and to recruit members for a new British anarchist militia.

Similarly damaging to Labor's cause was the letter's call for British progressives to rally in favor of U.K. government loan guarantees, trade credits and most-favored-nation trade status for the Unionist State. A particularly damning section of the letter read:

"An official reopening of commerce between our two countries will assist us in revolutionizing the British working class toward a successful uprising in struggling districts of Britain. Closer contacts between the British and American peoples through international travel and exchanges will likewise enable us to extend the propaganda of Unionism throughout Britain and into the Commonwealth."

A photograph of Progintern Chairman Zuckerman *in The Mail on Sunday* showed him as a man with cold, calculating eyes and coarse, cruel lips. The caption described him as a member of the Unionist Party Council of Three, a close confidant of Party Chairman Paul Twitchell, and an avowed enemy of British democracy.

Below the fold, the article quoted the head of MI5 as offering "five very good reasons" why he considered the Zuckerman letter to be genuine. Anonymous sources in MI6 and Scotland Yard echoed that assessment. Moreover, an unnamed senior official in MI6 revealed on background that the Unionist Party Central Committee had intercepted a secret proposal from the Progintern with wording very similar to that of Zuckerman's dispatch.

As might be expected, when *The Mail on Sunday* editors sought the U.K. Foreign Office's comment prior to publication, the office's press secretary declined to respond. But the same article cited a leaked copy of a demarche from the British Foreign Secretary to the U.S. Secretary of State denouncing the Zuckerman letter as a flagrant breach of the U.S. government's commitments not to commit subversion against Britain. Though the British demarche was not public information, it amounted to official confirmation of the published story.

Linder put down the newspaper after reading the incendiary article. He felt a peace of mind he hadn't experienced in weeks. Annabel couldn't help but notice the self-satisfied smile that spread across his face.

"All right now, Warren, what is it?"

He handed the newspaper across the table for her to read.

"Well, that seems rather neatly timed," she replied with an artful look before putting the article down to butter a piece of toast. "With the election just days away, it won't be easy for Labor to recover from news like this. This Zuckerman letter wouldn't be related to what you were doing in Acapulco, would it?"

"You might think so," he replied, employing a popular trope, "but I couldn't possibly comment."

Though Prime Minister McKay denounced the Zuckerman letter in no uncertain terms as a forgery intended to discredit him, his party lost the election in a landslide. The new Tory government under Prime Minister Bledsoe promptly scrapped Labor's draft trade agreement and suspended the restoration of full diplomatic relations. At the same time, it ordered the U.S. Trade Representative, Irwin Kreutzer, to depart Britain within seven days, though it allowed the trade office to remain open on a provisional basis.

Three days after the government ordered Kreutzer's expulsion, Linder and Dwight Calder were at their office when a messenger from the Trade Representative's office brought invitations for the two men to attend an informal farewell gathering for the departing official, to be held at Winfield House. The British government had allowed Kreutzer to occupy the estate, which for nearly a century had served as the U.S. Ambassador's residence in London, even though normal diplomatic relations between Britain and America did not currently exist.

"Wouldn't you say it's odd for Kreutzer to invite us, of all people, to his going-away shindig?" Calder asked his business partner with a look of perplexity. "I would have thought the list would be limited to people who worked to pass the trade agreement, not those who fought it. Do you think it's some sort of ruse to get back at us?"

"It's an official diplomatic gathering, according to the press," Linder countered. "I doubt the Unionists would want to risk another scandal by pulling any funny stuff there. I'm inclined to go, if only to see the look on Kreutzer's face. Are you game?"

Calder returned a mischievous grin.

"You don't think I'd let you go alone, do you?"

After presenting their invitations and identification at the compound's fifteen-foot iron gate, Calder and Linder drove up to Winfield House. The thirty-five-room red brick Georgian mansion sat on twelve and a half acres of land in Regent's Park, making it the second largest estate in London, after Buckingham Palace.

The two men followed dark-suited ushers to the receiving line, where Kreutzer's staff pretended not to know them. Kreutzer shook their hands and greeted them with a knowing smile and the single word, "Welcome."

"Thank you for including me," Linder replied. But Kreutzer's eyes were already focused on the next person in the queue. If the trade representative had something to say to him, he wasn't showing it. So Linder continued moving down the line.

"I don't like how he looked at you, boss," Calder said under his breath, a dark look passing over his face. "Were we fools to come?"

"Let's wait and see," Linder replied.

At the end of the hall, a staff member pointed them toward the right, into the Garden Room, where visiting U.S. presidents once entertained British royalty before historic state dinners. Until the 2020's, the room had been lavishly appointed with original paintings, antique furniture, decorative porcelain, and various other *objets d'art*.

But after a decade of Unionist misrule, including five years when the residence remained vacant during the suspension of diplomatic relations, nearly all the art works were missing and many of the original furnishings replaced by cheap copies. Linder noticed with chagrin that the parquet floors were moisture-damaged, the hand-painted wallpaper had peeled, and stray wires dangled in places from missing sconces.

Linder and Calder each snagged a flute of champagne from a passing server before scanning the crowd for familiar faces. Many in the room were Members of Parliament or Labor Party notables, while others were industrialists and financiers who had supported the ill-fated McKay trade deal. But more than a few were American émigrés who, while claiming to be anti-Unionist, had secretly backed the deal. Each time Linder spotted such a turncoat, he spoke the person's name into his mobile phone to record it. After twenty minutes, he was surprised at how many he'd identified, though a few fled his approach to avoid being confronted.

Not long after trading their empty glasses for fresh rations of champagne, Linder noticed Kreutzer across the room, standing among a half-dozen well-wishers and regaling them with some anecdote or other. A moment later, Linder caught Kreutzer's eye, prompting the official to wrap up his story and leave the group. He waded through the crowd until he stood with Linder and Calder in a sparsely occupied corner of the room.

"I detect your hand in that phony letter," Kreutzer began without introduction or even mentioning Linder's name. His eyes glowed dark and hot with a mature hatred.

"Then you've found something that no one else has," Linder deflected.

"It was a clever trick, but it won't stop us for long. MI6 is already walking back its earlier statements and is calling your letter a forgery. I'll soon be back in London, perhaps even as ambassador. You, however, are a marked man, Linder. Enjoy your moment of glory. It won't last long."

Chapter Twenty-Two: Fury in Captivity

> "Every anarchist is a frustrated dictator."
> –*Benito Mussolini*

WEDNESDAY, 9 NOVEMBER 2033

I t was shortly after dawn on a Wednesday morning in November when low-flying clouds of leaden hue swept down on London from the northwest and put a taste of rain in the air. Linder was at his desk reviewing his bank statements over a cup of coffee when he received a phone call from Barton Cao.

"I've been trying to reach Leonard since Monday and can't locate him," Cao began. "He hasn't responded to voice messages or texts either, so I went over to his flat yesterday afternoon. No one came to the door. The concierge told me Leonard left the building late Monday night with the Geigers. I asked her to let me in to Fury's place, but she claimed she didn't have a key. Actually, that's not surprising, considering the high-tech locks he's installed. I tried to pick one, but it was way out of my league."

"So what do you think has become of him?"

"I think that horrid Geiger woman finally wore Leonard down with her hogwash about how the League desperately needs him to go back and become their maximum leader," Cao replied. "I warned him time and time again not to listen to her, but you know how Leonard can be when he gets a wild hair up his ass. Sometimes I wish I'd followed through with my idea of having him break a leg to keep him at home."

223

"Don't blame yourself," Linder told him. "You did all you could. Nobody can stop a man who's determined to risk everything at a throw of the dice. Leonard wasn't about to settle down to a quiet retirement in Paris or Nice after the sensational life he lived. My guess is he couldn't resist the temptation to make one last splash by attempting to take over the League."

"Maybe so," Cao replied. "But I wish I hadn't left him at that woman's mercy. You could smell the treachery on her a mile away. I warned Leonard more than once to get rid of her, but he seemed insensible to the stench."

"And what do you think now about the handwritten note from Poirier that those two League stooges brought to Leonard?" Linder asked. "It always seemed odd to me that Jack didn't deliver the message in person. "Do you suppose he might have written the note under duress?"

"Well, if he did, then I've got an even bigger problem on my hands," Cao answered, looking away. "My niece and her husband crossed into Vermont with Poirier three days ago, against my advice. If the DSS has rolled them up, or if the League is under DSS control, Maria is in more trouble than I thought."

"I'm very sorry to hear that," Linder replied, feeling a sudden chill. "Let me know as soon as you hear from her, will you?"

But the damage was already done, Linder thought. He doubted that Cao would ever see his niece again. His sister April and her husband Jay, Paul Wagner, Leonard Fury, and now Maria Silva—all returned to American shores in hopes of finding a changed country. Not to mention the dozens of reports he had received about other returnees. Was it the DSS's handiwork, or could the League really be operating outside the DSS's grasp and moving steadily toward toppling the Unionist regime from within? Only time would tell, but the queasy feeling in his gut told Linder that the League's claims were just too good to be true.

For several days, Linder received no further word about Fury's fate from Cao or any other source. Nor did Cao hear anything more from Jack Poirier or Maria Silva. Linder and Cao each harbored a sense that something had gone terribly wrong.

Then, the following Sunday, Linder read in *The Sunday Times* that Fury was under arrest in Boston. The report, sourced *to The New York Times*, claimed that the rebel leader had crossed the U.S. border into Vermont using a forged passport. The Customs and Border Patrol arrested him with two unnamed accomplices as they sat for breakfast in a diner outside St. Johnsbury. Shortly after grabbing them, the officers took the prisoners directly to the federal courthouse in Boston for arraignment. The report noted that the U.S. Attorney's office promptly indicted Fury on a wide range of charges, including treason, insurrection, terrorism, seditious conspiracy, and illegal entry into the U.S. They intended to try him soon in a special national security tribunal.

The news enraged Linder, as it confirmed his suspicion that the League had duped Fury into returning with Doris Geiger's connivance. It also saddened him that anything he might do now to help his friend would not likely improve his situation. Having been tried in a national security tribunal himself, he knew that Fury's trial would begin soon, end quickly, and produce an almost certain guilty verdict. And despite the League's promise of a suspended sentence and a full restoration of rights, punishment would be inescapable— and swift.

Later that week, *The Times* confirmed Linder's expectation by reporting on Fury's trial, which had taken no more than an hour, and without his court-appointed defense attorney raising a single objection. The reporter who had attended the Boston trial noted that Fury appeared confused throughout the proceeding and declined to testify in his own defense, though it might be his last opportunity to speak up for himself in public. The judge found the defendant guilty on all counts but stopped short of imposing the death penalty "so that a desire for vengeance does not color the public's sense of justice." And, "in view of the defendant's cooperation with the state," the judge commuted Fury's sentence to ten years' penal servitude at hard labor, with eligibility for parole in three years.

On first glance, the sentence appeared surprisingly lenient, considering Fury's notoriety and the grave charges leveled against him. Still, for a man of Fury's age and poor physical condition, even three years in the camps amounted to a death sentence.

Yet, scarcely a week later, *The Times* reported that the judge now suspended Fury's sentence entirely, with the exception that the prisoner was to remain under indefinite house arrest in a "comfortable hotel-prison" located near one of Boston's federal courthouses. The article noted with some irony that Fury would enjoy privileges to use the building's gym and swimming pool and, though unmarried, was also allowed "conjugal visits." While the visitor went unnamed, Linder imagined it had to be Doris Geiger.

Was this not precisely what Poirier's note had offered Fury during the previous summer? Namely, that Fury could expect to receive a suspended sentence on past charges if he confessed publicly and recognized the Unionist regime? And that the deal would clear the way for him to lead the League? Yet, how conceivable was it that the League had the power to fix Fury's sentence through its agents in the Justice Department? Unless in truth, the group was an instrument of the DSS.

To Linder's dismay, other leading British newspapers soon began to report Fury's capture, with all of them in agreement that Fury had betrayed his side to throw in with the Unionists, perhaps having decided to do so even before leaving Paris. After the stories appeared, émigré morale plummeted.

To seek a fresh perspective on the meaning of Fury's apparent defection, Linder phoned Barton Cao.

"As I reflect on it, I'd have to agree that Leonard's behavior is consistent with the offer in Poirier's note," Cao concurred. "It looks more and more to me as if Leonard were a willing participant from the start. He's either a dupe or a traitor. Perhaps both."

"And isn't it interesting how, whenever someone mentions the League in connection with Leonard's disappearance, that person is silenced? The group's backers claim to be protecting the League from the DSS, but sometimes I wonder if they're really trying to protect it from people like us."

Linder's suspicions about Fury's motives for his alleged defection and the League's role in it intensified over the next few weeks, when rambling letters, ostensibly from Fury, reached the British press. The letters defended his actions, praised the Unionist regime, and denied that he had denounced any of his émigré associates to the DSS. But what stung Linder most were Fury's claims that the émigré movement "is dead both morally and politically," and that he considered the DSS officers whom he had met in captivity "closer to me spiritually than any of my former associates in the movement."

After reading excerpts from these letters, Linder wrote to Nelson Furness voicing his anger and disgust at Fury's behavior. He confessed to Furness that he considered this a sign of Fury's moral suicide and was considering retracting his earlier public defense of the man.

Furness replied the same day.

"I have always thought of Mr. Fury as a great American patriot despite his reprehensible methods. However, it is very difficult to judge the politics in another country, so I must reserve judgment. I advise you to do the same."

Linder reluctantly followed Furness's advice and made no public comment about Fury's actions. But not long after, Linder received a handwritten letter from Fury, evidently smuggled out from his "hotel-prison" in Boston, claiming that he had resisted cooperation with the DSS and that public accounts of his trial were untrue.

"You must understand what's going on, Warren," Fury wrote. "The regime is determined to break me so that they can parade me before the world to discredit the movement I led. I have refused to yield, even in the face of death threats and mock executions. That is because I hate the Unionists and their ideology too much to die. My only chance of escape now seems to be a prisoner exchange. Could you use your contacts in Whitehall to propose it? Of course, I realize that the chances of success are slim. But I must exhaust all options before resigning myself to my fate. For, as we both know too well, hope is what gets you in the end."

Linder read the letter a second time and a third. The proposal was entirely self-serving and made no mention of Fury's personal responsibility for his plight. For Linder to propose a prisoner exchange to the British government would achieve nothing except to discredit him. He held the letter in his hand for a moment while he felt his anger rise. Then he crushed the letter in his fist and tossed it into the fireplace.

It was a week later when Linder received an invitation from Allen Hackett, inviting him to lunch at his club, a traditional gentlemen's club located in the St. James district of the City of Westminster. The club occupied a rather undistinguished Georgian townhouse, built originally as a private residence.

Linder entered the lobby and announced himself at the front desk before turning off his cell phone to comply with club rules. Hackett arrived moments later and escorted his guest to the library, where they found a pair of overstuffed leather chairs near a window. A dozen or more other members and guests shared the room, mostly middle-aged men dressed in tweeds or business suits and who looked more like bankers, brokers, solicitors and corporate executives than the House Cavalry and Life Guards officers who had once constituted a majority of the club's members.

"I'm going to miss this place," the MI5 man announced after an exchange of preliminaries and small talk.

"How so?" Linder asked, puzzled at the remark.

"I'll be leaving next month for a posting at our embassy in Ottawa. Two years under commercial cover. Primarily targeting your friends, the Unionists."

"How exciting," Linder replied, taken by surprise. "Did you request it, or were you drafted?"

"Oh, it was entirely my idea. A bit unconventional, but a stepping stone to higher things, if all goes right."

"Then congratulations, Allen. I hope you'll stay in touch. After all, your new line of work will give us even more in common, no?"

"I should think so," Hackett replied with a broad smile.

"I hear that most of what British intelligence collects about the U.S. flows through Ottawa," Linder noted. "But also that much of that information has been unreliable of late. Could that be why they're sending you?"

The smile disappeared from Hackett's face.

"Who told you that?"

"Just between you and me, it was my partner, Dwight Calder," Linder replied. "He has a friend posted to the Ottawa mission. Without revealing any state secrets, his source has noted some baffling contradictions between the embassy's reporting on the U.S. and independent coverage. The source also noted some troubling lapses in security, and an overreliance on information from the League. I assume you're familiar with the League's Canadian reporting?"

"Completely. But, unlike certain intelligence services on the Continent, British intelligence has no formal liaison relationship with the League. So it hardly seems likely that we could be overly reliant on them." Hackett's manner was chill.

"Formal liaison or not," Linder went on, "it's not hard to see how the League's reporting on the U.S. may have come to overshadow material from other sources. Let's face it—intelligence services have an insatiable demand for intelligence about America. But collecting it is hard, and the bosses aren't always willing to spend the time, effort, and money necessary to do the grunt work. So they exploit the League's uncanny ability to make off with Unionist secrets and soon become addicted to the easy pickings. And the more material they accept from the League, the less actual spying gets done. After all, why risk running your own sources inside the U.S. when you can piggyback on the League's? They claim to have assets all over the country. What could MI5 possibly know about U.S. compared to the League?"

Hackett's lips curled into a sneer.

"So you think the League is pulling a fast one on British intelligence?"

"Maybe," Linder replied, "if your secret service falls for the League's story that the Unionist Party is evolving toward openness and democracy. Or that populist- nationalists are taking over the Party's grass roots."

"I can see how it's very much in your interest to say such things, Warren. If the Unionist grip on America were to relax, hard-line oppositionists like you would lose your *raison d'être*. Along with your donor base."

"All right, then," Linder parried, "if you won't admit that the reporting from your Ottawa team might have gone soft, let me offer an explanation you'll like even less. Calder's source cites rumors that the embassy may have been penetrated by a DSS mole who backs the League. Might that not be worth checking out?"

"I'll thank you not to besmirch the integrity of His Majesty's Secret Service, Warren. Especially in view of your own checkered career." An ominous hardness arose in Hackett's eyes.

"Insult me all you want, Allen. I admit I made a terrible mistake in joining the DSS as a young man," Linder conceded. "But I joined before it became what it is today. Which means I've seen up close how a security service can go astray. Take care that MI5 doesn't go the same way."

As much as it discouraged Linder to read Fury's vain and self-serving letter from prison, and to endure Hackett's disdain, he didn't remain dispirited for long. Two days later, Calder informed him that the chief of Brazilian intelligence, Gilberto Mendes, had come to London to speak before an international security conference and wanted to meet Linder for drinks the next evening to discuss Leonard Fury and other matters.

The news buoyed Linder's spirits, since Mendes's boss, Brazilian President Ruy Nascimento, was a staunch anti-Unionist and had more than once extended a lifeline to Fury. Perhaps Mendes possessed new information about Fury's captivity. Or wanted to support Linder's propaganda war. Either way, Linder was eager to learn what Mendes had to say.

The two men met at Mendes's hotel, the Savoy, where the security conference was taking place. Just before the cocktail hour, Linder entered the hotel's renowned American Bar and surveyed the crowd in the elegantly appointed room. He found the Brazilian seated near the entrance. Mendes was a trim, athletic-looking man whose deeply tanned face and black Van Dyke beard made him resemble one of those swashbuckling Portuguese explorers who first colonized Brazil.

"It is a great pleasure to meet you, Mr. Linder," Mendes began. "I have heard so much about you from my American friends."

"The pleasure is mine," Linder replied. "Brazil has been a stalwart supporter of American patriots living in exile. And your president was most generous to my colleague, Leonard Fury, at a time when his actions were widely criticized."

"Our goal is the same: to end the Unionist dictatorship in America. And it saddens me that events did not turn out better for Mr. Fury."

Here Mendes paused, took a deep breath, and raised his eyes to the ceiling.

"As you know," he went on, "it wasn't always easy to work with Mr. Fury, especially after his missteps at Cannes and Mexico City. Now my government looks very foolish for having supported him."

Linder nodded. "I feel the same way, especially after reports that Leonard cooperated with the Unionists in return for favorable treatment. While I don't fully credit reports from the state-controlled media, I do find those stories distressing."

"That's why we have asked the American Constitution League to use its influence with certain European governments to get Fury released," Mendes replied. "It will be an important test for them, to be sure, but success would lend the League much credibility. And now that Fury has renounced his opposition to Unionism, I should think that securing his release would no longer be impossible."

Linder's heart sank on hearing the Brazilian mention the League's name. But at that moment, a waiter interrupted the conversation to take the men's drink orders and Linder managed to hide his dismay. Mendes ordered single malt whisky on the rocks, while Linder asked for a rye Old Fashioned with extra bitters.

"And how has the League responded to your request?" Linder asked once the waiter was out of earshot.

"They have not, and I don't quite understand why." Here Mendes shrugged and cast a veiled glance at Linder.

"How odd. Has your service had many dealings with the League?"

"We've had an information exchange with them for about a year, begun under my predecessor. But lately I sense that we many have relied too much on the League's intelligence against the Unionists and failed to seek authentication from other sources. Not long ago I ordered our USA section to seek corroboration for their reporting. Since then, we've uncovered some odd discrepancies."

"By discrepancies, do you mean careless mistakes or intentional misdirection?" Linder pressed.

At this, the Brazilian's face clouded over.

"Both. The League's reporting on the U.S. military has been especially troubling," he explained. "This summer we received a high-level visitor from the League, a Mr. Quist. Until his visit, local representatives of the League had been willing to undertake almost any intelligence tasking we gave them. But when we insisted on receiving documentary intelligence of Unionist defense capabilities and of Progintern subversion in Brazil, Mr. Quist took a step back. He claimed that the League lacked the necessary sources. To recruit them, he demanded five million Brazilian *reals*, a considerable sum for us. Nonetheless, I agreed to pay if his information could be authenticated. A few weeks later, we received documents responsive to our request. Sadly, our experts judged them to be clever forgeries. Since then, we have begun a meticulous review of the League's earlier reporting and find much of it unreliable."

"My colleagues and I have had similar experiences with the League," Linder replied. "Is there anything else about them that causes you concern?"

"Several things," Mendes answered. "For example, I marvel at the ease with which their people claim to move across frontiers and hold secret meetings inside the U.S. Does no one else find it odd that the American authorities have not shut down an organization so openly talked about in intelligence circles? Yet, whenever someone raises doubts, the League dismisses them at once, accusing us of showing disrespect."

"I agree, it's a paradox," Linder replied, nodding in agreement. "But, if the League's information is so unreliable, how do you account for its outsized influence with foreign intelligence services like your own?"

"Perhaps it is because the League projects an image of a vast popular resistance. Those who support it accept this narrative, largely because they lack direct knowledge of facts on the ground. Which makes organizations like ours dangerously vulnerable to deception. Wouldn't you agree, Mr. Linder?"

Chapter Twenty-Three: Fury's End

FRIDAY, 16 DECEMBER 2033

It was past six on a Friday afternoon, with the sky charcoal gray under a canopy of low clouds, when Victor Barbosa summoned James Jenkins to his office at the Tyson's Corner DSS Annex. Jenkins had already gathered his work papers and was preparing to store them in his four-drawer safe over the weekend when the call came. Jenkins tossed the files hastily into the top drawer, slammed it shut, and bolted down the hall.

"So can I release him?" Jenkins asked the moment he reached Barbosa's office.

Jenkins had been Leonard Fury's chief interrogator throughout the latter's incarceration. But now that Fury's sentence was suspended and he was under house arrest in Boston, Jenkins had important work in mind for Fury. And it would require greater freedom of movement for the prisoner.

"Before we get to that, how strong is your rapport with Fury?"

"Better than expected, considering the circumstances," Jenkins replied. "I think he began to trust me once he realized I wasn't out to crucify him. Most days I'd come in to find him depressed. Usually, by the time the session ended, he'd appear relatively at peace. But a few days ago, Fury told me he felt death creeping up on him. I'm starting

235

to worry that, if we don't start making good use of him, Fury might do himself in. He wouldn't be the first."

"Well, his premonition may be closer to the truth than he realizes," Barbosa replied before stepping to the door and closing it.

"What do you mean?" Jenkins asked, swallowing hard.

"I just got off the phone with the deputy director."

"Uh-oh," Jenkins muttered under his breath.

"Yeah, I know DeWaart approved your plan for putting Fury to work for the League. But we've been overruled. Twitchell changed his mind; he wants Fury gone. The deputy director suggests we make it look like a suicide. So get back to me with a plan. As Fury's interrogator, you're the one who knows him best."

"Do you want the plan in writing?" Jenkins asked with a perplexed look, never having been asked such a thing before.

"Of course not," Barbosa answered, staring at him askance. "This is outside normal procedure. Haven't you ever been in on one of these deals?"

"No."

"Well, in case you didn't know, this is how one gets ahead in our business. If you succeed with your assignment, you'll get another. No paper trail, but the right people will know what you did. And that'll get you on the fast track."

Jenkins didn't have much time to figure things out. Barbosa summoned him the next morning to discuss exactly how he planned to execute Leonard Fury and make it look like *hara-kiri*. Shortly after lunch, his plan approved, Jenkins boarded a plane to Boston while Barbosa picked up the phone to the DSS's Boston Base to clear the way.

It was early evening by the time Jenkins arrived at the DSS field office, which occupied two stories in a nondescript building adjacent to one of Boston's federal courthouses. He exited the elevator on the twelfth floor, approached the front desk, and began to sign the visitor's log.

"That won't be necessary, Mr. Jenkins," the desk clerk told him. "These two gentlemen will show you in."

The clerk, a fifty-something corrections officer with a thick Boston accent, pointed to a pair of hulking guards who appeared to hail from one of the Pacific Islands. Neither would have looked out of place on the New England Patriots' offensive line.

"If you're ready, we'll show you to the prisoner's quarters, sir," Jason, the elder of the two giants said.

"Ready as I'll ever be," Jenkins replied, sounding grimmer than he intended.

The pair led him down a long corridor before turning left onto another. Then they unlocked a door that opened onto what resembled a budget motel suite. Jenkins stepped in, flanked by the two guards.

Leonard Fury rose from the recliner where he had been napping with an open book on his lap. He was dressed in faded jeans and a striped rugby shirt, with penny loafers on his bare feet. His face wore a surly expression.

"If you came to repeat your offer of better living conditions if I'd help you haul in more rebels, the answer is still no."

It was the answer Jenkins expected although, until recently, he had hoped to bring Fury around to a better one. He accepted the prisoner's response and continued with the script he had worked out back in Virginia with Barbosa.

"That's a pity, Len. Because we can't wait forever for you to come around."

"Then don't," Fury shot back. "I'd rather go back to my old cell in the basement than betray a single soul for you goons."

"Again, it pains me to hear you say that. Because I thought you were starting to see the light. Your old cell is still available, of course, if that's really what you want. I could send you down there now."

Fury shrugged and tossed the book he had been reading back onto the empty recliner.

"Go ahead, then. Do your worst."

At a nod from Jenkins, the two guards closed in on Fury, who was a head shorter than either of them, and seized his upper arms while Jenkins circled behind and pulled a black nylon hood over the prisoner's head.

"Okay, we're all going for a nice elevator ride," Jenkins announced. "If you come quietly, we won't have to put on the cuffs and shackles. Do we have a deal?"

"Fuck you," came the reply. But Fury let his arms go limp and didn't put up a struggle as the guards zip tied his hands behind his back.

They led him out into the corridor, rounded the turn and passed the reception desk without drawing a comment from the desk clerk. A bank of three elevators served the west wing of the building. The guards moved Fury past the third elevator toward a set of windows while Jenkins pushed the elevator call button. One of the windows was wide open. Jenkins felt a cool breeze on his face as he yanked the hood from Fury's head. With that move as their cue, the two guards then lifted the prisoner off his feet and flung him head first out the open window.

They watched him hurtle twelve stories to the stone courtyard below while Jenkins, fearing vertigo, turned away.

When Jenkins returned to Virginia and appeared for work on Monday morning, one of the Exile Division's administrative people appeared outside his office door as he prepared to twist the combination dial on his four-drawer safe.

"Ready for moving day?" the middle-aged woman asked him cheerily, but without explanation

"Excuse me?" Jenkins answered, turning around in mid-dial.

"You're moving across the hall to a bigger office. Hasn't anyone told you?"

Jenkins offered her a blank stare.

"Oops. Guess I jumped the gun," she replied with a coy smile. "You'd better go see the division chief. He'll fill you in."

So Jenkins left his office with the safe still locked and walked down the hall. He found Victor Barbosa sitting at his computer.

"Somebody just told me I'm being moved to a new office and that you could tell me why," Jenkins opened with a questioning look.

Barbosa rose abruptly with a smile on his face and stepped out from behind his desk to shake Jenkins's hand.

"Congratulations," he told the younger man. "You're the division's new European Branch Chief. Hence the office upgrade."

"Wow. That was quick."

"That's because your promotion was handled outside normal procedure. Need I say more?"

"No. But aren't you going to ask me about Fury?"

"I'm not," Barbosa replied. "And you're not to talk about it again. If anyone asks, send him to me. Okay?"

"Got it. Funny, though, how fast his death made it into the media. 'Severe depression,' according to *The Boston Globe*."

"Yeah," Barbosa remarked with a knowing look. "I suppose it was only a matter of time before he did himself in. But Fury is history now. Let's move on."

"Sure, but on to what?"

"Before you left for Boston, I said that if the assignment went well, you might get another. Want to hear about it?"

Jenkins hesitated. He hadn't yet adjusted fully to what he'd done in Boston. Things were happening just a little too fast.

"Shoot," he answered, knowing that he dared not show any hesitation.

"Who would you say was our number one enemy among the émigrés?

"Linder. No question about it."

"How would you like to be the one to bring him in?" Barbosa asked with a pointed stare.

Jenkins shook his head.

"We tried it in Basel. Then again in Acapulco," he reminded his boss. "It didn't go off so well."

"I'm not talking about using brute force this time. We'd want a deception operation, more like the one that brought in Fury."

"Sounds good in theory, boss, but Linder and Fury are entirely different animals. With Fury, we had a reckless old fool who was totally dependent on caretakers under our control. The only asset we ever succeeded in moving close to Linder was Fiona Bowles, and he made short work of her. So how are we supposed to persuade him to cross the border and deliver himself neatly into our hands?"

"First off," Barbosa responded, circling back around the desk to retake his seat, "Linder's situation isn't nearly as strong as it used to be. He's lost much of the money he had stashed away in Basel, which is forcing him to make cutbacks. And quite a few of his backers have drifted away. Our psych evaluation staff points out that Linder has also been weakened by his sister's return to America. As well as by our recent moves against him. Then there's Fury's defection, which hit him pretty hard. I could go on, but you get the idea."

"I hear you, but there's a different way of looking at those developments. I get a sense that his sister's return has hardened Linder's attitude toward us. If that's even possible. Look at what he did with the Zuckerman Letter. Now he seems to be cooking up something with Brazilian Intelligence. I wouldn't call him weakened at all. It's more like he's preparing a counterattack."

"Well, you may have something there," Barbosa conceded. "Still, I believe Linder's options have narrowed, and the League's rise has cut into his support base. That's why I think that, if we limit his options even further, there's a good chance he'll take our bait."

"And that bait would be?"

"An offer from the League. Not quite the same one they offered Fury, of course. But a series of inducements that will draw Linder in by degrees. What do you think, Jim? Are you game to give it a go?"

"Am I interested in taking Linder down?" Jenkins replied. "You bet. But what can we offer Linder that he'd find so hard to resist?"

"I think we should invite him to visit America to see for himself whether the League's claims are for real."

A few days after his talk with Barbosa, Jenkins aka Darrel Otis summoned Owen Quist to the DSS safehouse off Chain Bridge Road. Since Quist's trip to Amsterdam, Brussels, and Paris a year earlier, he had traveled to Europe several more times to meet with émigré organizations and foreign intelligence services, including those in Spain, Italy, and Greece. His most recent trip had extended his range to Brazil and Colombia, leaving him exhausted. And even though the DSS had intervened with Quist's boss at StatOil to preserve his career after having spent so much time away, Quist complained that the League trips were too frequent, lasted too long, and harmed relations with his wife.

Even when Quist was back in Washington, the DSS didn't leave him entirely alone. As the League's leading spokesperson, it fell upon Quist to help train other League emissaries for their overseas missions. And whenever the League brought foreign visitors to the U.S. for Potemkin village-style tours, it was Quist's duty to show them around.

Expecting resistance from Quist once he broached the agent's new assignment, Otis opened their meeting with flattery and a bribe.

"It's been two years since we began our work together, Owen, and over a year since your trip to Amsterdam. The Department would like to recognize your service."

As Otis spoke, he slid an unmarked letter-sized envelope across the low table between them. Quist opened it. Enclosed were an extra month's cash pay and a voucher from a high-end tour operator for a weeklong trip for two to Maui, including first-class airfare and accommodations in a five-star hotel.

"Thank you," Quist said with something between a squint and a smile as he read the voucher. "This will go a long way toward placating Denise for all the time I've been gone."

Of course, Denise Quist knew that neither she nor her husband had any choice in how hard he worked for the DSS, but that had never stopped her from griping about it. Nor had it inhibited her from taking for granted the extra perks and pay that Owen had earned for serving his DSS masters so well. Still, Quist hoped that the trip and the extra cash might help to buy her silence. At least for a while.

"You're welcome, Owen," Otis replied. "Now, I realize you haven't been thrilled about taking on so many responsibilities for the League this past year. But you play a very special role in our campaign against the émigré opposition. And you've done an outstanding job so far."

"Thanks for trusting me."

Though Quist's tone was less than enthusiastic, Otis went on.

"The League's impact on the opposition and its state sponsors has exceeded all expectations. Anti-Unionist activity in Europe is weaker now than it's been in years. Even the tenor of discussion among the émigrés has shifted. It's moved away from direct action toward more of a wait-and-see attitude. The League appears to have convinced all but the most rabid anti-Unionists that the winds of change are blowing and that the League represents the only internal opposition capable of challenging Unionist rule."

Here Otis paused to flash Quist a self-satisfied smile.

"So you called me in today just to thank me?"

"To thank you, and to discuss the operation's next phase."

"So my work 'exceeded all expectations' but that still isn't enough?" Quist sputtered. "How much longer do you think we can fool these people into thinking that the League can steal classified documents, hold secret meetings, and move agents in and out across the border without any pushback from the DSS? Didn't you read my report from Brazil? Nascimento's intelligence service isn't swallowing our B.S. any more. Brazil's intelligence chief attended a security conference in London last month and met with Linder while he was there. I'm sure they're up to something. The fact is that Fury's sudden death has raised too many questions. I think it's time the League started easing off."

Otis shook his head.

"Easing off is not an option," he declared emphatically while leaning across the table. "The League may be facing stiffer headwinds now, but the best defense is a strong offense. If we're worried about trouble from Linder's organization, it means we go after Linder himself. And for that, we need your help."

Chapter Twenty-Four: Setback

> "We showed weakness, and weak people are beaten."
> –Vladimir Putin

THURSDAY, 22 DECEMBER 2033

Two days after Jenkins left Boston, Linder read in a London morning newspaper that a "severely depressed" Leonard Fury jumped to his death from an unbarred twelfth story window in a Boston federal prison annex. The article, which cited the state-controlled New York Times, claimed that Fury left a suicide note in which he laid out why he took his own life. The note was so artfully phrased, and written in a style so clearly Fury's own, that even his mother was convinced of its authenticity. Excerpts from the note explained that the rebel leader had ended his life because he realized his "moral and political bankruptcy" and could no longer live with his conscience, "having taken so many lives in the service of a futile cause."

Over breakfast at their Mayfair flat, Linder confessed to Annabel how at odds he felt about Fury's end.

"It was Fury's own damn fault that he landed in Unionist hands," he began. "Whatever he expected over there, clearly things didn't work out as planned. When he realized the gravity of his mistake, he sent me a desperate note asking to arrange a prisoner exchange. At the time, the project seemed so absurd that I didn't even bother to send him a reply. But I was wrong. Now I realize that I let him down."

"But how do you know the note was even genuine?" she asked, as if to console him.

"Maybe it wasn't. But Leonard was my friend. I owed him better."

Later that morning, Linder headed off to meet with Dwight Calder at the latter's club. Linder had been to the Barksdale several times before and liked it better than Allen Hackett's club, though its atmosphere was a bit stuffier and its luncheon menu less appealing to his taste. The two men found each other in the lobby before climbing the flight of steps to the main dining room, where a waiter led them to Calder's favorite table.

"Whisky for you?" Calder suggested when the waiter asked for drink orders.

Linder looked around at the other tables. Seeing that he wouldn't be the only one indulging in spirits before lunch, he nodded yes. After all, it had been only a few hours since he'd heard of Fury's death, and his nerves felt a bit frayed. He closed his eyes for a moment and breathed deeply to calm himself.

"My usual, please," Calder informed the waiter. "And the same for my guest."

When Linder opened his eyes, he found the waiter giving him a concerned look before stepping away.

"So what's your assessment?" Calder went on when they were alone again. "Do you think Fury's dead indeed? Frankly, I find that hard to believe. It wouldn't surprise me if the DSS has him stashed away somewhere."

"That's possible," Linder conceded. "But I think it more likely they've executed him. I simply can't believe that Leonard had the sort of conscience that would drive him to suicide. He was so tremendously gifted at self-justification that I think he would have found a way to go on living even if it required turning logic on its head. My guess is that someone high up in the Party considered it inconvenient for Fury to go on breathing."

"Do you have any evidence for that?"

"Nothing solid. But I spoke to Barton Cao before leaving the office. He said he'd been pushing the League's Paris rep extremely hard to get Fury released. The rep told him in confidence that someone very high in the Party wouldn't allow it."

"But, by the same token," Calder argued, "Fury's death has conveniently gotten the League off the hook for failing to spring him loose. And it's eliminated the risk that Fury might expose the League as a creature of the DSS."

When their whiskies arrived, the two men hoisted glasses in tribute to their fallen comrade.

"I doubt we'll see another like Fury," Calder announced.

"I thought I knew him better than anyone," Linder reflected. "Now I wonder if I understood him at all."

The two men downed their whiskies quickly, shared a bottle of Beaujolais with their meal, and finished it off with a ration of Spanish brandy. When Linder arrived back at his apartment that afternoon, Annabel noticed that his step was unsteady, his eyes glazed and his speech slightly slurred.

"I see you've started with the whisky again," she noted with a disapproving look. "Is this going to become a trend?"

"No, it's just the odd one," Linder replied.

"Is it because of your friend Leonard?"

"Yes. I wouldn't have expected it. But you never know how much someone means to you until you lose them."

Annabel put a reassuring hand on her husband's cheek and kissed him before she stepped aside as he entered his study and closed the door.

On opening his laptop, Linder found a fresh message from Nelson Furness cautioning him, as before, not to judge Fury too harshly. A more complete story was bound to emerge, the former Prime Minister wrote, and, in any event, no man could look into the soul of another.

But Linder's disquiet would not go away. That night, before retiring, he noticed some lingering physical discomfort from his time spent in captivity that should have drawn his attention sooner. In addition to the dull ache in his joints from felling trees in subzero temperatures, there was a numbness in his fingertips and toes from frostbite, a lingering heartburn from three years of malnutrition, and the odd way his heart seemed to skip a beat from time to time. All this, plus the fact that, at forty-eight years, he was no longer a young man. How much more time, he wondered, did he have to make his mark against the Unionist tyrants?

After the lunch at Calder's club, Linder didn't leave his flat for several days. He spent most of his waking hours behind closed doors in his home office, coming out only to eat. He took no phone calls and said little to Annabel except at meals. He knew she was concerned about his mental state, but she kept her distance and didn't broach the subject of Fury's death. Only once did she mention that Linder might be drinking too much.

"Remind me what's the right amount," he snapped, regretting it immediately.

Annabel backed off and did not mention it again. Instead, she took to drawing Linder out with light conversation at each meal and sitting with him every morning and afternoon when she brought his coffee. Her only concession to worry was her decision to remove the 9-millimeter pistol from Linder's desk drawer while he slept, lest he think of using it on himself.

But Linder had never been one for self-condemnation. Most often, he acknowledged his errors and resolved to not to repeat them or despair over them. Nor was he inclined toward survivor's guilt. He had risked his life to escape the labor camps. Now he lived an affluent life in London while the men he left behind went on suffering. But was he obliged to sacrifice himself for their sake? Or would they prefer that he fight on? He knew what the good ones would want. It was just that the fight seemed harder and harder to win.

As for the League, whom he held responsible for luring Leonard Fury back to America, Linder felt conflicted. Part of him strongly distrusted the League, though he couldn't prove that it was a sham. The other part, like Fury, nursed an irrational hope that the group might somehow be genuine, or at least redeemable, and that it might someday play a role in overthrowing the Unionist regime. Above all, Linder wanted to make a difference with the time he had left, even if he might not live long enough to see Unionism fall.

Making a difference was important to Linder because, ever since his flight from Beirut, he had a sinking feeling that he was living on borrowed time. Even before the League's arrival on the scene, support for the émigré opposition movement had been waning. And now the League was steadily gaining dominance over that movement, largely at the expense of established émigré leaders like Fury, Cao, and himself. Even some foreign intelligence services that ought to have known better had gone over to the League. Worse yet, many émigrés who were no admirers of Unionism were nonetheless returning to America, seduced by the extravagant promises of the New Economic Plan.

As Linder emerged from his days-long funk, his thoughts for the future revolved more and more around the League. Above all, it was essential that he determine once and for all if the League were legitimate. If it were, he was prepared, however reluctantly, to throw his support behind it. If not, he would dedicate himself to destroying it. But what made him tremble to the marrow of his bones was that, to know which path was correct, he might have to cross the U.S. border and see for himself.

Not until the following weekend did Linder feel entirely himself again. He opened the windows in his office, threw open the shades, and returned all the soiled coffee cups and whisky glasses to the kitchen. The first phone call he took on Saturday morning was from Allen Hackett, freshly returned from Ottawa after his first few weeks of being posted there.

"I met some friends of yours in Ottawa," Hackett began.

"Is that so? Who might they be?"

"Jack Poirier and Maria Silva."

For a moment, Linder didn't know what to say. The last he'd heard from Cao, both Poirier and Silva were missing somewhere inside the U.S. after having entered with agents of the League.

"That's terrific news," he said at last, feigning enthusiasm at Hackett's acquaintance with the pair. "How are they?"

"In fine fettle. They came to Ottawa about a week ago and spent an entire day meeting with us. But Maria and her husband are back in London now. I've invited them to our London HQ for a debriefing tomorrow about what they they've learned. Would you like to join us for tea afterward? They're taking the evening train to Paris and wanted to experience a traditional English tea before they left."

"Certainly," Linder replied, amazed that Silva was in London. "Just name the place. I'll be there."

"Meet us at four in the Park Room at the Grosvenor House, Park Lane. They serve the best high tea in London."

Linder was still puzzled about the circumstances of Maria Silva's reappearance when he arrived at the Grosvenor House the following afternoon. He had called Barton Cao immediately after speaking with Hackett, and Cao told him that his niece had called him upon arriving in London the night before. Cao was brimming with questions for her and urged Linder to learn as much as he could about her time with the League so they could compare notes later.

Hackett, Silva, and her husband, Gordon Mook, were already seated in a corner booth when Linder found them in the Park Room, drinking tea and sampling from the assorted finger sandwiches, cakes and pastries heaped onto the restaurant's trademark three-tiered tower. Silva looked much the same as she had when Linder met her in Paris earlier that autumn. She wore little or no make-up, and her olive complexion appeared a bit paler than before, though perhaps it was just the ambient light. Perhaps she had also lost weight, though her gray pantsuit made that difficult to judge. Her husband, as tall and athletic as before, held out his hand to deliver a surprisingly tepid handshake for a man of his youth and physique.

Once Linder was seated, he ordered a pot of full-bodied Assam tea. Hackett opened the conversation by noting that, during her debriefing at MI5 headquarters, Maria had declared the League to be the only effective opposition group currently operating on American soil.

After a nod from Hackett, Maria then launched into a brief summary of the League's goals, organization, reach, and its recent successes and failures. Little of this was new to Linder, as he had received similar information from other sources. But here was someone who had crossed the border and seen the League up close. Just how strong were they? And what were their chances of overthrowing the Unionist regime?

"I must tell you that I speak now as an official representative of the League," she began with a masklike expression that gave nothing away. "During our time over there, Gordon and I dedicated ourselves to helping the League in any way we could."

"I see," Linder replied, sensing that Silva had just thrown up a barrier between them. "I respect your commitment to the cause, Maria but, to be frank, I'd much rather have your unvarnished personal opinion of the League than its official line."

Silva cast a veiled glance at her husband, and then at Hackett, before responding.

"And that's exactly what I will give you. Only you must understand that my opinion and the position of the League are entirely the same."

"And how does that square with your uncle's views of the League? You worked for him while you were in Paris, as I recall."

Silva bridled and for a moment her eyes flashed with anger.

"My perspective has changed since I left Paris. I'll be giving my uncle a full report on my return there."

"So what then is your net assessment of the League?" Linder pressed on, ignoring her evasions. "Is it a genuine opposition movement capable of dislodging Unionism? Or just a pack of wannabes working under covert DSS direction?"

"Oh, it's genuine, all right," Silva replied, choosing to disregard Linder's provocation.

"Then explain to me how the League manages to operate under the DSS's nose when every other opposition organization has been driven out of the country."

"Times have changed, Warren. The Unionist Party has weakened, while the League has had the benefit of starting out fresh, with an entirely new roster of members who were never compromised by the DSS."

"So what makes you think that the Party has weakened?

"Recent developments. Take the NEP. The broken economy forced the Party to implement major reforms, which were a massive departure from Party orthodoxy. Ordinary citizens noticed that, and they've smelled weakness."

"But how can ordinary people find out about the League if it's a secret organization?" Linder demanded. "The media are censored and DSS informants are embedded in every workplace, union, church, and social organization. How does one join the League, let alone commit a subversive act, without being arrested on the spot?"

"You have to remember," Silva pointed out coolly, "that the Party's power is concentrated in the hands of relatively few committed cadres, who live isolated from the masses. Rank-and-file members keep their mouths shut and wait to see which way the wind blows. And don't forget that the Unionist system is heavily dependent on largely apolitical middle managers and technicians carried over from the old administration. All those paper pushers get up and go to work each morning for the regime, but they're far from happy about it. They talk to one other."

Linder nodded. Much of what Silva said was reasonable, but somehow it didn't ring true coming from her. When he first met Silva, Barton Cao had described his niece as a headstrong young woman who made her own choices. And Linder had seen first-hand evidence of her independence and resourcefulness when she found a hiding place for Grace Kuroda in Paris's Quartier Asiatique. Yet now Silva claimed that her views matched those of the League. What had happened?

But rather than drill down into her answers, Linder nodded again, sipped his tea, and changed the subject.

"So what prompted you to stop in London on your way home?" he asked, assuming a more relaxed manner.

"I came because I have a message for you," she replied.

"For me?" Linder repeated, momentarily caught off guard. "From whom?"

"From the League's shadow foreign minister, Charles Bracken. He's an admirer of yours and would like to meet you. He's also keen to introduce you to other League leaders, but he isn't free to travel outside of North America. So he asked me to invite you to meet with him in Canada."

Linder responded with a smile that didn't extend to his eyes.

"Please thank Mr. Bracken for his kind invitation, but I'm going to decline. My confidence in the League hasn't yet reached the point where I can justify such a trip. And the next few months are going to be very busy for me."

A cloud drifted over Silva's face. She glanced once again at her husband, and then at Hackett, whose expression turned stony.

"May I ask what it is about the League that gives you pause, Warren?" the MI5 official broke in.

"Their lack of direct action," Linder answered, meeting Hackett's gaze head on. "The League has yet to demonstrate that they have the will and the capacity to seize power by any and all means. For example, where are the labor and student strikes? The demonstrations and sit-ins? The assassinations and bombings? Until the League comes out openly to confront the Unionists in tangible ways, I don't see much point in talking to them."

As someone who had some time ago renounced violent confrontation and embraced information warfare, Linder knew that his stance might seem inconsistent. But his aim was to put Silva and Hackett back on their heels. And he doubted that either would note the contradiction, since Linder also supported hard-liners like Fury and Cao.

"One more example," Linder went on, "why no cyber attacks? Even one big one would destroy the Party's aura of invincibility and sow panic among the apparatchiks. And why no sabotage? If I saw your people carry out a sustained program of direct action challenging the regime, I'd be much more likely to accept Mr. Bracken's invitation. In fact, seeing that my personal affairs are in a rather hellish state, if I truly believed that the League were up to the task, I might just chuck it all and throw in with them. In a few weeks I'll turn forty-nine and I want very much to see the Party fall before I die. To me, nothing else matters. At this point, it's all about action, action, action."

Silva's face assumed a thoughtful expression while she nodded in apparent understanding. Meanwhile, Hackett's was a frozen mask.

Chapter Twenty-Five: Warnings

> "Fear has its uses, but cowardice has none."
> *—Mahatma Gandhi*

TUESDAY, 24 JANUARY 2034

In January, Linder toured several East Asian capitals where large numbers of American émigrés had settled after the Unionist takeover. For three weeks, he gave near-nightly speeches to anti-Unionist audiences and met with major donors in Bangkok, Ho Chi Minh City, Singapore, Manila, Sydney, and Auckland. While the League hadn't yet made deep inroads among the émigrés there, word had spread that a new resistance group had emerged within America's borders, and that it promised to inject new life into the anti-Unionist cause.

Owing to his concerns about the steady growth of League influence abroad, Linder made an unplanned stop in Paris on his way home to consult with Barton Cao. Over dinner at Cao's favorite Vietnamese restaurant, the two men discussed Linder's Asian tour as well as news relevant to the émigré opposition in Europe.

"So what's the latest word from your niece?" Linder asked toward the end of their meal. "Has Maria's enthusiasm for the League waned at all?"

"On the contrary," Cao replied, making a grim face. "She has become a zealous League advocate, to the point of being tiresome. I assume you've read her recent debriefing reports that I emailed to you?"

"I have. And, as you said about Poirier a while back, if only a third of what she says is true, an entirely new phenomenon would seem to be emerging over there."

But the irony was heavy in Linder's voice.

"The question is," Cao noted, "are we to believe her any more than we would trust a conniver like Poirier?"

"I don't know, Bart. You're her uncle. Do you think she could have been conned? Or, worse, turned against us?"

Cao stared blankly into the distance before answering.

"Conned?" he repeated, as if considering the idea for the first time. "It's possible. But disloyal? I find that hard to believe. In many ways, Maria seems as anti-Unionist as she's ever been, though she favors the League's odds of ousting the Unionists more than ours. Still, sometimes, especially when she calls me late at night, or after she's had a few glasses of wine, I sense that she may have reservations about the League that she's not willing to share."

"Do you think Poirier may have colored her views toward the League?" Linder asked, shifting uncomfortably in his seat.

"It's hard to say. Maria isn't someone who's easily influenced. But I wouldn't put anything past Jack. And he's spent much more time with the League than Maria. Don't you think it's odd that he spends all his time in North America now and doesn't ever come back to France?"

"Not necessarily," Linder cautioned. "Remember, Jack has always been Fury's guy. But with Fury dead, he has little reason to spend time in Paris. In fact, I wouldn't be surprised if he were on the League's payroll by now."

Cao gave a knowing nod.

"That would make sense," he agreed. "And it also jibes with the fact that it was Jack who wrote the note inviting Fury to return to the U.S."

"And now it's Maria who's delivered the invitation for me to meet the League in Canada. Do you think I should even consider it?"

"I wouldn't, but then it's not my call. Have you talked to Annabel about it?"

"No. I didn't want to worry her, since I haven't decided yet."

"Well, if you did choose to go, what reason would you give her?"

"To give the League a proper grilling, I suppose," Linder answered after a moment's pause, caught off guard by the question. "If they didn't give a proper account of themselves, I could come home and expose them as a fraud."

"Yes, you could do that. But do you really think that would be the end of it? The League has powerful supporters. They would strike back at you."

"But what if I had the stronger case? What if I pointed out the League's failure to carry out cyber attacks, sabotage, or even peaceful demonstrations against the Unionist regime? It's a massive weak spot for them."

At that moment, Linder felt himself vacillate between the urge to get to the bottom of the League's story and his misgivings over the risks entailed in doing so.

"Of course it's a weak spot," Cao countered. "But if you're right about the League being under Unionist influence, taking them on could bring the DSS down on your head. Do you really want that?"

"Well, it wouldn't be the first time. If the DSS came after me for attacking the League, it would tend to prove my case. So let them try."

After wrapping up his business in Paris, Linder traveled to Geneva for client meetings, and then on to Lausanne, where he joined Annabel at the Lausanne Palace for a surprise visit to Caroline Kendall. That evening the couple enjoyed dinner with Caroline at a lakeside restaurant.

The next morning, Linder awoke before his wife and took an early shower. Afterward, he examined his face in the half-fogged mirror. With his forty-ninth birthday a few weeks away, he was highly conscious of having been alive for nearly half a century. To his dismay, the lines in his face had deepened into creases during recent years, and his dark brown eyes shone from ever-deeper sockets. All at once he felt the weight of his former captivity and his chronic state of stress ever since. How much fight did he have left in him? He still felt that his life's mission was to resist the Unionist regime, but that regime now seemed more and more like some impregnable fortress that could only be taken from the inside. And such a task, like the conquest of ancient Troy, would likely require some bold stratagem beyond any he had conceived to date.

Linder and Annabel ate breakfast in their room before catching a cab to the university, where Caroline had offered to show them around. One of the stops on their tour was the art atelier where Caroline had begun taking instruction in figure painting and landscape art during her summer break. At her cubicle in the atelier, Caroline showed Linder and Annabel her recent compositions, most of which were academic exercises consisting of intricate pencil drawings or nude figure sketches.

But what caught Linder's eye were a series of charcoal sketches of him that Caroline had drawn from imagination as part of an exercise in dramatic illustration. The assignment had been to imagine a protagonist and portray him or her in scenes that demonstrated heightened emotion or stress. Linder leafed through the stack of sketches, singling out several that appeared to show him a decade earlier. They pictured him in a Virginia interrogation prison soon after his arrest, then in a Yukon labor camp barracks, then cutting timber in the boreal forest, and later toiling in an underground tungsten mine. The images were uncannily accurate.

"How on earth did you dream up these scenes?" he asked. "You couldn't have captured them better if you'd been right there beside me."

Caroline let out a soft laugh.

"Don't you remember how I used to badger you endlessly to tell me stories about your work for the government, your life in the camps, and your escape? Well, when you told me your stories, I would close my eyes and visualize the scenes. I created a whole world in my mind that I can still see, any time I choose."

Then she brought out a folder with three more sketches. One showed a male figure with a black hood over his head and his hands zip tied behind his back, another with the figure being thrown head first out an open window, and a third with the figure lying face down in a shadowy courtyard.

"I drew these before I had any idea who the character was. I didn't realize he might be Leonard Fury until a month later, when I read about his death."

"But the official story is that he committed suicide. What made you think that he was pushed?"

Caroline offered Linder a shrug and an insouciant smile.

"It was just an idea I had at the time. I can't explain where it came from."

"Do you have any others like this?"

"Quite a few. That exercise got me started doing more illustrations based on intuitive flashes that I get from time to time."

"Do you have any more of me?"

"I used to, but I had to clean out my storage space a while back and discarded them by mistake. Why?"

"Call me superstitious, but I had experiences in the Yukon that made me a believer in all kinds of strange things. Anyway, if you get any flash images of me, please call me right away," Linder replied

"Sure," Caroline nodded. Linder responded with a smile. Annabel did not.

Chapter Twenty-Six: Decision

"Fortune favors the bold."
–Latin Maxim

MONDAY, 13 MARCH 2034

Soon after his return from Lausanne, Linder called on former Prime Minister Nelson Furness, who listened in silence as Linder informed him about the League's invitation to meet in Canada.

"I advise strongly against accepting," Furness replied at last. "What if the Unionists were to capture you in Canada, carry you across the border and claim that you defected like Leonard Fury? Even if you never collaborated with them, they could make it appear as if you had."

"Perhaps so," Linder replied, "but after the bad odor surrounding Leonard's death, who would believe them? Anyone who knows me would understand that I'm an implacable enemy of Unionism. The émigré community would blame the League for my disappearance. No one would trust it ever again."

"On that point you may be correct, Warren. But is it wise to stake your life on it? You have many good years ahead of you, a devoted wife, a fortune at your disposal, and an important mission to carry out If you were to fall into enemy hands, the anti-Unionist cause would suffer a heavy blow. Who else in your place would wage the information war or raise large sums for the cause, as you have done? No, Warren, we need you alive."

It was sound advice, but Linder was not yet ready to give up on the idea of confronting the League in Canada. Yes, it was risky. But how could he properly evaluate the League without questioning its leaders directly?"

That afternoon he phoned Benjamin Payne in Berlin and asked him if his Free American Patriots still held the League in high regard. If so, did Payne think it safe for Linder to meet with League representatives in Canada? Payne gave his sincere assurances that he and the FAP considered the League absolutely trustworthy and that Linder faced no risk meeting with them so long as he remained on the Canadian side of the frontier.

Linder also called Paul Wagner, the Kamas survivor whom he had met in Geneva two years before and with whom he had spoken several times since. Only after the call failed to go through did he remember that Wagner had planned to take his family back to Pennsylvania some months earlier. He resolved to check on whether anyone had heard from Wagner since, using the same sources he had used to check on his sister.

Linder spent the rest of the afternoon discussing the League with other émigré activists, most of whom thought favorably of the League and saw little risk in meeting with them in Canada.

The next morning he called Barton Cao.

"I'm considering a trip to Canada to meet with Charles Bracken and others from the League," Linder began. "Could your niece get in contact with Bracken and ask him to make the arrangements? I would arrive in Montreal around the twentieth."

"Must you hold the meeting in Canada?" Cao replied. "I would caution you to meet the League only in a country free of strong Unionist influence, which rules out Canada and Mexico."

"Bracken claims he has to stay close to the border because he can't be out of the country for long. That seems reasonable enough for a man in his position."

"It's your call, Warren, but if you insist on seeing Bracken in Canada, at least do it as far from the frontier as possible. Let him come to you in Ottawa or Montreal, but certainly not Toronto or

Windsor, where the U.S. is only a stone's throw across the water. And don't cross the U.S. border under any circumstances."

"Don't worry on that score," Linder stated emphatically. "I have absolutely no intention of going across."

"One other point," Cao added. "I don't like it one bit that your MI5 friend, Hackett, seems so eager for you to go. My Canadian sources tell me that British intelligence in Canada is riddled with DSS agents. And, as for my niece's ties to the League, I can no longer vouch for her. Frankly, Maria has become an enigma to me."

As he spoke that final sentence, the pain in Cao's voice was palpable.

"Are you saying that Maria is no longer to be trusted?" Linder asked with alarm.

"I can't say that. But if you've already decided to go, I'll tell her about your plans so she and Poirier can set things up."

Linder pondered Cao's response for a moment. Yes, he was beyond considering the trip now. He had decided to go. As for Maria, her role in the League was one of the points he intended to investigate. And when he was done, he hoped she would no longer be an enigma.

"Great. Anything else?" he asked Cao.

A pause followed.

"Actually, there is one thing I thought you'd want to know," Cao replied. "It's about your friend who worked at the American consulate here. Grace Kuroda."

"Is Grace okay? Last I heard, she was in Australia."

"Yes, she was," Cao repeated.

"Was? Can you be more specific?"

"Maria heard from a mutual friend in Sydney that Grace received a message a couple of weeks ago from her father. He wanted her help in escaping the U.S. Against everyone's advice, Grace traveled to Canada to work out a plan. After making a substantial down payment to some human traffickers, she awaited her dad in Windsor, Ontario, just across the water from Detroit. Then she vanished. I've asked my

Canadian sources to investigate, but they've come up dry. Other than concluding that her father's messages were almost certainly fakes."

Linder's heart sank. Kuroda was nobody's fool. How could she have let herself be taken in like that? Could Maria have played a role in it? And if so, did he dare go through with his plans to travel to Canada?

"I'm sorry, Warren," Cao went on. "Grace was a brave woman."

Linder had no words to respond.

Linder took lunch later that day with Dwight Calder at the Barksdale Club. Over a light meal, Linder informed Calder of his plans to meet Charles Bracken in Montreal and assured him that he would take all necessary precautions.

"I plan to stay in Canada less than a week," Linder explained. "Would you mind tending to our clients while I'm away? You needn't tell them where I've gone, only that I'm out of the country on business."

"Of course, Warren," Calder replied. "But how can you be sure that your precautions will be enough in a place like Montreal? The city is crawling with DSS agents. Why not meet in Bermuda, or the Caymans, or one of the other British islands in the Caribbean? At least there you'd enjoy a level playing field."

"Bracken says he and his people can't stray far from the border. I doubt the Caribbean would work for them."

"Does Furness know you're going?"

"He advised me against it."

"Then you must have some pretty strong reasons for going. Would you care to share them with me?" Calder was clearly nonplussed.

"Well, without listing them all, I'd say that a big reason is that my donor base is increasingly tapped out," Linder replied. "There's no denying it any more. My primary donors are tired of pouring money into émigré groups that have so few assets left inside the U.S. The smart money realizes that the Unionist regime is not going to collapse of its own weight. To bring it down will require major action from the inside. The League claims to have inside assets, but I've seen very few signs of it. If they could show evidence of genuine resistance, I think I could rally my donors for one last offensive against the regime. Which might earn me a seat at the table if the League succeeds."

Though Calder nodded, his expression did not brighten.

"Has it occurred to you that the reason you haven't seen any action from the League is that they have no inside assets?" he asked Linder.

"It's possible, but I would never consider meeting their leaders if I didn't think they had some sort of base inside. I have it from a reliable source that a number of high Party officials have lost confidence in Twitchell and are clamoring for change. Some of them, I'm told, are former Terzian backers concerned for their safety, now that the Gang of Three has pushed Terzian aside."

"Well, I can't begin to address that," Calder conceded. "I have no evidence of it either way. Is there anything else I can help you with?"

"Actually, there is," Linder replied with a contrite look. "Before I go, I'd like to leave you with this."

He handed Calder a sealed envelope.

"In the unlikely event that I don't return, I authorize you to release this to the media. But only after my death has been announced in the British press. Not a moment sooner."

On his return to the office after lunch, Linder placed another phone call, this time to Caroline Kendall in Lausanne. After catching up on recent events, Linder broached his primary reason for calling.

"Do you remember our conversation about those sketches you made of me?" he began.

"How could I not?" Caroline replied with a playful air.

"Do you happen to have any new ones?"

"Funny that you should ask. I drew another last night."

"Could you take a photo of it with your phone and text it to me?"

"No problem. Just a sec."

After a few moments, the photo arrived among Linder's text messages. He opened it, enlarged it to fill his screen, and gave it a closer look. The charcoal sketch showed him dressed in a foul weather jacket and fedora hat, stepping off a narrow wooden dock onto a low-slung motorboat floating on a moonlit lake.

"I don't recognize the scene," Linder asserted. "Could it be something that hasn't happened yet?"

"I don't know. But I had an uneasy feeling as I drew it. If I were you, Warren, I wouldn't board that boat."

"I'll take it under advisement. Meanwhile, my sweet, would you do me a favor and not mention this to Annabel? I may be traveling soon and wouldn't want to alarm her."

"If you insist," Caroline replied. "You don't plan to go anywhere near a lake, do you?"

That evening, Linder informed Annabel that he had received new evidence boosting his confidence in the League's legitimacy and that he intended to travel to Canada to meet with several of its leaders.

"But you've always expressed suspicion about the League," she replied with a puzzled look. "What changed your mind?"

"I received a personal invitation, delivered through a couple of colleagues of mine who've been spending time with them in the U.S. I believe the time has come to make a determination about the League, one way or another."

"You say you'll be traveling to Canada. You don't intend to cross the U.S. border, do you?"

"Surely not," he assured her, perhaps too vigorously. "I plan to meet them in Montreal, where it ought to be perfectly safe. But to put your mind at ease, why don't you come with me? Have you ever been to Montreal? It's a beautiful city, 'full of French charm,' as they say. I think you'd love it."

"When are you thinking of going?"

"Early next week. We could spend a couple of days relaxing in the Old City and then I'd go meet them for dinner somewhere. We could fly back to London over the weekend."

Linder could tell from the look in her eyes that Annabel wasn't keen on the idea.

"Will Dwight or anyone else from the opposition be coming with us? I don't like the idea of you meeting these people alone."

"I expect that Jack Poirier will be there. He's the old colleague who passed along the League's invitation. And possibly also Barton Cao's niece, Maria. You may remember her. She was the one who helped spirit Grace Kuroda out of Paris to Australia. But apart from the one business meeting, you and I would be on our own in Montreal and could kick up our heels a bit. "

"All right," Annabel answered, twisting the wedding ring around her finger. "I'll come. But I must confess, I don't have a good feeling about it."

She remained silent for several seconds before speaking again, now with a troubled expression.

"May I tell you a story?" she asked. "It's about Richard, my first husband."

"Of course. Go ahead," Linder replied, despite sensing trouble ahead.

"I've never told this to anyone," she went on. "But every week or so during the last six months that he and I were married, I had a recurring dream. In it, Richard came to me and said, 'I'm leaving you.' How I hated that dream! It was so upsetting! I confronted him about it several times, but each time he swore up and down that he would never ever divorce me. Then, a week after the last dream, he died of a stroke. That's why, before we travel, I must ask you this: You're not leaving me, Warren, are you?"

Chapter Twenty-Seven: Montreal

> "We will either find a way or make one."
> –*Hannibal Barca*

WEDNESDAY, 22 MARCH 2034

Linder and Annabel flew to Montreal the following Wednesday. It was a sunny morning and Linder was in an upbeat mood, looking forward to showing his wife the city's sights, dining in its celebrated French restaurants, and determining once and for all whether the League's claims held water. But once the couple passed through airport security and settled in the first-class lounge at Heathrow, Linder sensed that he was being watched by two of his fellow passengers, one a well-dressed middle-aged woman and the other a sturdy fellow in his mid-thirties wearing khaki trousers, white dress shirt and a cheap blue blazer. But both stayed seated when he went to the men's room and later to the bar for a quick drink. So he brushed off his sensation as a false alarm.

Nonetheless, the sense of being watched returned upon arrival in Montreal while he and Annabel picked up their checked luggage and met their hired driver in the airport arrivals hall. The hair on the back of Linder's neck pricked up once again as the driver led them out to the town car. While neither of the two suspects from the London airport lounge was in sight, he sensed that others might be watching. If well trained, they would be hard to spot. Still, he reassured himself, if any plot were afoot to snatch him, it was unlikely to go down until

269

later in his visit, closer to the time of his meeting with the League. And it was the sort of risk to which he had grown accustomed. Or so he thought.

As it happened, the ride to the Hotel Gault, a luxury property in the heart of Old Montreal, went off without incident.

Though Annabel hadn't seemed worried during the flight, she surprised Linder by confessing her unease soon after they sat for dinner at an elegant French eatery located a block from their hotel.

"I've seldom seen you so on edge," she began as soon as the wine was poured. "When you first described your reasons for coming here, you made it sound almost routine. Is there something you're not telling me?"

"Of course not," Linder replied, feigning surprise. "As I said earlier, I've come to hear out the League and decide whether they're to be trusted. No matter how things turn out, we'll go back to London this weekend and our lives will go on just as before."

"Except that your decision will carry a great deal of weight with your fellow émigrés. I can see how much you worry that the League is slowly taking over the anti-Unionist movement from within. But why must you alone shoulder the burden of stopping it? Why not let others take the lead for a change?"

"I did let others lead for the longest time. For years, Leonard Fury was the brightest star in the émigré firmament. But when his star fell, no one else was willing to step up and take his place."

"So now you've set yourself up as Unionism's Public Enemy Number One," Annabel complained. "Not that your former colleagues in the DSS haven't tried to destroy you before. But what does that portend for our future together, Warren? Must we forever live life looking over our shoulders?"

Linder reached out to take his wife's hand while offering her an encouraging look.

"The dangers to me now are no greater than they were a week or a month ago," he told her. "And this business with the League will resolve itself quickly, one way or another. Besides, the DSS won't dare make a move against me while they're so desperate to rebuild trade relations with the U.K."

"You sound so sure of yourself, Warren. But if sitting down with the League is nothing to worry about, then why have you been so careful to keep your distance from them until now? And why do I have such a bad feeling about it?"

Linder shrugged, smiled, and raised his glass to sniff the wine.

"Bad feelings are just a reminder to be careful. Rest assured, Annabel, I don't plan on taking any unnecessary chances."

Linder had chosen his words carefully. He would be taking chances, all right. And perhaps some very big ones.

The next day, Linder and Annabel ate breakfast at their hotel and set out on foot toward the Champ-de-Mars Park, Montreal City Hall, and the Bonsecours Market, guided by a detailed walking tour of Old Montreal described in their travel book. After a light lunch at an outdoor café, they were walking past the Notre-Dame Basilica when they heard a pipe organ. Once drawn inside, they took a pew in the rear to listen to the soaring finale of the Saint-Saens Organ Symphony, which lent a dramatic note to the work that Linder knew lay ahead. All at once, he felt very alone.

After leaving the cathedral, Linder and Annabel returned to their hotel for a glass of wine and an afternoon nap. When they awoke, both were in a more buoyant mood, having managed to put the previous day's anxieties behind them. But, soon after, their hotel phone rang.

"Hello, Mr. Linder? It's Harry Cowen, from the British consulate in Montreal. I have a message from Allen Hackett. May I come up?"

The call came as a complete surprise, as Linder had never told Hackett of his travel plans.

When Cowen arrived at the door, Linder invited him in and offered him a choice of wine or mineral water. The man was a pale, cerebral-looking fellow of about thirty, dressed in flannel trousers and a camel's hair sport coat. His eager demeanor reminded Linder of the British expression, "keen as mustard."

"Allen regrets that he wasn't able to come in person," the young diplomat began. "He was obliged to travel to Vancouver on short notice."

"Well, I hadn't expected to see him here, so it's not a problem. But, if you don't mind my asking, how did Allen know I would be coming?"

Cowen bared his teeth in a friendly grin.

"He found out from Jack Poirier. Jack's also been delayed, but he wanted to pass along some changes in your meeting arrangements. You see, Charles Bracken and the others whom you've come to see can't cross the border just yet. And when they do come, they won't have much time on this side. So they've arranged for a get-together tomorrow evening at a hotel that's a bit closer to the border. Jack will be there, along with Maria Silva, and Owen Quist. They can fill you in when you arrive."

"So how am I supposed to find them?" Linder bristled. It was an obvious bait-and-switch, and he didn't like it.

"I have a car. I'll swing by tomorrow afternoon to take you there."

"What kind of a place is it?" Linder asked, not quite willing to reject the new arrangement out of hand.

"It's a lakeside resort hotel called the Auberge Saint-Pierre. Quite nice, I assure you."

Linder cast a sidelong glance at Annabel, who drew a deep breath and frowned. Originally, he had told her that his meeting would take place in Montreal. Now it would be on the shores of a lake that likely formed part of the U.S.-Canadian border. Clearly, Annabel understood the increased risk but seemed resigned, as usual, to letting him have his way in such matters. Still, he couldn't help wondering what his wife might say if Caroline had shown her the sketch of him stepping off a dock onto a motorboat on a moonlit lake.

As soon as Cowen left them, Linder called Allen Hackett's mobile phone, which rang through to voicemail. Instead of leaving a message, he sent a text:

"Harry Cowen was just here. Is he one of yours?"

An hour later came the reply:

"Yes. You can rely on him."

"When is a good time for you to talk?" Linder texted next.

He received no response.

Dinner conversation with Annabel that evening was subdued, as Linder sensed that this was not the only last-minute change of plan he was likely to see during his visit. Annabel clearly distrusted the League, though Linder wasn't prepared to pull the plug on his meeting with them just yet, having come so far. And though Hackett had vouched for Cowen and there seemed no good reason to suspect him, he wasn't so sure any more about Poirier or Silva. And as for Quist and the League's other leaders, nothing seemed impossible.

It was late afternoon the following day when Cowen knocked on the couple's door once again to take Linder to his lakeside meeting. Linder identified Cowen through the peephole, but before he could reach for the door handle, Annabel seized his arm.

"I don't like you going so near the border with this man, Warren. At least, give me Allen Hackett's contact information in case anything goes wrong."

Linder nodded silently, found the contact entry for Hackett on his cell phone, and texted it to her. Then he took Annabel in his arms for several moments before letting her go and reaching again for the door.

"Please turn this way," she said. "I want to get a good look at your face."

He did as she asked and then opened the door.

"Take care of yourself," she said as Linder turned to leave with Cowen.

"No need to worry there," he replied. "That's my specialty."

The sun was low in the sky when Cowan's SUV reached the town of Magog on the northern shore of Lake Memphremagog. Though not visible from there, across the U.S.-Canadian border at the southern end of the lake was the town of Newport, Vermont. Cowen drove east along the lakeshore road until they reached the Auberge Saint-Pierre, a nineteenth-century two-story brick mansion with a modern annex that housed the inn's bar and restaurant. The parking lot was surprisingly full for late March, and Linder guessed that the restaurant might be the only one around that remained open through the off-season.

Cowen led Linder inside, where he found Jack Poirier and Maria Silva seated at the bar. Poirier, looking as fit as ever in khakis and a brown tweed sports jacket, gave Linder a hearty handshake and seemed unusually pleased to see him, given that the two men had never been close. Silva's handshake lacked energy by comparison and her smile appeared less confident than he remembered. But she still cut an elegant figure in a black silk jumpsuit that matched her jet-black hair.

"Owen should be along any moment," Poirier remarked after greeting Linder and Cowen. "What will you have to drink?"

"Oh, sparkling water will be fine. I'm still dehydrated from the flight over," Linder lied, preferring not to cloud his mind with alcohol tonight.

Poirier placed the order with the bartender, along with a light beer for Cowen.

"I'm really excited about putting you and Charles together," Poirier went on, referring to Charles Bracken, the League's shadow foreign minister. "He has so much to share with you about the League's progress."

"I'm sure he does," Linder replied. "But while I have you and Maria alone, I'm interested in hearing your impressions from being in the U.S. You went to investigate the League. So what have they accomplished? And how are they able to attack the regime from within when so many others have failed?"

Poirier and Silva looked at each other as if to decide who should speak first. Contrary to Linder's expectation, it was Silva who took the lead.

"I hardly know where to begin. I've spent over a month across the border, on three separate visits up and down the Eastern Seaboard. I've met dozens of League members, from the rank and file all the way up to senior leaders like Charles. I can tell you that they have members in virtually every important government department at the federal, state, and local level, especially in the big cities. They also wield influence in the labor unions, the media, and the universities. No matter what organization or institution I asked about, they were able to put me in touch with one of their people inside."

Linder offered Silva an approving nod. But how much of what she said could he believe? Had the people she met been bona fide League members embedded in those organizations? Or might they have been DSS stooges, trotted out on demand?"

"How genuine did these League people seem to you?" Linder inquired. "For example, did they seem concerned about being monitored or caught by the DSS?"

"Of course they did, at least in the sense that they observed proper tradecraft around our meetings. But I wouldn't say that they appeared overly worried."

"And how would you account for that? We all know how brutal the DSS can be toward spies and insurgents."

A cloud passed briefly across Silva's face as she cast a glance at Poirier.

"It's hard to say," she replied. "I put that same question to several League people. None of them gave me a completely satisfactory answer. But they all seemed to think that, if anything happened to them, the League would find a way to bail them out."

Linder was about to pose a follow-up question when Poirier interrupted, holding up his mobile phone.

"Hold on, a text just came in from Owen. He says that the others are delayed and that we should join them at their safehouse on the lake. There may also be another leader joining us from Montreal. Which means that dinner will be served at the safehouse, since Bracken's people have to return to Vermont later tonight."

"So we won't be dining here at the Saint-Pierre?" Cowen piped up, half in jest. "I looked them up on Zagat and they have a new chef who's supposed to be fabulous."

Poirier shot Cowen a look that was the equivalent of a kick in the shins. The younger man fell silent.

As for Linder, he didn't particularly care who cooked dinner or what was on the menu, but he did suspect that the sudden change of venue had been cooked up in advance. He turned to Cowen, who did not appear happy.

"Looks like it may be a longer night than we'd planned," he told the junior diplomat. "Will you be okay with driving back tonight, or should we book rooms at the Auberge and return in the morning?"

"Not to worry. I can handle the drive, so long as there's coffee along the way."

"Maria, how about your husband?" Linder asked next. "Will he be joining us?"

"No, Gordon had to stay in Montreal tonight," Silva replied without looking Linder in the eye.

Stay for what, Linder wondered? But he decided against asking to avoid appearing suspicious so early in the game.

Poirier settled the group's bar bill and the foursome retired to the parking lot, where Poirier instructed Cowen to follow him further eastward along the lakeshore road. Ten minutes later, the two cars pulled onto an unmarked gravel road and drove another quarter mile to a clearing on the lake. There they found a two-story shingled Cape Cod-style house that overlooked the water, complete with its own private boathouse and dock. Once the cars' headlamps went dark, the only light sources were the house's ground-floor windows and the crescent moon hanging low over Lake Memphremagog.

As the group stepped onto the front porch, the door opened and Linder saw a man whom he recognized as Owen Quist from prior descriptions. He was a huskily built man in his early fifties whose fleshy face was notable for its neatly trimmed beard and its dissipated mien. He was dressed casually in jeans and a navy zippered fleece over a pale blue dress shirt. Linder came prepared to distrust the man and in that regard Quist did not disappoint.

Quist led the visitors into the spacious living room, where a basic bar had been set up on a sideboard, with unopened bottles of gin, vodka, rye whiskey, red and white wine, mixers, and a twelve pack of Canadian beer. Quist was the only League representative in evidence. As if to address that fact, Quist greeted his guests with an apology.

"I'm afraid I've got some bad news. Charles Bracken informed me just before you arrived that he's been delayed en route, past the point where he could join us for dinner. And he won't be free to travel again until the middle of next week. Charles wanted me to tell you how sorry he is that you came all this way tonight without his being able to see you."

"And what about the other person, the one coming in from Montreal?" Poirier asked.

"No news yet. But, to be frank, I wouldn't count on him, either, unless we hear something very soon."

Upon learning this, Poirier and Silva made long faces, and it appeared to Linder that they were genuinely disappointed. Linder, too, felt let down by the news, though he had expected from the outset that the League might toss a curve ball or two his way to throw him off his game. When he realized that Quist had come alone, he suspected that this might be one of those tricks. It was a bad sign, to be sure, but not necessarily fatal to his plans. So Linder responded in the way that he had anticipated for such an event. He said nothing.

As if on cue, Poirier spoke to break the silence.

"So what's our Plan B?" he asked Quist.

"Well, we can always reschedule for next week, if Warren is willing to wait that long," the League representative offered.

All eyes turned to Linder, whose expression remained unchanged.

"Unfortunately, that won't be possible," Linder declared. "I've set aside several days for meetings, but not a week. I really must be back in London by Monday."

Now the ball was back in Quist's court. Would he let Linder go home or try to keep his fish on the line?

"In that case, might there be someone else in the senior leadership who could come out and take Charles's place?" Silva interjected.

"I've already checked," Quist answered with a discouraged look. "Both Charles and Simon Popovic, who also planned to join us here, are in Boston for meetings of the League's Political Council. Anyone that you'd want to talk to will be at those meetings."

At this, Silva and Poirier exchanged concerned glances.

"How about we all go down to Boston, then?" Poirier proposed in a voice several notes higher than before.

Alarm bells went off in Linder's head. Had this been their plan all along?

"Is such a thing even possible?" Silva asked with apparent sincerity.

Quist stroked his beard and struck a pensive pose.

"It might be," he said. "The motorboat that was supposed to pick up Charles on the other side is still standing by," he noted. "I suppose

I could redirect it to pick us up here instead. Once we're across, arranging a ride to Boston won't be a problem."

And there it was, the ruse to get him across the border. Linder looked away and caught a glimpse of the moonlit lake through the French doors. The room was completely silent.

"If that's what Mr. Linder wants, I'm happy to pick him up here next week and take him back to Montreal," Cowen offered, breaking the silence. "But I'm due at the consulate first thing tomorrow morning. So I'll need to know before I leave tonight."

"And I'm needed in Ottawa tomorrow," Silva added, without giving a reason.

Linder would have liked to know the nature of her business in the capital but decided not to ask. Not yet, at least.

All eyes now turned to Linder. And it was if they all held their breath waiting for his response. But he had no intention of letting them off so easily.

"I agreed to come to Magog, but no further," he declared in firm tones. "Entering U.S. territory is not a risk I care to take."

"I can certainly understand your hesitation, Warren," Quist stepped in, taking charge once again. "Even a year ago, I would have urged against it. But we've made such great strides this past year! We've now reached the point of forming a shadow government to replace the Unionist Party when it falls. Your participation in our planning would be extremely valuable to us."

"And if you're concerned about moving around safely once you're over there," Poirier added, "the League has that fully wired. I've made a half-dozen trips to the East Coast and the only time the police stopped us, it took just one phone call for them to send us on our merry way."

As if seeking confirmation, Poirier cast a furtive glance at Silva, who offered a nod and a tight-lipped smile.

"You know, perhaps we can make lemonade out of lemons here," Quist doubled down. "It seems to me that the best way for you to get a sense of the League's plans and capabilities would be to come to Boston and talk to our Political Council."

"Boston's awfully far away. I don't see how I'd have time, even for a short meeting," Linder responded with a deadpan expression.

The bait-and-switch was plain as day. The League had lured him closer and closer to the border and now they aimed to draw him across. Everyone in the room had to be in on the game. And if he refused to go along, what then? Would they take him by force? He had expected this moment, and he had planned for it. But would his plan work?

"Just suppose for a moment that we could make it happen," Quist went on, "What is the latest flight you could take and still get back to London in time for your work there?"

Linder decided to go along with the question.

"No later than Sunday evening," he replied.

"Okay, then, indulge me for a moment," Quist proposed. "Let's see, if we left tonight, we could be in Boston tomorrow morning. Once there, we could take a short nap, meet the leadership over an early dinner on Saturday, drive back to Canada overnight, and be in Montreal Sunday morning. If that works for you, I could call Charles tonight and ask him to arrange it."

"I don't know, Owen. That seems awfully tight," Linder answered, looking down and shaking his head. "And doing it on the fly leaves a great deal to chance."

"I fully understand," Quist assured him. "It's a lot to think about on such short notice. But wouldn't it be a shame for you to have come all the way from London only to stop on the threshold of playing a pivotal role in the League's future? I'm sure Charles and Simon are eager to include you in their plans."

"You could play a major role in the new national order, Warren," Poirier added, waxing eloquent. "No less than the role Leonard might have played if he hadn't lost his head before we could spring him free."

Out of the corner of his eye, Linder noticed Quist shoot Poirier a look that would have stuck six inches out the back of a more sensitive man. Did Poirier have no sense of irony in mentioning Fury's name after having helped lure the man into the DSS's clutches?

"I appreciate the offer," Linder answered, "but it seems like a bridge too far. Let me think about it over dinner and I'll let you know if I change my mind. Meanwhile, let's take advantage of the fact that you're all here to answer my questions."

"Yes, of course," Quist said, pretending not to be disappointed. "And I'm told dinner is ready. So why don't we adjourn to the dining room and continue our discussion there?"

A chorus of assent followed as each of the five freshened his or her drink and followed Quist to the dinner table, which had been laid by a local couple hired to cater the meal. Linder had spotted them only once, when they popped out of the kitchen to bring wine to the table. But if Bracken and Popovic had been delayed only at the last minute, which required moving the dinner from the Auberge Saint-Pierre to the lake house, how had Quist managed to find a caterer and have dinner ready so quickly? Something didn't add up.

Nor was dinner a slapdash affair. It consisted of roast duck medallions in red wine sauce, fresh asparagus, and fingerling potatoes. And the wine was an excellent St. Emilion, so delicious that Linder broke his rule not to consume alcohol that evening. Four bottles stood ready on the table, nearly a bottle for each person. Once the first glass went down and refills were poured, all tensions seemed to dissolve.

Linder asked Quist, Poirier, and Silva all manner of questions about the League, to which they responded with measured answers. Though he suspected that some of their responses were incorrect, he detected no transparent lies. The League seemed to have schooled its three spokespeople very well. Cowen also joined the discussion, pointing out how the volume of cross-border traffic had grown since the Canada-U.S. treaty and how border controls had become more lax. By the time dessert reached them, the five were swapping tales of old exploits, gossiping about mutual acquaintances, and sharing many a laugh.

Silva, in particular, seemed to relax noticeably the longer the meal wore on.

"You'd be amazed how closely the League has been working with friendly foreign intelligence agencies," she gushed at one point. "Canadian, Mexican, Brazilian, British, and many others. There's a torrent of information flowing out from the League while funds and tech support flow in. That's why Gordon and I relocated to Ottawa, to be closer to the action."

An uneasy look passed across Harry Cowen's face when she mentioned British Intelligence. Was the League's cooperation with the British more robust than Allen Hackett had let on?

Sitting back in his chair with yet another glass of Bordeaux, Linder put it all together. The League seemed better organized and more capable than he had thought. If left alone, it might soon complete its domination of the émigré opposition. Its effectiveness against the Unionist Party was another matter, however. Why had the League thus far not scored any major hits against the regime? Could the League be a creature of the DSS, either by design or by capture? Linder had ample evidence pointing in that direction, but no ironclad proof. If he went home to denounce the League, its followers would deny his claims, maintaining that he was peddling sour grapes. The only way to stop the League, and its possible DSS masters, would be to bring home irrefutable evidence of the League's perfidy. Or, alternatively, if he failed to return entirely—that, too, might serve as a kind of proof.

The conversation lagged for a moment and it seemed to Linder that the others were all staring at him. He let his eyes roam around the table. Then, as if reaching a decision at that very moment, he addressed them.

"Sorry, but I just can't take the risk of crossing, not on such short notice."

Linder turned his gaze to Quist, whose eyes held the look of a man who had just seen victory slip through his fingers.

Chapter Twenty-Eight: Crossing

> "There are decades where nothing happens, and there are weeks where decades happen."
> –*Vladimir Ilyich Lenin*

"

FRIDAY, 24 MARCH 2034

Once everyone had risen from the dinner table, Quist made a show of using his cell phone to call the men aboard the boat that was to have brought Bracken and Popovic across the lake to the safehouse.

"Change of plan," Quist told the boatmen in a clipped voice. "Your northbound passengers won't be traveling. Instead, please proceed to our location to bring us south. There will just be two of us."

Though Linder couldn't hear the smugglers' reply, he saw a fleeting frown cross Quist 's face before he hung up.

"The motorboat should be here in about ninety minutes," Quist announced. "For those who are traveling, this would be a good time to catch a short nap. Anyone else can do the same if you'd like. I just ask that you to stick around until the boat leaves the dock. Or you can spend the night upstairs. The bedrooms are at our disposal."

"No problem," Cowen replied. Silva nodded in agreement.

"I'll take you up on your offer of a nap," Linder added. "Harry and I will drive back to Montreal after you've gone."

"Suit yourself," Quist replied coldly before turning to leave.

Linder claimed the bedroom at the end of the upstairs hall and immediately sat at its desk to call his wife. But to his annoyance, the call went straight to voicemail. He checked his watch. The time was just before eleven o'clock. Had Annabel turned off her cell phone before going to bed? He broke off the call and tried again. Same result. So he left her a voice message.

"Hi, Bel. I arrived safely at the lake and am doing fine here. Our group had a very lively discussion over a fine dinner. We're all staying at a lovely Cape Cod style lake house, all glass and weathered wood shingles, with its own dock and boathouse. You'd love it. As for timing, I expect to be back sometime before dawn tomorrow. See you then. Love you to bits."

No sooner had he ended the call than he heard a soft knock at his door.

"Come in," he said.

Quist entered and quietly shut the door behind him.

"I just received a call from the person who was going to join us from Montreal," Quist began, appearing confident once again. "As it happens, he has just made it to Magog and his car will be here in a few minutes. Would you be willing to talk to him?"

"It seems a bit late for that," Linder answered coolly after a moment's pause, none too pleased at the sudden proposal. "But, sure. May I ask who this person might be?"

"I'd rather not speak his name out loud. But the two of you already know each other."

"Interesting. And do you also know him?"

"I don't," Quist replied. "Bracken just asked me to help him any way I could."

"Do Maria and Jack know him?"

"Not likely," Quist said. "Anyway, may I bring him up? I promise he'll come alone. His driver will stay outside with the car."

A few minutes later, Linder heard the crunch of car tires on gravel and looked out the window to see headlights approaching. It was a dark sedan, likely a livery car. Linder watched as Quist approached the vehicle and led the stranger inside. He was a dark figure of average height, dressed in an overcoat and a homburg hat pulled low.

Then came the creak of footsteps on the back stairs. Linder's door opened without knocking.

"Good to see you again," Irwin Kreutzer said as he removed his hat. His face wore the smile of someone who expected a warm welcome. "Surprised to see me?"

"Nothing you do could ever surprise me, Irwin," Linder replied in a level tone. "But why are *you* here, of all people. What's your connection to the League?"

"I support the League, though only a few in the organization's leadership are privy to that. So I agreed to come here on the condition that only you and Quist would see me."

"As I recall, you and I didn't part on the best of terms at your going-away party," Linder noted, gesturing for Kreutzer to take a seat. "I even recall you making a threat. So what's changed?"

The trade envoy removed his hat and coat and seated himself on the room's only armchair. Linder took the straight-backed wooden chair at the desk.

"Oh, I think we can safely put all that business behind us now," Kreutzer replied with a serene smile. "Do you remember my predicting that I'd be back in London soon as U.S. ambassador? Well, it's official now. So whatever turn that events might take, I'll be in an excellent position to control my future. Now that your Zuckerman Letter has been officially discredited, I'm not one to hold pointless grudges."

"How high-minded of you," Linder answered without expression.

"Anyway," Kreutzer went on without looking Linder in the eye, "what I'm about to propose to you is far more important than anything happening now in London. Tell me, Warren, do you intend to travel to Boston tonight to meet with the League leadership?"

"I don't."

"May I ask why not?"

"I told them I wouldn't cross the border, and I won't. If they want to talk, they can meet me here on this side."

Kreutzer offered a sympathetic nod.

"And what is your current assessment of the League, Warren? Are you confident that they are capable of overthrowing Twitchell and the Unionist Party within the foreseeable future?"

"Not from what I've seen," Linder replied. "To topple a firmly entrenched government, you need more than an organization. You need a movement with serious grass-roots support. I just don't see the League having that yet."

"They have more than you might think, Warren. If you went to Boston, I believe you'd be surprised."

"Then where are the demonstrations, the labor strikes, the civil unrest? At least, in Fury's day, he staged the occasional bombing or assassination to remind everyone that a functioning opposition still existed."

"I wouldn't attribute the lack of civil unrest to the League's lack of popular support. I'd call it a failure of leadership. Perhaps if Fury had taken over the League as chairman, things might have been different. But he never made it that far."

"And why not, if the League is so powerful?" Linder asked. "Fury was under their protection, wasn't he?"

"Yes, but he made the mistake of confiding his plans to untrustworthy persons, who betrayed him to the DSS."

"The Geigers, you mean?"

"So it seems," Kreutzer agreed. "The League might have managed to shake Fury free, but he lost heart and killed himself first."

"So what makes the League's prospects so different now?"

"Three things. Unified émigré support and a charismatic new leader. Both of those come from you. And support from a powerful faction of disaffected Party insiders. That comes from me."

Linder stifled a laugh.

"You expect me to bring the hard-line émigrés on board, just like that?" he asked.

"Yes, in return for being made League chairman."

"And the Party insider faction? What's that all about?" Linder challenged.

Kreutzer removed a creased sheet of paper from his inside suit pocket and unfolded it.

"Here, see for yourself."

The note contained neither an addressee's name nor a signature, but Linder recognized the handwriting from his work on the Zuckerman Letter. It was that of Ted Terzian, Twitchell's one-time rival in the Unionist Council of Three, who was slowly being eased out of power in the Politburo. Or perhaps the letter was a forgery. Linder scanned the text quickly. Among other things, it proposed full amnesty for all U.S. émigrés charged with anti-Unionist activities, the restoration of civil rights to those who returned voluntarily to America, and favorable treatment on oil and gas leases and other government contracts to foreign companies domiciled in countries that dropped sanctions against the United States.

"So the letter is from your man, Terzian?" Linder asked.

"Yes. Ted handed it to me personally to pass on to you."

"Pretty dangerous piece of paper for you to carry around, I'd think."

"Not so much here in Canada. I'll be burning it shortly, anyway."

"So does this mean that Terzian would scrap the Unionist agenda if he got in?" Linder probed.

"Definitely," Kreutzer agreed, leaning forward with elbows on his knees. "The first thing he'd do would be to sack all the Twitchell loyalists, replace them with his own people, and give the Party a new platform. He'd also draw heavily on League members to fill administrative positions. With some prominent émigrés, as well. Do you think you could win over your constituents with a program like that? Would they join forces with Ted and the League to take on Twitchell?"

"Maybe," Linder replied. "But how do I know Terzian will follow through? And that the League will have the strength to carry him over the top? And how can I be sure that he wouldn't cast me and my people aside once he got what he wanted?"

"Why not ask Ted yourself? And why not sit down with the entire League Political Council to see if they're made of the right stuff? They're all meeting in Boston this weekend."

"I already told you. I'm not going. And why should I believe you, of all people, that I'd be safe there if I did?"

"Because this is a once in a lifetime opportunity to get in on the ground floor of regime change, Warren," Kreutzer replied. "Terzian doesn't want you on board just to bring in émigré support. He wants you because you hate DeWaart and the DSS just as much as he does. He couldn't say this in his note, but he wants to make you head of the DSS when he comes in. Not to oppress dissidents, as DeWaart does, but to dismantle the DSS brick by brick, as few other people are capable of doing."

Linder threw his head back and laughed.

"Now that's something I could get behind," he told Kreutzer. "But all I have from you and Terzian right now are vague promises. To go inside, I'd be putting my life in your hands."

"You'd be in no more danger than any of the other people the League has brought safely in and out of the U.S. You'd be traveling with Quist and Poirier, who do this regularly. I'd fly in tomorrow from Montreal to meet you."

There was a look of earnestness on Kreutzer's face that Linder had never seen before, and that was wholly uncharacteristic of him. What was he to make of it?

"Look, Irwin, it all sounds very exciting. And, sure, I'd join forces with the devil himself to get rid of Twitchell and his crew. But why do I have to decide right this moment? Why can't it wait?"

Kreutzer looked from side to side into the semi-darkness, as if worried that he might be overheard even here, before replying in a near whisper.

"Because Ted doesn't have time to spare. He expects Twitchell to move against him at any moment and wants to make sure he can count on émigré backing before the balloon goes up. Believe me, if you get on board, you can pretty much write your own ticket once we take over."

"So let me see if I have this straight," Linder replied as he stroked his chin. "Terzian is making his power move under cover of the League, and the League wants a show of international support so that people don't see all this as just a palace intrigue among Politburo insiders."

"I think you're also overlooking the substantive policy differences between Twitchell and Ted. Remember that the New Economic Plan was originally Ted's idea, and it was he who forced Twitchell to adopt it. Ted has always been a reformer, and he's been bringing other reformers into his camp while Twitchell has been jockeying for absolute power. Believe me, Ted is the only person inside the country who has any chance of unseating Twitchell. So are you in or out?"

"If it's a fight between Ted and Twitchell, I'm definitely with Ted," Linder replied. "But why can't I just tell you that now and go home to support the League from London?"

"Because Ted insists on meeting you face to face, since he wants you to lead the DSS. He wants to make sure the two of you see eye to eye. But since the only way you can bring the émigré opposition on board is from your base in London, he absolutely guarantees your safe return."

Linder rose from his chair and took a moment to gaze out the window.

"All right," he told Kreutzer, "for the sake of argument, let's assume that I might be willing to meet Terzian south of the border. How and when would a meeting happen?"

"Quist and his people would escort you across the lake and into Boston. I would catch up with you there and take you to Ted before your meeting with the League. Afterward, Quist would escort you back to Montreal the same way you came."

"And if I decline the offer?"

"Ted would find someone else and you'd be out for good. No second chances."

"So can I have some time to think about it?"

Kreutzer let a moment go by before answering. A faint smile played on his lips.

"Of course, Warren," he answered, softening his tone. "You can give your answer to Quist in the next hour or so and he can pass word to me on the road." He looked at his watch. "Your boat arrives in about an hour."

Kreutzer stood up and approached Linder with his right hand outstretched. Linder took it. A moment later he watched from the window as Quist walked Kreutzer to the waiting car and remained in the driveway until the vehicle's red taillights were out of sight. Then Linder left the room to meet Quist as climbed the back stairs.

"Okay, I'm convinced," he told Quist. "Save me a seat in the boat."

It was a high-stakes gamble, but if Kreutzer was right, it might be the best shot he'd ever have to bring down the Unionist regime. And if he disappeared after crossing the border, it would be clear to all that the League was a hoax.

Upon returning to his room, Linder rifled the desk drawers for writing materials. Upon finding a sheaf of copy paper and a few envelopes, he put pen to paper, writing Annabel a message whose opening lines read:

"My beloved sweetheart, I am writing you again even though I texted you earlier this evening. The reason is that my plans have changed. It has become absolutely necessary that I cross the border and travel to Boston on business."

It was a difficult note to write, as he could not offer all his reasons for entering the Unionist State. And while he remained confident that he was making the right choice, if it turned out wrong, this message might be his last. He felt a sudden pang of regret, having assured his wife that he would never return to America so long as the Unionists reigned. To break his promise was bad enough. And if he failed to return, Annabel would feel doubly betrayed. But what about the members of the anti-Unionist movement who looked to him as leader? And the men he left behind in the camps? Did he not owe a duty to them, as well? Kreutzer was offering him the best chance he was likely to get to topple the Unionist regime. A better shot would not likely come his way. How could he not take it?

After finishing the note to Annabel and sealing it in an envelope, Linder spent the rest of the hour in silent meditation. When Quist called out that the boat had arrived, Linder stuffed Annabel's letter in his jacket pocket and returned downstairs, where he sought out Harry Cowen.

"I've decided to make the crossing after all," he told the younger man in a low voice. "And I've written a letter to my wife, to be opened only if I fail to return. Would you do me a favor and keep it in a safe place till I come back? And if I don't return on Sunday, would you wait a day or two before delivering it to Annabel at our hotel?"

"Certainly," Cowen answered, glancing over Linder's shoulder to see if anyone might be listening. He put out his hand where it wouldn't easily be seen and discreetly accepted the envelope. "I'll lock it away in my office safe and give it back to you when we meet on Sunday."

Though Linder couldn't be sure, something about Cowen's demeanor made him believe that the young man was sincere. But even if he weren't, it was a risk Linder was prepared to take.

It was half past midnight when the group finally gathered downstairs. Quist's first action there was to take Linder aside and ask him to leave behind his wallet, cell phone and any other identifying objects, like an engraved watch or ring.

"You'll be traveling under an alias for your own protection," Quist explained. Cowen collected the items and promised to hand them back on his return.

"What alias will I be using?" Linder asked.

"We took the liberty to create a alias travel document for you on the chance that you might be coming with us. A U.S. passport under the name of Vincent Stephens is waiting for you on the other side."

It was a clever stroke and Linder couldn't help wondering what made the League so confident that he'd go along. He hadn't agreed to make the crossing until the last moment. What if he'd refused?

"How did you put the document together so quickly," he challenged. "I never even gave you a photo."

"Our document techs do this sort of thing all the time. They can grab images off the internet and create a passport photo in a flash."

"How about border security?" Linder went on. "What if we're stopped and questioned on the water?"

"That's not going to happen," Quist replied with a sly smile. "Here on the northern frontier, the U.S. Border Patrol is far more interested in capturing Americans trying to escape than in stopping illegal entries from Canada. That's why Canadian cannabis growers use the lake to smuggle in their hydroponically grown weed into the U.S. rather than brave the cameras, ground sensors and armed patrols installed along the land routes."

"How about after we make landfall?" Linder persisted. "What's our chance of being stopped on the road to Boston?"

The smile returned to Quist's face. To Linder, who had crossed many a border in his time, the man's confidence appeared excessive. But Quist had a ready answer for this, too.

"Don't worry," the League official answered. "If you knew the government's security setup the way we do, you'd laugh. Their national ID system is a joke. First off, the database is offline half the time. And the new biometric ID cards are so easily hacked or corrupted that, outside the big cities, DHS has gone back to issuing old-fashioned paper IDs. Out here in the boonies, nothing at all is digital any more and there's a thriving black market in forged documents. In the unlikely event that we're stopped on the road to Boston, your Vincent Stephens passport will do the job just fine."

The temperature was scarcely above freezing when at last Quist led Linder and Poirier out the back door of the house onto a gravel path leading toward the dock. By now the moon was barely above the horizon, behind low clouds. Nothing but stars lit the earth, reflecting dimly on the water. The men walked slowly in the dark, their ears attuned to every little noise over the crunch of the gravel. Linder pulled his fedora down on his head against the cold.

Then, through the clatter of shoes on the dock, they heard the whoosh of a vessel closing in at short range. It was a low-silhouette motorboat, about twenty-five feet in length, its charcoal-hued carbon-fiber hull scarcely visible in the darkness. The driver circled around and pulled alongside the dock, pointing the craft's bow out toward open water.

The crewman tossed the bowline to Quist, who cleated it quickly and helped Linder and Poirier climb aboard. The crewman then handed each passenger a blue foul weather jacket and a life preserver

"Put the jacket on first and then the life preserver over it. It's cold out there on the water," the man said in a lilting Canadian accent before reaching out to retrieve the bowline.

Only then did Linder remember the image that Caroline had drawn of him in a foul weather jacket and fedora hat, stepping off the wooden dock into the motorboat. His heart sank.

The moment the three passengers took their rear-facing seats behind the two-man crew, the boat took off, slowly at first, then accelerating rapidly, but with scarcely a sound from the inboard engines.

"What kind of boat is this, anyway?" Linder asked Quist over the noise of water rushing against the hull.

"It's all-electric. Stealth design. And faster than anything else on the lake. Can you smell the cannabis resin on the deck?"

"Not in wind like this," Linder replied, zipping his jacket up to his chin over his overcoat to keep from shivering.

The passage from Magog to the outskirts of Newport took scarcely over an hour. The entire way, Linder saw no other boats on the water. Toward the end of the crossing, the craft veered left, slowed to half speed, and skirted the shoreline for several minutes. At one point, they passed an illuminated buoy with a sign that read, "United States Boundary. Illegal to Enter U.S." with pictographs showing firearms and illegal drugs. Further ahead was another illuminated sign with the word "Warning!" written in bold letters and the words "If you are entering the United States without presenting yourself to an Immigration Officer, you may be arrested and prosecuted for violating U.S. Immigration and Customs Laws." Linder recalled having come across a similar sign a decade earlier upon entering the Montana wilderness just south of the Alberta border.

"Are we there yet?" Linder asked Quist after passing the signs. "I don't see any lights onshore."

"No, we have another ten minutes to go. Right now we're taking advantage of a surveillance blind spot."

Ten minutes after crossing the international border, with the town lights of Newport in the distance, the boat drew up silently onto a sandy beach. Quist lowered himself from the bow first and pulled the lightened boat forward so that Poirier and Linder could step ashore without soaking their feet. Then he gave the bow a shove and the boat rotated slowly before peeling away at high speed to the south.

Without a word, Quist motioned for his two companions to follow him off the beach onto a dirt path that climbed a gradual slope for a hundred yards before joining a two-lane blacktop road. At the junction, shielded from view by a dense grove of pines, stood a silver Chevy SUV. Quist opened the rear door for Linder and Poirier to climb in before opening the front passenger door to seat himself. An instant later, the driver pressed the ignition button and switched on the headlights. In the glow of the dashboard display, Linder could see that the driver was Gordon Mook. So much for Silva's claim that her husband had urgent business in Montreal. Had she intended then to lie about Mook's whereabouts, or was he on a mission kept secret even from her?

"Thanks for coming to fetch us," Quist told Mook once they were on their way. "I apologize for the last-minute change in plans."

"Not a problem," Mook replied without turning his head to look at Quist.

"Mr. Linder, this is for you," the driver said next, holding up a manila envelope for Linder to take.

Linder accepted the envelope. Inside was a U.S. passport prepared in the name of Vincent Stephens. The photo was his, but who had snapped it?

Poirier then handed him a pocket LED flashlight.

"Study the passport closely and memorize its details," he said. Then Poirier described the route they would take to Boston. First, Mook would drive south on I-91 to the outskirts of St. Johnsbury, Vermont, where they would stop for coffee and Mook would separate from them to return to Montreal. From St. Johnsbury, Quist and Poirier would take turns driving along I-93 all the way into downtown Boston.

❖   ❖   ❖

The three travelers left Mook behind at the coffee shop and resumed their drive to Boston with Quist at the wheel. Despite several attempts, Linder was unable to sleep. Seeds of doubt kept sprouting in his head. Would Kreutzer show up as promised? Was it all an elaborate trap? To distract himself from these negative thoughts, Linder took advantage of the opportunity to question Quist and Poirier on several matters not covered during dinner the night before. One was the death of Leonard Fury.

"As you might expect," Linder began, "I have a hard time swallowing the official narrative about Leonard's end. So tell me, what does the League think happened to him?"

"Well, I can't claim to know all that Charles or Simon might know," Quist replied, turning around in his seat to face his questioner. "But, from what I've heard, Fury really did take his own life. Our people were monitoring his prison conditions closely. And I honestly believe that we could have gotten him out if given a little more time. But we had no idea how badly depressed Leonard had become over being sentenced to hard labor. He seems to have lost hope that he'd ever be free again."

Linder nodded but he didn't believe a word of it. Fury had been captured by the enemy before and had never despaired. His cardinal trait was defiance. While he might have looked depressed to an outsider, suicide was simply not in Fury's DNA.

"I don't get it," Linder objected. "Leonard had to know all along that, once he turned himself in, they'd demand that he make a public confession. It was a key element of the original deal the League offered him in the note the two Canadians delivered to Paris. So why would his show trial throw him into such a tailspin?"

This time Poirier fielded the question.

"It's impossible to know Leonard's true motives for jumping to his death. But it seems clear to me that he was no longer of sound mind when he did it. Perhaps it was a combination of factors. I was as shocked as anyone that he let himself be so shamefully abused at his trial. All I can say is that he must have had a lot on his mind after leading the kind of life he did."

Inwardly, Linder bristled at the disdain implicit in Poirier's remarks. The man had worked for Fury for years, had been entrusted with many sensitive missions, and was rewarded handsomely for carrying them out. Who was Jack Poirier to judge his late boss? But this was not the time and place for Linder to defend Fury's character. Rather, the occasion called for the opposite.

"For years I'd been one of Leonard's greatest admirers," Linder replied. "But I believe what you say makes sense. You see, Leonard was a conspirator *par excellence*. He couldn't get through a single day without plotting some dark scheme. And he was quite unscrupulous in his pursuit of power, money, women, and the means to a cushy life. In the end, it seems to me, Leonard's motives were not as principled as he led people to believe. Maybe that's why he lacked the inner resolve to keep going at the end. Perhaps if he'd had an organization like the League to back him up a year or two ago, things might have turned out differently."

The statement was intended to show respect for the League, if perhaps at Fury's expense. The ploy seemed to have worked, because both Quist and Poirier looked relieved that Linder hadn't doggedly defended Fury. To sustain that impression, during the next hour Linder confined his questions to more innocuous topics.

As they crossed the border from Maine to New Hampshire with Poirier in the driver's seat, Linder voiced surprise that the tollbooths were unmanned. Even the EZ Pass scanners seemed inoperable, as cars zipped through in every lane without so much as slowing down.

"What's with the broken scanners?" he asked. "Weird that the government is giving up all that toll revenue."

"Welcome to socialism. Nothing works," Poirier answered. "Besides that, there just aren't enough privately owned cars and trucks left to make toll collection profitable. And government vehicles are exempt, of course."

"So where did all the private vehicles go?"

"Sky-high licensing fees and outrageous fuel and electricity prices made the cost of owning a car prohibitive. In the cities, most people use public transit, despite the overcrowding and unreliability. And, in the suburbs, jitney vans have largely filled the gap."

As if to prove Poirier's assertion, when they entered Boston's northern suburbs during the morning rush hour, the highway filled rapidly with ride-sharing vans, panel trucks, rattletrap buses and swarms of noisy, exhaust-spewing motorbikes like those that abound in Third World cities. The closer they came to center city, the more Boston resembled Cairo, Bangkok, or Manila.

Along the waterfront, Linder noticed dozens of identical newly constructed concrete apartment blocks, replacing those that were condemned after the catastrophic New England floods a decade earlier.

"Well, at least the government managed to put up some new apartments for the flood refugees," he observed. "And they don't look too shabby, either."

"Good thing you don't have to live in one," Poirier responded in an acid tone. "The city government rations living space based on square footage per occupant. It's like living in a coat closet."

As they entered Boston's downtown commercial district, they passed scores of tent cities, despite the new public housing units. On entering a formerly gentrified area of South Boston, Linder noted with sadness many vacant storefronts, broken windows, and trash heaps that marked the community's fallen state. Yet, amid the squalor,

Poirier pointed out an upscale retail store whose proprietor was just then rolling up its metal security shutter.

"What's that one?" Linder asked.

"It's a Progress Store," Poirier replied with thinly veiled disgust. "Think of it as a Unionist Party commissary, much like a military PX, that sells hard-to-find and luxury goods. But only to people who show a Party membership card or have special government scrip to spend. Ordinary citizens aren't even allowed inside."

"So where do the locals shop? I don't see any supermarkets or bodegas."

"Oh, there are still a few of those, but unemployment, low wages, and stingy government handouts mean that the average family can't afford much more than food and rent. For most other things, people haunt the flea markets. Look, there's one, on the right, in the schoolyard over there. The collapse of manufacturing and the shortage of imports means that people resort to barter or selling off heirlooms to pay for things they can't do without."

Nostalgia for the Boston that Linder had known as a young man turned to revulsion as Poirier drove along litter-strewn streets where sullen, listless residents milled about or squatted idly on front stoops. Quist's SUV passed a bakery where queued-up shoppers swiveled their heads to follow a shiny sedan that stopped further down the street outside a police station. For a few moments, resentment smoldered in their eyes. The shoppers' faces seemed to question what right the people in the sedan had not to waste their time waiting in queues. Then the flame of resistance flickered out and their eyes swung around again to stare at the backs of heads just before them. Justice was one thing, but at the front of the line was bread.

A few minutes later, Poirier parked the SUV outside a three-story white clapboard townhouse where he claimed his younger brother lived when not on the road for his job. It was a modest dwelling, unmistakably working class, but respectable. Once inside, Poirier suggested that the three men take a short nap before their scheduled afternoon meeting with local League members for an informal walking tour. All agreed, and Poirier led them upstairs, offering each his own bedroom. It had been a long night in the boat and on the road and Linder was eager to sleep despite his senses still being on high alert.

Yet the moment Poirier was out of sight, Linder slipped into Quist's bedroom and closed the door behind him.

"Have you heard from Kreutzer? When are we going to see him?"

Quist answered with an expression that conveyed an unmistakable sense that something was wrong.

"No word just yet," he replied, quickly turning away. "His plane may still be in the air. Let's get some shuteye and check again later."

Linder didn't like that at all.

Chapter Twenty-Nine: Boston

> "The fight ain't over till you've thrown your last punch."
> —*Muhammad Ali*

SATURDAY, 25 MARCH 2034

Linder awoke shortly after one in the afternoon when he heard loud voices and a door slam downstairs. Upon entering the living room, he found Poirier and Quist seated with two strangers, one of them a moon-faced African American with a coffee-and-cream complexion, rotund figure, and pudgy hands. The latter visitor rose to greet Linder with a benign smile.

Linder returned his smile. Grilling Quist on when he'd be able to meet Kreutzer would have to wait.

"Warren, I'd like you to meet Roy Scovill," Quist began. "He's a good friend of my brother's. Roy was elected to Boston City Council last year after fifteen years with the police union. Now he runs a program similar to the old Oath Keepers, educating police and first responders on the difference between legal and illegal orders, and training them to refuse those that are unconstitutional. You can imagine how much trouble that would have gotten him into even a couple years ago."

"So why would it be different now?" Linder observed with a skeptical mien. "The Party has been running roughshod over the Constitution from day one."

"The citizens are what's changed," Scovill answered, still smiling. "They want clear rules that apply to everyone, not just the favored few. And they want the police to enforce the law fairly."

"Fascinating," Linder replied, pretending to believe what he'd been told.

Then Poirier introduced Linder to the other stranger, a middle-aged man dressed in salmon-hued trousers and a white polo shirt with upturned collar, who had the look of an over-the-hill frat boy. His face was imprinted with a sly, know-it-all expression that Linder generally associated with plaintiff lawyers and insurance salesmen.

"And over here is my old friend, Jerry Jacobs. Jerry has a day job in the City Attorney's office, but he also happens to own a string of restaurants around Boston. Jerry has been invaluable to the League. He knows all the city's movers and shakers and understands how things get done in this town. Which also helps explain how Jerry has come to own five restaurants—or is it six, now, Jerry?"

"Six, as of last week, Jackie boy. Tonight you'll be eating in one of them," he announced with his hands folded behind his head and his feet propped up on the room's cheap coffee table.

"Sounds like business is booming," Linder offered with a respectful nod to Jacobs, despite ample evidence to the contrary on his drive through Boston. "What would account for the economic upsurge—the NEP?"

"No doubt about it," Jacobs replied. "New England is a lot like post-Soviet Russia. The apparatchiks who remained in office at the end of the Soviet era discovered they could become fabulously wealthy by selling off public property left under their control. What you see in Boston today is the same sort of gold rush. A once-in-a-lifetime opportunity—for those who know how to play it."

"And how do the policemen and first responders in your organization feel about that?" Linder asked, turning to Scovill. "Presumably, your members entered government service to serve their fellow citizens, not to line their pockets."

"Sure, but most are so beaten down by now that they don't dare raise a stink about the corruption," Scovill replied. "Sometimes it amazes me that so few people are capable of thinking for themselves."

"Then how does your organization find anyone willing to defy unlawful orders?"

"Our members are mostly older guys who knew right from wrong before the Party came to power. Many of their grown-up kids have also joined. Other than that, I'll admit it's been an uphill battle for us to recruit younger members."

Linder offered an understanding look. But there was something about Scovill that set off alarm bells. It wasn't so much what he said, but rather his manner of speaking and how he carried himself. Linder recognized it because such a manner was so common among DSS officers he had known. There was no hesitancy or reserve in their demeanor, just the arrogance of knowing that they had nothing to fear because the full force of state power stood behind them.

Quist and Jacobs, however, were quite unlike Scovill. Their eyes bore the telltale traces of fear, possibly because they had started out as ordinary citizens who were co-opted or extorted into clandestine service. Poirier, however, was different from all three. Far from resembling a DSS officer or even a coerced informant, he appeared to be a true believer in the League.

Linder listened carefully as Scovill went on to explain how the League set about attracting new members. It was a smooth and confident presentation that struck Linder as being perhaps too glib. Several times, when pressed for specifics to back up his claims, the former police union leader gave answers that lacked the granularity and color that one would expect from someone who had once been a cop on the beat.

But discussion was cut short when Quist proposed that the group grab a bite from one of the food trucks that had recently set up in the neighborhood. Across from a hospital, the men found a truck serving cheap tacos and burritos. As they ate, Linder noticed a sleek European sports car drive past. It was the first foreign-made passenger vehicle he had seen since leaving Canada. A few minutes later, a shiny new Japanese luxury sedan also swung by.

"What kind of person drives a car like that?" Linder asked in surprise. "Are there still drug pushers operating in the Unionist utopia?"

"Hardly," Quist replied with an amused look. "These days, drugs are handed out like candy at the free clinics. No, those guys are NEP men, our *nouveau riche*."

"People whom the Party used to arrest for illegal speculation," Jacobs added in an ironic undertone. "Now it's hands off. Go figure."

"Give those NEP men a few years, and they'll be opening businesses that employ thousands," Linder mused. "A rising tide lifts all boats, I suppose."

"Maybe so, but it's going to take some getting used to," Quist added.

For someone supposedly dedicated to ousting the Unionist Party and bringing back free markets, Linder found Quist's tone a bit too grudging. How was the League to restore American prosperity without creating individual wealth? Nonetheless, Linder let the remark pass.

When the men finished their food, Jacobs led them further on their walking tour around the neighborhood, stopping at a bare-bones ice cream parlor, a bustling flea market, and a newly reopened Catholic church. South Boston was a shadow of its former self, but signs of rebirth were all over. Clearly, the NEP was making a difference to ordinary Bostonians.

A half hour later, Quist, Poirier, and Linder said goodbye to the two locals and went back to the safehouse. As soon as they returned, Linder took Quist aside.

"Any news from Kreutzer?"

"Not yet," Quist replied with an uneasy look. "But he knows where we are. Don't worry, he'll find us."

Two hours later, there was still no sign of Kreutzer. Time was running out if the trade rep was to take Linder to meet with Ted Terzian before sitting down with the League leadership. Linder cursed Kreutzer for leaving him in the lurch, but he also cursed himself for letting himself get into such a situation. Now he would have to meet with the League without knowing whether he had Terzian's backing. Would Kreutzer ever turn up?

At six, Jacobs arrived in a gleaming black town car and declared with evident pride that it belonged to a new limo service he had started. After greeting his three passengers, he drove them to his flagship restaurant, Mateo's, where they were scheduled to dine with members of the League's Political Council. The place was a remarkably upscale Italian restaurant, located in a well-scrubbed enclave of Boston's North End, where Jacobs noted that many emerging entrepreneurs now lived. Most of these, he reported, opposed the Unionist regime and some had even donated to the League.

Jacobs dropped off Linder, Poirier and Quist at the eatery's front door and promised to return after dinner upon receiving their text message. As Linder crossed the sidewalk, he paused to look up and down the street and spotted six or seven people who seemed out of place. Once indoors, he also noticed a handful of possible security types posing as customers, both at the bar and seated at the restaurant's front end. Such a heavy security detail for an event held on the League's home turf gave Linder pause. Were these people sent by the League to protect the Political Council or were they DSS operatives sent to keep close watch on the council's notorious guest? Or perhaps do something much worse?

Linder took Poirier by the elbow and pulled him aside.

"Who are all these people?" he asked, inclining his head toward the bar. "Are you sure they're all with the League?"

Poirier followed Linder's gaze to the bar.

"They have to be ours," he replied, dismissing Linder's concern. "Don't worry about it."

But Linder was not reassured. As if Kreutzer's no-show hadn't been enough. Even so, it made little sense for the DSS to arrest him now, when they could have done so immediately upon his entry in the U.S. or at any time thereafter. Yet, what if their plans had changed?

In the next moment, Quist led the group past the bar to a private dining room at the rear where three men in business suits huddled beside a table set for six. A pair of cocktail waitresses stepped forward immediately to take the newcomers' drink orders.

Only after the waitresses left the room did Quist offer to make introductions, starting with Charles Bracken, the League's shadow foreign minister. Bracken was a tall man in his middle fifties with the slender physique of a runner and the face of an ascetic. He had spent nearly a quarter century in the U.S. Department of State, rising to the level of ambassador in several small Middle Eastern countries before the Unionist takeover forced him into early retirement. Thereafter, according to Quist, Bracken had cooled his heels as a tenured professor at Princeton until finding a new calling with the League. Now, as the League's shadow foreign minister, he was responsible for fostering relations with nations that favored regime change for America.

Linder gave Bracken a close look as they shook hands, seeking to divine whether the man was a true believer in the League or perhaps a DSS stooge. But while Bracken held his gaze and showed no sign of deception, it wasn't sufficient for Linder to judge either way.

Likewise with former Lt. General Simon Popovic, a majestic figure who stood several inches taller than Linder and, though in his mid-sixties, looked as if he could still crush the obstacle course at West Point, where he had once served as superintendent. According to Quist, Popovic had sided with the Unionists during CWII but soon after fell out with Party General Secretary Twitchell and was pushed aside. During the Blue Terror, he had gone into hiding and emerged only recently to recruit a network of former military officers to support the League. As a result, Popovic was now the League's chief of personnel, although Linder could not easily picture so vigorous a man in so sedentary a role. But if Linder harbored doubts about Popovic's true function within the League, the general's demeanor didn't give much away.

The third council member, Sax Hayward, posed a different problem. Quist had presented Hayward as a retired Navy admiral from an upper crust Boston family who had refused to emigrate after the Unionist takeover. And Hayward looked the part, with his ramrod-straight posture, buzz-cut hairdo, and chalk-stripe business suit. According to Quist's introduction, Hayward had worked on Wall Street after leaving the Navy, until his firm's collapse in the Great Bust. By virtue of his presumed financial acumen, he was now the League's finance chief. But something in Hayward's mannerisms and speech reminded Linder far more of his former bosses in the DSS than any high-ranking naval officers or Wall Street financiers he had known. Even more telling was Hayward's reaction when, after claiming to have attended boarding school at Exeter, Linder announced that he also had studied there, and asked Hayward the name of his dormitory, the year he graduated, and whether he had taken classes from certain of Linder's old instructors. The blank look on the admiral's face before attempting to fast-talk his way out of the situation spoke volumes. Linder had a sense that he'd seen Hayward's face somewhere before, and it wasn't at Exeter.

Now that he stood face to face with these three members of the League's Political Council, Linder wondered why they had wanted to meet with him at all. These were supposedly ranking members of the League's shadow government who had a great deal to lose if caught conspiring against Unionist rule. Meanwhile, Linder was arguably Unionism's Public Enemy Number One, a notorious DSS renegade and escaped prisoner who had been sentenced to death in absentia twice. Yet, here they all were, meeting semi-openly in a posh restaurant that catered to local bigwigs and NEP men, acting as if they had no fear of exposure. What was wrong with this picture?

Once each man had a cocktail in hand, except for Linder, who stuck to club soda, the six continued getting acquainted with one another until the servers arrived with the soup course. Once they sat down to eat, the topics of discussion remained largely anodyne, since unvetted servers were flitting in and out at frequent intervals. But throughout dinner, it became increasingly difficult for Linder to imagine that the League was a genuine opposition group. Their claims to operate outside the reach of the DSS and to have informants placed throughout the Party and the government apparatus seemed more and more far-fetched. He remembered the warnings from Barton Cao, Bob Bednarski, and the Brazilian intelligence chief, Mendes, as well as the misinformation that Mendes had detected in the League's reporting. Nor could Linder ignore how the League had lured Leonard Fury to his capture.

Did they really expect him to go home and sing the League's praises? And if he did the opposite, how long before they came after him? No, it wasn't enough to go back and declare the League a hoax. He had to completely destroy the League's credibility, no matter the consequences.

As soon as the waitresses finished serving coffee and cleared the remaining dishes, Quist kicked off the business portion of the meeting by asking Bracken to deliver a progress report on the League's latest efforts to bring down the Unionist regime. Bracken rose to deliver his report while pacing back and forth behind his seat, a habit likely developed during his days as a professor.

"Thanks, Owen. I'd like to focus my comments on three areas of strategic weakness for the Unionist regime and how we are exploiting them. The first is disunity among Party leaders. Second is unrest among the people and Party cadres. Third is the fragile economy. Bracken then spent the next twenty minutes delivering an arid lecture that had his audience checking their watches and doodling on their notepads.

Next, Quist called on General Popovic to talk about the League's plan to win over the armed forces and police. The plan seemed sound enough, though fraught with obstacles.

After that, Quist asked Admiral Hayward to speak briefly about the League's finances.

"Unfortunately, contributions from overseas have been disappointing," Hayward began. "It seems that many émigrés object to the League because of their pre-existing loyalties to other resistance groups whose leaders have been slow to embrace us. Would you care to comment, Mr. Linder, and perhaps offer your guidance on how to increase the League's support from overseas?"

The stony expression on Hayward's face when mentioning other resistance groups made it clear to Linder that the admiral counted him among the foot-draggers. But if Hayward's remark was meant to put Linder on the defensive, it failed. Linder took a sip of coffee and paused to pat his lips ever so gently with his napkin before responding.

"Thank you for inviting me to speak," Linder began, doing his best to appear sympathetic toward his hosts. "But you see, the difficulty with raising money today is that just about everyone's house is on fire. Which means that the League can't reasonably expect to solve its funding problems overseas. No, you'll have to find the lion's share of your funding right in your backyard. As for wealthy foreign donors, like Nelson Furness in Britain, or Gordon Butts in the Netherlands, they might be willing to chip in if they could be confident in bringing Unionist power to a complete end. But big donors have been keenly disappointed in the past by resistance organizations, including my own. Which means that the League has no real choice but to put out the fire in its own house first."

Everyone around the table seemed taken aback at the bluntness of Linder's remarks. Hayward's expression, in particular, grew dark.

"But you've seen with your own eyes how destitute the people are," Hayward replied straight away. Over the past year, we've received contributions from a growing number of rising NEP men, but there's a limit to what even they can give. Nearly all their capital is tied up in their businesses. That's why we've been counting so heavily on our émigré friends."

"Desperate times call for desperate measures," Linder replied without flinching. "Having said that, I come to you with a proposal that could bring in some very substantial sums. But my methods are crude and might repel you."

The room went silent as all eyes settled on Linder. The time had come to put the League's leaders to the test.

"The idea is this," he went on. "I propose that you use your available manpower and skills to remove a selected list of highly marketable art works and antiquities from America's leading museums. You would then send these treasures across the frontier to Canada and Mexico and, from there, to dealers in Europe and Asia for sale. My associates and I would be happy to put you in touch with suitable dealers, if you like."

"But we aren't thieves!" Bracken sputtered, aghast at what he'd heard. "What would our people think if they knew that the League was plundering America's national treasures?"

"You mustn't tie your hands with pointless sentimentality," Linder scoffed, laying both palms firmly on the table. "America's major museums still hold treasures of immense value, despite the impoverished state of the U.S. economy. I speak of Old Master paintings, Impressionist art, and pre-Columbian artifacts. Many of these items are compact in size and can be easily concealed for transport. While it's difficult to steal from the museums' public displays, their basements are overflowing with superior works of art, already packed and crated. Bring them to Montreal or Tijuana or Ciudad Juarez and I will personally arrange for their sale at the highest possible prices."

Without waiting for a response, Linder pulled from his jacket pocket a folded list of candidate works to be taken: Dutch masters, paintings of the great Italian and Spanish schools, Italian and Flemish primitives, modernist works, antique coins, sketches, engravings, and miniatures.

"How can you even suggest such a scheme?" Quist objected. "For years you've have held yourself out as an ethical opponent of Unionism. How can you justify despoiling the American public of its cultural heritage?"

Linder cast a cynical smile at Quist before looking askance at the chagrined expressions of the other Political Council members. Both Bracken and Hayward seemed to have difficulty controlling their outrage.

"So are you revolutionaries or not?" he challenged back. "Are you not willing to win by any and all means necessary?"

Judging from their indignation, Linder concluded that the answer was no. But if not revolutionaries, what were they? Some tame species of reformist? Or Unionists impersonating revolutionaries at the DSS's behest?

"Come now," he taunted them, "a true revolutionary, like Lenin, Trotsky, Mao, or Fidel would seize any opportunity that brought him closer to his goals."

By way of contrast, these League men seemed petrified of how others might view them. A moment later, several voices spoke out at once, with Hayward's rising above the others.

"But it would ruin the League's reputation if word ever got out! We are not museum robbers!"

Linder brushed off the objection.

"When money is needed, one's reputation must sometimes suffer," he replied with a shrug. "But, in this case, the risk of discovery is small, as only a few of your colleagues need to know about the plan. And, in any case, after you seize power, you can justify it any way you please. Or say nothing."

"But that's not the point," Quist dissented. "What you propose is just plain wrong."

"Oh, please. Be realistic," Linder responded. "The Unionist nomenklatura have been siphoning off state assets for years to pad their offshore bank accounts. What's sauce for the goose is sauce for the gander. Except, in your case, the money would be going toward a worthy cause."

This was a deliberate taunt intended to expose anyone inclined to defend the Unionist leadership. But nobody spoke up to deny what all knew was true. So Linder decided to push them harder.

"All right, then," he went on. "If you don't want to sell off surplus artwork, you could also raise cash by partnering with a truly serious foreign intelligence organization, like the Brazilians or the Russians. Either one would be prepared to pay handsomely for hard intelligence about the DSS and the Progintern. They'd also pay very well for well-sourced intel from inside the FBI, CIA, DHS, or the Pentagon."

"We've talked to the Russians. It went nowhere," Popovic answered with a scowl and a vigorous shake of his oversized head. "They asked for the moon and offered peanuts in return. Besides, what you're describing entails significant risk."

"Oh, so it's risky, is it?" Linder taunted. "Of course it is! But, never mind, what can't be stolen can often be fabricated. I'll give you an example. In Britain, the Zuckerman Letter was a forgery, but it gave the Tories a huge electoral win. Why not try your hand at peddling some high-quality forgeries of your own?"

Linder looked around the table and was met with stony silence.

"And while you ponder that," he went on with a cavalier smile, "allow me to mention that I have some modest influence with members of London's tabloid press. I expect they'd be delighted to run a series on the secret lives of your Unionist elites. Surely you must know of some juicy scandals involving the Gang of Three. Not only do the tabloids pay very well, but dragging the reputations of men like Twitchell through the mud would be a terrific way to tarnish Unionist prestige. Of course, this would require genuine evidence, like photos, sound recordings, bank statements, and the like. But surely, with a network like yours, you should be able to manage it, no?"

"I daresay we could," Bracken sniffed. "But such behavior would lower us to the level of our oppressors. We are a shadow government, for God's sake, not a gang of paparazzi!"

As if Linder had not yet provoked his hosts enough, he let out a deep laugh. Whoever these men were, they were clearly not revolutionaries. He decided to rile them further.

"It seems to me, Mr. Bracken, that you and your colleagues are altogether too scrupulous. You'll never succeed in overthrowing the Unionists if you hold yourself to the rules of conventional morality. Take terrorism, for instance," he said, turning his smile into a leer. "Leonard Fury once told me that an agent of his failed to detonate a bomb in a crowded subway car because children were seen riding in it. Leonard would say that, if you insist on upholding such lofty principles in a life-or-death struggle, you will never achieve your ambitions."

"So you would have let the bomb explode?" Popovic protested.

"Not I, but a true revolutionary would. Because once you adopt violence as your method, you must make every target count. For example, why not assassinate Zuckerman or Kanchuk, or even the tyrant Twitchell himself, to destroy the regime's aura of invincibility? Killing any one of them would unleash utter chaos, creating the very opening you need. It's exactly what Leonard would have done in your place."

"But that would bring a new round of Blue Terror down on our heads!" Hayward burst out, his eyes bulging and face flushed.

"So what?" Linder asserted. "Imagine how strongly the people would rally to the League's cause! The resulting loss of life would be a mere fraction of the carnage that the Unionists will inflict on the people so long as they remain in power."

"But why even talk of terrorism, Warren?" Poirier spoke up in an agitated voice, having remained silent through most of dinner. "You renounced violence years ago and turned instead to information warfare. Isn't what you're proposing a complete about-face for you?"

"Not really," Linder replied after taking the last sip of his lukewarm coffee. "Besides, when has the League ever renounced violence? It seems to me that assassination remains completely open to you. As well it might, since you don't seem to be very effective at non-violent tactics. After all, where are your strikes and demonstrations?"

At this, Quist bristled visibly.

"Oh, you're offended, Owen?" Linder went on. "Then tell me, where are those strikes? And where are your boycotts, your sit-ins, and your candlelight vigils? Every day I check the posts of local dissident networks on the Dark Web. Nowhere do I read about the League organizing mass actions. Have you forgotten your Alinsky? How does one go about overthrowing a regime without first organizing mass protest?"

But the question went unanswered. Linder's audience seemed at a loss for words. The only one who even met Linder's gaze was Jack Poirier, and his face was white with alarm.

Linder could see now that he had vexed the group quite enough. And he had gathered more than enough evidence to show the League wasn't serious about crushing Unionism. The question now was, what would they do with their troublesome émigré visitor? Did they dare let him go home after having laid bare their weak spots and demanded action?

"All right," Linder added at last, fixing his gaze on Quist. "I think I've made clear where the League needs to improve if it wants to attract more émigré support. And I'm happy to help you move forward in those areas if that's what you want. So why don't we call it a night?"

Quist let out a deep breath and his face took on the look of someone who has survived a close brush with disaster but can't quite understand why.

"Yes," he agreed. "I'm afraid we've run out of time. Unless anyone objects, the meeting is adjourned."

The men from the League rose from their places without comment, pasted on fake smiles, and proceeded to thank one another for their contributions to the meeting, while not deigning to look at Linder. It was as if his provocations were already forgotten.

But Linder, far from being dismayed at their outrage, felt deeply satisfied. He had thrown the League's top people into confusion and no longer harbored any doubt that the organization was all hat and no horses. While they hadn't liked being confronted with their weakness, they had little reason to fear his return to London. That was because the League had the louder voice now and could shout him down at any time. Or silence him by violent means, if it came to that.

On the other hand, if Linder disappeared in the Unionist State while under their care, his followers would hold the League responsible. After what had happened to Leonard Fury, nobody who knew Linder would believe that he had defected to the enemy. And that would certainly be true once Dwight Calder released the letter that Linder had left with him for such an eventuality. Checkmate? No. Perhaps only stalemate. But, either way, the League would never be the same.

The sun hung low on the horizon when the private diners stepped outdoors into a chill wind blowing off Boston Harbor. The three Political Council members huddled together and spoke to one another in low tones as they waited for their rides to draw to the curb. Were they fretting over what might happen to them if a tape or a transcript of the meeting fell into the wrong hands? Or were they plotting how to dispose of their nettlesome guest?

Linder scanned the crowded street and spotted the very same suspicious characters he had seen outside the restaurant when he entered hours before. Now that the meeting was over, would they swoop in and bundle him off in an unmarked van? He checked his watch and saw that the meeting had lasted longer than planned. If the League were to let him catch his return flight to London the following day, he and Quist and Poirier would need to begin the long drive back to Vermont very soon.

But before Linder had time to ponder what ill might happen to him, Jerry Jacobs's shiny black town car pulled to the curb. A moment later, Jacobs stepped out with a welcoming smile to open the car doors while Linder and Poirier climbed in.

"Man, I've never seen so much security for a League event," Jacobs observed once they were on the move. "Must have been a pretty important meeting, eh?"

"I should say so," Poirier replied. "Still, the security presence seems a bit over the top. I reckon the leadership doesn't want to take any chances, given what's been happening all day."

"What do you mean?" Linder asked, startled by Poirier's comment. "Is something going on that I don't know about?"

"It's not in the news yet, Warren, but Hayward told me during the break that Ted Terzian has fled the country and just surfaced in Brazil. Apparently, he was plotting some sort of coup. The DSS has been rounding up his minions all afternoon."

Linder drew a sharp breath and felt his pulse racing. "Have they hauled in anyone connected to the League?"

"Not that I've heard," Poirier replied, without alarm. "But I doubt they'll catch any of our kind playing footsie with that scoundrel. There's not a dime's worth of difference between Terzian and Twitchell, if you ask me."

"So you don't think any of the League's people would have backed Terzian against the Gang of Three?"

"Not bloody likely," Jacobs echoed with a bitter laugh as he eyed Linder in his rear view mirror. "We want to get rid of the whole lot of them."

So where did that leave Kreutzer, Linder asked himself. Under arrest? In hiding? Or might he have been collaborating with the DSS all along? His heart sank. What did Quist know about Kreutzer's fate? And where was Quist now?

Preston Fleming

Chapter Thirty: Arrest

> "We'll ask the man, where do you stand on the question of the revolution? If he's against it, we'll stand him up against a wall."
> *—Vladimir Ilyich Lenin*

"

SATURDAY, 25 MARCH 2034

O wen Quist watched Jacobs's town car pull away from the curb with Linder and Poirier inside. As soon as it was out of sight, Quist made his way back to the private dining room where the Political Council members had met. There he found his case officer, James Jenkins, alias Darrell Otis, also alias Roy Scovill, seated at the table while speaking with someone on his mobile phone.

"Okay, I'll wait for your call," Otis said as he ended the conversation.

Quist took a seat beside the DSS officer and made a quick look around before speaking.

"Who in God's name ordered such heavy security around the meeting site?" Quist demanded. "Linder's no fool. He must have spotted it right away. The Political Council wouldn't have done something like that on its own. Someone else up must have ordered it."

"I'm afraid you're right," Otis replied, shaking his head in dismay. "It seems there was a snafu at headquarters. Someone there ordered Linder's arrest and I didn't find out in time to stop it."

"Arrest Linder?" Quist sputtered. "That's nuts! If Linder doesn't show up in London, the exiles will immediately blame the League, especially after the mess with Fury. We'll never be able to show our faces again!"

"I understand, Owen. But tell me this," Otis countered. "Hayward claims that Linder said some pretty shocking things in there. Like urging the League to assassinate the General Secretary. Did he really say that?"

"That and more," Quist replied with a pained look. "The only positive spin I can put on it is that Linder wanted to test our resolve and provoke the League into taking more aggressive action. But I'd hate to see a transcript of the meeting find its way to the White House."

"Me too. Unfortunately, right now I can't rule that out."

Quist recoiled. He could only imagine the firestorm that would ensue if General Secretary Twitchell knew everything that Linder had proposed during the meeting. It wouldn't matter that the League leaders were operating under instructions from the DSS or that they had rejected Linder's proposals out of hand. Twitchell was paranoid. Everyone connected with the meeting would be accused of treason. Quist imagined himself being hauled off in chains and thrown into a dark cell down the hall from Linder's. He imagined his wife losing her job and being jailed for conspiring along with him. None of what he'd done for the DSS over the past two years would save him now. All his sacrifices would be for nothing.

Before Quist could speak again, Otis's phone rang. He stepped away from Quist and answered the call but said little in response. When Otis hung up, his expression was grim.

"That was Barbosa. He said the arrest order came straight from the deputy director's office. He's trying to get it rescinded but doesn't hold out much hope. He wants us to go back to the safehouse and await further instructions. And in the event the arrest older stands, you and I will be the ones assigned to take him down."

Quist's heart sank. A moment later, he heard a knock on the door and a swarthy young man with a lean and wiry physique appeared.

"You wanted me, boss?" he asked, sticking his head and shoulders inside.

"Yes, Ali," Otis told him. "Would you mind bringing the car around back? I'll be with you in a minute."

Quist gave Otis a questioning look as the man turned to leave.

"Oh, that's Ali Jafari," Otis explained. "Ali was on the team that picked up Leonard Fury and is also one of the men assigned to arrest Linder. If the order gets lifted, we'll hear about it first from Ali."

A few minutes later, Jafari pulled up at the restaurant's rear door in the SUV that had made the drive from Canada and drove Otis and Quist to the South Boston safehouse. While en route, Otis took another phone call, which Quist guessed was likely from Victor Barbosa. As before, Otis listened carefully but spoke few words. When the call was finished, a determined look came into his eyes.

"Okay, Owen, here's the plan," he announced. "The arrest is back on, but it's to occur as Linder is leaving the city. I want you to go in and take Poirier aside. Tell him you've agreed to give Ali and me a ride to North Station on your way out of town with Linder. Ali and I will wait for you here. When we're all ready to go, I want you to take the wheel and have Poirier ride shotgun. Ali and I will sit in back with Linder so we can cuff him as we approach the station. From there, we'll take Linder to the DSS prison annex, where they'll book him into a cell. Is all that clear?"

"Perfectly," Quist replied, though he wished it weren't.

"And you, Ali?" Otis demanded.

"I'm on it, boss," Jafari replied with a sinister hardness in his dark eyes.

"Okay, then, let's go. And just so you know, a backup vehicle will be right behind us. Popovic and Hayward will bring up the rear in their own car. We'll meet them all afterward at the safehouse for a quick debrief."

❖   ❖   ❖

When Quist arrived at the safehouse apartment, Linder was drinking coffee in the kitchen with Poirier and Jacobs. Linder noted with interest that, as soon as Quist entered the room, Poirier and Jacobs put down their coffee cups and glanced pointedly at the wall clock.

What was their hurry, Linder wondered? Could they know about his secret meeting with Kreutzer, or was there another reason for their haste? If only he could get Quist alone to ask him what he knew about Kreutzer's current situation and why he hadn't shown up to meet them. But there were too many people around.

"Sorry I'm late," Quist told them, showing no signs of urgency. "I ran into Roy Scovill and a friend of his outside the restaurant. They needed a ride to North Station, so I said we could give them a lift. It's only a couple of minutes out of our way. I hope you don't mind."

"Not a bit," Linder offered with a magnanimous smile while hiding his rising angst. "We've still got plenty of time." The others nodded but said nothing.

They rose together and Quist led Linder and Poirier out to the SUV, taking the driver's seat for himself. Linder sat in the back seat, sandwiched between Scovill and Jafari.

Soon they were on their way north toward Summer Street, crossing the Fort Point Channel and heading toward Boston's commercial center. No sooner were they past the channel than Linder spoke up.

"Do you mind if we stop just ahead so I can buy a postcard?" he asked. "I'd like to send it to my wife as a souvenir."

Poirier looked across to Quist, who gave a quick nod before responding.

"Not a problem," Quist told Linder. "In fact, it might be a good opportunity to pick up a few bottles of water for the trip."

So Quist stopped the car outside the nearest bodega while Poirier escorted Linder inside. When the latter two returned with their purchases, Linder sat alone in the back seat to fill out his postcard while the others lingered outside to drink the bottled water Poirier had brought. To Linder's relief, no one watched when he put down his pen, removed his gold wedding band, and used it to scrawl an invisible message across what he had already written on the card.

Once the SUV was on the move again, they stopped one last time for Linder to drop his postcard in a letterbox, with Scovill standing a few steps away. Linder heaved a secret sigh of relief when he saw the card disappear. Then he and Scovill returned to the car.

That was when it happened. The moment the car was in motion, Scovill and Jafari seized Linder roughly by the shoulders, slammed his head forward and slapped handcuffs on his wrists. Linder uttered a sharp cry of surprise and pain but, as the sidewalks were empty, no one outside the SUV could possibly hear him. He did not resist. This was it. The game was up.

"Okay, Quist, to the annex," Jenkins alias Scovill ordered on a note of satisfaction when the deed was done. "And step on it."

Then Jenkins texted the location of the mailbox to Sax Hayward in the chase car to have the box opened and Linder's postcard retrieved.

A few seconds later, Jenkins felt his mobile phone vibrate. It was Hayward.

"We'll take care of the postcard," the admiral told him. "Is the target fully under control?"

"Affirmative," Jenkins replied. "We're taking him to the annex as we speak."

"Thank heaven!" Hayward blurted out. "My God, what a horrible man!"

After surrendering Linder to uniformed guards at Boston's DSS prison annex, Jenkins left Jafari behind to complete the necessary admissions paperwork while directing Quist to drive him and Poirier back to the South Boston safehouse. When they arrived, Hayward and Popovic were already seated on the couch, passing back and forth a bottle of whiskey that Jacobs had brought from the limo. The two Political Council members were already oily-faced and red-eyed from drink, their speech loud and slurred.

"Now you've done it," Popovic complained to Jenkins as he stepped into the room. "We were this close to controlling the entire émigré opposition movement," he declared, forming a tiny gap between his thumb and forefinger.

"And now it's game over," Hayward joined in. "Along with the millions in hard currency the League was raking in from its foreign partners. So kiss it all good-bye, fellas, along with any hope of scoring a bonus or promotion for what we've accomplished. No, from now on, we'll be known as the boneheads who killed the goose that laid the golden eggs."

"Come on, fellas. You're blowing things all out of proportion," Jenkins asserted. "It's not quite that bad. Here, hand me that bottle," he said next. Then he grabbed a tumbler from the table and wiped its rim on his sleeve before pouring three fingers of whiskey into the glass.

"Is there any chance Linder might be released?" Poirier broke in, perhaps realizing that the League's collapse might also be very bad for him. "If we could spring the guy before tomorrow morning, it might still be possible to make it look like the League is on top of the situation."

"I see where you're going, Jack. But there's absolutely no chance of a release now," Jenkins replied. "As I've said before, the arrest order came straight from the top."

"Then how are we supposed to explain Linder's disappearance to the outside world?" Quist demanded. "The only reason he went to

Canada was to meet the League. Won't everyone blame us for his going missing?"

"No. Because headquarters is working on a Plan B," Jenkins rebuked him. "It's not perfect, but it might be enough for us to dodge the bullet."

"How so?" Quist pressed.

"Victor is thinking of staging a botched border crossing. Again, it's not perfect, but weird shit happens all the time at the border. And most people find error and incompetence easier to accept than conspiracy."

Poirier stroked his chin and cast a pensive glance back at Quist. As Fury's right-hand man, Poirier had made many crossings to and from the U.S. over the years and could be expected to know a thing or two about conditions at the border.

"I suppose it might work," Poirier mused. "But we'd have to move fast if we intend to claim that whatever happened to Linder took place on his way into the U.S. and not out. And that he entered on his own, without the League's help. Otherwise, the League would look responsible for losing him."

But Hayward wasn't buying it.

"I think it was a mistake to bring Linder here in the first place," the ersatz admiral said. "How could we even think of bringing a traitor like him into the country, giving him our full dog-and-pony show, and then sending him home to report on what he'd seen without some assurance that he wouldn't put the League in jeopardy? Sure, go ahead and give the border crossing idea a try, but I don't see it fooling anyone for long."

"Well, at least it might buy us time to interrogate Linder and weigh our options," Jenkins responded, throwing up his hands. "Besides, it's for headquarters to decide now, not us. I'll be down there tomorrow. Let's see how things go then."

An hour later, Jenkins had just arrived at his temporary desk in the DSS's Boston field office when his mobile phone rang again. It was Barbosa.

"Can you talk?" the division chief asked. "Where are you?"

"Boston. At the office."

"Where's Linder?"

"In his cell," Jenkins replied. "Why, have you spoken to the deputy director? Has he approved Linder's release?"

"I just left DeWaart. It was he who ordered Linder's arrest, on instruction from the White House. Apparently, when the General Secretary found out that Linder urged the League to assassinate him, he went ballistic. At this point, releasing Linder is out of the question."

"Are you serious?" Jenkins protested. "All because he made some stupid suggestions that nobody in the room took seriously?"

"I wish I weren't," Barbosa answered. "But Twitchell wants Linder dead. Remember, the guy already has two death sentences on his head."

Jenkins felt sick at heart. Not only would Linder's summary execution ruin the League's reputation among the émigrés, but it also meant no lengthy interrogation, and thus no way to manipulate Linder into mitigating the damage he had caused to the League.

"So what's next?" Jenkins demanded. "Are we supposed to hand Linder over to the executioners? If we do, sooner or later it will be all over the news. And the émigrés will demand to know how the League could have let such a thing happen."

"Stop right there," Barbosa barked. "We're not handing Linder over to anybody. Twitchell has given us a week to interrogate him. After that, we're to carry out the sentence in-house."

Jenkins swallowed hard. A week was better than nothing.

"All right," he replied. "We'll start the questioning right away. But how do we gloss over his disappearance in the meantime?"

"We'll run with the border incident. The pieces are being put in place as we speak."

"Unfortunately, the border story may no longer work," Jenkins noted on a downcast note.

"Oh, really? Why is that?" Barbosa challenged.

"Linder sent a postcard to his wife from Boston. Hayward was supposed to retrieve it from the mailbox, but the mail carrier got to it first. The card is en route to Linder's wife as we speak, and we have no idea what he wrote on it."

"Well, that's just terrific," Barbosa groused. "Any other good news? Don't hold back."

"Just this: How do you want to handle the interrogation? Should we send Linder down to Virginia?"

"No. Better to keep him up there. And I want you to do the questioning yourself. Nobody else. Depending on how Linder responds, maybe there's still a chance to salvage something from the League before the wheels come off."

Chapter Thirty-One: Missing

> "All battles are first won or lost in the mind."
> –*Joan of Arc*

SUNDAY, 26 MARCH 2034

Annabel hadn't heard from her husband since his Friday night voicemail, but she didn't begin to worry in earnest until her return from Sunday breakfast in Old Montreal. This was the day when Linder was due back in Montreal. The moment she entered the hotel room, she took a seat and dialed Linder's mobile number. As before, the call went straight to voicemail.

Only then did the loneliness that Annabel felt over the weekend begin to envelop her in soft folds. Since her husband left for the border, every hour of separation from him seemed like two. Though she longed to talk to someone about it, she dared not. Instead, she called the lakeside hotel in Magog whose name Harry Cowen had mentioned when describing the upcoming meeting with League representatives.

"Bonjour, Auberge Saint-Pierre," the male desk clerk said upon answering the phone.

"Excuse me, but do you speak English?"

"Of course, *madame*. How can I help you?"

"I'm checking to see if my husband has checked out of your hotel. He was supposed to be spending the weekend there for a business conference."

"Certainly. If you could tell me your husband's name…."

"It's Warren Linder. Spelled L-I-N-D-E-R. He would have arrived just before dinner on Friday evening."

A long pause followed before the clerk spoke again.

"I'm sorry, but we haven't had any guests by that name this weekend."

Annabel drew a sharp breath, feeling as if she'd missed the bottom step of a staircase. At a loss to say more, she thanked the desk clerk and hung up.

For the next hour, Annabel glanced over the Sunday newspapers and waited by the phone. Then she packed her suitcase in the hope that Warren was already on the way to her, allowing the television news to run in the background. After that, she sat down to read a novel. Two hours later, she ordered a room service lunch, having decided against ordering meals for two.

By the time she finished lunch, it was too late to reach the airport in time to check in for her return flight. She called the airline to cancel both reservations before informing the hotel desk clerk that she intended to keep the room for another day.

Annabel slept fitfully that night, waking up with every random noise, hoping it was Warren at the door. In the morning, she called the British consulate in Montreal. She asked to speak with Harry Cowen, only to be told he was out of town. Next she called the British Embassy in Ottawa and was put through to Allen Hackett. She explained to him that Linder had traveled to Lake Memphremagog with Cowen and had failed to return by Sunday noon, as promised. Now neither Linder nor the young diplomat was anywhere to be found.

"Could you get in touch with your man and find out what happened to my husband?" she asked Hackett.

For several seconds there was no reply.

"It's highly unusual for Cowen to be out of pocket," he replied without addressing her request.

"I don't care how unusual it is, Mr. Hackett. All I care about is that my husband has gone missing while in the British Foreign Ministry's care. So are you going to find your colleague and have him tell me where my husband has gone?"

"Of course I will, Mrs. Linder," the MI5 man replied in a deferential tone. "Will you be staying at the Gault a while longer?"

"Yes. For the duration," she declared.

On Tuesday, Annabel didn't leave the hotel until mid-afternoon when, out of boredom and anxiety, she decided to go for a walk in Old Montreal. She ended up eating a late lunch at a bistro cum wine bar and drinking considerably more wine than she had intended. After a tiring walk uphill back to the hotel, she found a picture postcard slipped under her door. It was in Warren's handwriting, dated and postmarked on Saturday, saying only, "Greetings from Boston." On the reverse side was a photograph of the city skyline as seen from Boston Harbor.

Immediately Annabel pulled her cell phone out of her handbag and called Allen Hackett in Ottawa. Hackett listened without comment while Annabel described the postcard in detail.

"We need to talk," he responded coolly. "I'll come to you tonight. There are flights to Montreal every hour. Expect me at the Gault some time after dinner."

As promised, Hackett knocked on Annabel's door just after eight. As soon as he sat down across the coffee table from her, he delivered shocking news that totally eclipsed any thought of the postcard.

"Today I received important new information about your husband. It now appears that he traveled across the border by motor launch late Friday night with representatives of the League, against my advice.

The group planned to return early Sunday , but the boat failed to pick them up. So, instead of crossing the border via Lake Memphremagog, it seems they attempted to drive across at an unguarded spot in the forest near Newport, Vermont. Canadian border guards reported hearing gunshots and later saw uniformed Americans carry bodies to an ambulance. From a distance, it wasn't clear if the bodies were wounded or dead."

"Where did you hear this? I've seen nothing in the media or on the internet." Suddenly Annabel felt her heart turn to water.

"I got it from Cowen, who was at the lake house when they boarded the motorboat. He returned Sunday to pick them up, but no one was there. Apparently, your husband had told Cowen to wait a day or two before sounding the alarm if he failed to return. As for the border incident, the Embassy has excellent contacts with the Canadian police. We asked them to check any unusual activity at the border and they told us about the shooting."

"What about the ambulance? Have the police been able to find out whom they carried away? "

"No," Hackett answered. "The American side refused to comment, saying it was a matter of national security."

"But why on earth would Warren enter the U.S. at all? If Cowen was with him at the lake house, shouldn't he have some idea why Warren went? And who traveled with him?"

"All good questions," Hackett replied, nodding gravely. "And now that Cowen is on the way back to his office, I plan to sit down with him in the morning and ask him. Meanwhile, would you be so kind as to show me the postcard you received from Boston?"

Annabel removed the card from her handbag and handed it over. Hackett examined the card carefully before holding it under glancing light from a nearby table lamp.

"It looks as if there might be additional impressions in the area where the writing appears," he noted. "Would you mind if I took the card with me to have our experts analyze it?"

"Analyze it for what?"

"For secret writing. Your husband was a trained spy and would know some techniques."

But Annabel was not in the mood to take Hackett's word at face value, not when this same man had goaded her husband to come to Canada in the first place, remained conveniently absent throughout his visit, and then reacted strangely on being told of Linder's disappearance.

"I wish I could help you, Allen, but this postcard is all I have from Warren right now," Annabel replied. "I'm not willing to part with it. Perhaps later, if it becomes absolutely necessary, but not right now."

Though the postcard might indeed hold valuable information, she didn't trust Hackett enough to leave it with him.

"Of course. I understand," Hackett replied.

"When you talk to Cowen tomorrow," Annabel went on, "could you also ask him where I might find the lake house where he and the League people met for dinner? Warren described the place to me in a voicemail, but not well enough to locate it without directions."

"Certainly. I'll ask Cowen for that and any other details that he might have. You can expect my call in the morning."

But Wednesday morning came and went without any communication from Hackett, and when Annabel called his cell phone, he didn't pick up.

It wasn't until late afternoon that the MI5 man returned her call, claiming that he was on his way to the airport and couldn't talk for long. As for the lake house's location, Hackett said Cowen had followed another car there in the dark and doubted he could find the house again, since the gravel drive from the main road was unmarked. If Annabel tried to find it on her own, she would be wasting her time. Nor did Cowen name the people who there with her husband. But

Hackett promised to keep Annabel informed as soon as he learned more.

Something in Hackett's tone, along with the fact that his call was both belated and evasive, left her feeling uncomfortable. For example, if Cowen had remained at the lake house long enough to see Linder leave by boat, why couldn't he name the others who presumably stayed with them through dinner until the boat came?

Later that day, something else added to Annabel's sense of unease. While checking a news site, she found a story from an American wire service claiming that three suspected smugglers had been stopped by the U.S. Border Patrol while attempting to enter U.S. territory via a disused forest road east of Lake Memphremagog. Two of the border-crossers were killed in an exchange of gunfire, while the third suffered serious wounds and was life-flighted to a Vermont hospital. U.S. authorities were withholding the suspects' identities pending further investigation.

But the date given for the incident wasn't early Sunday morning, when Warren was scheduled to return to Canada, and when Hackett's alleged border incident occurred, but late Friday night, when Linder had supposedly left by boat for Vermont. Both accounts couldn't be right. Someone wasn't telling the truth.

Early Thursday morning, Annabel woke with a dogged determination to find the lake house on Lake Memphremagog despite Hackett's advice against it. Through the Gault's concierge, she hired a driver familiar with the lake resort and set off before noon for Magog. Her first stop was the Auberge Saint-Pierre, where the owner confirmed his desk clerk's assertion that Warren Linder had never checked in as an overnight guest. While the bartender remembered seeing someone meeting Linder's description at the lobby bar on Friday evening, the guest hadn't stayed on for dinner.

But Annabel wasn't ready to give up so easily.

"I believe that Warren and his friends may have gone on to a Cape Cod-style lake house with its own boathouse and dock," she went on. "Might you know of such a lake house near here?"

The hotel owner shook his head.

"There must be a dozen properties like that along the lake's northern shore, *madame*. You'd best talk to Angie Lavelle at Magog Lakeside Retreats. She's the leading real estate agent around here. If anybody would know the house, it would be her."

So Annabel instructed her driver take her to the east side of town, where they found the middle-aged real estate agent seated alone at her desk. Annabel repeated her description of the house, adding that its gravel driveway was likely unmarked. On her computer, Lavelle showed Annabel photos of a dozen lake houses and printed out a list with their addresses, each keyed to a local map. Then she checked her most recent rental listings.

"It looks like none of these houses has been rented out this month. Of course, you could check Airbnb or VRBO to see if any of them are listed for rent. But neither vendor will tell you whether the properties were rented out last weekend."

Annabel spent the rest of the afternoon cruising along the lakeshore road, checking out the most promising candidates among the listings that Lavelle had given her. She snapped photos of several with her cell phone but none matched all the features in Linder's voicemail description. She even went to the town marina to see if she could hire someone to take her for a short cruise along the shoreline to identify the lake house from the water. But the marina was closed.

With the sun sinking low above the sparkling lake, Annabel ordered the driver to stop at the Magog police station as a last resort. There she explained to the duty officer that her husband had gone missing over the weekend after visiting the town.

"I reported his disappearance to the police in Montreal," she explained. "But when I heard about the shooting Friday night at the border, I thought he might have been caught up in it. Since you're much closer to the action than the Montreal police, could you do me a favor and check to see if anyone has released the names of any people shot along the frontier that night?"

The duty officer, a well-nourished, florid-faced man sliding toward retirement age, nodded sympathetically and entered a series of keystrokes on his computer. Then he gazed at the screen and pecked at the keyboard again.

"I see the news report, *madame*, but we have no record of any border mishap in our district. Not Friday, not Saturday, and not Sunday."

"You mean no reports of shots fired along the Derby Line, and no sightings of bodies being removed by ambulance from the U.S. side?"

"Not a peep," the officer replied. "Which is odd, because if shots had been detected by our acoustic sensors, one of our patrol cars would have been dispatched immediately, no matter which side of the border the action was on."

"Well, thank you, officer," Annabel answered with a downcast expression. "I suppose no news is good news when it comes to something like this."

And perhaps it was good news, because if neither Hackett's account of the incident nor that of the Unionist wire service was accurate, then it seemed far less likely that her husband had been killed or wounded at the border. She pondered the idea for a moment before the policeman nudged her out of her reverie.

"Would you like us to contact you if something turns up?"

"Yes, please," she answered, giving him her name and cell phone number and details of her hotel in Montreal.

But before returning to her car for the drive back to Montreal, Annabel stopped to take one last look across the shimmering moonlit lake toward the American side. She thought of her husband's appeal to her two years earlier in London.

"Promise me one thing," he had told her then. "Promise that you'll never go to America. Whatever happens, however great the temptation, even if I should write and ask you to join me there, you must never go. Not ever."

But if Warren was so firmly set against it, why did he go himself without telling her? And if he went anyway, where was he now? Because, despite her distress at his disappearance, and at hearing of the border incident, Annabel simply could not accept the possibility that her husband was dead.

Annabel was beyond hungry by the time the driver dropped her off at the Hotel Gault. Upon reaching her room, she immediately ordered a room service dinner. But while waiting for her food to arrive, she decided to call Allen Hackett one more time. He answered on the second ring and listened patiently while Annabel reported on her visit to Magog. She told him how she had traced Warren to the bar at the Auberge St.-Pierre but had failed to locate the lake house where he had gone afterward. What she left out of her account was her visit to the Magog police station.

"There's one thing that still confuses me," she added. "Did you see the wire service story last night about the border incident? It said shots were heard along the land border on Friday night, not Sunday morning. Now why would they report that way if your sources show Warren entering the U.S. on Friday night by boat, and being intercepted Sunday morning on land?"

A long pause followed.

"Because the Unionists are notorious liars," Hackett replied at last in a patronizing tone. "First off, it's more acceptable for their border troops to be seen shooting foreign intruders entering the country than American refugees fleeing it. Second, the Party hates to admit that thousands of its citizens risk their lives every year attempting to escape. The Party would much prefer to lie about Canadians wanting to break in."

Annabel found the answer dubious but didn't argue the point.

"So you still think the border incident happened on Sunday morning?"

"On balance, yes."

"What about Warren then? Do you think he might have been killed or wounded there?"

"I really don't know," Hackett answered in a tone that Annabel also found less than sincere. "But I wouldn't lose hope. For all we know, your husband may not have been captured at all and may still be at large. After all, he's a highly trained intelligence officer—if he's free he'll find a way home. Perhaps he's only been delayed. Besides, if the Unionists had really caught so notorious an enemy as Warren, I'm confident that they would have trumpeted the news by now."

"I suppose there's some consolation in that," Annabel answered, while feeling deflated not to know more. "But before I let you go, I have one more request. Could you send Harry Cowen to see me? I really would like to question him about what he saw in Magog on Friday night."

"I'll see what I can do. Harry is on the road a great deal these days with consular work and I'm not his immediate supervisor, so I can't guarantee it."

Shortly afterward, the conversation ended with Annabel doubting she would ever see Cowen again.

On Thursday morning, Annabel received a surprise visitor, but it wasn't Harry Cowen. It was a plain-featured woman of about thirty years, slim, with glossy black hair and features that suggested Asian ancestry. She wore a confident expression along with freshly pressed jeans and a black V-neck cashmere sweater under a waxed cotton utility jacket.

"Hello, Mrs. Linder. You don't know me, but I was with your husband the night he left Magog for Boston. May I come in?"

A flurry of conflicting thoughts ran through Annabel's mind as she gave this young woman the once-over. Nobody had mentioned that a female had been at the Auberge Saint-Pierre or at the lake house on Friday night. Was she from the League? And what was her relationship with Warren?

"Of course, please do," Annabel replied before opening the door wide for the stranger.

"My name is Maria Silva." the woman said, holding out her hand. "I'm Barton Cao's niece. Warren and I met in Paris at my uncle's apartment. Perhaps he mentioned my name?"

"Yes, now that I think of it, he mentioned what a fine job you did in hiding that poor woman who worked at the American consulate in Paris," Annabel replied, warming up to her visitor. "Please have a seat. Would you like some tea or coffee?" she asked, pointing to a pair of thermal carafes on the sideboard as she and her visitor chose seats on opposite sides of a low table.

"No thank you," Silva replied.

"You mentioned that you were with Warren the night he crossed the border. Are you part of the group that invited him to Magog—the League, as they're called?"

"Not exactly. You see, my uncle sent me and one of his contractors, Jack Poirier, to Canada last year to investigate the League. Over the course of several months, we traveled to the Unionist State many times and came to know League members in cities up and down the East Coast. While we weren't League members ourselves, my uncle's organization and the League shared common goals, so we cooperated with them."

"So what brought you to the meeting at Magog?"

"With your husband being so close to my uncle, the League thought that perhaps Jack and I could put your husband at ease about crossing the border to meet members of the League's Political Council."

"And you were comfortable with that?" Annabel challenged, her pique suddenly rising. "You trusted the League to keep Warren safe?"

"I did. You must understand that Jack and I had tested the League in every conceivable way during the time we worked with them. Not once did we feel ourselves in danger. Of course, we realized that your husband was far more important a figure than either of us. So we couldn't entirely rule out that the League might have been penetrated by the DSS and their invitation to Warren might constitute a trap."

"And now?" Annabel pressed. "Do you still trust the League? And what do you think happened to Warren once he crossed the border? Did he travel by boat, or over land, as the media reported?"

"He arrived in the U.S. by boat. Of that I am sure," Silva replied. "I know because I saw him board it. Also, it was my husband who picked him up on the other side of the lake. Gordon drove him and his two travel companions to St. Johnsbury, where he let them have the car so they could drive on to Boston. Gordon returned to Montreal the next day."

The woman's statements rang true, and Annabel felt unable to hold any sort of grudge against her.

"And who were the two companions?" she pressed the younger woman. "Were they League people?"

"Only one," Silva replied. "Owen Quist, the League's principal liaison with foreign opposition groups. The other was my uncle's contractor, Jack Poirier, who's not formally a League member. But Jack has become such an advocate for the League by now that he might as well be considered one of them."

"So what do you think happened to Warren? Has anyone from the League told you more?"

Silva shook her head and remained silent for a few seconds. Annabel used the time to study the younger woman's face more closely. It was plain yet handsome, with steady blue eyes that left an impression of earnestness.

"No, with Jack and Owen gone, no one I knew was privy to what went on in Boston. All I know for certain is that Gordon picked up Warren and the other two men from a boat on the Vermont side and drove them further south. As for what happened to your husband later, I can only speculate. Except that every day my speculations grow darker. Now I regret that I didn't warn him against going."

It was an admission that couldn't have been easy for Silva to make, and so it aroused Annabel's empathy, albeit mixed with an anger that seemed not fully fair.

"But what could have made him cross the border after insisting for so long that he wouldn't?" Annabel asked, addressing the question as much to herself as to Silva. "Was it difficult to persuade him to go?"

"Yes, it was. At the end of our meeting he announced that he would not take the risk of crossing. Then, the next thing I knew, he was preparing to board the boat. I was baffled as to why."

So was Annabel. Could Linder have had reasons he hadn't shared with her, reasons that outweighed his long-standing resolve against venturing into the U.S.? Reasons that transcended his promise to come back safely to her? If so, what could those reasons have been?

But there was one more issue she needed to raise.

"What of the news reports, then?" Annabel asked, doing her best to suppress her unease. "Could Warren have reached Boston but been killed at the border on his way back?"

To Annabel's surprise, Silva brightened at the question.

"I highly doubt it," the younger woman replied with a knowing smile. "If your husband had died in Unionist custody, the DSS surely would have identified the body quickly and used that information to broadcast news of his death. After all, Warren topped the Party's enemies list and was sentenced to death not once but twice. No, if a border incident had taken place and anyone had died, it was probably someone else."

"Thank you, Maria. I hadn't thought of it that way. It's small consolation, but it's better than nothing."

Silva rose and sat beside Annabel, drawing an arm around her shoulders.

"It troubles me immensely that I didn't do more to stop your husband from crossing," she said at last, with regret showing in her eyes. "If he doesn't return soon, I intend to suspend my work for the League to go find him. Until then, you and I can communicate through my uncle in Paris. But now it's time for you to leave Montreal. I fear for your safety the longer you stay here."

Chapter Thirty-Two: Waiting

> "Everyone is a moon, and has a dark side which he never shows to anybody."
> —*Mark Twain*

SATURDAY, 1 APRIL 2034

Saturday was Annabel's first full day back in London. But she returned as a changed woman. Before meeting Warren, she had been a carefree soul, fond of comfort and the good things in life, and with a tenderness for all God's creatures and the world's beauty. Upon marrying him, however, Annabel stepped into the world of intrigue and physical danger that her husband inhabited. She adjusted remarkably quickly to living under the DSS threat and being spied upon, even after the attempt to kidnap her in Mexico. Through it all, she had never doubted that Warren would somehow keep them both safe. But now Warren was gone, rather than being fearful, she felt a growing rage against the people who had taken him from her.

Shortly after breakfast, she decided to distract herself by calling Caroline in Lausanne. The call went through on the second ring.

"I hope I reached you at a good time," Annabel began.

"I'm on my way to the library," the younger woman replied. "But call any time. Where are you calling from? London?"

"Yes. I'm sorry I couldn't give you more details about Warren's situation before I left Canada. And, frankly, I'm afraid I don't know much more now than I did then."

Annabel then offered Caroline a brief account of what she had learned about Warren's disappearance, including what Maria Silva had told her in Montreal.

"But why on earth would he have risked going over?" Caroline asked.

"I don't understand it, either. Right now, my main goal is simply to find out where he is and get him back."

"Would you like my help? I could come to you in London."

"Thanks, but that's not necessary," Annabel replied with firmness. "Stay in school. As soon as I learn anything new, I'll let you know."

"You're sure?"

"Absolutely."

Later that morning, Annabel received an email from Allen Hackett in Ottawa that, if it were to be believed, offered a ray of hope about her husband:

"Just received word from a reliable source that Warren was not killed at the border per press reports. Indeed he is safe, and efforts are underway to arrange his return. Will advise when I know more. Latest from Cowen is that Warren left a letter for you before leaving Canada. It is being sent to you by overnight service. Meanwhile, I ask that you share this message with no one and refrain from any inquiries to the British government until further notice from me."

Remarkably, the letter of which Hackett spoke arrived later that day, along with Warren's wallet and cell phone left behind intentionally at Magog. Annabel opened the package with shaking hands. Tears welled in her eyes upon seeing her husband's crabbed handwriting. The letter read as follows:

"My beloved sweetheart, I am writing you again even though I texted you earlier this evening. My plans have changed. It has now become absolutely necessary that I cross the border and travel to

Boston on business. I am leaving tonight and will be back with you by midday Sunday.

"I want you to know that I would not have undertaken the trip were I not convinced that there is little to no risk attached to it. I write this letter only to cover the possibility that some improbable mishap might occur. If it does, I urge you not to intervene, as any steps you take would likely make matters worse. Knowing you, Annabel, I am certain that you will rise to the occasion, keep a level head, and do whatever is necessary to keep my affairs in order while I am away.

"Naturally, no one must get an inkling of what has occurred. Please trust that I am doing what I must do, and that, if you were with me, you would approve. You are in my thoughts always. God bless you forever. I love you beyond all words. Warren."

Annabel read the letter through a veil of tears. As the late winter sun sank over the Thames, its rays lit the room with beams of lurid red. Her worst fears had come to pass. Despite assurances that he would never do so, her husband had followed his sister and brother-in-law, in addition to Leonard Fury, Grace Kuroda, and Paul Wagner, back to America and into Unionist hands.

All through the weekend, Annabel scoured the internet for any news that might be relevant to her husband's disappearance and kept her mobile phone close at hand. She left the apartment only for food, and sleep was next to impossible.

So it was with great relief that Monday morning she received a call from Warren's good friend, Barton Cao. The Paris-based opposition leader had just arrived at Heathrow on business and asked if he could call on her that afternoon.

This gave Annabel a compelling reason to tidy up and buy groceries and fresh flowers, which occupied nearly the entire morning. When Cao arrived, he brought sympathy and kindness but, alas, no news of her husband. But when Annabel showed him the letter that Warren had written at the Magog lake house, Cao's expression turned grave.

"The letter is almost certainly genuine," he began. "But I'm completely baffled by Warren's decision to enter the U.S. Surely, he knew that the League could not be trusted. The idea that he faced no risk in crossing the border is preposterous. He must have had some other thought in mind that I'm not aware of."

"Odd that you should say that," Annabel replied. "It's very similar to what your niece said when she visited me just before I left Montreal. During our talk, she told me of her connection to the League and the fact that she had been at the Magog lake house when Warren and the others left for Vermont. I asked her why she thought Warren had gone over. Her answer was that he seemed to have persuaded himself."

A look of hopeful surprise appeared on Cao's usually impassive face.

"You mean you saw Maria just a week ago?" he asked.

"Yes. Didn't she tell you?"

He shook his head and sadness replaced the hope in his eyes.

"I haven't heard from Maria in many weeks," he confessed. "I was the one who sent her there, but she stopped following my instructions very early on. So I can no longer vouch for her reliability. For all I know, she may be under DSS control. Did she give any indication of what she thought happened to Warren?"

At this, Annabel forced a thin smile.

"She said she didn't know, but she doubted that he'd been caught or killed at the border. That's because, if the DSS held him, they would have identified him right away and bragged about his capture."

"Did Maria say anything about her own plans? Does she intend to come back to Paris any time soon?"

"Nothing definite. But she did say she felt guilty about Warren's disappearance and thought she might go to Boston to look for him."

Cao's face fell.

"But she also left open the possibility of returning to Paris and promised to visit me on the way if she did," Annabel added. "In the meantime, she said I could communicate with her through you."

Only the last part was true. Because if Maria were to make good on her pledge to visit Boston, Annabel suspected she and Cao might never see the young woman again.

"Yes, of course," Cao answered, pasting on a half smile. "The moment I hear from her, I'll be sure to let you know,"

"I imagine you've also read the reports about the border incident near where Warren crossed," Annabel went on, changing the subject. "What's your take on it? Do you think Warren could have been captured on his way back to Canada?"

"Such reports mean nothing. The DSS can insert any story it wants in the controlled media."

"I agree," Annabel noted, crossing the room to fetch a file folder. "But do you know an Allen Hackett, posted to the British embassy in Ottawa?"

"Only from what Warren has said about him. And from Maria," Cao replied with a wary look. "Since her arrival in Canada, Maria has been working with Hackett to investigate the League. I still don't know quite what to make of him."

"Then maybe you should see this."

Annabel showed Cao the email message in which Hackett claimed that Warren was not killed at the border but rather was safe and sound. And this, she noted, had come days after Hackett told her that Warren had been intercepted at the border. She also voiced her unease that the MI5 officer had urged her not to approach the British government.

"I think he's playing for time," Cao declared after reading Hackett's message.

"Another thing," Annabel added, retrieving Linder's Boston postcard from her purse. "Hackett asked if he could borrow this to test it for secret writing. I refused."

Cao accepted the card from Annabel and held it under a lamp in glancing light, as Hackett had done.

"There's definitely something beneath the cover message. Would you trust me to have it tested? I can have results by this time tomorrow and promise not to damage the original."

Annabel hesitated for a moment. She hadn't felt comfortable giving the card to Hackett, but Cao had been one of her husband's closest confidants.

"Yes, please take it and do what you must," she told him.

"By the way, does Warren wear a ring? A wedding ring, perhaps?"

"Yes, a simple gold band, like mine," she added, holding up her left hand.

Cao was as good as his word, ringing Annabel the next afternoon to set a time to return Warren's postcard. When he did, he showed her the faint block letters that Linder had imprinted on the card with his gold wedding ring, perpendicular to the message "Greetings from Boston."

The hidden text read: "League is fraud. Arrested 3/25."

Annabel was devastated.

"But Hackett said Warren was safe! What am I to do now?"

"You've got to publicize his arrest right away," Cao urged. "That's the only way to create public pressure for Whitehall to demand Warren's release. Do you have any contacts in the media?"

"No, but Warren's business partner does."

"Good. Then put him to work."

As soon as Cao was off the phone, Annabel called Dwight Calder and explained the situation. He dropped everything and came right over to work with her on a draft letter to *The Evening Standard*. The gist of the letter was that the League had enticed Linder to return to America for a secret meeting with its leaders, based on its now-doubtful claims of having built an internal resistance movement capable of toppling the Unionist regime. The letter added that Linder had posted a secret message to his wife shortly before his arrest claiming that the League was a fraud. In closing, Annabel's letter demanded that the Foreign Ministry contact the Unionist leadership to demand Linder's immediate release.

"Do you think they'll publish it?" Annabel asked Calder as soon as the draft was complete.

"I can't guarantee it, but I'd say the chances are good," he replied. "I have a friend at the paper who owes me a favor."

"If they publish it, do you think it will have any effect?"

Calder bit his lip and paused as if to put the best gloss on his answer.

"I won't lie to you, Annabel. The Unionists don't swap spies and they rarely admit to holding a political prisoner unless they decide to trot him out for a show trial. Still, it's worth a try."

On Wednesday, Annabel's letter appeared in *The Evening Standard*, along with a one-paragraph correction to an earlier story about Linder's disappearance. The correction cited new evidence contradicting earlier reports that Linder may have been killed or captured along the Canadian border. It pointed instead to Linder's apparent arrest in Boston while meeting with members of an obscure domestic opposition group calling itself the League.

Annabel spent the rest of the week alone except for her part-time cook and housekeeper. She had no desire to go out. Likewise, nearly all her friends kept their distance after sending flowers and making sympathetic noises over the telephone. Even worse, the London to which she had returned seemed a different place from the one she had left. All around town, people were laughing, talking, joking, flirting, and going about their daily lives, apparently without a care in the world. Traffic roared in the streets. Evening came and theaters opened at the usual time, as if her husband hadn't disappeared from her life and her heart hadn't shattered.

Finally, on Friday, the last day in the fateful month of March, she summoned up her courage and made a dinner reservation at the Beaumont Hotel, near Grosvenor Square, where she and Warren had dined and stayed many times. But during the short cab ride the world seemed oddly distant. And upon entering the hotel lobby, she felt like a ghost returning to haunt a place where it had once known joy.

Nonetheless, she made her way to the Grill Room, one of her husband's favorites for its traditional American menu, and asked to be seated in the same booth where she and Warren often sat. The room was a comforting place, with its dark wood-paneled walls, burgundy leather upholstery, and Art Deco flourishes. She ordered the steak *tartare* appetizer and lamb chops, along with a glass of Burgundy, and kept her mind busy imagining the private lives of the other diners.

The outing proved to be a pleasant distraction, if not wholly enjoyable without Warren's companionship. But the meal's warm afterglow turned to ice as she passed through the lobby and glanced into the bar, thinking she might linger for a nightcap. For there, seated at the rail, she caught a glimpse of a small man staring at her with a triumphant smirk on his lips. The face was vaguely familiar but she couldn't make the connection until after she had quickened her step and moved past the registration desk. Only then did she recognize the man as Samuel Nadler, the pesky accountant who had followed her and Warren around Paris while they visited Leonard Fury the previous summer. But why was Nadler here and what did he want?

Chapter Thirty-Three: Interrogation

> "The limits of tyrants are prescribed by the endurance of those they oppress."
> –*Frederick Douglass*

SATURDAY, 25 MARCH 2034

T he building that housed the DSS Annex in Boston formed part of a downtown office complex occupying an entire city block. A decade earlier, during the Great Blue Terror, DSS firing squads had worked around the clock in the building's cavernous cellars to execute enemies of the state. The DSS now used a portion of those cellars as a regional interrogation prison.

Linder knew the building by reputation only. Even so, it made his skin crawl to be taken inside and to ride the freight elevator to the third subbasement. On exiting, Jafari ordered him politely but firmly to undress. Then three uniformed prison guards and a middle-aged female paramedic conducted a thorough strip search, treating his limbs and bodily cavities as inanimate objects. They also searched his clothing, examining every seam and fold of each garment for contraband. When finished, Jafari made a list of each item found on Linder's person, including garments and pocket litter, and instructed Linder to sign it. Afterward, Linder felt utterly alone.

In that moment, Linder's thoughts were suddenly transported back to the Virginia interrogation prison where he had landed a decade ago after his rendition flight from Beirut. His arrival then had been a similar nightmare, and he recalled his realization that, from this moment on, nothing would belong to him, not even his body. At any moment the authorities could empty his pockets, remove his clothing, or poke their gloved fingers into his mouth or up his rectum. Throughout his imprisonment in Virginia, and later in the labor camp system, he never got used to the strip searches. Each one was a fresh humiliation.

Over time, however, Linder learned to follow the Stoic philosophers in treating his captors like the weather. They could cause problems for him, like a storm, but a storm did not humiliate. He alone could humiliate himself by doing something that brought on shame or regret.

Once Linder's inventory of possessions had been registered and packed away for storage, the guards asked about his clothing sizes and issued him an orange prison jumpsuit, white socks, cotton underwear, and open-heeled synthetic clogs. Next the orderly checked his clipboard to see which cell would be Linder's.

"So, what crimes have brought you here?" the orderly asked with a bored expression before pressing a buzzer to open the security door.

"I have no idea," Linder answered. "Why don't you tell me?"

"This one's done 'em all," the paramedic chimed in with a derisive smile. "He's the fugitive traitor they warned us about."

"Right, then," the orderly responded. "Don't you try anything here, pal, or it'll be straight to the punishment cell."

Linder paid the orderly no mind. He knew from experience that the entire entry procedure was designed to throw the prisoner off balance and leave him without hope. So he dismissed the threat from his mind as the guards shackled his wrists and ankles and linked the shackles to a chain fastened around his waist. Then they pulled a black nylon hood over his head and marched him through a series of damp, chill corridors that smelled alternately of mold and disinfectant. All along the way, one of the guards jangled his keys, most likely to warn the other prisoners that a new man was in tow.

When they stopped, Linder heard the keys jangle again as a cell door opened.

"You're in cell 73. From now on, you'll be known as Prisoner 73, except during interrogations. If you use your real name out in the hallway or in your cell, you'll land in the punishment block."

Linder was familiar with this tactic. It was meant to strip the prisoner of his identity, keep him from knowing the names of others held at the facility, and thus advance the process of dehumanizing him.

The guards unshackled Linder and removed his hood before leaving him alone in the cell. The place measured about six by ten feet, windowless, with walls of unpainted gray concrete and a floor of beige composite resin. Its only fixtures were a steel door fitted with a spyhole and a food delivery slot; a rectangular lighting panel high overhead; a stainless steel toilet-and-sink combo; and a steel bunk bolted to the floor. Stacked neatly on the vinyl-covered mattress were a set of threadbare white cotton blend sheets and pillowcase, a gray polyester blanket, a slender pillow, and a terry towel and washcloth. Beside them were an enameled steel mug and bowl.

Linder strained his ears for sounds from the corridor. Nothing. That didn't surprise him, however, as this wasn't some medieval dungeon or Third World fingernail factory, where the screams of torture victims were allowed to echo down the corridors to terrorize other prisoners. It was an isolation ward intended to keep detainees secluded from one another during their secret intelligence exploitation.

That night, no one came to disturb him. After a while, the overhead lights dimmed but did not go out entirely. All manner of confused thoughts ran through Linder's mind as he lay on the unyielding prison bed. And despite having concluded rationally that he might be there for a very long time, he still nurtured the irrational hope that someone might be on the way to him at any moment to announce that a terrible mistake had been made.

Early Sunday morning, Linder awoke to a noisy crackle like the static from an overhead speaker and opened his eyes with a start. Just above the door, he spotted the built-in loudspeaker and imagined that the unit probably contained a concealed microphone and video camera, as well. Sitting upright in his bed, he also noticed that he had a headache and a bitter taste in his mouth that he couldn't quite place.

Now that the facts of his arrest and captivity were undeniable, he acknowledged the extreme unlikelihood that the Unionist regime would ever release him. After all, he was a renegade DSS officer who had spent a decade working to overthrow Unionist rule. For such an enemy, there could be no amnesty, no parole, and no prisoner swap, and not even a return to the labor camps. After his interrogation, he would be executed or somehow made to disappear. But Linder was at heart an individualist who believed in personal responsibility and rejected any notion of victimhood. To feel sorry for himself or appeal for mercy was beneath his dignity.

Still, there remained the matter of his interrogation. He had been through it before, and in fact had sat on the other side of the table at various times in his government career. But interrogation was not something to be taken lightly. According to an old saying from the Soviet gulag, interrogation is like seasickness. At first you think you'll die, and then you're afraid you won't. How long would this one last? And how should he comport himself? To comply or resist—that was the question. If he resisted, how soon before his strength failed? And then what? Could he find a way to hasten death, or would he end up dissolving into a disgusting heap of jelly and do whatever was asked of him?

What might Annabel think of him if she ever learned how he had behaved? Or his followers. Would they ever be allowed to find out? No. Only if he capitulated.

Linder thought of the maxims of the renowned Jewish psychiatrist, Viktor Frankl, who had survived captivity at Auschwitz. Several of these, as he recalled, were:

"Those who have a 'why' to live can bear with any 'how.'"

"The last human freedom is to choose your attitude."

And: "The point is not what we expect from life, but what life expects from us."

So, if the end was near, what did life expect of him? What meaning could he give to his final days? Linder had spent the past decade atoning for his actions in the DSS. And he came to Boston intending to expose the League and to thwart its goal of subverting the legitimate anti-Unionist opposition. Now that he had fallen into DSS hands, they would likely try to make him betray that movement and endorse the League. Would he be strong enough to resist?

Linder crossed the cold floor in his bare feet and lifted the hinged door to the food slot, which was empty. Returning to his seat at the foot of the bed, he racked his brain to recall the fundamental principles of interrogation, as he had learned them during his early intelligence training. The DSS interrogation scheme was patterned in most respects after the one used by the CIA, the Russian FSB, and most other modern security services. Based on classic Soviet interrogation doctrine, the system relied upon sleep deprivation, social isolation, environmental manipulation, and the omission of basic nutrients from the diet, all intended to gradually weaken and demoralize the prisoner without resort to physical beatings or torture. For some prisoners, psychoactive drugs were also part of the mix.

In addition to having studied interrogation techniques, Linder had also learned how to resist those techniques and had been afforded ample opportunity to practice such resistance during his years of captivity. But he had been younger then, and stronger, and had not yet attained a level of notoriety sufficient to bring the full weight of the DSS down upon his head.

For captured soldiers and spies, the usual goal for resisting interrogation was to protect time-sensitive military secrets, like imminent military actions, and to allow fellow operatives to evade capture. American counterintelligence doctrine generally assumed that most U.S. soldiers and spies would spill their guts within forty-eight hours after capture. Thus, heroic resistance was deemed pointless unless the prisoner had a reasonable chance of escape or rescue within a day or two. In Linder's case, no imminent threat to plans or persons demanded his ongoing resistance. Similarly, his chances of escape or release were remote.

So what was the point of resisting? To avoid shame and humiliation? To win better treatment? To inspire others? Or merely to spite his enemies? All these seemed valid enough, but which motivation would stand up best under pressure? That was a question he couldn't answer. All he could do was prepare for the ordeal, no matter how long it—and he—might last.

Linder's training and experience told him that, regardless of duration, the key steps to resisting a modern interrogation were to study one's conditions in minute detail; record the passage of time; set a daily routine; maintain physical and mental discipline; and call upon a higher power for strength. For while one's captors could bring enormous resources to bear against any one prisoner, their time and attention were finite. As a result, throughout human history, certain exceptionally determined prisoners had been able to hold out for astonishingly long periods through superior force of will. Regardless of the methods deployed against them, some prisoners simply would not break.

At last, Linder's concentration lapsed when the food trap banged open. On its interior shelf he found a foil-wrapped energy bar and a bottle of metallic-tasting water. He ate the bar slowly before washing it down with water. Then he dressed, made his bed, and launched into a series of exercises that included push-ups, sit-ups, and burpees. He was halfway through the burpees when the food trap opened a second time and a voice from the other side rang out.

Not long after Linder's arrest on Saturday evening, the chief of the DSS's Exile Division, Victor Barbosa, directed James Jenkins to take personal charge over Linder's interrogation. Accordingly, Jenkins remained in Boston and set up shop in the Boston Field Office. The first thing he did the next morning was to call Barbosa to present his interrogation plan. Barbosa listened to the plan in silence.

"The General Secretary has put us in a bind," Barbosa replied at last. "The longer Linder remains missing, the more his people will blame the League. What we need is an alternate narrative. My choice would be for him to confess that he was on his way to Boston meet with insurgents when he was captured at the border. That would help protect the League's reputation. Failing that, I think our best option is to put out word that he was killed on his way in."

This took Jenkins by surprise.

"Really? Shot on Friday night?" he probed. "How would that work? It's already Sunday."

"It's not ideal, but it'll do. Backstopping for the shooting story is already in place. After you and I spoke last night, I sent a team from our Vermont field office to the Canadian border, posing as insurgents. Early this morning they staged a fake shootout with the Border Patrol at a place where the Canadians would be sure to hear the gunfire. Then our people brought an ambulance to the scene and carried away two survivors on stretchers and another two in body bags. A reporter at the Boston Globe was given the story this morning and posted it to the Globe's website."

"But how does that get the League off the hook?" Jenkins persisted. "Linder's inner circle will know that the League invited him to Canada. Won't his people hold the League responsible if he doesn't come back?"

"Not as much as if we announced his arrest," Barbosa replied. "Even though our story is coming out a day late, the border incident muddies the water and will buy us time. A week is all we need."

"And all we have, if the General Secretary has his way."

"Well, there you have it, Jim. If Linder doesn't cooperate, the League operation will start to unravel. A leak here, an investigation there, and before you know it, three years of hard work will go up in smoke. We'll have to recall our field agents and make the League dissolve into the night."

""All right," Jenkins yielded, though not happy about it. "Now I know what I'm supposed to do. But what reason does Linder have to cooperate with us? He must know by now that he doesn't have long to live—two death sentences *in absentia* will see to that. So why should he destroy his reputation and demoralize his followers by collaborating? No, I think he'll hold out as long as he possibly can. And after his experience in the camps, a week in solitary should be a cakewalk for him."

"Prisoner 73—to questioning!"

The voice on the opposite side of his cell door carried a thick Boston accent. When the door slid open, two muscular guards stood in the corridor. One ordered Linder to face the wall while the other shackled his wrists and ankles and slipped a black hood over his head. Next the pair seized him by the shoulders and frogmarched him down the hall to a stairwell, which they climbed to the next floor above.

A minute or two later they entered an overheated room. There the guards removed Linder's hood and directed him to sit on a straight-backed metal chair just out of reach from a bare metal table that, like the chair, was bolted to the floor. The room was dimly lit except for a bank of spotlights shining into Linder's face from behind the table. At first the interrogator stood behind the lights, observing Linder but saying nothing. When he emerged from the glare, Linder could see that the interrogator was a light-skinned black man of middle height and rotund build, dressed in a gray jumpsuit without insignia. Linder gave him a closer look and recognized the man as none other than Roy Scovill, the Boston City Council member whom he met the day before at Poirier's safehouse.

"Who are you and why are you keeping me here?" Linder challenged before the man had a chance to sit down.

"My name is Darrell Otis, and I've been assigned to ask you some questions."

"Oh, then you're not Roy Scovill, the name you were using yesterday?"

"No. From now on, I'm Otis."

"Suit yourself," Linder answered.

James Jenkins, alias Otis alias Scovill, took a seat on the edge of the steel table and opened the file folder he had brought.

"And you are Warren Linder. Or would it be Vincent Stephens?"

"The first. Stephens was just the name on the passport they gave me in Vermont."

"I see," Otis went on. "So you entered the country under a false name. And by what means did you enter?"

"By boat."

"From where?"

"Canada."

"Can you be more specific?"

"Near the town of Magog, in Quebec," Linder added.

"Did you report to an immigration facility for processing on arrival in the U.S.?"

"Not that I recall."

"Then you entered the country illegally."

"If you say so."

"What was the purpose of your visit, Mr. Linder?"

"I was invited to meet with members of a local non-profit in Boston. I think you know the one."

"So I do," Otis answered. "Why then do you suppose you find yourself under arrest?"

"You tell me," Linder replied, taking odd pleasure in the fact that Otis's torso momentarily shaded the glare from his eyes.

"Your file shows prior convictions for treason, seditious conspiracy, advocating government overthrow, espionage, sabotage, terrorism, receiving stolen property, money laundering and—what a surprise—tax evasion. Quite a record."

From there, the interview advanced only inch by inch, with Linder giving truthful answers but offering not a single word more than was asked. Otis, if that was his name, showed occasional impatience but brought it quickly under control. Linder remained imperturbable. After about ninety minutes, Otis ordered him back to his cell.

In the afternoon, the guards brought Linder in once more for questioning. Now Otis displayed a more severe side.

"Are you aware that you stand convicted of capital crimes and have been sentenced to death *in absentia*?" he asked.

"So I've been told."

"Maybe now would be a good time to put that at the top of your mind. It's my duty to inform you that an order for your execution remains pending. Only by fully cooperating with us do you have any chance of surviving it."

Linder remained silent. Of course the DSS would say this. But that didn't make it true.

"Are you ready to answer all questions truthfully and to the best of your ability?" Otis demanded.

"Go ahead and ask. I'll say what I can."

Otis offered Linder a doubtful look.

"Fine, then," he went on. "Let's start with émigré-sponsored violence against the U.S. government. What can you tell me about it?"

"That was Fury, not me," Linder replied. "I never supported his paramilitary work, though I did give him money sometimes for his personal use."

"How about your own cross-border operations? What can you tell us about your collaborators in the U.S.?"

"I don't have any. That's why I decided to come here in person."

"Then how about the people who work with you remotely? Can you share their names?"

"Such people don't use their true names. And even if they did, I've promised them confidentiality."

Otis offered a weary expression.

"Of course," he remarked. "So why not provide whatever pseudonyms or codenames you have for them?"

"Same reason," Linder replied with a crooked smile. "Because I promised."

A series of questions followed, touching on the activities of émigré organizations other than his own, to which Linder responded with claims of ignorance. When he did offer a response, he sounded more like a paid consultant than a prisoner under interrogation. But Otis wasn't showing all his cards, either. Exactly what level of cooperation would be enough to stave off the execution order? And for how long?

Otis questioned Linder for another hour before sending him back to his cell. There Linder napped until the food slot opened. By now he was famished and wolfed down his dinner of overcooked macaroni with watery tomato sauce. Soon after, the guards took him outdoors to the exercise yard, a fenced-off area the size of a basketball court, where Linder walked the perimeter for twenty minutes until the guards took him away.

Later that night, conditions in the cell remained suspiciously benign, with the temperature comfortably warm, the overhead lights dimmed, and a low hiss-like white noise issuing from the cell's loudspeaker. But Linder knew the honeymoon wouldn't last. That was because the DSS's interrogation protocol, like the Soviet one on which it was based, imposed a step-by-step withdrawal of comforts and privileges designed to wear down a prisoner's mental and physical resistance. The goal was to induce a state of acquired helplessness and despair. So Linder counted sheep to help him fall asleep, expecting that each succeeding night would be rougher than the one before. Unless, of course, he capitulated.

Linder didn't have long to wait before experiencing downgraded comforts. During his second night in the interrogation prison, the cell's temperature dropped sharply. And at wakeup time, the overhead speaker spewed out horrendously loud Europop music of the most irritating kind. Breakfast consisted of a grayish gruel, served lukewarm, whose starchy texture made it scarcely palatable. Soon after, the cell temperature rose rapidly from warm to blazing. Linder couldn't help but admire the genius who had dreamt up this oppressive scheme. At some deep level, he found himself already growing anxious over the discomforts he might suffer next.

Fortunately, Linder could console himself with recollections from recently published interviews with released Unionist prisoners that certain rules went into effect several years earlier to protect DSS detainees from the worst sorts of abuse inflicted during the Blue Terror. Physical beatings and mock executions were now taboo in DSS facilities. And interrogations were not permitted after ten at night. Even shouting at prisoners was verboten—the official DSS interrogation manual called for "rapport building" and "psychological methods." Not that the rules were always observed. But, as Linder was a high-value prisoner, his interrogator would likely abide by the new regime. For a while, at least.

The guards summoned Linder at the usual time for his second morning of interrogation. Initial questioning centered on the months following his escape from the Yukon, including his activities in Utah, how he managed to locate Philip Eaton's cached treasure in Ohio, and how he transported it, along with his sister, his friend Jay Becker, and his ward Caroline, from Ohio to the U.K. Most of this material had been covered in Linder's book and his public statements. He answered Otis's questions, but with little detail and at an excruciatingly sluggish pace. At last the examination moved on to Linder's most recent relocation to London and his interactions with MI5 and other British police and security organs.

The afternoon session focused on the Anglo-American Freedom Committee and Linder's propaganda outlet, the Anglo-American Information Bureau. Here, Linder was more generous with his responses, offering choice tidbits about his non-violent activities, though not compromising anyone who worked with him. But when Otis pressed him to discuss his finances, Linder refused. They funds he had left now would belong to Caroline.

Perhaps for this reason, the questions took on a harder edge as they delved into the various techniques that Linder had used to propagate his anti-Unionist messages. Linder understood that the DSS would have compiled an exhaustive dossier on him and the AAIB, and that Otis would draw liberally from it in crafting his questions, which jumped forward and backward in time, the better to trip him up.

At the session's end, Otis presented a printed summary of the previous day's interrogation for Linder's review and signature. While broadly correct, the transcript slyly manipulated the prisoner's actual words to make them sound more incriminating. It also used inflammatory language wherever possible. For example, Linder's "friends" became "accomplices," and his "activities" became "criminal activities."

Linder refused to sign the summary.

"Need I remind you that you've been convicted of capital crimes and that an execution order remains open against you?" Otis blustered, clearly frustrated at his lack of progress.

"Okay, I consider myself reminded."

"Your fate is entirely in your hands," Otis went on. "Cooperate fully and your sentence could be commuted to as little as ten years imprisonment. And not in a labor camp, but in a conventional prison, where you'd stand a fair chance of survival. Who knows what could happen in that time, Linder? Perhaps an amnesty. Or a prisoner swap. You'd be a fool not to play ball with us."

"Except we both know that I'd never get out alive," Linder countered. "If you don't like my answers, why don't you go ahead and shoot me now?"

Otis said nothing. He closed the file folder containing the previous day's unsigned interrogation summary and rose to leave. By offering Linder a chance at a commuted sentence, he had apparently hoped to plant seeds of doubt in the prisoner's mind. But how could Linder possibly trust Otis's offer, having made so many empty promises of his own when he had been the interrogator? And if he accepted the offer, what further price might he be forced to pay? How could he live with himself if he gave the Unionists what they wanted?

After the session, Linder returned to his cell, where dinner was a watery fish soup with a revolting odor. An hour later, the guards took him to the exercise yard for his walk. But for the rest of the evening, a disturbing thought nagged him: What if he really did have a choice over his fate?

Chapter Thirty-Four: Death Notice

> "Our anxiety does not come from thinking about the future, but from wanting to control it."
> –*Kahlil Gibran*

MONDAY, 10 APRIL 2034

Two weeks passed without Annabel receiving further word about her husband's fate. Then, on the Monday after her solo dinner at the Beaumont, a new email arrived from Allen Hackett in Ottawa. This one was as confusing as it was disturbing. The text read:

"I am presently on my way to London and hope to be with you shortly. The latest information on your husband indicates that my earlier reporting to you was not entirely accurate. The correct part is that Warren appears to have been captured by Unionist forces while en route back to Canada early Sunday morning. The mistaken part is that, while alive and uninjured, he cannot be said to reside in friendly hands. In any event, please take no further action until you and I meet."

Three days later, Annabel had heard nothing more from Hackett, whom she presumed would have arrived in London by then. Bearing in mind Barton Cac's suspicion that Hackett was more interested in keeping her quiet than in helping her, Annabel recalled Hackett's earlier mention of his favorite London hotel and decided to take matters into her own hands. So she made a reservation at the Royal

Horseguards Hotel, located a short distance from MI5 headquarters at Lambeth Bridge, and checked in Thursday evening.

"I'm expecting a friend this weekend," she told the desk clerk while he was looking up her reservation. "Might you be able to tell me whether Allen Hackett has checked in yet?"

The clerk, a rail-thin young man with an officious manner, gave her a close look before responding.

"Yes, I see Mr. Hackett arrived earlier this week," he replied. "Would you like me to ring him for you?"

Annabel feigned a yawn and glanced at her watch.

"No, it's rather late and I'm spent from traveling. Can you tell me at what time he usually takes breakfast when he's here? I'll try to catch him in the morning."

"Just a moment and I'll check," the clerk answered, entering a few keystrokes on his computer to pull up Hackett's restaurant charges. "Yes, it looks as if he comes down early most mornings, around seven."

"Thank you," Annabel said, accepting her room key from the clerk and heading toward the elevator.

The next morning she waylaid Hackett at the entrance to the breakfast room.

"Good morning, Allen," she greeted him with a matter-of-fact smile. "May I join you?"

"You?" he gasped upon seeing her, and then looked around to check if anyone had seen them together. "Yes, good morning, Annabel," he added after regaining his composure. "Lovely to see you. Shall we take a table in back so that we can talk without being disturbed?"

"As you wish."

After they were seated and the waitress had poured their coffee and pointed them toward the breakfast buffet, Hackett apologized for not having been in touch.

Annabel acknowledged the admission with a nod but said nothing.

"I don't know quite how to put this, Annabel," he went on before taking a sip of coffee, "but my superiors have instructed me to suspend contact with you. They say it's improper for a member of the British secret service to keep company with Warren Linder's wife, in view of the publicity surrounding the man's disappearance. You really shouldn't have taken his case to the media, you know."

"I don't see how I had much choice."

"I understand your feelings, Annabel, but now that you're here, there is something you could do that might help matters all around," he went on with a tentative expression.

"And what might that be?"

"The service would appreciate your handing over any of Warren's papers that deal with the League. These mustn't be allowed to fall into unfriendly hands. And they could also put you at some risk."

Annabel shook her head.

"You won't get anything from me without a court order," she asserted. "Which I doubt you'll seek. But while you're here, what can more you tell me about Warren? Is His Majesty's government doing anything behind the scenes to free him?"

"We know little, other than that he is presumably in Unionist custody, most likely in Boston. But rest assured, our networks in North America are doing all they can to locate him."

"Sure, of course," Annabel scoffed. "But if that's all you can offer, what right do you have to tell me not to act on my own?"

"All I am at liberty to say, Annabel, is that your best chance of getting your husband back is to lie low and wait. It would be most unwise to interfere with any measures that the British government might take behind the scenes."

Then he gulped down what remained of his coffee and left.

Annabel stayed on for another half hour to partake of the hotel's traditional English breakfast. But before returning to her room, she stopped at the registration desk and slid a note across the counter, sealed in a hotel envelope.

"Would you mind leaving this for Allen Hackett?" she asked the desk clerk.

"Certainly," he replied before looking up Hackett's name on his computer. Then, finding it, he drew a sharp breath. "I'm afraid Mr. Hackett checked out, just a few minutes ago."

"Did he say where he was going?"

The clerk shook his head.

On the ride back to her flat, Annabel racked her brain for clues that Hackett had been dishonest with her from the start and might have played a role in Warren's disappearance. For example, there was Hackett's absence from Montreal when she and Warren arrived there. Then she recalled his conflicting claims about Warren's whereabouts, and the elusive behavior of his young associate, Cowen. Not to mention Hackett's requests for her to give him Warren's postcard and any of his papers connected to the League, and for her to remain silent about her husband's disappearance. She hadn't agreed to any of his requests. And yet, despite it all, Annabel somehow retained an instinctive trust in Britain's secret services. She still found it extremely hard to believe that a senior MI5 officer could meet her eye with a deliberate lie on his lips.

On returning to her flat, Annabel called Dwight Calder to tell him about her meeting with Hackett and to warn him against giving MI5 any of Warren's documents absent a court order.

"By the way," she added, "I haven't heard a word from the Foreign Office since our letter to *The Evening Standard.* Can you think of anyone in Whitehall whom we could nudge to work on Warren's behalf?"

"Not at the moment," Calder replied, "but let me investigate further. Perhaps Nelson Furness can suggest a name."

"Could he propose another contact in the media, as well, to help keep Warren's story alive?"

"I'll check on that, too, and get back to you."

On Monday, Calder reported back to her after speaking with a senior diplomat at the Foreign Office, on Furness's recommendation.

"Nelson's contact claimed that the most that his office can do in your case is make a routine inquiry about Warren through routine consular channels," Calder told Annabel. "No public statement, however, or anything that might cause a stir."

"How about Nelson's friends in the media, then. Any luck there?"

"I'm afraid not. Nobody will touch the story. Your best bet is to go back to *The Evening Standard*. Perhaps they'll take pity on you and post a further update."

"I'll give it a try," she answered, gritting her teeth in frustration.

After leaving several callback messages at the newspaper, she finally reached the reporter who had arranged to publish her letter to the editor and the one-paragraph correction about Warren's arrest.

"No, there's no way we can run another update unless substantial new information surfaces," the reporter explained.

"Then how about interviewing me as a human interest story? Surely, your readers would be interested to know what it's like to have one's spouse disappear into the maw of a totalitarian regime. And Warren is hardly the only British resident to have suffered that fate."

"Such an interview was already proposed. The editors nixed it. However, there is one other thing we could do for you, though you may not like it."

"Try me."

"Well, since you're the next of kin, we could publish a death notice for your husband any time you choose."

"But Warren isn't dead! He can't be dead!" she burst out.

"I'm so sorry if I've offended you, Mrs. Linder. Please forgive me for even suggesting it," the reporter replied in an apologetic tone. "But please feel free to call me should you change your mind."

For the rest of the week, Annabel felt like a caged lion. Her options seemed exhausted and, wherever she went, she ran into a deafening wall of silence about her husband.

Soon she encountered another problem. For while Warren's final letter had asked her to keep his business affairs in order, he had neglected to leave her a written power of attorney to act on his behalf. At first, Calder had managed to work around her lack of authority over Warren's accounts, but the longer the latter remained missing, the more difficult it became for Calder to manage his business partner's finances. At last, Annabel accepted Calder's suggestion to consult Warren's solicitor.

"Isn't there some other way for me to have authority to sign contracts and approve transactions on Warren's behalf?" she asked her husband's legal advisor.

"I'm afraid not, other than by going to court. And even that won't likely work without proof of death."

"But Warren isn't dead!" she exclaimed. "And even if he were, the Unionists might never acknowledge it!"

"Well, in that case, your only recourse is to seek a guardianship under the Missing Persons Act. The Presumption of Death Act won't be of much use to you because, for that to apply, you'd need to wait seven years before seeking relief."

"What if, for the sake of argument, we had proof of death? What then?"

"In that case, we could conduct a routine estate administration," the solicitor explained. "Fortunately, we already have a properly executed will to do that. As I recall, Warren's will names you as executor and leaves all of your husband's property to his ward Caroline, apart from sums to be set aside for his missing sister and for you. After a routine court hearing, you could take control of Warren's personal assets in relatively short order."

"And what about Caroline's trusts?" Annabel inquired. "Will proof of death or a court hearing be required for those, too?"

"Fortunately, not. Caroline is an adult now, and the remaining trusts that benefit her all have corporate trustees that can make disbursements to her without any further action from Warren."

"Well, Caroline will be happy to hear that. I'll be sure to tell her right away."

At the end of the conversation, Annabel felt as if she was no further along than when she'd started. What she wanted was her husband back, not his money or the ability to manage his business. And only the Unionists could hand him over.

Annabel slept poorly that night, caught as she was between the Unionist regime's silence, the court's probate requirements, and *The Evening Standard's* offer to have her declare her husband dead, though not officially.

But in the hazy consciousness that precedes awakening, she had an idea. What if she published the notice of Warren's death, not for the purpose of seeking guardianship, but to pressure the Unionists to either admit that they held Warren or confirm his death?

After weighing the decision over her morning coffee, she called *The Evening Standard* reporter and told him she would send over a draft death notice later that morning. Two days later, the announcement appeared in print. The text read:

"Warren Linder. Died March 26, mortally wounded by gunfire from United States Border Patrol troops at Derby Line, Vermont, while seeking to cross into Canada. Linder served as an officer in the United States Central Intelligence Agency and the Department of State Security before being convicted of treason and sentenced to hard labor at a series of corrective labor camps in North America. After escaping from one such camp in the Yukon Territory, he made his way to the United Kingdom, where he wrote a best-selling memoir and became a leader of American émigrés opposed to the Unionist regime. Linder is survived by his wife, Annabel, his sister, April, and his former ward, Caroline Kendall."

Though *The Evening Standard* published nothing further about Linder's death, several London tabloids came out days later with sensationalized accounts of his exploits. Among those exploits was Linder's alleged role in publishing the later-discredited Zuckerman Letter that precipitated the fall of Prime Minister Robert McKay's Labor government. Neither the Unionist regime nor any of its controlled outlets commented on the tabloid stories.

Soon after, however, the death notice ignited an entirely new round of media coverage. That was because Linder had given Dwight Calder a sealed letter shortly before leaving for Montreal with orders to release it to the press immediately upon public announcement of Linder's death. The *Evening Standard* obituary triggered that release, and Annabel was astonished to read in the Sunday papers that her husband had gone to Canada with the express intention of putting the League to the test. Either that group was a *bona fide* insurgent organization or it was a hoax under DSS control. Though Linder's letter did not specify whether he intended to enter the U.S. as part of his mission, it declared that, should he fail to return from Canada, American patriots must hold the League responsible and reject anything that the League or its representatives might say to exonerate themselves.

The publication of Linder's letter about the League and the resulting media speculation over his disappearance left Annabel bewildered. She confronted Calder over why he hadn't told her about the letter. Calder's answer was that he had wanted to, but that Warren had given him explicit instructions not to release the document to anyone until his death had been announced to the public.

Chapter Thirty-Five: Decline

> "It requires more courage to suffer than to die."
> *–Napoleon Bonaparte*

TUESDAY, 28 MARCH 2034

On Tuesday, the third full day of his captivity, Linder rose to the din of heavy metal music blaring from the cell's loudspeakers. He had slept only intermittently because the cell had turned bitterly cold during the night. And perhaps from lack of sleep, or possibly hunger, or the stress of confinement, his limbs felt weak and his mind befuddled.

He had an hour to wash, shave, dress, clean his cell and make the bed before his guards opened the food trap. When breakfast came, it was the same drab gruel as the day before, except for being thinner and colder. Nonetheless he forced it down, if only to keep up his strength. He was struggling through his calisthenics when the guards summoned him for interrogation.

The morning questioning picked up where the previous afternoon session had left off, covering Linder's latest opposition activities in London and abroad, including his alleged efforts to torpedo an Anglo-American trade agreement by means of the since-discredited Zuckerman Letter. As to the trade agreement, Linder admitted to lobbying vigorously against it, as reported in the British press. As for the Zuckerman Letter, he denied taking any hand in it.

To compensate for his lingering brain fog, Linder adopted the tactic of speaking slowly and answering in as many words as possible to avoid misstatements and to buy time. Otis soon caught onto this, however, and alternately scolded, threatened, and cajoled the prisoner

377

to offer up more signal and less noise. Perhaps as a consequence of his foot-dragging, Linder received no lunch that day. And during the afternoon session, Otis stepped up his browbeating.

"Let's face it, Linder," he snarled. "You're no hero. You're a traitor to your country and a Judas to the Department. Everyone around you knows what a shitheel you are. Even your sister couldn't stand being with you. Which is why she ran away, in hopes of leading some semblance of a normal life in Utah."

Stung by the taunt, which he knew contained a grain of truth, Linder replied, "If April and Jay are truly enjoying a normal life in Utah, I couldn't be more pleased for them. But, in two and a half years, I haven't had a word from either one. So you'll excuse me if I suspect they've been sent to the camps. And if I'm wrong, why not let me talk to them? You'd be a lot more credible if you did."

"I'm afraid that's not possible," Otis declared with a grimace that passed for a smile. "Remember, to the rest of the world, you went missing at the border and are presumed dead."

"All right, have it your way," Linder replied, meeting Otis's gaze. "But if I'm a dead man, why should I bother talking to you? Bring on the executioner and let's get it over with."

Otis seemed not to have expected this reaction from Linder. For a moment, he seemed at a loss to respond. When he did speak, it was on a note of exasperation.

"Listen, Linder, I don't understand why you're making things so difficult for yourself. I've offered you a clear way out of this. Cooperate and you'll have a chance to get on with your life one day. You won't even have to report against any of your people, if that's what's holding you back. Just go along with our story of how you landed here."

"Sure. So you can keep your phony League alive," Linder snapped back. "Sorry, but no dice."

The afternoon interrogation ended soon afterward. That evening, dinner consisted of tasteless chicken noodle soup and stale saltines.

Linder stopped his exercise walk after ten minutes when the drizzle turned to a hard rain. At bedtime the overhead lights dimmed, but for the next hour the cell temperature rose steadily until Linder was bathed in sweat. He threw off his blanket, then his sheet, and finally sat bolt upright in bed.

All at once his hatred for the Unionist Party, the DSS, and Darrell Otis boiled over. All Linder could think of was how to beat them at their own game. Should he fake cooperation and recant later, claiming duress? He considered the idea, then rejected it for fear the DSS would publicize his initial capitulation to demoralize the opposition, as they'd done with Fury. But how else to spite them, except by resisting to the point of death? Must he choose between being a dead hero and a live coward?

Linder awoke on the fourth day of his interrogation to the sound of a John Philip Sousa march. But which one? Was it the *Washington Post* or *Semper Fideles*? Or maybe *The Thunderer*? He ought to know and that bothered him. Yet somehow he couldn't help but smile and went on nodding his head to the beat. Was he losing his grip?

The morning interrogation began with some follow-up questions on his anti-Unionist activities in London before moving on to his work in Europe, particularly his contacts in Paris with Leonard Fury and Barton Cao. Otis was particularly interested in finding out when and how Linder first learned about Owen Quist's trip to Berlin to meet Benjamin Payne and the Free American Patriots.

"Leonard told me about it few days after it happened," Linder said, seeing little harm in responding. "His main man, Poirier, went to Berlin because Leonard didn't care to."

"And why not?"

"Probably because he detested Payne and trusted Poirier to act as his proxy. As I recall, Leonard didn't put much stock in the League back then."

"And what were your thoughts about Poirier at the time?" Otis probed. "You'd known him for several years, hadn't you?"

"We crossed paths now and again. He certainly wasn't the brightest bulb. But he'd done a lot of cross-border work for Leonard and was considered an experienced operator."

"How about later, when you met Quist at the lake house in Magog? Who did you think Poirier represented then? Because, by that time, Fury was dead."

"I couldn't really tell. Supposedly, he had begun working freelance for Barton Cao. But by the time I saw him in Canada, he seemed to have gone all-in for the League."

"And the Silva woman? Did she answer more to the League or to her uncle?"

The question puzzled Linder. Why the interest in Silva? Did the League have its hooks into her, too?

"How should I know?" he snapped. "Everybody was singing the League's praises that night. They all urged me to go to Boston."

"So why did you decide to go? Because they pushed you? Or had you already made up your mind?"

Linder hesitated. It was Kreutzer's visit that had pushed him over the edge. But it was against Linder's principles to rat on a fellow conspirator, even one so suspect as Kreutzer. If the trade rep had been arrested in the roundup of Ted Terzian's alleged coup plotters and had confessed on his own to the Magog meeting, that would be one thing. But Linder had no evidence of that. And even if Kreutzer had escaped capture, the DSS wouldn't hesitate to lie and claim that he had confessed, just to trick Linder into implicating him. So he said nothing.

Otis repeated the "why" question, but Linder remained silent. After circling around again without drawing a response, the interrogator looked at his watch and adjourned for lunch.

When the session resumed that afternoon, Otis returned to the question of why Linder had crossed over.

"So, if it wasn't persuasion, what was it? Morbid curiosity? Too much wine? A momentary lapse in judgment?"

"All of the above, I suppose," Linder evaded.

"But certainly you didn't expect to be arrested," Otis pressed.

"No, I didn't."

"Yet you'd warned your friend Fury repeatedly not to cross the border. What made you think you'd fare any better?"

Linder offered no answer. Otis went on.

"What if I were to tell you that your advice to Fury was completely on target? And that he should never have trusted the League?"

"How do you mean?"

"What I mean to say is that the League has been a creation of the DSS from the start," Otis replied, leaning forward with his elbows on the metal table. "Quist has been our agent all along. Your original instincts not to trust the League were right on the money. While old-line émigré outfits like yours, Fury's and Cao's were losing members and hemorrhaging money, the League was busy gaining a stranglehold over the entire anti-Unionist movement."

Linder felt as if his heart might stop. While he had long suspected that the League had been co-opted or penetrated, he never imagined that the DSS had created it out of whole cloth.

Otis leaned back and offered Linder a knowing smile.

"You were right to snub the League. That is, until your old friend, Irwin Kreutzer, dropped by to see you at Magog. What a game-changer!"

It was the second blow of a one-two punch. Linder reeled from it.

"Okay, so you knew about Kreutzer coming to the lake house," he replied, pulling himself together. "So what?"

"It's not just that we knew about his visit. We're the ones who made it happen—the Exile Division. Kreutzer is one of ours, too."

"But Kreutzer is Terzian's guy," Linder sputtered. "And Terzian hates the DSS."

"Sure, but Kreutzer's been collaborating with us for years. Hell, you should know that from your time working together at the London Embassy. It was we who sent him to you at Magog with that cock-and-bull story about Terzian joining forces with the League. It was our last shot at luring you across the border without waiting months for another crack at you."

It was as if someone had knocked the breath out of Linder's lungs. Had Kreutzer really betrayed him? And was it revenge for the Zuckerman Letter?

Perhaps seeing how badly shaken Linder was, Otis pressed home his advantage.

"Through the League, the DSS now controls virtually all significant intelligence about the U.S. reaching Western intelligence from the inside. We're beyond the point where you or Cao or anyone else can stop what we're doing. And don't think that your disappearance will set us back. The game is over and you've lost. The only sensible thing now is to save your skin by recording a statement describing how you screwed up at the border and urging your followers to go forward with the League."

But Linder had not forgotten how, as a DSS officer, he, too, had resorted to the most outrageous lies to break a prisoner's will during interrogation. Otis's story seemed too pat to be true.

"Yeah, I suppose I could give you a statement," Linder answered in a languid tone after recovering his poise. "But why would anyone believe something extracted from me under duress?"

"Because they wouldn't be hearing it from us," Otis explained with a predatory smile. "Your statement would surface as a clandestine recording smuggled out to the Canadian media."

Linder let out a bitter laugh.

"So you expect me to turn over all my followers to the League, just like that? How dumb do you think I am?"

"Come on, Linder, is it so bad a deal?" Otis persisted. "The League has already gained effective control over the émigré movement. You can't change that. Why not make the best of a bad situation? All we ask is that you admit you made a wrong turn at the border and ask your people to support the League until it finds a way to bring you home."

"Except that it won't do that."

"Not any time soon, anyway," Otis conceded with a shrug. "Not after you called on the League to assassinate Party leaders and pillage America's art museums. None of that went down very well with the White House."

The DSS man slid a manila folder across the table to Linder.

"Here, take a look at this statement and let me know if it's something you can accept."

But Linder didn't look. Instead, he glanced down at the floor and spoke in a barely audible voice.

"You said that, if I cooperated, you could get the court to commute my sentence down to ten years, served in a conventional lockup. Can you guarantee that?"

Otis shook his head.

"Only a judge can do that. You'd have to give us your statement first and then throw yourself at the court's mercy."

"Fat chance of that," Linder replied, pushing the folder away.

Because, no matter how much he wanted to believe that making a deal could save his life, Linder simply couldn't bring himself to sign a document that would insure the League's victory.

Otis didn't argue. He simply took the folder and left the room.

That evening, after a dinner of cold rice and beans and a stroll in the exercise yard, Linder thought back to the meeting at Mateo's where he had berated the League's Political Council for not selling off stolen artwork, mounting demonstrations, or assassinating Party leaders. Such inflammatory recommendations were bound to provoke the League leaders' outrage. So why had he pushed them so hard?

His original goal for the Magog gathering had been to assess the League's legitimacy and its capacity to bring down the Unionists. After meeting with Kreutzer, that goal had expanded to learn whether, by joining the League, it might serve as a power base from which he could play a key role in a new Terzian-led regime.

All at once, Linder caught his breath. Suddenly he realized how the DSS had drawn him in. Had they discovered in him the same flaw that they had identified in Leonard Fury? Had both he and Fury, seeing their chances of overthrowing the Unionists slipping away, been too eager to grasp at any chance, however remote, to strike a mortal blow at the regime? Seen in that light, it seemed to Linder that perhaps he and Fury had each fallen into the same trap. Pride, ambition, and a lust for revenge were their undoing.

Chapter Thirty-Six: Maria's Return

> "Men, it has been well said, think in herds; it will be seen that they go mad in herds, while they recover their senses slowly, one by one."
> *—Charles Mackay*

WEDNESDAY, 19 APRIL 2034

A few days after the posthumous message that Linder had entrusted to Dwight Calder appeared in *The Sunday Times*, Annabel called Barton Cao in Paris to ask whether the resulting backlash against the League had prompted anyone to come forward with fresh news about her husband.

"Nothing new, I'm sorry to say," Cao replied. "But I do have word about my niece, Maria. She's left Canada and is stopping in London before coming home to Paris. She asked me to give you the name of her London hotel."

The hotel was in a shabby area of southeast London and bore an unfamiliar name. That afternoon, Annabel appeared unannounced at Maria's room. But when the door opened, the younger woman seemed a different person than the one Annabel had met in Montreal. Her face was drawn and haggard and her eyes bore a hunted look. Her self-confidence seemed shattered, like someone who had been held captive or initiated into a cult.

Maria invited Annabel into the small room, whose windows looked onto a dark courtyard, and offered her a seat on the room's only chair, while Maria sat at the foot of her unmade bed. She was still dressed in her pajamas.

"My uncle told me you'd be coming," Maria began. "I wanted to see you before I return to Paris, as my time may not be entirely my own once I get there."

Annabel offered Maria a nod with a reassuring smile.

"When we met in Montreal," she told the younger woman, "you said you hadn't heard anything about Warren since your husband saw him in Vermont. Have you learned anything about Warren's situation since then?"

Maria gave a downcast look and shook her head.

"No," she said in a voice barely audible.

"You also said you were thinking of looking for him in Boston," Annabel went on. "Have you done that?"

"No," Maria replied, raising her head to meet Annabel's gaze. "The League refused to take me across the border."

"On what grounds?"

"They said it would disrupt their own investigation into the matter. But when I asked who their investigators were and what had been discovered, they wouldn't tell me. And afterward I noticed that I was being followed. So I slipped out of our Ottawa flat late one night, took a taxi to the airport, and caught the next flight that would connect me to Heathrow. I told Gordon to follow as soon as he could."

"Does that mean you no longer trust the League?"

"I wouldn't go quite that far," Maria replied, biting her lower lip. "Gordon and I have worked with them for the better part of a year. Some of our most valued friends are in the League. We've risked our lives for each other more than once. But lately I sensed the leadership didn't trust me any more."

"How so?"

"Because now I'm required to tell them everything I'm doing. Only, sometimes I don't. Like when I visited you at the hotel in Montreal. Every time I've tried to investigate something on my own, they've accused me of 'acting against discipline.' Then, when I told them I wanted to take time off to visit my uncle in Paris, they forbade it. God knows what they'll think of me, now that I've run away."

"So is there nothing else that you can tell me about Warren now that you are on your own?" Annabel asked.

Maria let out a long sigh and fidgeted with her purse, which lay beside her on the bed.

"Only bits and pieces," she replied. "For example, on the night before your husband was scheduled to come back to Canada, I asked Harry Cowen if I could drive out with him to pick up Warren in Magog. Harry acted surprised, as if I should have known better than to ask. Then he told me that Warren had been arrested in Boston but urged me not to tell anyone that he said so."

"Do you think Cowen was telling the truth?"

Maria drew a deep breath and held it for an instant before speaking.

"I have no reason to doubt it. That was on Saturday, the night of the arrest. So Cowen had to have gotten the news from someone in the know. But if the DSS picked up Warren, why did they let Jack and Owen go free? It had to be a setup. Someone in the League must be working for the DSS. But now I feel as though I have Warren's blood on my hands for not warning him. The only way to erase the stain is to rescue him. But that seems impossible. As much as I want to, I don't dare go back."

At that moment, the two women heard a noise outside the door, followed by rapidly retreating footsteps. Maria rushed to open it, as if expecting to confront an eavesdropper outside. Then she shut the door quickly and turned to face Annabel.

"Someone was out there and may have been listening to us. You should leave—now."

"But who could…"

"Please, go," Maria insisted. "I hope we meet again, in better days."

Then she opened the door and let Annabel out.

❖   ❖   ❖

That evening, Annabel called Caroline to fill her in on recent events and to share her growing sense of unease. Caroline confessed that she, too, had felt rather on edge lately.

"Why, has anything happened?" Annabel asked on a sharp note of concern.

"No, nothing like that. It's just a feeling."

"What kind of feeling?" Annabel persisted. "You haven't had any more strange visions lately, have you? Like the ones you had of Leonard Fury lying face down in the courtyard?"

"No, nothing like that," Caroline assured her. "But I did make a sketch of Warren about a month ago. I texted a photo to him, but he didn't recognize anything in it. So I didn't think much of the sketch at the time."

"Do you still have the photo in your images folder? Could you send it to me?"

"Sure, give me a moment."

"What did the sketch show?" Annabel asked while Caroline searched her phone for the image.

"It was a charcoal drawing of Warren, seen from behind, standing on a wooden dock at night, about to step into a motorboat. The water was very still, so it might have been a lake or a river. Okay, found it. Wait for my text."

Annabel opened the text message and enlarged the photo. All at once her blood ran cold.

"I've seen that dock," she said quietly. "It was at one of the lake houses I looked at in the town where Warren went to meet the League. Do you have any more sketches like this?"

"Yes, one other but, again, I didn't bother showing it to Warren because I wasn't even sure it was him. The sketch was of a man sleeping on his side, on a narrow bed or cot, with his back turned to me. The room was tiny, almost like a jail cell. I'm sorry I didn't say anything, but I didn't want to worry you. I thought maybe the drawing was of someone else and I kept waiting for that person to appear to me again."

"Can you remember when you sketched it?"

"Yes, it was on a Friday night," Caroline answered, "sometime in late March. I remember that because, since then, nothing else has come through."

Chapter Thirty-Seven: Finale

> "Those who foresee the future and recognize it as tragic are often seized by a madness which forces them to commit the very acts which make certain that what they fear shall happen."
> –*Dame Rebecca West*

THURSDAY, 30 MARCH 2034

Thursday was Linder's fifth day of interrogation. When the wake-up music came on in the morning, it was some discordant twelve-tone monstrosity from Schoenberg or Alban Berg that made it impossible for Linder to think straight. But mental distress was just the start. Moments later, shivering from cold and hunger, Linder's legs buckled on attempting to rise from bed. Even worse, his eyes seemed glued shut and his mouth filled with cotton. Then everything went dark.

A guard must have noticed Linder collapse to the floor, because a few minutes later a female paramedic arrived at his cell. She took Linder's pulse, listened to his breathing, and told him to get dressed and lie in bed until summoned for his morning interrogation. Linder did as he was told but felt no better for it.

The interrogation session began on time, with questions about Linder's key partners in the anti-Unionist movement, including Dwight Calder, Nelson Furness, and Barton Cao. Linder offered vague answers, mainly owing to fatigue. He rallied only when asked to explain why he had decided to renounce Leonard Fury's insurgency in favor of Alinsky-style agitation. On that topic, Linder was prepared to ramble on for hours, and would have done so had Otis not interrupted him. The interrogation eventually reached an impasse when Otis demanded derogatory information on his business partner, Dwight Calder.

When Linder refused, Otis pressed him to report on several others in the émigré movement and received the same response. Though Linder refused in each case to rat on his friends, he shivered through much of the session, nodded off frequently, and could barely hold himself erect. Perhaps for that reason, the interrogation ended early. That evening, Linder skipped his walk in the exercise yard after being unable to force down his dinner of lumpy potato soup and mold-encrusted cheese.

He remained awake for hours after the overhead lights dimmed, puzzling over how he might have handled his meeting with the League's Political Council differently. But answers eluded him until, as the cell's temperature transitioned from torrid to frigid, he slipped into an unsettled sleep.

That same evening, James Jenkins alias Darrel Otis was awaiting dinner at an Irish pub a block away from the DSS's Boston field office when his cell phone rang. It was Victor Barbosa.

"Your week is almost up, Jenkins," Barbosa began. "Unless you can get your man to see things our way, his end is nigh. What's your endgame to bring him around?"

"I think he's playing for time, hoping for a prisoner swap," Jenkins replied. "I've got to break that expectation. Tomorrow I'm taking him to the brink."

For a moment Jenkins heard nothing on the other end of the line.

"Okay, but don't wait too long," Barbosa's reply came at last. "Rumors about him and the League are rampant in the London press. And nobody over there is swallowing the border skirmish story. God help us if word gets out that your man is alive and kicking in Boston."

On Friday, the sixth day of interrogation and the last day of March, Linder awoke with a premonition of death. Whether by coincidence or design, today's wake-up music happened to be shamanic drumming, soft at first, then rising to a crescendo so loud that it nearly rattled his teeth.

Linder struggled to wash, dress, and make his bed. But this morning he found no breakfast in the meal slot, only a bottle of foul-tasting water. When the time came for his morning interrogation, a guard surprised Linder by bringing him his civilian clothes and ordering him to put them on. When he'd done so, the guards shackled him, pulled a hood over his head, and took him up two flights of stairs to a cold and drafty corridor where he endured the bite of handcuffs and leg irons fastened more tightly than usual.

Through a half-open door, Linder heard a heated argument outside, followed by the sound of weapons being loaded and rounds chambered. Then his hood was removed and he found himself standing before an exasperated Otis.

"Okay, Linder this is it," the interrogator barked. He wore a brown leather flight jacket over a blue oxford cloth shirt and khaki trousers instead of his usual gray jumpsuit. "Your last chance. Are you going to cooperate or not?"

"Get lost," Linder replied without thinking. But when Otis motioned for the guards to take him outside, Linder added. "But before you do, I'd like a pen and paper so I can write something to my wife."

Otis scowled and shook his head.

"No."

Suddenly it occurred to Linder that Otis might not be bluffing about this being the end.

"Surely, the Department didn't expend so much effort on my capture just to shoot me after a few days of questioning," he countered, doing his best to hold down a sudden sense of dread. "Getting me to talk was always going to take time. You knew that."

But Otis merely walked away, leaving Linder in the corridor with his two guards. After five or ten minutes, the pair led their prisoner out the door and into an underground parking garage. Two full-sized SUVs awaited with open doors. The first held two rough-looking strangers. The second had a driver and passenger in front, while in the back Linder spotted Otis and Ali Jafari, the swarthy young fellow who had helped to arrest him the previous Saturday.

The guards pulled Linder's hood on again, seated him between Otis and Jafari, and stepped back as the SUV drew away from the curb. It was clear what was going to happen next. They were taking him to some secluded spot to be shot.

En route, Jafari squeezed a finger between Linder's wrists and his handcuffs to make sure that he couldn't wriggle out. Linder could hear raindrops falling on the car's roof while the windshield wipers swept back and forth. But then the car slowed to a halt and the front-seat passenger answered a phone call before stepping out into the rain. During his absence, Jafari and the driver swapped filthy jokes.

At last the agent who'd taken the phone call returned to the car.

"Something's wrong with the other car," he said with a discouraged look. "We've got to go back."

And after a short drive, both SUVs returned to the underground garage, where Linder was left hooded and shackled in the corridor with guards for another half hour, wondering whether the next drive would be his last. When the door to the underground garage finally opened, Linder recognized Otis's voice.

"Take the prisoner back to his cell. No further action this morning."

Linder realized at once what had happened. Nothing had been wrong with the second SUV. The whole episode had been staged. For while the new DSS interrogation rules might prohibit the standard mock execution, in which a fake executioner pulls the trigger on an unloaded pistol aimed at the prisoner's head, the longer-form version was still allowed. That is, without threatening outright to shoot Linder, Otis had led him to believe that death was imminent. And though it was a lie, it worked, to a degree. The stress of expecting death at any moment had taken a toll. Linder's legs could barely support him as he trudged back to his cell.

But the morning's torments were not yet over. A few minutes later, the guards returned Linder to the interrogation room. Otis seemed to sense Linder's weakness and pushed him hard from the start.

"Don't be a schmuck, Linder," he urged. "Why die for nothing? Why not humor us and admit you got caught trying to cross the border? There's no shame in that. If you agree and you credit the League with working toward your release, we could go ahead and transfer you to a regular prison. And, who knows, maybe down the road someday we could swap you for one of our own guys and let you go home to your wife."

"So you want me to bless the League and deny everything I've been working for?" Linder parried. "No way."

"I hope you realize, Linder, that your time is running out. If you don't help me right now, I can't save you from your execution order. It'll happen."

"Then let's go to court. I'll take my chances there."

"You don't know our judges," Otis answered with a hardened expression. "Besides, you've already been sentenced. The law says you're already dead."

The back-and-forth went on for a while, with neither side ceding ground. By the time Linder returned to his cell, he was so exhausted that he couldn't recall half of what he'd said. He wolfed down the energy bar that he found in the meal slot and dropped onto his bunk, fully spent.

While Linder napped, Jenkins alias Otis sat in his temporary office on the DSS field office's sixth floor updating the prisoner's daily interrogation summary. He had just begun to prepare his notes for the afternoon session when his phone rang. He knew before he picked it up that the caller would be Barbosa.

"How did it go?" the division chief began.

"He's on the ropes, but not down for the count," Jenkins replied. "We go another round in a few hours."

A long pause followed.

"Today is the seventh day since his arrest," Barbosa pointed out. "The General Secretary gave us a week."

"But it's only his sixth day of interrogation," Jenkins objected. "I thought we had one more day."

Barbosa gave a skeptical grunt.

"I'd have to confirm that with the White House," he replied. "They'll want to know if the extra day will make any difference to the outcome. If you had till tomorrow, how confident would you be of bringing Linder around?"

Now it was Jenkins's turn to hesitate.

"I don't know," he conceded. "To be honest, sometimes I think the bastard has resigned himself to the inevitable."

"All right. Then I see no point in dragging things out any further. Let Twitchell have his execution by the end of the day. If the League collapses, so be it. The operation has had a terrific run, but the time has come to put it to bed."

During Linder's afternoon nap, he experienced nightmares more vivid than any he had faced for years. In one, he relived his arrest a decade earlier in Beirut, and then his interrogation in Virginia. In another, he experienced hard labor in the Yukon once again, escaped through the wilderness, and made his way two thousand miles further south to Utah. Each dream seemed like a chapter from a past life. Yet he felt oddly at peace.

When the guards summoned him for his afternoon interrogation, he could barely stand and required support to shuffle down the corridor.

Otis began the session with a final attempt to enlist Linder's cooperation.

"It's your last chance," the DSS officer warned. "We've prepared a script for you to read aloud and have the cameras ready to roll. We'll even let you edit the wording so that it sounds more natural to you. When you're done, you can start serving your ten years in a conventional prison. What do you say?"

Linder didn't answer right away. The problem wasn't that Otis was asking him to lie. He had lied his way out of so many tight spots in his life that telling one more lie wasn't a problem. The problem was that Otis was also lying. His promises meant nothing. So why humiliate himself and let down his fellow exiles by endorsing the League when the DSS would likely kill him, anyway? Why not end it right now?"

"Sorry, no deal," he told Otis.

The DSS man turned his back on Linder and left the room. A moment later, the guards unshackled Linder's ankles from the floor and returned him to his cell. That evening, he was served a better meal than usual, consisting of meatloaf, mashed potatoes with gravy, and green peas. Also, the cell's temperature reverted to normal while the loudspeakers fell silent. It was clear to Linder that serious change was afoot. Yet he felt at peace.

On a scrap of paper he wrote, "Tomorrow is my birthday. I expect I may not live to see it, but I'm not afraid. Of course, it's impossible not to fear death at some level. But I'm too stubborn, too much the untamed beast, not to believe I'll survive somehow. And, if that's what I truly expect, then, right up to the last split second of life, I won't have any fear of dying. What a concept! Fury would have loved it! I'll have to tell him all about it if we meet again on the other side."

Linder signed the paper, rolled it up, and stuffed it into a crack in the wall in the hope that another prisoner might find it someday and thus confirm that the late Warren Linder had spent his final days in DSS custody.

Not long after, the guards summoned Linder for his walk in the exercise yard. Feeling a bit stronger after his nap and the nourishing dinner, he rallied. As he stepped outdoors, he felt a chill wind blowing dead leaves in swirls around his feet. The air smelled of rain, wet earth, and rotting leaves. For a moment, Linder wondered whether he would lie buried under earth like this when winter turned the rain to snow. He breathed deeply while listening to the sound of the wind gusting around him. He imprinted these sensations on his memory.

Knowing that whatever happened to him now was largely beyond his control, Linder relaxed and waited for one of his guards to open the exercise yard's security gate. However unfair his execution might be, he recognized that he had little right to complain. During his years in the Exile Division, he had sent scores of his countrymen to remote camps like the ones where he had done time. And where his victims had drawn the same quantum of justice as he.

At that moment, instead of opening the gate, one of his guards seized Linder from behind and looped a slender cord around his neck. Linder felt it tighten, gasped for breath, and struggled with animal ferocity. But in less than a minute, his arms weakened, his vision narrowed, his chest stopped heaving, and it was over.

Chapter Thirty-Eight: Epilogue

> "The moving finger writes; and having writ,
> Moves on: nor all your piety nor wit,
> Shall lure it back to cancel half a line;
> Nor all your tears wash out a word of it."
> *—Omar Khayyam*

FRIDAY, 12 MAY 2034

In early May, just over a month after Linder's execution in Boston, photographs of his body, allegedly killed in a border shootout with U.S. troops, were leaked to a Canadian newspaper. Upon reading the news, Unionist Party surrogates praised the Border Patrol for having dispatched so notorious an enemy, but they did not mention a date of death. Anti-Unionists expressed skepticism about the border incident story but, given the quality of the photographic evidence and the newspaper's reputation, few could doubt that Linder was indeed dead.

With help from Dwight Calder and Nelson Furness, Annabel Linder organized a memorial service for her husband, to be held ten days later. When friends and followers walked the gravel paths of Mayfair's Mount Street Gardens toward the Grosvenor Chapel, past potted palms and beds of shaded tulips, they mourned not only Warren Linder and all that he had meant to them. They also mourned all that they had once been, as Americans, but no longer were and might never be again.

Few prominent Britons attended the memorial service. Furness was the conspicuous exception, as he delivered the eulogy. In it, Furness made clear that Linder never betrayed the anti-Unionist movement. He had not entered U.S. territory to defect, but rather had been lured over the border by deceit. He cited as evidence the written statement that Linder had left behind with his partner, Dwight Calder, citing his suspicions about the League.

And what had become of the League since Linder's death? Vanished. Evaporated into thin air, its members having fled Britain, gone into hiding, or surrendered to British police.

For days after the Canadian newspaper article about Linder, the London press churned out lurid stories of Linder's life and exploits. But the controversy surrounding his disappearance also deeply divided the émigré community. Some attributed Linder's death to his own failures and secretly rejoiced to be rid of such a troublemaker. Those more active in the anti-Unionist movement blamed the DSS and the League for Linder's death. Of these, many also accused the British Foreign Office and MI5 of complicity with Unionist agents and demanded an investigation. Owing to the public outcry, MI5 recalled Allen Hackett and Harry Cowen to London, where they were quietly relieved of duty. Neither man attended Linder's memorial. Nor was the newly installed American Ambassador to the Court of St. James, Irwin Kreutzer, among the mourners.

One of Linder's close friends who did attend the memorial was Colonel Barton Cao. After the service, Cao joined Annabel, Caroline, Calder, Furness, and a handful of Linder's closest friends at the widow's flat in Mayfair. After most of the guests had gone, Calder invited Cao and Furness to join him and Annabel for a private talk in the drawing room.

"Colonel Cao has completed an investigation of your husband's final days and would like to share it with you, Annabel," Calder told the widow. "Are you ready to hear it?"

"Certainly," she replied while motioning for the men to sit. "Please go ahead."

Annabel felt drained after hours of putting on a brave face to friends and well-wishers. But if Cao had anything new to say about Warren's fate, she wanted to hear it.

"Thank you, Annabel," Cao began. "You should know that my conclusions are based for the most part on the following evidence: Warren's messages to you from Magog and Boston; the statement he left with Dwight before leaving London; my interviews with informants and with defectors from the League, including Jack Poirier and my niece, Maria; and public reporting."

"Nothing from British Intelligence?" Furness inquired.

"The British government has not seen fit to cooperate," Cao replied. "You may draw your own conclusions from that."

"I already have," Calder interrupted. "And they're not flattering. But do go on."

"Yes," Cao continued. "What seems clear is that Warren left the Magog lake house by motor launch late on Friday night, March 24th, and arrived in Vermont early on Saturday morning with Poirier and Owen Quist. The three men then made the drive to Boston, arriving by noon of the same day. On Saturday evening, after meeting with members of the League's Political Council, DSS officers arrested Warren, almost certainly with the League's connivance. All indications are that the DSS interrogated Warren in Boston for a week and executed him on or around Friday, March 31st."

Cao cast a glance at each of the others before continuing.

"What's not clear is why Warren decided to cross the border. He assured Annabel before leaving Montreal that he wouldn't. Yet his final message to her from Magog on Friday night said that his plans had changed and that it was absolutely necessary for him to enter the U.S. While assuring Annabel that that there was little or no risk to it, he also noted that, if he were detained, his 'new friends' were powerful enough to get him released. So the mystery remains: What happened at the lake house that made him change his mind, and what happened in Boston that made his plans go awry?"

"But you said that Jack Poirier was with Warren when they crossed the lake," Annabel interrupted. "So wouldn't he have participated in meetings at the lake house? Wasn't he able to shed any light on why Warren changed his mind?"

Cao shook his head.

"Poirier told me that Quist was doing his best to convince Warren to go to Boston but didn't make much headway. Then, after their meeting broke up, Warren suddenly decided to go, anyway, as if he'd persuaded himself."

All at once Annabel felt light-headed.

"How very odd. That's almost exactly what Maria Silva said when she visited me in Montreal."

"She told me a similar story on her return to Paris," Cao added. "But I'm sorry to say that Maria won't be available to answer our questions."

"And why is that?" Annabel asked, a note of alarm entering her voice.

"Because my niece returned to Canada three weeks ago to contact friends in the League. She was very disturbed about what happened to Warren and vowed to get to the bottom of it. But she still couldn't bring herself to believe that the League was a hoax."

"So have you been in touch with Maria since she went back?" Annabel pressed.

"As soon as I found the note she left me," Cao continued, "I called Poirier in Ottawa and had him search for her. He tracked her as far as Montreal, where he lost her trail. Two days later, he learned from informants that she turned a gun on herself as she faced capture in Vermont. It seems she finally learned the truth about the League. The hard way."

"So you think the League was a hoax?"

"I suspected it early on and shared my thoughts with Warren. He tended to agree, but wanted to gather more evidence. It's my belief that he didn't make a final decision until after he sat down with the League's leadership in Boston. According to my sources, Warren made a series of highly provocative demands that would have tended to expose the League as a creature of the DSS. After that, perhaps they felt they couldn't afford to let him go."

"That would help explain why Warren left me his sealed statement before leaving for Canada," Calder observed. "He must have known that, if he disappeared while in the League's hands, as Fury had, his followers would never trust the League again."

"Are you implying that everyone associated with the League was a witting DSS agent?" Furness challenged.

"No, surely not everyone," Cao replied. "Some were unwitting dupes, I suppose. But any League member who was allowed to come into contact with Warren almost certainly would have been under DSS direction."

"Including Maria and Jack Poirier?" Annabel asked.

"Not Maria. I think her belief in the League was genuine. As for Jack, the jury's still out. But the longer he stays away from Paris, the less I'm inclined to trust him. Unfortunately, in the deception game, no one can be sure who is on the opposing side until the game is over."

Victor Barbosa entered the fifth-floor offices of the Exile Division's newly downsized League Task Force amid rows of pallets that held file storage boxes awaiting transport to an off-site repository. The skeleton crew of DSS officers that had remained on duty to wrap up the League operation was being relocated to smaller quarters down the hall. Upon stepping inside, Barbosa found James Jenkins and Ali

Jafari reviewing a checklist that catalogued the storage boxes by file number and level of security classification.

As Barbosa had predicted toward the end of Linder's interrogation, it didn't take long after the prisoner died in DSS custody for the League operation to begin unraveling. With each passing day after Linder disappeared, the League fell under greater public suspicion. Rather than remain passive and risk having foreign security services roll up the DSS's foreign-based operatives, or having those operatives panic or defect, Barbosa ordered his undercover officers and agents working for the League to quietly make their way back to the U.S.

Mere co-optees who had agreed to work for the League without being aware that it was a DSS-controlled enterprise were cut loose to fend for themselves. Many of these panicked when police accused them of being agents of a foreign power. Accordingly, within a few weeks of Linder's disappearance, Britain's MI5, France's DGSI, Germany's BfV and other European internal security agencies managed to compose a mosaic of how the League had been able to subvert the émigré opposition movement so successfully and to lure those same security services into a one-sided collaboration.

Accordingly, once the League's overseas organization dissolved, its sprawling task force at DSS headquarters became redundant. By now, most of its officers and support staff had been reassigned over time to other duties, leaving Barbosa, Jenkins and Jafari behind to tie up loose ends.

"I've come here both to congratulate and to commiserate," Barbosa announced as he perched on the edge of a vacant desk amid boxed files. "The League was a wild success while it lasted. But to be perfectly honest, its downfall has left the Exile Division in shambles."

Jenkins shot his superior a puzzled look.

"But you scored a medal and a promotion, boss. How bad can that be?"

"My promotion is just on paper, so I can qualify for a higher retirement payout. I'll be leaving the Department by the end of the year."

"So is that good or bad?" Jafari piped up with an irreverent grin.

Barbosa looked at him askance before turning back to Jenkins.

"You know, the League might still be alive today if Twitchell hadn't discovered that Linder was in country," Barbosa mused. "Until then, the General Secretary endorsed whatever we wanted to do against the émigrés. Things might have gone on that way indefinitely if Linder hadn't challenged the League to assassinate none other than Twitchell himself. And if somebody in Boston, who shall remain nameless, hadn't reported it to the White House. But what's done is done. From now on, if an émigré poses a credible threat, Twitchell wants us to liquidate the bastard immediately. Otherwise, we're to leave the émigrés alone. Period."

Jenkins snorted.

"So much for Exile Division as a career choice."

"Oh, you needn't worry on that score, Jim," Barbosa replied. "Let me know what other division you'd like to work in and I'll make sure you land there. By the way, you'll also be getting a promotion for your work with the League."

"Well, thanks!" Jenkins replied, suddenly bucking up.

"You might also find it interesting that there's an outfit that's taken a hit even worse than ours. I hear that Twitchell has also decided to dissolve the Progintern. This week he's going to deliver a speech that will replace the Party's long-term goal of 'World Unionism' with 'Unionism in One Country.'"

"My God, what could have brought that on?" Jafari broke in with a mischievous snicker.

"The Zuckerman Letter, apparently. Linder's handiwork stung the White House badly. The hope is that scrapping the Progintern will put foreign leaders at ease and boost foreign trade and investment."

"Got to hand it to Linder," Jafari quipped in response. "His sacrifice play killed both the League and the Progintern at one stroke. Pretty nice work for a guy everybody thought was washed up."

"You call it a sacrifice play, but was it really that?" Barbosa asked next. "Maybe Linder understood that his days were numbered and that he had nothing left to lose. After all, he was already under two death sentences and not in the best of health."

Jenkins shook his head.

"No, I don't think so. Remember, I promised to commute his sentence to ten years imprisonment, along with eligibility for a spy swap. Any other prisoner would have leapt at that offer. He couldn't possibly have known that Twitchell ordered him dead and that the commutation was never going to happen."

"Then why do you suppose he turned your offer down?" Barbosa persisted. "Could he have thought you were bluffing?"

"I don't know. Maybe he just hated us too much to give in. Or didn't want to betray his followers. Or maybe he refused out of pure cussedness."

For a moment, no one spoke. Then Jafari broke the silence.

"Well, whatever his reason for holding out, he guessed right," the junior man opined. "Because if he'd knuckled under, it would have been for nothing. At the end of the week, he'd have been dead, anyway."

Barbosa gave Jafari a sour look but didn't reply. Instead, he rose from the desk as if to leave, and addressed a final question to Jenkins.

"I see you brought Quist in yesterday for his exit briefing. How is he doing, now that his work for us is over?"

"Oh, well enough, I suppose," Jenkins replied. "He's relieved to be back full-time at his day job with StatOil. But things aren't so happy at home. It turns out that his wife, the fair Denise, has left him."

"I'm sorry to hear that," Barbosa answered with a perplexed expression. "Did he say why?"

"The usual reasons, in our line of work. Too much time away from home. Too much secrecy. And the feeling that undercover work had turned her husband into someone she no longer knew."

"Ah, yes. The wives always end up paying the price, don't they?"

"Not in Quist's case, it seems," Jenkins replied with a thoughtful look. "You may remember that the main reason he agreed to work with us at the start was so he could marry Denise."

"Then he got what he wanted, no?" Barbosa suggested.

"Yes, except in the end it was the key to an empty room."

– END–

Author's Biographical Note

I decided to write novels at age fourteen, during my first year as a boarding student at Exeter. My English instructor, a World War II combat veteran, advised those of us who wanted to follow the path of Melville, Conrad, and Hemingway to first go out and live some adventures so that we could write stories that people would want to read.

My adventures started in the Middle East and continued in Washington, Europe, the Russian Far East, Maui, Utah, New York, and Boston. Particularly in the Middle East and Russia, I saw failed states and failed societies but was often surprised at how much their people had in common with Americans.

This made me think about whether America might someday suffer its own kind of societal failure. During the 1930's, Americans watched Germany, Italy and Russia and asked, "Could it happen here?"

Today, one might look around and ask the same.

I wrote *Forty Days at Kamas, Star Chamber Brotherhood, Exile Hunter*, and *Exile Endgame* to illustrate how America's failure might come about. In deciding to publish the *Kamas* novels independently, my greatest concern was that the novels gain a readership before the events they described came to pass.

In writing *Maid of Baikal*, I wanted to look on the positive side and show how a single enlightened and charismatic figure might inspire a country's political and military elite to become worthy of governing, and thus lead their country forward to freedom and prosperity. In the historical figure of Joan of Arc, I found a template for how this might be achieved even under the most adverse conditions. I pray that America will never fall so low as to require an American Joan to ride to its rescue.

Root and Branch describes the danger of excesses from the country's national security establishment in the event of a severe national emergency. While the scenario described in *Root and Branch* is a narrow one, I believe that the novel illustrates how close our government has already come to a general trampling on Americans' rights and liberties.

A FINAL WORD: When you turn the page, Kindle's "Before You Go" feature will give you the opportunity to rate this book and share your rating and comments on Facebook and Twitter. If you enjoyed the book, please take a moment to let your friends know about it. Better yet, post a Reader Review on Amazon.com, or on Goodreads.com or LibraryThing.com. If the book gives others a few evenings of enjoyment, they'll be grateful that you reached out to them. As will I.

Please also keep in touch with me and learn about my upcoming novels by following me at PrestonFleming.com, on BookBub.com and at Facebook.com.

With best wishes, Preston Fleming

Books by Preston Fleming

DYNAMITE FISHERMEN
Spy Thriller. "Civil disorder in 1980s Beirut. An extraordinary novel, each page as eruptive as the city providing the setting." KIRKUS REVIEWS

BRIDE OF A BYGONE WAR
Spy Thriller. "CIA agent in Beirut fears his past has caught up to him. An intelligent thriller teeming with vigor." KIRKUS REVIEWS

FORTY DAYS AT KAMAS
Dystopian Political Thriller. "A brutal portrait of a dystopian America, full of dramatic irony and shocking revelation." *KIRKUS REVIEWS*

STAR CHAMBER BROTHERHOOD
Dystopian Political Thriller. "Dystopian thriller about a prison-camp survivor enlisted to assassinate the camp's warden. A full-bodied thriller relayed by a consummate storyteller." KIRKUS REVIEWS

EXILE HUNTER
Dystopian Political Thriller. "Pure energy in print form, whether the characters are being pursued or simply talking." KIRKUS REVIEWS

MAID OF BAIKAL

Historical Fiction. "A Russian war story that lives and breathes from a writer at the peak of his powers." KIRKUS REVIEWS

ROOT AND BRANCH.

Dystopian Political Thriller. "Intelligent and indelible. A shrewdly written tale with a robust cast of characters and a frightening intifada in the U.S." KIRKUS REVIEWS *(KIRKUS STAR RECIPIENT; KIRKUS BEST 100 INDIE BOOKS OF 2020)*

ABOUT THE AUTHOR

Preston Fleming writes realist thrillers set in exceptional times and places, from Siberia during the Russian Civil is War (MAID OF BAIKAL), to explosive 1980s Beirut (DYNAMITE FISHERMEN), to a near-future gulag-style labor camp in Utah (FORTY DAYS AT KAMAS). His experience as a diplomat, lawyer and corporate executive, combined with his ultra-lean writing style, lend rare authenticity to his stories. All of Preston's eight novels have received praise from KIRKUS REVIEWS and other publications. Preston is a native of Cleveland, Ohio, but left home at fourteen for boarding school and has been on the move ever since. Today he and his wife live in Utah's Wasatch Mountains.